CONRAD EDISON AND THE FIRST POWER

OVERWORLD ARCANUM BOOK FIVE

JOHN CORWIN

RAVEN
HOUSE

BOOKS BY JOHN CORWIN

THE OVERWORLD CHRONICLES

Sweet Blood of Mine

Dark Light of Mine

Fallen Angel of Mine

Dread Nemesis of Mine

Twisted Sister of Mine

Dearest Mother of Mine

Infernal Father of Mine

Sinister Seraphim of Mine

Wicked War of Mine

Dire Destiny of Ours

Aetherial Annihilation

Baleful Betrayal

Ominous Odyssey

Insidious Insurrection

Assignment Zero (An Elyssa Short Story)

OVERWORLD UNDERGROUND

Possessed By You

Demonicus

OVERWORLD ARCANUM

Conrad Edison and the Living Curse

Conrad Edison and the Anchored World

Conrad Edison and the Broken Relic

Conrad Edison and the Infernal Design

Conrad Edison and the First Power

STAND ALONE NOVELS

Mars Rising

No Darker Fate

The Next Thing I Knew

Outsourced

For the latest on new releases, free ebooks, and more, join John Corwin's Newsletter at www.johncorwin.net!

OVERWORLD OVERTHROWN

Victus Edison controls the Overworld.

On the run from wandslingers, bounty hunters, and the brutal magitsu master, Garkin, Conrad feels powerless to put an end to the nightmare. Nightliss, Ivy, and the other Seraphim they rescued from Victus's demon foundry can't use magic, and even if they could, Victus has an army of battle mages and monsters ready to crush them.

But a voice from the past may be the key to saving the future. Conrad discovers a link to a power passed down from Moses that might help him overcome impossible odds. If he can survive long enough to wield it, there is one last hope for the resistance.

The first power.

CHAPTER 1

Two strangers flew into the small Colombian town of Los Angeles just after lunchtime. They landed their flying carpets outside El Rey Del Tequila, the lone cantina in the middle of town, and went inside.

"Howdy, barkeep." The man with icy blue eyes sat at the bar, placed his wide-brimmed hat on the counter, and said, "I'd like some sweet iced tea, if you don't mind."

His female companion removed a similar hat. A long brown ponytail spilled out down her back. "Make that two." Her genteel southern accent danced on a razor's edge.

The bartender shook his head. "Sorry, we no have tea, *senor* and *senora*." He pointed a thumb to the right. "Cafeteria, *por favor*."

The man flashed his teeth. "Very well. *Dos cervezas*."

The bartender looked back and forth between the pair, then filled two mugs with beer and placed them on the bar. Neither of the strangers touched their drinks. Instead, they turned in their chairs and surveyed the cantina.

The man wore an immaculately groomed beard and a crop of thick hair above shaved temples. Tattoos snaked from beneath his shirt and around his neck, curling into strange patterns that seemed to move of their own accord. The woman gripped the beer mug and took a long draw, revealing tattoos radiating from the back of her hand and along her fingers.

My stomach twisted in knots as I watched the scene from the relative safety of a house not more than a hundred yards from the cantina. I looked up from the screen on the arctablet and watched the expressions, or lack thereof, on Kanaan's face. The magitsu master blinked, but betrayed no concern.

"What are they doing here?" I asked. "Los Angeles, Colombia is in the middle of nowhere."

"They definitely aren't just passing through." My best friend, Ambria, didn't take her eyes off the screen. "They're up to something."

My other best friend, Max, frowned. "Maybe they're tourists heading to El Dorado."

"Doubtful." Kanaan put a hand under his chin. "They have the look of bounty hunters."

"If that's true, why would they come all the way down here?" I asked.

"We require mobility. Staying within reach of an arch waystation allows us to travel anywhere." Kanaan studied the people on the screen. "A good bounty hunter knows we would avoid crowded places where watchful eyes could spot us. That leaves only a handful of waystations: El Dorado, Three Sisters, Grand Nexus, to name a few."

"I hate being on the run." Max turned back to the scene at the bar. "Every time a stranger comes through town, it puts my nerves on edge."

Kanaan looked down the hallway. The light from an open portal glowed from one of the bedrooms. "I will go to the control room at El Dorado and make sure no one is there."

2

An omniarch allowed a portal to be opened anywhere without the need for another arch at the other end. When we'd come into Los Angeles a month ago and requested refuge, the citizens had been happy to help. They'd set us up in the former home of Bella Pizarro, one of the first people to help Justin Slade when he'd stumbled into town all those years ago.

Kanaan had left a portal open in case we needed a quick getaway, and also as a convenient way to bring through the half-dozen people we'd rescued from my evil father, Victus. While it offered us a means of escape, it also meant that if Victus's people searched the control room, they'd find the active gateway that led straight to us.

The two strangers sat in the cantina for another five minutes then got up and left. I switched to the outside cameras Kanaan had installed around town. The man stopped in the middle of the dusty street, raised his wand, and fired a bolt of light into the air.

The streak exploded into a shower of colors. Thunder rumbled in the clear sky and the few people in the street stopped walking to stare. The man joined the woman on a white bench outside the grocery store and waited as a crowd slowly gathered.

Antonio Pena, the local sheriff strode up to the men, a hand resting on the butt of his wand. "Is there something I can help you with?"

The man stared at the sheriff for a moment without answering. He slid a foil package from within his robes and put a black cigarette in his mouth. The woman flicked her wand and a flame lit the tobacco.

The man inhaled. Blew out a smoke ring. "Matter of fact, maybe you can." He nodded at his companion and waved a hand toward the sheriff.

The woman produced a yellowed piece of parchment and unrolled it for all to see. *Wanted Dead or Alive.* Beneath those words hung a picture of me glaring angrily at the onlookers, and then, *Conrad Edison.*

"You seen this boy?" the man asked the sheriff.

Antonio blinked a few times. Shook his head and met the eyes of the man. "Who are you?"

The man stood and brushed off his leather duster. "Talbot and Delilah, at your service."

"Bounty hunters." It wasn't a question. Antonio gestured at the gathering crowd. "We prefer the quiet life here, my friends. Please, enjoy our hospitality but take your bounty hunting somewhere else."

Talbot ignored the request. "None of you have seen this boy?" He flashed his teeth around the cigarillo. "A million tinsel for his capture."

Eyes widened at the large sum, but no one volunteered information.

"Perhaps you didn't hear me," Antonio said firmly. "That boy is not in our town, and we don't want you bothering us with questions. If you can't abide by my request, you are welcome to leave."

Delilah slid another parchment from inside her duster and unrolled it to display the image of a glowing orb. I zoomed in so I could read the text beneath it.

Let it be known that the bearer of this order hereby has the authority to carry out their official duties, granted by the Arcane Council.

Beneath were the signatures of several council members.

Talbot pointed his cigarillo at the document. "Says here we can ask questions and do whatever we need to hunt down this dangerous fugitive and his gang."

"This town hasn't been under the jurisdiction of the Overworld or the Arcane Council since the war," Antonio replied. "That document is as worthless as the parchment it's written on."

Delilah raised an eyebrow. "You think you're above the law?"

"Sheriff Pena is the law!" someone in the crowd shouted.

Talbot's hand blurred to his waist and back up. A magic bullet rippled from the tip of his wand and slammed Pena in the shoulder. The sheriff rocked back a step. Looked down. Blood pooled across his robes. He dropped like a stone.

Shouts and cries rose from the crowd. Wands came out, glowing with energy.

Talbot's hand blurred again. Shots rang out. Wands splintered and flew from hands. Delilah fired silvery blasts from her wand, knocking people off their feet but not killing them. The crowd scattered.

A loud whistle and a shout stopped many of them in their tracks. "Hold it right there," Talbot said. He nudged a groaning Pena with his foot. "Now, unless you want to end up like your sheriff, I recommend you come to your senses and accept my authority."

"You shot the sheriff!" A woman shouted. "Does the council condone assault?"

"I reckon they condone just about anything to get Conrad Edison in custody." Talbot grinned and spun his wand. It slid neatly into the holster at his waist without him so much as looking at it. "Just a moment ago, you all felt mighty safe hiding behind your sheriff, thinking there's only two of us and a whole mess of you." He winked at Delilah and she smirked back.

"We come from a long line of wandslingers." Talbot flicked the wands from the holsters on his hips, spun them up, sideways, threw them in the air, and caught them. In one smooth motion, he slid them back where they came from. "Ain't a one of you here that could best either of us."

Delilah laughed. "Not even the whole lot of them could."

"My sister and I are gonna get some sweet iced tea from your cafeteria down the road," Talbot said. "You've got until noon to help us find the fugitives."

"But we don't have sweet ice tea," someone protested.

Talbot's eyes flashed. "Then you'd better learn how to make it fast."

He and his sister unfurled several more parchment posters, tacking each one to the side of the cantina until a row of nefarious faces stared out at the crowd. Each one read the same as mine, but the names and faces were different.

Maxwell Tiberius, Ambria Rax, Kanaan, Galfandor.

Ambria gasped. "Oh, no, we're all wanted!"

"Who are these wandslingers?" Max asked.

I looked up with a start and realized a crowd had gathered around me—Ambria, Max, Asha, Lily, Baxter, and dangling by a web overhead, Shushiel.

Asha grimaced. "I've heard of them, but never believed the stories until now."

"Stories?" Max asked.

"About how fast they are with their wands." Asha shook her head slowly. "That poor sheriff didn't even have a chance. I'm glad the deputy wasn't around to get shot."

I turned to watch as Talbot spoke to the populace. "What spell did he use?"

Asha mimicked a gun with thumb and forefinger. "A bullet spell."

Max scratched his head. "You mean bullets like noms use in their guns?"

"Almost." Asha took out her wand and focused on the tip. A small cone of aether gathered. "All it requires is a bit of aether coated by air and a burst of willpower to provide the thrust." She aimed at the wall. The aether zipped through the air, leaving silver ripples in its wake. It thudded into the adobe wall, leaving a small hole.

"Whoa, it's like a mind bullet," Max said.

Lily hugged herself. "What do we do now?"

I'd been thinking about this for a while and seeing the wanted posters only made the decision clearer. "You and Baxter should go home." I kept the camera pointed at the posters. "They don't even know you're with us."

"Victus killed Harris," Lily said. "He must know we're with you."

"Victus never saw you with us," I said. "For all he knows, Harris came by himself."

Baxter shook his head. "But we have to avenge Harris. I can't just let Victus get away with it!"

"In case you hadn't noticed, we're alone and outnumbered." Max slumped into a nearby chair. "There's no way we're getting near Victus anytime soon."

"It's not just about being safe," I said. "It's also about having people back at the university to tell us what's going on."

"You mean spies?" Baxter's eyes lit up. "I can be a spy if it means we can kill your dad."

I grimaced, but let the unintended barb pass. "That doesn't mean I want you doing something stupid."

"Conrad, it's me." Lily put a hand on her chest. "I don't do stupid."

"Then it's settled." I tore my eyes from the arctablet screen and motioned the others to follow me. We went into the bedroom where a shimmering portal hovered just off the floor, and walked through it. We emerged from an omniarch in the El Dorado control room. Even though the ancient city was clear of husked angels and shadow people, it was still under interdiction to keep noms from stumbling upon it.

Kanaan wasn't in sight, but another portal hovered in a neighboring omniarch, the back of a building visible through the gateway. *He must have gone to look at the bounty hunters in person.*

Red slashes marred the silver rings around the next few omniarches, but the fourth one down was marked green, meaning it functioned. I concentrated on the grassy field behind Arcane University and willed a gateway to open. A vertical silver line formed between the columns and tore a hole in the air. The fringe of the Dark Forest appeared like a view through a window.

I held out a hand to Baxter.

He paused, took my hand and shook it. "I hope we kill your father soon." Baxter let go and stepped through the portal. His body seemed to warp as if viewed through a curved window, and snapped back into shape on the other side.

Lily wiped tears from her eyes. She hugged me and Ambria, then kissed Max on the cheek and pressed her head to his chest. "Be careful, okay?"

Max's face turned red. "Um, sure." He patted her head awkwardly. "Play it smart, okay?"

Lily looked up at him and smiled. "You're braver than I thought, Max." She hopped onto tiptoes, pecked a kiss on his lips, and dashed through the portal, leaving my friend with a flummoxed look on his face.

Shushiel rubbed my arm with a foreleg. "Conrad, I would like to go to the Dark Forest and speak with my family. Perhaps they can help. Can I open a portal inside the forest?"

"Of course." I closed the open portal and let the ruby spider open another. The portal flicked open into a small glade. Grunts and the thud of heavy feet emanated from the other side.

"What is that?" Max whispered.

I poked my head through the portal. The world warped and snapped back into place. Beyond the glade in the giant trees of the Dark Forest stood a horde of monsters. Standing at least ten feet tall, thick muscles bulging beneath green skin, the creatures stood in formation, their frog heads twitching back and forth.

I jerked my head back from inside the portal and faced my friends. "It's a small army of frogres."

Max's mouth dropped open. "An army of frogres?"

"How odd," Shushiel said. "They usually fight anything they encounter. I have never seen them gather peacefully."

"Victus must be gathering them," Ambria said. "This is not good news."

"Nothing is these days." I rubbed Shushiel's soft red fur. "We may need the ruby spiders sooner than we thought."

Shushiel rubbed my arm. "I will do whatever I can to help. I am sure Shasha will help."

Max's eyes brightened. "That would be great!"

"Is Shasha the spider leader?" Ambria asked.

"Her eggs bore the first generation of all the giant spiders, ruby, cobalt, and golden. But Victus took her children away." Shushiel sank sadly.

"That's horrible." Ambria hugged the spider. "Did she ever see them again?"

"She saved the ruby and the golden, but her cobalt offspring was not saved." Her eight eyes blinked. "They have never forgotten this."

Ambria frowned. "I didn't even know there were different kinds of giant spiders."

"Can the other spiders camouflage like you?" I asked.

Shushiel waggled her mandibles side-to-side. "Only those of us who inherited that specific gene. Most cannot. Why?"

"I hoped we could get more spies." I touched her foreleg. "We need all the help we can get."

"Then I will go." Shushiel rubbed each of us with a leg. "I will contact you with my pendant when I need to return."

I held out a hand. "Wait, is it safe with all those frogres out there?"

"They will never even know I am there." She stepped through the portal and shimmered into a nearly invisible blur with her active camouflage. I waved goodbye and closed the portal.

Asha touched my arm. "If Victus is assembling an army of frogres, no one is safe."

"I hardly even know what being safe feels like anymore." It felt as if it was us against the entire Overworld.

CHAPTER 2

We walked back toward the portal Kanaan had used to travel into town. I peeked through and recognized the back of the hair salon across the street from the cantina and cafeteria.

"Don't go through, Conrad." Ambria tugged my arm. "Kanaan knows what he's doing."

"I sure hope so." Max leaned against an inactive omniarch, face tight with worry. "These wandslingers look as dangerous as Garkin and his battle mages."

"I don't know, I think Kanaan could beat these two," Ambria said. "They might be fast, but Kanaan is faster."

"Kanaan isn't looking for a fight," Asha said. "What we need more than anything is time."

"And hope Percival can restore the memories of Ivy Slade and the others?" I backed away from the gateway, a bad feeling brewing in my stomach. "Victus isn't just sitting around. If he's gathering a frogre army, what else is he doing?"

"Not making infernus, that's for sure." Max managed a weak smile. "We destroyed the foundry so he can't clone more government officials. Now, if only Ivy and the other Seraphim could use magic, we could blow his stupid army to bits."

Victus had kidnapped dozens of ordinary Arcanes and created demon clones of them—infernus—that he used to take over the government from the inside. He'd also imprisoned half a dozen very powerful individuals: Galfandor, three unidentified Seraphim, Ivy Slade, and someone we'd all thought long dead—Nightliss.

Galfandor had only recently been added to Victus's collection and was recovering nicely from a torn soul. Ivy Slade, Nightliss, and the other Seraphim had been under preservation spells for years and lost most of their memories and the ability to channel magic. Percival was hard at work finding potions to combat the amnesia, but hadn't had much luck. For now, they were staying with Stan, halfway around the world in Italy.

My cousin, Ansel, had been one of the first victims, his soul damaged so badly he'd become comatose. Kanaan had taken him and others with extensive soul damage to a temple in Nepal where the healers focused on soul magic. If anyone could heal Ansel, Kanaan assured me they could.

I stared through the gateway at the back of the hair salon, tempted to go through and spy on the bounty hunters, but it was a bad idea. Kanaan was the expert here. I turned back to the other gateway leading to Bella's house and stepped through. The world curved like a fishbowl and snapped back into place.

I walked to the arctablet and sat down to watch the camera feeds. The bounty hunters still waited in the cafeteria, sipping iced tea and looking out the windows. They seemed very sure of themselves, which made me wonder if they possessed information about our whereabouts. I wondered what would happen at noon if the citizens didn't produce us.

Ambria brewed a pot of tea and poured me a cup. She sat down next to me. "Would you like to take a walk through El Dorado today?"

"A walk?" My forehead pinched. "There are bounty hunters in town and you want to go for a walk?"

"It might take our mind off things, plus it's miles away from here." She stirred her tea with a spoon. "It would also be nice to enjoy a day off instead of training with Kanaan or running for our lives."

"Well, yeah, I guess." We'd trained non-stop with Kanaan since coming here. My muscles didn't get nearly as sore as before, and my casting while under pressure was noticeably faster. "But what if something happens while we're out?" I shook my head. "I wouldn't be able to enjoy myself."

Max dropped into a chair holding a wide, framed picture. In it, a group of people posed in the cavern of the El Dorado waystation. "Look what I found!" He pointed to a petite woman hugging a tall man in a leather duster. "That's Bella, and the person next to her is the infamous Harry Shelton!"

Ambria's eyes widened. "Is that Justin and Elyssa?"

Max moved his finger to the right to a muscular teen with thick hair, his arm around a beautiful fair-skinned woman. "Yep." He shook his head. "Don't recognize the others though."

"Wow." It was so strange seeing these heroes of Eden posing casually for pictures. "Wasn't that around the time they cleaned all the shadow monsters out of El Dorado?"

"Yep." Max shivered. "This is so cool. We have to make sure these pictures are preserved for history."

I looked back at the arctablet to see what, if anything, was happening blocks away from us. Talbot checked a pocket watch and tucked it back into his duster. Three hours left until noon. Time seemed to slow to a crawl. To pass the time, we looked through the photo album Max found and kept a careful eye on the monitor.

My eyelids grew heavy with boredom and I leaned back in the chair to rest a moment.

Two stars blaze in the void, but I feel no heat on my face. They drift toward me, beams of white and blue light arcing between them like electricity. A ghostly wail grows louder, and a terrible sense of unease spreads through my body. I try to move, but I'm transfixed. In seconds, the boiling surface of the stars will touch me and burn me to ash.

I jerked and shouted in alarm.

Ambria and Max jumped up. A stack of picture albums spilled from their laps and onto the floor.

"What in the world is wrong with you?" Max knelt to pick up an album. "You scared me half to death."

"I-I must've fallen asleep." I blinked and saw the afterimage of twin stars in the split-second of darkness.

"Another bad dream?" Ambria said.

I sighed. Nodded. "At least this one wasn't about Harris dying." I still couldn't shake the image of Victus burning a hole through the boy's chest. Just the thought of it clenched my chest with fury and regret. His death was only one of many that haunted me. Images of Cora dying from cancer, visions of Delectra mortally wounded in my arms, mass graves and ravaged corpses dogged my thoughts constantly. Sometimes it was all I could do to shut out the noise.

"It's not your fault." Ambria sat back down next to me and patted my arm. "Harris thought he could beat Victus. He was wrong."

Kanaan stepped from behind us, silent as a ghost.

Max and I shouted in alarm. Only Ambria retained her composure. "Where have you been?" she asked.

"Watching and waiting." The magitsu master leaned against the wall. "Talbot and his sister are not alone. A large force of mercenaries just portaled in at the edge of town."

My insides went cold. "They must know we're here."

"I am not certain of that." Kanaan studied the scene on the arctablet. "Altash told me no others had been to the El Dorado waystation, and the tunnels leading from the surface are blocked. This means no one else saw the portal we use to go back and forth."

"They certainly couldn't have seen us in town," Ambria said. "We never leave the house except to train, and even then, we usually stay in the waystation."

"Agreed." Kanaan checked the time. "It is possible they plan to comb the town with the mercenaries."

Asha grimaced. "I hope things don't get violent."

"It was plenty violent when they shot the sheriff," Ambria reminded her.

On the tablet screen, the door to the cafeteria opened and a tall man with a staff entered. It took me a moment to recognize Leopold, the leader of the city council. "We want you out of town immediately," he told the siblings. "You may think you're above the law, but you can't beat all of us."

Delilah snorted. "You folk don't have what it takes to beat us, even if you wanted to." She swigged the rest of her iced tea and stood, pushing the edge of her duster back behind her wand holster. "And I know you don't want to fight us. You want to hand over the kid and his accomplices and let us be on our merry way."

"Whoever those people are, they aren't here." Leopold's hand tightened on his staff. "Now, kindly leave before I give the order to storm this place and arrest you."

My stomach twisted. "Does Leopold know about the mercs outside town?"

Kanaan shook his head. "Unlikely."

"He's going to get his people killed if he starts anything!" Ambria said.

Kanaan's eyes twitched, as if he'd just seen something bad. "Pack your things, now."

"Why, what did you—" I didn't finish my question, because a blade flashed. Leopold screamed and looked down at his hand, impaled on the table by a dagger.

Delilah laughed. She tore the staff from the Arcane's hand and threw it to her brother. Talbot caught it in one hand and set it on a table while sipping his tea. Delilah gripped the screaming Leopold by the collar of his robes and looked back. "Time yet?"

Talbot checked his pocket watch. Held up a finger. "Three, two, one." He lowered his finger. "It is now."

Delilah yanked the knife from Leopold's hand and laughed as he screamed louder.

"I said, pack now." Kanaan's voice was urgent.

"I never unpacked," Ambria said.

"Same," I said, unable to tear my eyes from the screen.

Delilah slammed Leopold down on a long table. The cafeteria owner cried out and vanished through a door in the back. Talbot drew a dagger and held it under Leopold's throat. "You will tell us if the boy and his companions are in town, or I will make you tell me."

A trickle of blood ran down Leopold's neck where the dagger nicked it. Blood poured from the wound in his hand. Eyes watering with pain, he hissed, "This is illegal. If you do anything to me, a hundred people will rush inside and kill you."

"Naw, you see, we brought backup." Talbot grinned. "Got a squad of battle mages already enroute."

Leopold's face turned a shade of green. "The boy isn't here. How many times do we have to tell you?"

"Just so happens, I have a pretty good idea he is." Talbot cleaned the blood off his knife and slid it into a sheath on his back. With his other hand, he slid a small piece of parchment out of his pocket. He unfolded it to show a crimson stain in the middle of a drawn compass. Part of the stain formed an arrow pointing southeast. "We followed a blood tracking spell. The blood was old, so it wasn't as precise as we'd have liked, but it led us down here. We know he's close."

Delilah paced around Leopold, hand on her wand holster. "We know the boy wouldn't go to La Casona in Bogota. Too many eyes." She shook her head. "It doesn't take much sense to figure he went to El Dorado."

Leopold wrapped a robe around his wounded hand. "Why are you terrorizing my town? El Dorado is an hour away."

"Because a growing boy's gotta eat." Talbot waved an arm toward the window. "Your little town here is the perfect place to hole up. It's a small town filled with the same Arcanes who helped Justin Slade back when he was a fugitive."

"If your fugitive went to El Dorado, he could use an omniarch to go anywhere he wants for food." Leopold somehow managed to keep his wits despite the blood soaking his robes where he'd wrapped it around his hand. "There's absolutely no reason to come here."

Talbot shrugged. "That's a real reasonable argument, sir, but the spell terminated when we walked into town. That means he's close, or was." He jabbed a finger in the other man's chest. "That means you'd better tell me where he is, or you'll lose an ear or two."

I shivered and turned from the unfolding scene. "Is that my blood?"

"Yes." Kanaan grabbed the arctablet off the table. "Get your things and meet me at the portal. I suspect Leopold is about to break."

"But how did they get my blood?" I thought back to the battle at Cumberbatch's house. I didn't remember bleeding.

"I suspect they only recently acquired the blood," Kanaan said. "Blood tracking is slow, but it does not require a month. The blood must be alive for the spell to work."

"I'd like to know where they got his blood," Ambria said.

"The mystery can wait," Kanaan said. "Get your things and go."

We didn't need any prodding. I grabbed a backpack stuffed with my meager belongings, stopped to grab as much non-perishable food from the pantry as I could, and raced to the portal. Something rammed on the front door. Wood splintered and the house shook.

Ambria and the others waited on the other side of the portal, waving me on.

Talbot's voice rang out. "Conrad Edison! I know you're here, boy. Come on out."

I leapt through the portal, stumbled, and nearly fell. When I turned around, I saw Talbot and Delilah racing toward the portal, wands drawn. The gateway winked off, leaving us alone in the arch control room.

"That was close!" Max said. "How in the world did they find us so fast?"

"Bella's house is not far from the cafeteria." Kanaan regarded the omniarch for a moment.

"Don't we need to get out of here?" Max said. "They know we're in El Dorado."

Asha looked up and down the rows of arches as if expecting an attack at any moment. "They can't physically walk down here, but if they have access to an omniarch, they could be here in a heartbeat."

"Not if they don't have a picture to go by," Ambria said. "Unless they have a clear image, we're safe."

"Are you kidding me?" Max said. "Bella's house is full of pictures of this place!"

"We have to go to Granddad Stan's." A spell glowed at the tip of Asha's wand. "It's the only place they won't find us."

"But we lose a major advantage." Kanaan hesitated. Nodded. "The rest of you go to Stan's. I will go to another waystation with omniarches so I can bring you through when needed."

"Is that really a good idea?" Ambria said. "We need you, Kanaan."

Come here, boy. The whispered words startled me so much, I nearly jumped. *Into the cavern.* I looked around at the others, but they were too busy yelling at each other to see my distress. *Conrad, come.* A gentle force pulled on my senses. While my friends argued about what to do next, I slipped away and headed toward the control room exit.

When I peered into the main cavern, a great form stirred. Purple scales uncoiled and the earth dragon, Lulu, slithered across the floor toward me. Her giant red companion, Altash, opened an eye, but did not stir.

Lulu lowered her lean muzzle to the ground. Even her eye dwarfed me.

"Did you call me?" I asked in a small voice.

Your times comes. We cannot lend our direct aid and break the oath that keeps the nemesis at bay.

"My time for what?" I struggled to understand what this ancient creature meant. "You can't help us against Victus?"

Forge your spirit well, for you face the void of the rift alone.

She opened her massive maw to reveal rows upon rows of sharp teeth. My heart thudded faster. The pulse roaring in my ears. The dark pit glowed azure blue. Heat washed over me, and I wondered if she meant to roast me alive. The light blinded me. My skin felt as if I stood beneath the heat of a thousand suns.

I held up my hands and cried out. "No!"

Just as suddenly, I stood alone, cold and confused. I blinked away the bright spots in my eyes. Lulu was no longer in front of me. I looked to the center of the cavern and my heart dropped. The earth dragons were gone.

"I don't understand." I turned in a circle, but the place was completely empty. The skin on my pale arms glowed pink from the intense heat. Otherwise, there was no sign the dragons had even been here.

Shouting from inside the control room jerked me back to my senses. I raced inside and saw relief sweeping the faces of my friends.

"Where did you go?" Ambria asked when I rejoined them.

"The dragons, they—" I didn't have a chance to complete my sentence.

"AT LAST, WE MEET." Talbot and Delilah stepped out of a portal near the large map spanning the front wall. Talbot held out his arms in greeting. "Perhaps the great Kanaan would like a go at me? Might as well get this over with so I can collect my bounty."

"Go, now." Kanaan gripped Asha's arm. "Keep them safe. I will contact you soon." Before anyone could object, he walked toward the pair of bounty hunters, both of his wands drawn.

"No!" I shouted.

A gateway split open in the omniarch. Max grabbed me and dragged me through before I could chase after Kanaan. Asha and Ambria followed close behind, blocking me from going back in. The gateway snapped shut, leaving us in a field of wheat.

I jerked free of Max's grip. "Why did you leave him? We could have taken them!"

"That wasn't the real Kanaan going to fight, Conrad." Asha gripped my shoulders and made me look her in the eye. "He used his illusion trick to slow them down."

"An illusion trick?" I instantly felt sheepish. "How do you know that?"

"Because he showed me how to do it." Asha performed an elaborate pattern with her wand and tapped herself on the head. She ran away into the wheat field and vanished from sight. An invisible hand touched me and Asha reappeared. "You see?"

"Whoa, that's neat!" Max mimicked the wand pattern, but a tap on his head failed to produce an illusion. "Can you teach me that?"

"It's quite advanced." Asha smiled. "Then again, you're my best students."

Ambria grabbed my arm. "Conrad, where did you run off to a moment ago? I thought we'd left you behind!"

"The big purple dragon, Lulu, she called me."

Max's eyes flared. "What? The dragons never talked to us before."

I showed them my slightly sunburned skin. "I thought she was going to burn me." I told them Lulu's grim words and how she and Altash vanished.

Asha grimaced. "You'll face the void of the rift alone? What's that supposed to mean?"

I shook my head slowly. "I guess it means we're totally on our own."

Ambria's eyes saddened as she looked at the countryside all around us. "Yes, I think we are."

Her words punched me in the gut. Our world had turned upside down in a heartbeat. Victus controlled the Arcane Council. He'd cloned dozens of people with demon golems and even now assembled an army of monsters. It felt as if nowhere was safe from him.

And now we were helpless fugitives trapped in the middle of nowhere.

CHAPTER 3

I pushed the dragon's words from my mind. It seemed unnecessarily cruel to call me into the cave just to tell me that we couldn't count on their help. *Nothing has changed. The dragons never offered us help before.* Which made the entire incident too incongruous to ignore. My burned skin itched—more salt in an already painful wound.

Why say anything at all? Why not simply leave?

Asha put a hand on my shoulder. "I know this is hard on all of us, but we'll get through it." She looked up a grassy hill to a white stone house beneath a red-leaved oak. The sun sat low on the horizon, evidence we'd jumped forward several time zones. "For now, I just want to see my Granddad Stan and rest."

An old man stepped out of the front door and did a double-take. He waved and started walking toward us, a slight limp slowing him. A spotted leopard bounded out of the door after him, and behind in the doorway, a petite woman with curious green eyes peeked out.

The sight of Nightliss melted away some of my melancholy. Even though she couldn't remember much, her sweet personality and calm demeanor were like an island of peace in a sea of chaos.

"Guess the wards already told him we're here." Asha jogged through the wheat, long, dark hair trailing behind her. She was nearly the mirror image of our mother, Delectra, a fact that pleased and haunted me all at the same time.

We caught up to her and took turns hugging Granddad Stan. Though he wasn't actually mine and Asha's grandfather, he'd raised Asha as his own at the request of our desperate mother once she'd realized Victus's monstrous plans for her.

The leopard morphed into a young woman with black bands around her private bits. "Why are you here? I thought we agreed it was safer to stay away."

"Yes, I told you I need plenty of time." Percival stood outside the house, arms crossed, eyes narrowed. "What if they track you here?"

"We had no choice." Asha told them what had happened.

"Somehow, they had a sample of my blood." I held up my hands in a shrug. "I have no idea how they got it, but I think the blood is too old to track with anymore."

Guilt flashed in Percival's eyes. "Oh, dear."

"Oh, dear what?" Max said.

"I took a blood sample from Conrad over a year ago." He tapped a finger on his chin. "Put it in a preservation spell so I could study the effects travelling in the Glimmer had on the human body. Someone must have discovered the sample."

Ambria's mouth dropped open. "Did you take samples from us too?"

Percival shook his head. "No. And I only took a small sample from Conrad. It would only be enough for one tracking spell."

"I hope, or else we'll have a lot more company soon." Natalia bared her teeth. "Why did you come here of all places? You had an omniarch. You could have gone anywhere. Now you're hundreds of miles from the nearest waystation."

"Kanaan sent us," Asha said. "He said he'd stay close to a waystation so we could come back through a portal when it's safe."

"Well I hope that's the case." Natalia sighed. "Might as well come in for tea and biscuits."

"I could definitely use some biscuits to calm my nerves." Max rubbed his stomach. "Going on the run makes me hungry."

Ambria snorted. "Blinking your eyes makes you hungry, Max."

"Sure does." Max headed up to the house. "I'm a growing boy."

"I don't care why you're here," Stan said. "It's good to see you."

Nightliss greeted us at the front door, green eyes curious. "Hello again." She waved at me and smiled.

My knees felt weak, and my heart beat a little faster. She looked so young for such an ancient being, and the amnesia gave her an aura of innocence.

Ambria nudged me in the ribs. "She's way too old for you."

I flinched and managed a sheepish grin.

"Hey, Ivy!" Max's face flushed when the pretty blond girl smiled back at him.

"God, you two and your hero worship." Ambria sighed and went into the kitchen.

"My memory is still awful!" Ivy grabbed Max by the shoulders and shook him. "I need to remember so I can use magic again. God, I just want to blast those baddies to dust." Her gaze caught on me and her lips twisted into a guilty look. "Don't worry, Conrad, I'll let you vaporize your evil daddy if you want."

Max staggered back, dizzy from the shaking.

"That's very sweet of you." I sat on the couch and tried to relax, but my nerves were taut. Nightliss sat next to me and touched my hand. Heat flushed up my arm. All thought vanished from my mind, filled instead with the presence of this lovely angel.

"What happened?" she asked.

It took a moment to find my voice. "Bounty hunters found us."

She scowled. "This is not good."

"Can you do any magic yet?" I asked.

Nightliss held up a hand. A small ultraviolet globe flickered and puffed away. "Something is wrong. I know how to do it, but it is like a wall between me and my power."

"You mean your memory isn't the problem, it's something else?"

She nodded. "I remember bits and pieces. I see flashes of war. A tall dark-haired boy turns into a demon. A woman who looks just like me, but is blond and fair-skinned."

"Daelissa, your twin sister." I knew everything the history books said, and a bit more thanks to books we'd discovered in Moses's hidden vault. Nightliss's hand moved away from mine. I wanted to touch it again, to hold it. *She is so beautiful.* I cleared my throat, aware that my jaw hung slightly open as I gazed at her angelic face. "Um, do you remember anything about the Crystoid Incident?"

Nightliss pursed her lips and tapped a finger on her chin.

She's so cute!

"No. Everything is jumbled in my head." She stopped tapping her chin and cocked her head slightly. "Are you okay, Conrad?"

I flinched. "I'm sorry, I, um..." My mouth and brain stopped communicating, leaving me witless. For a moment, I forgot about my itchy, sunburned skin.

Nightliss's forehead pinched with worry. She wrapped an arm around my shoulder and hugged me. "You have been through a lot today. You should rest and relax."

I melted into her caress. She smelled like honey and flowers. "Yes, I should." I saw Ambria standing against the far wall, a teacup in her hands. Her eyelids fluttered as she turned away. *She must be as tired as me.*

"Here, lie down." Nightliss put my head in her lap and stroked my hair. "Sleep, Conrad."

It wasn't even that late in the day, but everything seemed so right in the world that I couldn't resist. I yawned and sighed with contentment.

Blazing comets streak from the void straight at me. Energy dances along their surfaces. A low, throbbing hum vibrates me to my core. Rising above it all, the keening wail of the dead rakes cold chills along my spine.

"Are you really sleeping?"

I jerked upright and caught a cross gaze from Percival.

"It's still early afternoon in the time zone you just came from." He clapped his hands. "Chop, chop. I need to speak with all of you, because I can't proceed without help."

I groaned and stood so I wouldn't be tempted to lie back in the lap of an angel.

"Do not push yourself so hard, Percival." Nightliss stood next to me, her head rising just above my shoulder. "You do not rest enough."

"Don't use your sleep magic on me!" Percival backed up a step.

Nightliss frowned. "It is not magic."

Percival sniffed. "Well, whatever it is makes young Conrad here behave like a brainless fool."

Ambria laughed and quickly covered her mouth.

"Do you have any lotion for sunburns?" I asked.

Percival took my hand and examined the scabs forming on the back. "Can't you children take care of yourselves at all?" He huffed and walked away. I wondered if I'd driven him away with my request, but he returned with a small bottle of pink lotion. "Put this on to soothe your skin."

I took it gratefully.

"I'll do whatever it takes to beat Victus." Max's voice carried across the room where he sat next to Ivy. "You can count on me."

"Oh, Max, you're the bestest!" Ivy squeezed him in a hug so hard, his eyes bugged.

Rather than crying out in pain, a dreamy grin spread across his face.

A loud fart broke the silence.

Ambria gasped. "Goodness, Max, that's rude."

"That wasn't me!"

Ivy giggled and Ambria burst into laughter.

"I couldn't help it," Ambria said between bouts of laughter.

Max groaned. "Was that a fart spell?"

"No, it's just a spell that makes noises, Max." Ambria sniffed the air. "See? No foul odor like your regular farts."

Ivy chortled. "That's hilarious!" She kissed Max on the cheek again and he moaned with pleasure, all thoughts of the fake fart forgotten.

"Bloody hell." Percival rolled his eyes. "This room is positively seething with pubescent hormones. If only I had a cure for that!" He snapped his fingers. "Now, where did Asha get off to? I need help!"

Asha stepped out of the kitchen, teacup in hand. "Here I am, at your beck and call, Percival."

The healer nodded in satisfaction. "Yes, I quite like the sound of that."

I could practically feel the heat rolling off Nightliss even from three feet away. Somehow, I resisted the urge to touch her and managed not to think of her face for a few seconds. *What is wrong with me?* I recovered my wits and rejoined the conversation. "What do you need from us, Percival?"

"Ingredients." He unrolled a parchment and shoved it in my face.

Absorbent acorns

Devil pupfish oil

White avocado

Toasted snails

Elephant tears

I took the document and raised an eyebrow. "You want me to go to the local apothecary?"

"No, of course not." He set hands on his hips. "If I could get these locally, I would, but they are quite rare."

"Are they for memory loss?" I asked.

"No, for memory blocks." Percival motioned us to follow him and went into a room with a whiteboard spanning the back wall. On it was the diagram of a brain with several red Xs on it. "Each of the victims was given a blocking potion to not only cut them off from their memories, but to place a bottleneck in the part of the mind that harnesses willpower."

Nightliss took the lotion from me and began rubbing it into my arms where the burn was the worst. I did my best not to moan with pleasure as the stinging subsided.

Ambria stepped up to the whiteboard and peered at the markings. "I thought willpower was part of the soul."

"Yes, yes." Percival touched his chest. "Our soul rides in this meat wagon we call a body." He tapped his head. "It interacts with our brain, which forms a metaphysical bond we call the mind. If the physical side is blocked, the soul cannot form that perfect bond with the physical realm."

"That's why we can't use our magic." Ivy slapped a hand to her forehead. "Because Victus screwed with our brains."

"I've never heard of such a potion," Asha said. "Are you certain that's the cause?"

"Are you a healer?" Percival asked.

Asha's jaw tightened. "I minored in healing."

"Then you barely have more than a layman's perspective."

Asha seemed to struggle internally with a response.

Ambria held up her wand. "Percival, why don't I slice open your hand and we'll see if you can heal it before Asha heals hers?"

Max grimaced. "Just like in class when she burned her hand and then healed it?"

Percival blanched. "What sort of insanity is that?"

Asha grinned. "It was a lesson on anesthetic magic." She took out her wand. "Shall I burn your hand and see if you can numb the pain?"

"Absolutely not!" He jumped back a foot.

Ivy burst into laughter. "Oh, wow, look at his face. What a scaredy-cat!"

Asha held up a hand and Ambria high-fived her. Natalia skipped up to them and added her own hand to the mix.

"Oh, me too!" Ivy held up her hand and the other three slapped it.

"Should I also strike your hands?" Nightliss asked. "What is the meaning behind it?"

Max sidled up to me. "What in the world is going on with them?"

I shook my head. "I think the girls are bonding."

"Dangerous."

I nodded. "Especially for us." I cleared my throat, but it didn't stop the laughing women. It was odd seeing Asha transform from serious professor, to long-lost sister, and now this giggling girl.

Max clapped his hands. "Hey, let's get some order in here."

Ambria whispered something in Ivy's ear and the pair giggled.

Max's face turned bright red. "Are you talking about me?"

They only giggled harder.

I sighed and pulled Percival into the adjacent room for some quiet. "Where can I get these ingredients?"

"The only place that will have them is the ingredients room in Arcane University." Percival put a finger on the first item. "Unfortunately, I have no idea if you'll find devil pupfish oil there, but it is absolutely vital."

"Where can I find it if it's not there?" I asked.

He shrugged. "This potion originated with monks in Tibet. It's possible they might have ingredients at one of their temples."

"Noms discovered a magical potion?"

He nodded. "They do stumble across magical discoveries now and then."

I tried to imagine how far away Tibet was without a portal and failed. "So, either we find a way to sneak into Arcane University, or we have to travel to Tibet and hope they have it?"

"I know of an apothecary in Kathmandu that could possibly have it, but let's hope Gideon Grace stored some for a rainy day." Percival grimaced. "I dislike that self-righteous ass, but he does keep an excellent inventory."

I looked around. "Where is Galfandor, by the way?"

Percival motioned toward the back. "He's still on his daily walk."

"But it's getting dark," I said.

The healer tutted. "Galfandor is not in a good place, Conrad. He feels like he failed the school and everyone else by getting kidnapped so easily by Victus."

"He didn't know half the Arcane Council was in Victus's pocket." I sighed. "None of us did, and once again, my clever father outsmarted us all."

"Well, get me these ingredients, and we'll restore Nightliss and Ivy to their former glorious selves." A grin split Percival's narrow face. "I'd love to see them blast Grint and Quiff to bits!"

Esmerelda Quiff and Agatha Grint were secret allies of my father when he was the Overlord, and had survived the purge of his associates after his staged death. Several other council members had no doubt been replaced by infernus, demon golem clones my father had perfected with the help of Aerianas and her brother, Zarin.

It was because of those very people that getting these ingredients would be incredibly difficult. "We don't have access to an omniarch portal anymore. How am I supposed to sneak past university security and get into the ingredients vault?"

Percival's grin vanished. "I have no idea."

"Alternatives?" I said.

"The university is a long journey by broom, but I can assure you that Kathmandu is much farther." Percival shook his head. "There must be some way you can get in."

I took out my arcphone and dialed the symbol for Kanaan, hoping he'd remained close to a portal waystation.

He answered after several rings. "Conrad, you are safe?"

"Yes, but we need an omniarch."

"Impossible for now." The video turned on. Kanaan stood in a dense jungle. "I am in Australia, near the Three Sisters waystation. I tried to portal inside, but it was blocked. It would seem Garkin has blocked access to many waystations."

"Are you stuck there?" I asked.

"For now." He stroked his beard. "For what do you need an omniarch?"

I told him about Percival's potion.

"Go to Vivachi in Venice. They have many ingredients."

Percival stuck his head in front of my screen. "Not these ingredients. I already sent them a query. In fact, I sent queries to all the top dealers, and none of them have even half of what I need."

"What about Kathmandu?" Kanaan said.

"They don't use arcphones, so I have no way of knowing." Percival shook his head. "We certainly can't use any public waystations."

"Correct," Kanaan said. "I am certain they are under surveillance." He pursed his lips. "Conrad, ask Asha for advice. She will know what to do."

"Don't you have advice?" I said. "How do I sneak past the security wards at the university?"

"Your teacher is wise and powerful. Listen to her." Kanaan's face flickered away and the call ended.

It seemed we were on our own.

CHAPTER 4

Percival grunted. "Asha's about as wise and powerful as an old shoe."

I grabbed Percival's arm. "Asha could kick your butt anytime, so don't talk that way about my sister!"

His eyes widened. "I'm sorry. I just get so tired of hearing Stan talk about her all the bloody time! Asha this and Asha that, and oh, she's so talented." He made a mouth with his hand, opening and closing it rapidly. "Fine, I get that your adopted granddaughter is a million times smarter than me, but, please, dear god, just let me be inferior in peace!"

I looked with surprise at the tears in the corners of the healer's eyes. "I'm sorry, I didn't know you felt like that."

Percival waved an arm toward the other room. "I'm trying my best to heal these people, Conrad. I worked so hard in school to be the best. I experimented and read until my eyes watered, but I was never the best. While everyone else graduated with honors, I barely passed. The only class I excelled in was potions." His shoulders slumped. "My father was a great healer. My brother is a talented medic with Science Academy. All I ever wanted was to be the best at something."

"You're pretty amazing with potions," I said. "Your experiments leave a little to be desired."

"But they can be effective." Percival shrugged. "Provided the patient survives them."

"Look, I'll tell Stan to stop bragging on Asha so much." I held up a hand when it looked like he was about to object. "But I won't let him know it's because of you, okay?"

Percival abruptly hugged me. "Thank you, Conrad." He left before I could say another word.

"Well, that was an awkward conversation to walk in on," Ambria said from behind me.

I jumped and spun to see her standing in the doorway. "How much did you hear?"

"Oh, all about how Stan brags on Asha." She giggled. "Poor Percy."

"I feel bad for him," I admitted. "It's like seeing him in a whole new light."

Her face sobered. "I remember the way his brother, Arthur, looked at him. It was like he was disappointed." Ambria gave a *what can you do?* shrug.

I told her about my call to Kanaan and where we'd have to go for the ingredients.

"Great." She squeezed my hand. "Do we have to do it now?"

I squeezed her hand back and shook my head. "No. We need to see what Asha thinks."

"It's so lovely out here in the countryside. Do you think we could take a walk or something tomorrow? Maybe just enjoy a day before we dive back into danger?"

I nodded. "Sure. I'll grab Max and we can make a picnic of it."

Ambria's eyes grew sad. "I thought maybe just the two of us, like old times." The light from the overhead glowball hit her eyes just right and flecks of gold glittered in her hazel irises.

How did I never notice how pretty her eyes are? I remembered that she wanted an answer. "I mean, sure, if you want."

She hugged me. "Thanks."

We went back into the other room. Galfandor had returned from his walk and greeted me with a sad smile. "Good to see you, Conrad. I am sorry to hear you had to leave Colombia."

"Me too." I touched Asha's arm to get her attention. "Percival needs some rare potion ingredients from Gideon Grace's vault. Do you have any idea how we can sneak in and steal them?"

"Oh, my, that is a rather difficult assignment." Galfandor stroked his long beard. "Unless they have completely redone the wards, I know of two backdoors that you might use to gain access to campus."

"We put the key to the ingredients vault back in the desk at your house," Ambria said. "Is there a way to sneak in there?"

"Doubtful," Galfandor said. "I think it unlikely they haven't warded the place."

"I can get past just about any ward or lock," Stan said. "Get me near that potions vault and I'll get us in."

"What if we have to run for our lives?" Asha shook her head. "This mission is too dangerous."

"I recommend sending a small party," Galfandor said. "There are disillusionment traps all around campus designed to dissolve illusion disguises and set off alarms, so you will have to use stealth."

"Or, we could use wigs and makeup," Ambria said.

"Have you ever wondered why no one on campus uses much makeup?" Galfandor said. "It's because those very same wards will set off an alarm if they detect excess alterations to appearance. After I discovered Victus and Delectra had been in disguise among us for so long, I'm afraid I went overboard in securing campus."

"Yes, but they used the Eye of Juranthemon," I said. "It physically transformed them into Sideon and Esma." Just speaking the name of my favorite teacher stabbed me in the heart. Esma had been my mentor. She had also been my mother, Delectra, in disguise. Victus had killed her shortly after this revelation and I still had a hard time coping with it.

Galfandor seemed to sense my shift in mood, for his voice softened. "Which is why I also added DNA to the disillusionment traps that would reveal Victus in case he ever tried it again." He sighed. "In any case, you will have to resort to stealth since any means of disguise will only set off an alarm."

"I'll go by myself," Asha said. "Cumberbatch saw me with Kanaan, but he's dead. I don't think Victus knows I'm part of the gang."

"Unless Grint or Quiff saw you at the mansion with us," I reminded her. "Besides, you've been gone for a month. You can't just show up on campus and expect no one to ask questions about where you've been."

"I'm going too," Ambria said.

Max held up a fist. "Me too."

"I want to blast some baddies," Ivy said. "I'm in."

I held up my hands. "Whoa, people. Didn't you hear Galfandor? It has to be a small party."

Asha tapped a finger on her chin. "I have a few ideas." She looked over at Galfandor. "I'd love your input and help."

"Of course," he said.

I put a hand on her shoulder. "What about me?"

"Conrad, you've been through a lot for someone your age." Asha's eyes filled with concern. "Let the adults handle this."

"I agree, young man." Galfandor leaned heavily on his staff. "I let you put yourself in danger too many times because I suspected you might turn out like Victus." He patted my arm. "You've proven yourself to be anything but your father's son."

"You can't just cut me out," I protested. "If it wasn't for me and Max and Ambria, you'd still be in one of Victus's preservation chambers."

"It wasn't just the three of you," Asha said. "Shushiel was there. I helped. Natalia helped. It was a team effort." She held up a hand to stop my reply. "Harris is dead because he thought he could handle Victus. I won't let you make the same mistake."

My hands clenched. "Harris was mental! I'm not!"

Galfandor nodded. "Yes, yes, we know. But I will not send children into the very heart of danger."

"What rubbish!" Ambria put herself between me and the former head-master. "You never had a problem with it when you thought we might turn out to be evil."

"Look, *children*." Asha's eyes flashed. "If any of you can beat me in a duel, I'll gladly take you with me. The truth is, you're still students. Your faces are plastered on posters all across the Overworld and you wouldn't have a chance of defending yourselves against experienced battle mages. Odds are, Victus's minions don't know I'm connected with you. That gives me a better chance to get in and out of the university without shots fired."

"For now, you should rest, relax, and let the adults do the heavy lifting." Galfandor offered a smile, but his face looked too weary to support it.

I could tell arguing would get us nowhere, so I spun on my heel and went outside. I sat beneath the red-leaved oak. Fields of wheat swayed in a gentle breeze. A flock of sheep dotted a far-off hill. Everything seemed so peaceful this far from the chaos threatening the Overworld. I took out my arcphone and looked glumly at the blue dot on the map. We were in the middle of nowhere.

"Please don't be mad, child." Galfandor leaned on his staff, looking older than I remembered. The tearing of his soul by one of Zarin's ripper wyrms had taken a heavy toll.

"In case you hadn't noticed, I'm not a child anymore." I tried to keep the anger out of my voice, but failed.

The old man chuckled. "Quite true." He caught a leaf as it fluttered down in front of him. "I imagine your grandfather would be rather proud of you in his own way."

I frowned. "Damien Shelton?"

"I'm sorry, your great-grandfather, old Ezzek Moore himself."

"He's the father of Sasha Moore?" I knew very little about my extended family tree. "I thought he was a more distant relative."

"Ezzek, Moses, or whatever alias he had at the time, had surprisingly few marriages or children over the centuries." Galfandor looked out into the gathering darkness. "He was a bit of an enigma."

"So I've heard." I'd read everything I could on the first Arcane, from the tidbits about his role in the First Seraphim War as Moses, to his great accomplishments as Ezzek Moore, founder of Arcane University, the Arcane Council and more. The final chapter in his life as Jeremiah Conroy hardly seemed to fit in the same book. He allied with Daelissa and switched sides only after trying to kill Justin Slade several times.

Then Daelissa killed him before the final war even began, burning him to ash in front of the very mansion where Galfandor lived before Victus kidnapped him. Every time I'd walked past that place, I could almost feel a tingling in the air, as if part of Moses's spirit still resided in that bit of hallowed earth.

"You and Asha are quite likely his last remaining direct descendants." Galfandor turned his gaze back to me. "I think he would be proud of what you've done, but caution you to listen to those who are older and wiser."

How would you know? I barely kept that retort to myself, but didn't want to argue.

Galfandor continued. "I'm glad you want to help, Conrad, but please don't be angry with your sister for keeping you out of this."

I nodded and faked a smile. "I won't. Thanks."

The old man nodded then turned and headed into the house.

Not more than a moment later, Ambria plopped down next to me. Max walked around the tree and sat cross-legged on my left.

"Did he give you a pep talk?" Ambria said.

I nodded.

Max grunted. "Did it work?"

"It's not fair." I plucked a blade of grass and tossed it to the mercy of the wind. "We did everything ourselves before, and now they think we're too young."

"They're being idiots," Ambria said. "We didn't survive this long on luck."

"Conrad, I like your sister, but"—Max looked around as if Asha might be lurking nearby—"she's a dumb adult like Galfandor."

"I know how we could get back into the university ourselves," Ambria said.

Max and I twisted our heads toward her. "How?" we asked in unison.

She let us hang for a moment before answering. "Underborn."

"Are you crazy?" Max's eyes flared. "He's just as bad as Victus."

Ambria shook her head. "I don't agree. Plus, he has several relics of Jura that could help us."

"Underborn help us?" My forehead tightened. "How in the world do you figure that?"

"Well, I'm not absolutely certain, but I don't think he wants Victus in charge any more than we do." Ambria held up her hands to ward off arguments. "Look, it's worth a try."

"Last time I checked, the only place to contact him is in the Grotto." Max raised an eyebrow in challenge. "How do we get all the way across the pond to Atlanta without using an arch?"

She raised both of her eyebrows. "We don't."

"Huh?" Max and I once again synchronized our responses.

"We ask Gwyneth Augustus to take us to him." Ambria tapped on the arcphone in my lap. "You still have her contact information, right?"

"Unless she's changed it, yes." I opened my contacts and found her symbols—the arcphone equivalent of a phone number.

Max put a hand over the phone. "Before we contact her, why don't you explain exactly how Underborn can get us into the potions ingredients room without dying."

"He has the Map and Key of Juranthemon." Ambria made a twisting motion with her hand. "We just link a door to the one in the ingredients room and it'll take us straight there. No risk at all."

"Except for the Underborn part," Max said. "I mean, he might just kill us because he's an assassin and all."

Ambria sniffed. "He's not evil, just conniving."

"Nothing with him is free," I reminded her. "What will we owe him if he helps?"

She shooed my objection with a wave of her hand. "I have no idea, but it will probably be better than letting Victus have his way with the Overworld."

"Can't really argue with that," Max said.

I nodded. "I guess it makes sense."

"Of course it does," Ambria said. "I came up with it." She met my eyes. "Unless you've dredged up some better ideas from your parental archives."

My father had once ruled the Overworld as the Overlord. Ivy Slade had led a revolt and overthrown him. Before they could be captured, Victus and Delectra faked their deaths, binding their souls to mine by using a demon. When Rufus Cumberbatch released the binding and brought them back to life, fragments of their souls remained stuck with me for so long, I'd started calling them Vic and Della just so I could differentiate the voices in my head from those of my living parents.

I'd recently freed myself of them, but vivid memories from my parents' perspectives still remained lodged in my subconscious. Through meditation, I could access them in all their horrifying details. Most of Victus's were too awful to ever want to see, so I avoided looking. My scars were deep enough already.

I shook my head. "Ever since seeing him combine human fetuses with animals, I get sick to my stomach just thinking about it."

Ambria's eyes softened. "I know it's awful, Conrad, but the more we know about Victus's past, the better we can counter him in the future."

"Did you try using keywords?" Max said. "Focusing on something specific might narrow it down."

"Like what?" I plucked another blade of grass. "I don't think any of his memories will help us get into the ingredients room at the university any easier."

"Maybe Delectra knew of a secret passage." Ambria suggested.

"Yeah, think about secret passages," Max said.

I sighed. "Fine, I'll try." I'd already suffered through memories of my mother being tortured and humiliated when she'd tried to escape Victus. I didn't know what memories of hers could possibly be worse. I closed my eyes and shut off the outside world, just as I'd been taught to do in school. It was almost automatic now, thanks to so much repetition, but the waking terrors of my past clawed at my resolve.

I saw Harris scream as Victus blasted a hole in his chest. Watched a demon devour the lycan, Brickle. Smelled burning corpses. Watched my own hand slice a man to ribbons with Fireblade. It took everything I had to empty my mind.

Finally, I looked inward at the dark abyss. *Mother. Secret passage to the ingredients room.* It felt strange using keywords as if my mind was a search engine. *Mother, show me the secret passage.*

Victus stands in front of me, a crooked smile on his handsome face. "Finally, we have found the secret passage."

"I told you it was here, master." *A short, bald man grins, revealing crooked, yellowed teeth. Already, the caustic demon possessing him corrupts his flesh.*

"Well done, Herbert." *Victus barely looks at him.* "You are an excellent finder."

I look left at the narrow crack in the cliff wall. "It looks too small to enter."

Victus grunts. "I'll widen it later, but I want to see the inside." *He walks to the wall, turns sideways, and crabwalks inside.*

Herbert follows closely behind.

I don't want to go with him, but darkness coils around my mind and pushes my will to the side. Unable to resist, I slide into the crevice. It's so narrow, so tight, I fear I might become lodged inside. "How did the old fool fit through here?" *The voice hardly sounds like my own, a distant part of my mind realizes. Demonic impulse controls me now. I want to care, but I can't.*

When I reach Victus, he stands at the edge of a starry void. It is as if we have reached the edge of the earth and beyond is the infinity of space.

He tosses a rock into the void and it lands on an invisible bridge. "We've found it!" *Victus turns to me, face flush with joy.* "The answer to immortality lies on the other side." *He points to a crack in the void just on the other side.* "The legendary Glimmer exists!"

"Then let us go, my love." I cast a spell to dust the invisible bridge with aether. It sparkles for a span of hundreds of yards. "I want to live forever."

Victus kisses me passionately. "Soon we shall, my sweet." He turns and takes a step onto the bridge.

A haunting whine rises. Two stars detach themselves from far above and drift down toward the bridge, growing larger with every second.

Victus turns to Herbert. "What are those?"

"I don't know, master." Herbert scowls up at them. "I did not venture any further than this ledge when I arrived."

"Shall I?" I aim my wand.

Victus nods.

I unleash a torrent of destruction at the orb on the left. The energy merely dissipates on impact. "Perhaps it's a ward of some kind." I use the strongest dispel I know, but the orb continues drifting over the path with its mate.

Victus steps back. "Herbert, cross the bridge."

"But—master. My body—"

"We can always get you a new body." Victus thrusts a finger to the bridge. "Cross it!"

Herbert gulps, but steps out onto the bridge. The whining hum from the orbs grows louder with every step. When he's halfway across, the orbs vibrate, surfaces pulsating.

"My love, I don't think—" A gout of blue energy arcs from the orbs and into Herbert before I can finish my sentence.

Herbert screams. His body seems to catch fire from the inside, consumed by blue flames. The sickly yellow mist of the demonic spirit within drifts where the body once was. Before it vanishes back to Haedaemos, the orbs change color to an angry red. A cascade of energy nets the demon spirit.

Horrific shrieks rise above the wail of the orbs and the demon soul vaporizes.

The orbs abruptly revert to blue and drift away to rejoin the other stars. All that remains of the demon is a fine black dust settling into the void.

I gasped and opened my eyes back to the real world.

"Didn't work?" Max said.

"Sort of," I said.

"You only closed your eyes for a second." Ambria quirked her lips. "I thought it took longer than that."

"The memories don't take long," I said. "It's getting to them that usually takes a moment or two."

"Keywords do help." Max grinned. "See, I told you this would be useful."

"Not exactly." I told them what I'd seen. "It was the first time Victus and Delectra entered the crack in the world that leads to the Glimmer."

"I always wondered what those rift guardians would do if someone tried to cross." Max shuddered. "Now I know."

I touched my throat out of habit, but the chain with the anchor stone fragment was gone, taken back by Cora to keep me out of her realm, the Glimmer.

The shattered realm was home to a massive green moon known as the anchor stone. It held together the many realms, Eden, Seraphina, Sturg, Draxadis, and Aquilis, to name a few, and kept them from drifting too far apart in the celestial divide. Its aura granted eternal life even as it erased emotion and humanity. Victus had been after a piece of the anchor stone so he would be immortal.

We'd stopped him and driven him out.

"It seems your keyword of 'secret passage' didn't work entirely as we'd hope." Ambria sighed. "Do you want to try again?"

I shook my head. "Maybe later." I didn't want to admit how much it drained me to push aside existing nightmares only to awaken new ones.

The faces of the dead haunted me night and day, no matter what I did to push them away. I wondered how anyone found peace. *How does Kanaan do it?*

Max scratched his head. "How is it you have memories of Delectra's that happened after you got her soul shard? I thought you were limited to memories from before then."

"Somehow, the soul shards stayed linked to Victus and Delectra," I said. "Some of the visions I used to have before I lost the shards felt as though they were happening in real time."

Ambria shuddered. "I'm so glad they're gone."

Max grimaced. "Agreed." He looked down at my arcphone. "Well, since that didn't work, let's switch to plan B—Gwyneth."

Relieved to let buried memories lie, I dialed the symbols.

Gwyneth's face flickered onto the screen after several rings. "Conrad, you're alive?" The sound of wind nearly drowned out her voice.

The sight of her pretty caramel face and piercing green eyes stole my voice for a moment. Ambria punched me in the shoulder to knock me from my stupor.

"Yes, still alive." I frowned. "Why do you ask?"

"Rumor was you and your friends died in Colombia after a firefight with some hired wands." Her lips spread into a lovely smile. "I'm so glad to see you're alive."

"Where are you?" Max said. "It sounds like you're in a cave."

"Yes, that's right." Gwyneth panned the camera to show a steep rock face above and below her. The light from the phone drowned in a sea of pitch after only a few feet. She turned the camera back toward her. "I'm on the trail of some rare relics."

"Relics of Jura?" Ambria asked.

"Possibly." Gwyneth's forehead pinched. "So, what's up?"

Max turned my hand and phone toward him. "We want to talk to Underborn."

Ambria turned the phone her way. "We need his help."

"Oh, is that all?" Gwyneth tugged on an orange rope that seemed to be the only thing holding her onto the cliff. "Unless your backs are against the wall, I'd avoid asking him for anything. I agreed to help him on a temporary basis, but his contract had a clause I overlooked and now I'm his little errand girl."

"Are you relic hunting for him?" Ambria asked.

Gwyneth's face filled with regret. "Unfortunately, yes. And if you go to him for a favor, he'll just keep dangling carrots in front of you until you're so deep in debt, you'll owe him for the rest of your life."

I turned the phone back toward me. "I think he and I have a mutual interest in keeping Victus out of power."

"Underborn doesn't think that way," she said. "Unless Victus is bad for business, he doesn't care who's in power."

Ambria jerked my hand toward her face. "Look, we just need to borrow the Map and Key of Jura. We have to get into Arcane University without being detected so we can get into the ingredients room."

"And that's exactly how you'll end up owing Underborn." Gwyneth sighed. "If you want my advice, I'd say use any other means to get what you need without asking Underborn. There are bounty notices plastered everywhere on the Overnet. He knows you're on the run and desperate. Don't for a moment think he won't take advantage of that."

"Is he really that okay with Victus taking over?" I couldn't hide the disgust in my voice. "My father won't be good for business. I can guarantee you that."

"You can't guarantee it, Conrad." Gwyneth groaned. "God, now I know how my mom felt when she tried to talk me out of doing something stupid. Look, I wish I could make you believe me, but I guess you'll have to find out for yourself. If you really want to contact him, I'll point you in the right direction, but don't hold me responsible if you sign away your lives."

Deep in my gut, I knew she was right. Unless Victus posed an immediate threat, Underborn wouldn't lift a finger to interfere. In fact, he might offer help to my father just so he could gain favor. It wasn't that Underborn was evil. If anything, he was a chaotic neutral, dealing with direct threats to himself as necessary while taking advantage of everyone else. Given our present situation, we couldn't hope that he'd be generous enough to loan us the map and key without plenty of strings attached. The only reason I'd had a somewhat beneficial arrangement with him the last time was because the Heart of Jura had been in a place only I could safely reach—the Glimmer.

On the other hand, I knew of a relic he might be interested in. "What if I offered him the Dagger of Jura?"

Gwyneth's eyebrows rose. "The dagger of invisibility?"

"Yes. Plinth used it to reach the Glimmer." I arched my brow. "It's still there and only I can get it." I didn't mention that the Glimmer was still closed off to me.

Her lips formed a line. "I'd leave it there for now, Conrad."

My mouth dropped open at her disinterest. "Why?"

"Because someone else is aggressively searching for all the relics of Jura." Gwyneth shook her head slowly. "I mean, there's always been competition to retrieve valuable artifacts, but this is unlike anything I've seen."

Ambria crossed her arms. "Explain."

Gwyneth tested her rope and looked down before answering. "You've heard of the Reliquisti Order, right?"

"Heard of them, yes," I said.

"Think of it like an honor organization for great relic hunters." She turned her wrist toward the camera to reveal a tiny, but ornately drawn R tattooed on the skin. The edges seemed to hover slightly off the skin like a three-dimensional image. "I was inducted because I found the Lost Room of Jura."

"Is that an automatic in?" Ambria asked.

"Finding an exceptionally rare artifact in the wild usually is," Gwyneth said. "The rules are simple: Don't steal from other Reliquisti. All bets are off if several hunters are after the same relic."

Max frowned. "Where are you going with this?"

"Three major relic hunting organizations, all of whom are members of the Reliquisti, have been robbed blind of everything relating to Jura." Gwyneth paused as if to let that sink in. "That has never happened before."

"I assume they had good security," Ambria said.

"The best." Gwyneth bit her lower lip. "Whoever is doing this is the best thief I've never heard of. Even Underborn wouldn't dare steal from members of the Reliquisti, and he's not even a member."

Max's eyes brightened. "Hey, do you still have the Lost Room?"

"Not with me, no." Gwyneth shrugged. "Underborn locked away all his relics until we find out who's behind the thefts."

Max groaned. "He didn't even give you the map or key to use?"

Gwyneth shook her head. "No, he's not letting them out of his sight. I'm afraid that no matter what you offer him, he won't let you borrow anything."

"We can't beg, borrow, or steal our way into that ingredients room," Max groaned.

Once again, we were stuck.

CHAPTER 5

I was about to end the call when Gwyneth's eyes brightened. "Underborn did give me this." She tugged on a silver chain around her neck and pulled a U-shaped ornament from beneath her shirt.

"He certainly doesn't have an eye for art," Ambria said. "I could've made you something nicer out of bottle caps and paper clips."

Gwyneth chuckled. "It's not an ornament, it's a mini arch."

"A mini arch?" Max scratched his head. "You couldn't even fit a mouse through that thing."

"It expands to full size and can take me to any arch with the matching symbol." She turned it to the side to display a tiny Cyrinthian symbol.

I'd seen the same symbol engraved on an arch in the control room at El Dorado and in the one at Queens Gate. "Do all control rooms have arches with the same symbol?"

She nodded. "You have to focus on the symbol for the specific waystation for it to work. I have several memorized."

Ambria tilted her head slightly. "Are you offering the use of your mini arch?"

Gwyneth tilted her head to the side. "You said you need to get into Arcane University, right?"

Ambria smiled. "Yes."

"I can get you into the control room at Queens Gate." Gwyneth held up a finger as if an idea just occurred to her. "And, I can get you through the secret passage Underborn installed in the control room so you can bypass the main entrance altogether. Once you're in, you can take the mini arch and use it to get back to the control room."

"Great idea!" Max said.

I held up a hand. "Why bother with secret entrances? If we can get into a control room, we'll just use an omniarch to portal wherever we need."

Max slapped his forehead. "Duh, why didn't I think of that?"

Ambria clapped her hands. "We could portal straight into the ingredients room!"

"Do you remember what it looks like inside?" Max said.

She nodded. "Vividly."

I couldn't stop from grinning. "This is going to be a lot easier than I thought."

"Oh god." Gwyneth sighed. "You just jinxed it, Conrad."

Ambria and Max laughed.

"Um, I hate to ask you this, but when can you help us?" I waved a finger at her background, not that she could tell. "I mean, you're on a mission."

"I'm another hour from the bottom of the crevice," Gwyneth said. "Once I'm there, I have to navigate a few puzzles and traps to reach the relic, provided I'm even in the right place." She took out a palm-sized glowball and lit it. A single loud ping echoed and numbers appeared above the glowing orb. Gwyneth turned the camera to show the darkness below. Her hand released the glowball and it fell, pinging every so often until it vanished.

The camera turned back to Gwyneth. She held a hand to her ear, listening to the pings. "Make that an hour and a half."

"I do hope you don't die," Ambria said, "because we really need your help."

Max grimaced. "What awful phrasing."

I turned the phone back to me. "So, we'll hopefully see you in a few hours? A day?"

"Three hours if this is the wrong place, or tomorrow morning if this is the right place." She flashed a grin. "I'd better get going."

I imagined the traps and pitfalls that might await her. "Please be careful."

"And do let us know if you run into delays," Ambria said.

"Good luck!" Max shouted.

"Thank you." Gwyneth's image flickered off.

"I certainly hope she doesn't die," Ambria said.

Max pursed his lips. "Why don't we use the Dagger of Jura to complete our pantry raid? Invisibility would be perfect."

"We'd have to get into Queens Gate, onto the university campus, and into the Glimmer," I said. "Unless Evadora happens to be visiting the Fairy Gardens, we have no way of getting past the rift guardians." I shrugged. "Besides, from what Plinth told me about the dagger, every second you hold that thing is agonizing." I already felt agonized enough that I couldn't expect help from Evadora or Cora.

"Like you're being stabbed over and over." Ambria shuddered. "I don't think I could walk all the way across campus feeling like someone is murdering me."

"Yeah, but maybe Percival could make some painkillers. Then we wouldn't feel a thing!" Max looked back and forth at us as if waiting for congratulations on his great idea.

"It's a cursed relic, Max." Ambria rolled her eyes. "The pain probably cuts right through painkillers."

"Besides, we won't even need it since we can portal into the ingredients room." I paused as terrible thoughts swirled in my head. "Provided Gwyneth doesn't die on her quest."

"If she doesn't come through, we're gonna need a backup plan." Max stood and brushed off his pants. "Every minute we're stuck here is a minute Ivy could be blowing up our enemies." He turned and stalked back toward the house.

I closed my eyes and let a gentle breeze wash over me, a futile attempt to untie the knots in my gut. A warm body pressed against me, arms wrapped sideways around my shoulders. The vice around my chest loosened and my insides seemed to unwind.

"Are you okay, Conrad?" Ambria asked.

I nodded without opening my eyes. "I'm worried about Gwyneth. I'm worried about Nightliss, Ivy, and the others. I'm worried about Victus's monster army and his evil plans." I opened my eyes and looked up at the stars. "It's not like I can do anything to stop him right now."

"That's true." Her breath against my ear raised the hairs on my neck, but in a good way.

It reminded me of the first hug she'd given me after our escape from the orphanage. How good it felt then and now to have a true friend. "Thank you for always being there for me," I said.

Ambria leaned her head on my shoulder. "It's difficult, but I try."

I chuckled. "True."

She squeezed my hand. "I can tell you're still upset about Cora closing you out of the Glimmer. Would it help to talk about it?"

Evadora had come to me not long after I'd brought Cora back to life and taken back my necklace with the anchor stone. She told me Cora needed to concentrate on restoring her powers and regaining control of the Glimmer. Apparently, my visits were too much of a distraction. I wondered if the immortality aura from the anchor stone had already drained emotion from her and caused her not to care or if it was something else.

My heart hung heavy just from thinking about it. "I loved Cora so much, and she loved me. I just don't understand how she could go from being my mom to being a complete stranger."

"Coming back to life and losing her memories had that effect." Ambria sandwiched my hand between hers. "I just know that any day now she'll remember everything."

"Every day in the Glimmer erases emotions and humanity." The weight in my chest felt almost unbearable at the thought of losing Cora forever. "Even if she remembers, she won't be able to care or love." I pulled my hand free and stood up, unwilling and unable to keep talking about this. "Let's go inside and eat."

Ambria looked up at me with big eyes. "I'm sorry, Conrad. I didn't mean to—"

My phone rang. I frowned and whipped it out of my pocket. *Lily. Why is she calling?* I answered and her face appeared on the screen.

"Conrad!" Lily slumped with relief. "I just wanted to make sure you all were okay."

"Yes, we're fine for now." I saw a bookshelf behind her. "Where are you?"

"My dorm room." She turned the camera in a circle to show a room packed with books and parchment, then returned it to her face. "I don't know how much longer I'll be in school, though."

Ambria got up and put her cheek next to mine so she could appear on Lily's screen. "Why's that?"

"Grint and Quiff have totally taken over the curriculum." She threw up a hand. "They've practically thrown out all the normal books and replaced them with ones they call the New Ordinated Standard—that's capitalized, by the way."

"Are the professors okay with that?" Ambria asked.

"Several quit, but they've already been replaced." Lily's shoulder's slumped. "There's no sign of the Overlord, but I have a feeling he's pulling the strings around here."

"So he hasn't publicly declared himself a ruler." I didn't get my hopes up. He could comfortably control his puppets without ever coming out of the dark.

"I believe your father learned that sometimes it's easier to control the government from the shadows than by proclaiming yourself the dictator." Lily's lips pressed together. "Security is heavy everywhere, and the perimeter of the Dark Forest is blocked off. I haven't been back long, but I've seen enough to know that things are changing for the worst."

Ambria scowled. "Victus probably closed off the perimeter to build his monster army."

"A monster army?" Lily's eyes grew wide.

I told her what I'd seen. "The university is too dangerous. You should probably leave."

Her lips pressed together. "Or maybe you need me here more than ever."

I thought about telling her to leave again, but what if she could help? "Did anyone wonder why you and Baxter were gone for so long? Did anyone say anything about Harris?"

"Oh, Baxter didn't stick around. He left school and I haven't heard from him since." Lily sighed. "I faked an excuse note from my parents explaining that I came down with aetheritis and it took me a month to overcome it."

"What's aetheritis?" Ambria asked.

"It's an extreme version of magic poisoning," Lily said. "There's no cure for it except for plenty of rest and no magic." She smiled. "Quiff didn't even seem suspicious."

I frowned. "Why did you give the excuse note to Quiff?"

"Oh, I forgot to tell you. Winona Lutz, the Minister of Education, assigned Quiff as the new headmaster of Arcane University." She rolled her eyes. "It's ridiculous."

Ambria's forehead pinched. "Did they say anything about Harris?"

"No, I haven't heard even a whisper about it." Tears formed in Lily's eyes. "I'm sure Quiff and Grint know Victus killed him, but they're keeping it a secret."

"Without a body, it's not like they could say he accidentally died either." Ambria shivered. "It's so morbid. I can't bear to think about it."

"Quiff put recruitment posters all over campus," Lily said. "They're starting a Young Arcanes League."

"What in the world is that?" Ambria asked.

Lily made a face. "It claims to be self-defense training to protect Arcanes from vampires, lycans, and other undesirables, but it's obviously an indoctrination tool. Xander Tiberius is supposed to give a speech tomorrow about a new adult organization called Arcanes First."

I blew out a breath. "I don't like the sound of that at all."

"It's just the start." Lily looked over her shoulder toward the door. "People are showing their true colors. I don't even trust my roommate anymore."

"What do you mean?" Ambria asked.

"A bunch of students are really happy about the changes. They say it's time to get rid of the undesirables." Lily's forehead pinched. "All sorts of terrible things happened while I was gone. A group of shifter students was attacked by Arcane students a week ago. Most shifter kids have already left the school, and vampires are fleeing Queens Gate."

"It's just going to keep getting worse," Ambria said. "Be careful."

Lily nodded. "I will."

I decided it was worth the risk asking for her help, just in case Gwyneth didn't come through. "One other thing. Percival needs supplies for potions he thinks can help Ivy and the others."

Lily's eyes grew wide. "Do you need me to get something for you?"

I shook my head. "Hopefully, no. We have another plan that should minimize the risk, but it's possible that it won't work and I'll need a backup. Do you know of any way to get into the ingredients vault?"

Lily tapped a finger on her chin. "Professor Grace might help me."

"Really?" Ambria sniffed. "Why would that horrible man help you?"

"Because he believes—" Lily choked up. "Harris was his golden boy, and I'm Harris's friend."

I tried not to think about the way Victus's spell had punched a hole in Harris's chest, or how he'd gloated over the boy's corpse, but the images replayed in my mind no matter how hard I tried to forget them. "Do you really think Grace will just let you take any ingredients you want?"

Lily waggled a hand in a so-so manner. "Maybe. It can't hurt to ask."

"It could tip him off that you're up to something," Ambria said.

Lily tilted her head. "What exactly do you need, Conrad?"

I gave her the list Percival gave me. "From what I understand, these are rare ingredients. I don't know if that will make Grace more suspicious or not."

Ambria snorted. "Everything makes that man suspicious."

"Don't do anything unless I call you back," I said.

Lily nodded. "Understood. Good luck."

"Thanks, Lily." I offered a smile. "Right now, we need all the luck we can get." We said our goodbyes and ended the call.

Ambria and I remained silent for a while, looking out at the moonlit countryside, consumed by our own thoughts. Ambria eventually broke the lull. "I hope Kanaan is okay."

"I doubt he's in any danger," I said. "I hope he contacts us soon, though."

We went back inside. Most of the household had gone to sleep. Since we'd lived in another time zone for the past month, I still wasn't tired. Ambria went into her room to do some reading. I went into the kitchen for a snack and found a silver-haired Seraphim drinking a cup of tea. She and the other two Seraphim hadn't spoken a word of English when we'd rescued them. Unlike Ivy and Nightliss, the trio preferred to keep to themselves.

She looked up from a cup of tea, her matching silver eyes glinting in the light, but said nothing.

"Hi." I sat down across from her and buttered a slice of bread.

"Percival tells me you are looking for way to help us."

I reeled back in surprise. "You speak English now?"

She nodded. "Some. Apparently, we knew English before."

"We?" I asked.

"My companions." She pointed up. "I do not remember their names, but I feel as if I knew them." She shrugged. "I do not remember Ivy and Nightliss."

I leaned forward, interested. "You remember bits and pieces?"

"Yes. I know we come from another realm." She motioned with her hand again, as if pointing out the direction of said realm.

"The Grand Nexus is broken, so you probably won't be going back to Seraphina anytime soon."

She shook her head. "Not Seraphina. Olympus."

This revelation had me at a loss. "Are you certain?"

"Very certain." She took a sip of tea. "We lived on Olympus. We traveled to many realms. I can imagine some of the places, but not the names. Sturg, is one, I think. Draxadis." Her eyes narrowed in concentration. "There is another place with much water."

"Does Olympus have an Alabaster Arch?" I asked.

She shook her head. "An arch? No." Her eyes widened. "Ah, I remember it—yes, a small orb. The Chalon!" She moaned as if in pleasure. "Yes, that was it. We opened gateways to many worlds through Voltis. No need for an arch. All worlds lead to Atlantis and Olympus." Her eyes flared again. "Atlantis!"

I was completely lost. "You mean the mythical city that sunk into the ocean thousands of years ago?"

She hugged herself, eyes closed as if reveling in pleasure. "Your questions helped me remember, even if only a little."

"Tell me more about Atlantis and Olympus," I said.

"I can see Atlantis far below Olympus," she said without opening her eyes. "It is all that remains of the original Earth before the shattering into realms."

The bread dropped from my fingers. "Part of the world before the Sundering is still left?"

"Everyplace leads back to Atlantis." The Seraphim opened her eyes. "If only I could get back to Voltis." She looked around, gaze distant, then abruptly focused on me. "What is this place?"

"Italy?" I said. "Eden?"

"Eden!" She clasped her hands together. "Yes, Eden! Where is Voltis here?." She said something in another language and squeezed her eyes shut. "The center of the triangle?" After a moment she shook her head and opened her eyes. "If we could get to the triangle, we could return home."

"The triangle?" My bread had landed butter side down on the table, but I didn't care anymore. "Back up a step—you can get to Seraphina from Atlantis?"

She nodded. "Every realm leads there."

The breath caught in my throat. If she was right, that meant once she remembered how, she could take us to Seraphina and Justin Slade.

CHAPTER 6

"Who are you?" I asked.

The Seraphim paused, taken aback. "Pizza." She shook her head. "No, that is why we came. I am"—she gasped and looked at me—"Purah."

I blinked a few times trying to understand how she'd gone from pizza to Purah and wondered if she even knew what she was talking about. "Purah is your name?"

"I believe it is." She pressed a hand to her chest. "It feels right."

"What did you mean you came for pizza?" I asked.

"Eden has pizza," she said slowly, "and we came many times for pizza."

I hadn't eaten a lot of pizza, though admittedly it was one of life's more enjoyable foods. Cora had taken me for pizza and hamburgers when she was my foster mother.

"What is your favorite topping, Conrad?" Cora smiles from across the table.

My mind, as usual, is slow to respond. I struggle to come up with an answer.

"Use association to remember, Conrad." Cora touches my hand. "The last time I ate pizza, I..."

"The last time I ate pizza, I enjoyed..." An image sprang to mind of me eating pizza with mushrooms and olives. "Mushrooms and olives!" I clapped my hands together, so pleased to recall such a clear picture even with my dull mind.

Cora giggles. "Then that is what we shall get on our next pizza."

I blinked back to reality. *It's like using keywords to search memory.* Purah stroked her long silver hair, eyes lost in thought. I cleared my throat to get her attention. "Let's try word association."

Purah frowned. "I do not understand."

"The last time I wanted pizza, the others said..."

Purah raised an eyebrow. "The last time I wanted pizza, the other said —" Her lips pursed. "The last time I wanted pizza, the others said..." She repeated it over and over, eyes closed.

I dared not interrupt, instead, picking up my bread and inspecting the buttered side. It was a mess, so I tossed it and wiped off the table. I selected a fresh slice and began buttering it. A jubilant shout startled me so much, I flailed and flung my snack across the room.

"Sithain said, 'No anchovies this time.'" Purah leaned forward. "Gallifer said, 'But anchovies are my favorite!'"

"Your companions are Sithain and Gallifer?" I'd never heard those names before and wondered if anyone else might recognize them.

Purah stroked her hair and beamed. "Yes. You have done well, mortal."

Her sudden imperious tone rankled me. "Mortal?"

Purah frowned. "You are a temporary being, are you not?" Her English had gone from broken and accented to clear and precise. It was as if the fog surrounding her language skills had evaporated.

I didn't like her tone, so I lied. "No, I'm immortal."

"Oh." Her eyebrows lifted and some of her previous accent returned. "I thank you for your assistance."

"Then I ask you for a favor in return," I said.

"Name it."

"When you return home, I would like assistance reaching Seraphina. Perhaps you would let me borrow the Chalon."

Purah nodded. "Granted." She stood. "I must tell the others what I have remembered. This is a joyous occasion and requires pizza." Without another word, she left.

I didn't know where she planned to get pizza in the middle of the countryside, but that wasn't my problem. I could barely contain my own excitement. *We don't need the Grand Nexus! We have a way to bring back Justin Slade and the others!*

Moments later, Purah and her companions entered the kitchen, laughing and talking.

"This boy helped you?" The blond Seraphim put warm hands on my shoulders.

Her touch didn't soothe me like Nightliss. Instead, I felt uneasy.

"Yes." Purah coiled a strand of silver hair around her finger. "Sithain, meet Conrad." She looked at the man with the cloud of black hair. "Gallifer, meet Conrad."

"We owe you much thanks," Sithain said in heavily accented English. "Purah told us your request."

"Yes." Gallifer's voice was deep and booming. "Travel to Seraphina."

"Provided, of course, I can remember where we placed the Chalon." Purah seemed to deflate a bit. "There is much to remember, but this is a good start."

"If all goes well, Percival's potion will help even more." I fished another slice of bread from the breadbox and buttered it.

"Then we hope for your success." Purah held up two fingers and channeled a tiny sphere of glowing white that fizzled after only a moment. Her lips curled into a snarl. "Without my powers, I am weak."

"Do you remember anything else about your past?" I asked.

The trio looked at each other, shook their heads.

"Pizza," Gallifer said after a moment of silence.

Sithain nodded vigorously. "Agreed. We must find it."

Natalia walked into the kitchen. "I keep hearing the word 'pizza'. What's going on, and can I have some?"

"We must find pizza," Purah said.

"Won't find any nearby." Natalia cracked her knuckles. "Thankfully, I keep some premade dough and could probably whip you up a pie in no time."

"Delightful." Sithain rubbed her hands together. "We would be eternally in your debt."

I WOKE up late the next morning, tired from staying up and eating pizza with angels and a felycan. My damaged skin was itchy and peeling, so I put on more of the pink lotion. The backs of my hands itched the worst so I slathered it on extra thick.

After giving it a moment to dry, I went downstairs to the kitchen. A few cold pieces of bacon sat on a dish on the table, so I helped myself. Stan stepped in the back door and took off his rubber overshoes.

"Raining cats and dogs." He grinned. "Makes doing the chores harder."

I looked out of the back window at the chicken coop and the flock of sheep in the pasture. It reminded me of the fateful day a man had tried to kill me by mind-controlling sheep and chickens. Instead, I'd accidentally killed him. That led us to Queens Gate and his house where we'd discovered he was Ambria's older brother, Levi Rax.

"You look troubled, Conrad." Stan put a hand on my shoulder. "Anything I can help you with?"

I shook away the memories. "No, just thinking about the farm at the orphanage."

He grimaced. "Well, no child slaves on this farm."

I laughed. "That's good to know." I looked around. "Mind if I take some eggs and make some toast?"

"Absolutely not. Help yourself." Stan turned on the gas stove and put a pot of water on it. "I'll have some tea ready in a few minutes."

Ambria and Max stumbled into the kitchen moments later, both of them looking as if they hadn't slept a wink.

"Do I smell eggs?" Max rubbed his tummy. "I could eat a whole dozen."

Stan chuckled. "Guess we'd better double the food order."

As I put more eggs in the frying pan, I saw Ivy and Nightliss walking from the direction of the pasture. Their soaked hair and clothes hung heavy, but they carried on an animated conversation, completely oblivious to the drizzle and continued to talk unabated when they burst into the back door.

"Ladies, you're tracking mud." Stan put his hands on his hips. "I'm too old to clean up after everyone."

Ivy stopped in her tracks. "Oh, I'm sorry! Bigdaddy would be so angry right now." She sighed. "I wonder where he is."

Max grimaced and shot me a look. He'd told me that her Bigdaddy had been Jeremiah Conroy, one of the many incarnations of Moses, dead now for years. None of us had the heart to tell her, and hoped she didn't react badly when her memories came back.

Nightliss took off her soaked shoes then got down on her hands and knees and began wiping up the mud with a towel.

Stan sighed, but couldn't help but smile. "I don't think these angels are used to cleaning up."

Max looked horrified. "Nightliss, please! You're the Templar Clarion. I'll clean it up."

Nightliss looked up at him, green eyes sparkling with amusement. "Even the Clarion must follow house rules."

My heart melted in the glory of her smile. *She is so beautiful.* I knew how hopeless it was to pine after someone like her. She was thousands of years older, and I was still just a boy. Her eyes found me and I nearly swooned.

"Good morning, Conrad." Nightliss stood, holding the muddy, dripping towel. "Asha and Galfandor wished me to say goodbye for them."

I blinked out of my stupor. "They what?"

"Did they leave?" Ambria looked out the back window. "They didn't even tell us!"

"How could they leave without telling us?" I stood next to Ambria at the back window and felt my heart sink. "Did they say anything else, Nightliss?"

Nightliss looked confused. Her eyes wandered between me and Ambria. "No, I am sorry they did not say anything else. Is there something wrong?"

Ambria growled. "I guess the only thing that's wrong is that we're kids."

Max came over and stood between us. He put a hand on each of our shoulders and quietly said, "Well, I guess that means we have to rely on Gwyneth."

I checked the time and saw how late it was. Either Gwyneth had forgotten about us or something terrible had happened.

Ambria must have noticed the look on my face. "You haven't heard anything from her?"

I shook my head. "Nothing yet." Since the kitchen was getting crowded I motioned my friends to follow me into the family room where we could be alone. "On the other hand, I found out something very interesting last night."

Max's eyebrows rose. "What do you mean found out something interesting?"

I told them about my conversation with Purah, Sithain, and Gallifer.

"You've got to be kidding me," Max said. "They have a way to travel between realms that doesn't require an arch?"

"If this is true, we have all the more reason to go get those potion ingredients for Percival." Ambria put a hand to her forehead. "We wouldn't have to rely only on Ivy and Nightliss to help us. We'd have the entire Eden Army behind us."

"Unless Aerianas defeated Justin in Seraphina." Max winced as if he wished he hadn't said that. But he was right. We had no idea if Justin Slade and his army were still alive.

I pulled up Gwyneth's contact information and stared at it, wondering if I should call and see if she was okay. *What if she was somewhere dangerous? What if her phone rings and it gets her killed?* "Maybe I should just let her call when she's ready."

Max nodded. "Yeah, you're probably right. I would hate to distract her at a crucial moment."

Ambria also nodded her agreement. "She did say there's no telling how long it might take her."

Max rubbed his belly. "I'm going to go get some more bacon and toast."

Ambria grunted. "Maybe you should just eat a few spoonfuls of lard. That might keep you full longer."

He stuck out his tongue and left.

Ambria went to the front window, leaned on the sill, and looked forlornly at the rain. "There goes our picnic."

I put a hand on her shoulder. "We could always have a picnic inside.".

"Yeah, but a picnic inside isn't as much fun."

I wasn't sure what to do with myself at this point. Without Kanaan around to train us, I decided to go into my room and do some reading. I took out my arc phone and pulled up one of the Arcnology books written by Adam Nosti. After couple of hours, I couldn't take it anymore.

Though I was afraid of what I might see, I decided to revisit Delectra's memory about the crack in the world. I didn't think it would help with our current quest, but maybe it would help me find another way back into the Glimmer. I couldn't bear not seeing Cora for so long.

I closed my eyes and retreated within, picturing the rift.

Meditation always came at a cost. Images of blood-spattered bodies, of screaming victims and burning spells flashed like faded pictures in the back of my mind. I'd grown used to pushing past them so I could use magic, but they were always there, like spiders crawling in my hair.

Any time I used magic, I had to push through that barrier of nightmares to reach the silence of the void so I could aetherate and focus my will. Even then, I heard the whispers of the dead.

I focused on the rift. *Show me more.*

I TREMBLE in fear at the edge of the void. Victus means to kill me, of that I am certain. The demon he'd sent across was annihilated, flesh and spirit. What will become of me if these guardians attack?

Victus pushes me onto the invisible bridge. "Step forward, dear. If my theory is correct, you will not die."

Moments earlier, he removed the infernal totem from around my neck, allowing the demonic influence in my mind to wane. To bring back more of the real me. Gone is the cold, evil woman. Back is the vulnerable Delectra. The foolish girl who allowed herself to be duped by a charismatic man. Perhaps I should welcome oblivion instead of this prison of flesh.

"Perhaps if you explain this to me, I can help." I don't even have a wand. Victus took it from me in case I try to escape.

He reveals the same smile he used to seduce me all those years ago. He's so handsome, so magnetic, and so terribly evil. Victus points to the rift guardians. "Moses created those things, but they transcend everything I know about magic. They are not aether. They are not wards. They seem to be alive."

"Yes, and they will kill me," I remind him.

"Moses, as Ezzek Moore, was your grandfather. You share his blood. Somewhere in that lovely soul of yours flows the power of the first Arcane." Victus offers his kindly smile again. The kind he uses to get what he wants. "I believe the guardians will let you pass."

"The first power." Serena steps between us and looks up at me with curiosity. "Do you really think she can touch it as Moses did, even with the demon stains on her soul?"

"I am certain. That is why I allowed the demonic taint to fade from her." Victus pushes me onto the invisible bridge. "She will survive."

The wail of the guardians echoes faintly through the stars as they notice my attempt at trespass. My legs freeze, but Victus shoves me hard. I fall and scrape my knees on the invisible stone.

"Go, woman!" Victus motions me on.

I stand. Blood trickles from the wounds in my knees. A few steps more and I'll stand where the guardians vaporized the demon. A barrier forms at my back.

I spin and try to go back, but Victus extends his wand, using a shield spell to force me onward.

"Please, no!" I pound on the invisible barrier. Tears stream from my eyes. "Victus, stop!"

The guardians swoop down. I press my back to the shield and face them as their wails reach fever pitch. Arcs of plasma surge toward me.

Something snatches me backward. I land hard on the bridge. Rough stone skins my elbows and hands. Tears drip from my eyes and blood pools beneath my new wounds.

Victus sneers down at me. "Useless woman."

"Completely removing the demon influence might allow her to touch the first power, Victus." Serena looks down at me dispassionately—the gaze of a scientist at a lab rat. "With that power, you would be unstoppable."

"I don't want her to have it." Victus jabs a finger at his chest. "I want it for myself."

I try to crawl between them. To escape my tormentors. But Victus cuffs me on the back of the head. He fastens the choker around my neck—the infernal totem. Needles press into my skin. The nauseating sensation of demon essence seeps into my veins. Soon, I'll be his little monster again.

I jerked from the memory, my face wet with tears that still trickled down to my chin and dripped off. *Mom, I'm so, so sorry you had to live like that.* Victus nearly killed her in his attempts to cross into the Glimmer. I really wanted to know more, but if it meant reliving another horrible memory, I didn't think I could do it.

The void. Those words stirred Lulu's words from my memory. *You stand alone at the void of the rift...or something like that.* Did it have something to do with the rift between our realm and the Glimmer? Or had her words been metaphorical? I tried to work through it with logic, but the memory of my mother awakened more terrors from my past.

Images of her holding a knife to my throat, of my father gloating, flashed into my mind's eye. I gasped in fright and wiped tears from my face. I needed to recover with something mindless.

I composed myself and went into the kitchen. I wasn't hungry, but I didn't want to be alone anymore. There was only one person who could cure this melancholy feeling. I made a couple of brisket sandwiches, and poured some water into the canteen. Stan helped me find two pairs of galoshes and raincoats and let me borrow his biggest umbrella.

I found Ambria lying on the couch reading while Natalia played Monopoly with Nightliss and Ivy in the middle of the family room. I waved at Ambria to get her attention. "Are you hungry?"

She sat up and groaned. "Not really, but I suppose I could eat."

When we got into the kitchen I handed her raincoat and pointed to a pair of galoshes. "Put those on."

Ambria raise an eyebrow. "Were going out in the rain?"

I nodded. "I thought it would be nice to go out for a walk."

She smiled. "I think anything is better than listening to Ivy yell at everyone when they're beating her at Monopoly."

Ivy screamed in the other room. "I will not go to jail again!"

We looked at each other and burst into laughter.

I put on a pair of galoshes and a raincoat and opened the back door. It was raining quite heavily, the water flying sideways in sheets. "Ladies first."

Ambria giggled. "Aren't you the gallant one?" She pulled the hood of the raincoat up over her face and hunched against the wind as she stepped outside. Thankfully the long raincoat and tall galoshes seemed to protect her from the elements.

I stepped up behind her and closed the door. Hooking an arm in hers I guided her down the gravel path toward the pasture. Despite the raincoat, water still got in past the hood and trickled down my neck. Some of Ambria's hair drooped wetly out of the edges of her hood. We walked for about five minutes and finally reached the tree where I had prepared our picnic.

The large umbrella had blown away and now lay in the middle of a flock of curious sheep. The soaked picnic blanket covered the basket with the sandwiches. I ran over, peeled away the blanket, and opened the basket. Aside from the canteen of water everything inside was a soggy mess.

Ambria burst into laughter. "Did you really try to arrange a picnic in the middle of a thunderstorm?"

I closed the basket and nodded. "It wasn't raining this hard when I arranged it. I thought it would be nice."

Ambria wiped her eyes. "Besides saving me from a lifetime of slavery at an orphanage and rescuing me from all sorts of other evildoers, this is probably the nicest thing anyone has ever done for me."

I laughed. "Well, you and Max have saved me plenty of times." I rolled up the soggy blanket, and picked up the basket. Ambria and I walked toward the sheep. The woolly creatures walked toward us, bleating, bells jingling on collars around their necks.

"They must think we're bringing them treats," Ambria said. She reached into the basket and pulled out the soggy sandwiches. "I wonder if sheep like brisket."

"I doubt it but they'll probably eat the bread." I took one of the sandwiches and tossed it to the sheep. The lone ram of the herd trotted over and nibbled at the bread.

Ambria threw hers in the opposite direction and laughed with delight when the rest of the flock chased after it. She splashed through the mud and grabbed the large umbrella as the wind threatened to blow it away again. When she picked it up, a strong gust nearly lifted her off her feet before she was able to close it.

We stood in the gusting rain watching lightning split the horizon and feeling the rumble of thunder in our bones. Ambria took my hand and kissed me on the cheek. "Thank you, Conrad. I know things didn't go exactly to plan, but I've had a wonderful time."

Warmth spread through my cheek. I looked over at the one person who'd been with me every step of the way since our escape from Little Angel Orphanage. She'd blossomed into such a pretty girl. She was like a sister to me. Without her, life would be unbearable.

I wanted to say something, wanted to let her know how I felt, but a sudden buzzing in my pocket startled me. I fished inside the raincoat and pulled out my arcphone.

At last, the call I'd been waiting for was here.

CHAPTER 7

"**I**t's Gwyneth," I said.

Ambria blinked rapidly. "Oh, finally." She sounded disappointed for some reason. She took out her wand and cast a shield spell to keep the rain off the phone.

I looked at the shimmering barrier and snorted. "Maybe I should've used magic instead of an umbrella to protect the picnic."

I answered the call. Gwyneth's face appeared on the screen. Purple and blue underlined her left eye. A long scratch down her cheek on the same side hinted that her quest had not entirely gone to plan. "Are you okay?"

She nodded wearily. "It could've been much worse, believe me. The worst part is there wasn't even a relic there. It was all part of an elaborate trap designed to mislead anyone else looking for the relic."

Ambria's forehead wrinkled with concern. "A trap? What hit you in the face?"

"A small rock, thankfully." Gwyneth touched her left eye and winced. "If a much larger one had hit me I wouldn't be speaking to you right now." She held up a hand as if to ward off further questions. "Look, I can tell you all about it when I see you. For now, I need to know how to find you."

I wasn't quite ready to trust her with the location of Stan's house, so I gave her a location that was a comfortable distance away, but still easily reachable for us by regional train. "Meet us at the leaning Tower of Pisa."

Gwyneth hesitated, nodded. "I can't blame you for not entirely trusting me, Conrad, but I promise I will do all I can to help you."

"When can you meet us there?" I asked her.

"How does six o'clock this evening sound?"

I did some quick calculations in my head. Nodded. "We'll see you on the south side of the tower at that time." I ended the call and sighed with relief. "Thank goodness she survived."

Ambria looked at the time on my phone. "How long will it take us to reach Pisa?"

I'd already looked at the train schedule online. "About four hours by regional train."

"Then we better get going." Something gurgled. Ambria's eyes flared with surprise as she put a hand on her stomach.

I laughed. "Maybe we should eat some lunch first."

She nodded vigorously. "Yes, we should."

We went inside, had a quick bite to eat, and found Max playing checkers with Stan. Max looked at us expectantly. I nodded.

This is the tricky part. "Stan, we want to sightsee today. Could we get a ride to the train station?"

Stan looked out the window at the gray skies and pouring rain. "Not exactly the best day for that. Weather is supposed to clear up for tomorrow. Why don't you wait until then?"

"Uh, I don't mind the rain," Max said.

I shrugged. "Yeah it would just be nice to get out of the house even if it's raining."

Stan hesitated. Shrugged. "Sure. Let me get my raincoat."

While he was getting that the three of us grabbed our wands, satchels with extra clothes, and any other supplies we might need, then waited inside the black Range Rover in the garage.

"Wish we had brooms," Max grumbled. "Trains are slow."

Ambria sniffed. "I don't fancy flying in the rain, so a train is perfect. Besides, we left our brooms in Colombia."

Stan shuffled into the garage and hopped in the driver's seat. "Where you kids going today?"

"Just thought we'd ride the trains around," I said.

The garage door was already open, so he backed out. "You have money?"

I nodded. "I learned it's good to keep money on me in case of emergencies."

Stan chuckled. "I'll bet you've had a few of those." He steered onto the gravel road and headed toward town. "Do you have any Euros?"

"Um, a few." I hoped I could exchange pounds for the other currency somewhere.

We reached the train station about half an hour later and said our goodbyes to Stan.

The locks clicked down before we got out. Stan turned in his seat and gave us stern looks. "I know you're not going sightseeing."

"But—"

He shushed me. "I figure I can't do much to stop you if you really want to go chasing after Asha and Galfandor, but I would like you to listen to me for a moment."

Ambria sighed. "I know we're just kids, but we've been through a lot, Stan."

"Yes, and you know how to handle yourselves." Stan patted her hand. "You're not dummies, but you don't have a lot of experience. I think Asha and Galfandor know what they're doing. I think you'd be better off staying at home, but I know trying to talk you out of this won't work. Just think before you leap, and call me if you need any help, okay?"

"You probably could've told Natalia to keep us at the house," Max said. "She's stronger than all of us."

Stan snorted. "Natalia's got a mind of her own. She probably would've joined you."

I held out a hand. Stan took mine and shook it. "Thank you, Granddad Stan."

He squeezed my hand. "Of course, son. Take good care of yourselves."

Ambria leaned through the gap between the seats and hugged him. "We will."

Max shook his hand, and we got out. As the Range Rover pulled away, I realized I clenched something in my hand. I opened it and found a transit pass inside. "Stan must have slipped it into my hand," I said.

Ambria smiled fondly. "It feels good having someone watch out for us."

"Yeah, it's kinda strange." Max stared wistfully as the car vanished into the rain. "Hope we don't get ourselves killed now."

Ambria groaned. "Don't be so negative."

I went into the small train station and used the transit pass to get us three tickets to Pisa. We sat on a bench outside and browsed the Overnet on my arcphone for news of the Overworld. The official site of the Arcane Council flashed a hologram of my face with the word *WANTED* in all caps above my phone.

A young woman sitting on a bench across from us gasped in surprise. She asked us something in Italian, but I couldn't understand her.

Max grabbed the phone and banished the hologram. "They must've used a script to make it pop up like that." He growled. "I hate pop-ups."

"How did you do that?" the woman asked in broken English.

"Experimental phone," Max said.

She frowned. "What app?"

The trained squealed into the station and saved us from further questioning. The cars looked mostly empty so we chose one near the middle and sat in the back away from a lively group of old people. One of the men held out a bottle of wine to the woman on his right. She took a healthy swig and passed it on.

"Italians certainly know how to live it up," Max said. "It's the middle of a work day and they're drinking like it's the weekend."

"I've never seen much outside of England." Ambria leaned back in her seat and sighed.

"Uh, the Glimmer?" Max said. "The Grotto, Queens Gate? Should I go on?"

"I mean of the normal world, Max." Ambria folded her arms and delivered a cross look. "It would be nice to travel to a land where the wild creatures aren't trying to kill me for once."

Max grinned. "Then let's stay away from Australia."

His casual mention of the Glimmer returned my thoughts to Cora. I'd missed her terribly after she died—so much so that I'd traveled to the ends of the Glimmer so I could resurrect her. Now that she'd walled herself off from me, she might as well be dead again.

Max nudged me with an elbow. "What's the glum face for?"

I shook my head. "Just thinking of Cora."

"Yeah, what's her deal?" Max grunted. "We nearly died bringing her back to life and now she won't even see us anymore."

Ambria squeezed my hand. "I'm sure once she gets her powers back under control, she'll be happy to let us visit again." She let go of my hand and tapped my phone screen. "Let's look at something funny online."

"Yeah." I swallowed the lump in my throat and tried to forget about Cora for the time being. I wasn't in the mood for mindless reading, so I opened a web browser and went to the Overworld News Network website. The video stream automatically started to play.

A lovely blond woman with glowing red eyes smiled into the camera. "Little Jimmy, his parents, and most of the church congregation are expected to survive the demon-summoning accident, and Custodians are onsite providing complimentary mind wipes to those who want to unsee the horrors a crawler can inflict on living beings."

A square-jawed man in teal robes chuckled. "You might say they had a hell of a time, Darcy."

Darcy giggled. "Yes, indeed, Dennis. At least we know little Jimmy got plenty of exorcise yesterday."

Dennis guffawed. "Along with most of the church congregation." He turned to the camera, the levity abruptly vanishing from his features. "In other news, Primus Tiberius has announced new school reforms. All history texts are now updated to the new standard, telling the true story of Justin Slade and how he engineered the downfall of the Overworld government."

"That's right, Dennis." Darcy looked down at a stack of parchment in her hands. "New reports indicate that had the Overlord not banished Slade and his minions to another realm, they might even now rule us all as slaves."

Dennis's brow furrowed. "With more on that report, here's Blaine Stevens."

A picture of Justin Slade, his face morphing into demon form flashed onto the screen. "Corruption. Power. Absolute destruction." A young news reporter appeared, face grim. "According to revised history, Justin Slade was a hero. But students at Arcane University discovered a treasure trove of original documents revealing that this so-called savior, was anything but."

A young girl sitting in a chair read from a piece of parchment. "Justin Slade wanted absolute control of everyone. He liked to morph into demon form and eat virgins." She looked with worried eyes at someone behind the camera. "That's what it says on the documents we found."

The scene switched to that of an office. A man in gray Arcane robes sat before a shelf of leather-bound books and looked seriously at someone off-camera. "He was driven by greed, lust, and the need to destroy anyone who opposed him."

The camera switched to Blaine now sitting in a chair across from the man. "Do you think his people rewrote history to make him seem like a hero, Professor Hobbes?"

"Absolutely." Hobbes stared directly at the camera. "In fact, the same people rewrote history to make the Overlord, the man who actually saved us from Slade, look like the villain." He shook his head sadly. "It's time to put Arcanes first. I pray Primus Tiberius can fix the mess we're in now."

"Are you kidding me?" Max swiped the video off my screen. "What is that rubbish?"

"Isn't it obvious, Max?" Ambria scowled. "Victus is rewriting history. When he comes out of the shadows, he'll be welcomed as a savior."

Max scowled. "But who in the world would believe this rubbish?"

"The ones who want to believe." I stared out the window at the passing scenery. "We just have to hope people don't believe the propaganda."

"People are sheep," Max said. "They read something or see something and think it's true."

"Don't we have videos of our own we could get out there?" Ambria said.

"We can't exactly get it on the Overworld News," Max said. "Maybe one of the social websites would work, but I don't have many friends on them."

I hoped people wouldn't blindly trust the news, but with Xander Tiberius in charge of the Arcane Council, he had the power to sway people by force if necessary. We might have disabled the foundry, but only Victus knew how many people he'd replaced with infernus. We literally couldn't afford to trust anyone, not even people we thought we knew.

When the train pulled into the station at Pisa, we got out and stepped into the street. I couldn't help but feel a bit disappointed at the rundown buildings and graffiti defacing an old red brick wall across the road. I couldn't even see the famous leaning tower from where we stood. The gloomy weather didn't help.

Ambria took out her wand and cast a small invisible shield a few feet above her head to act as an umbrella. Max and I did the same then consulted my arcphone for directions. The scenery improved the closer we got to the Pisa Baptistery and the church near the tower. Despite the sprinkling rain, dozens of people posed with the leaning tower in the background, arms outstretched as if holding up the tower.

"I'll bet that never gets old to the locals," Max said sarcastically.

Ambria looked around with wide eyes. "Isn't it beautiful?"

The great domed baptistery, the sprawling church, and the leaning tower were works of art, even if not as amazing as some of the buildings in Queens Gate and the Grotto. I tried to take a moment to enjoy the change in scenery, but my gaze drifted to the south side of the tower where Gwyneth would meet us in just over an hour.

I caught the narrowed gaze of a woman from beneath a red umbrella. Her eyes looked up above my head and then at my face. She turned to a man next to her and nodded at us, spoke in a language I didn't recognize. The man gave us an apologetic look and pulled her away.

"What was that about?" Max said.

"Probably wondering why we aren't getting wet." I pointed above my head. "Thanks to our invisible umbrellas."

Ambria shrugged. "It's better than getting soaked."

Max rubbed his belly. "Speaking of umbrellas, I'm starving."

Ambria's forehead wrinkled. "What does that have to do with umbrellas?"

"Nothing, really." Max shrugged. "I just couldn't think of a good segue."

"Can't expect Max to think on an empty stomach," I said with a grin.

"Or ever, for that matter." Ambria pointed to a pizzeria just down the street. "Let's try the local cuisine."

The pizza we shared was nothing spectacular, but it stopped Max's stomach from growling and gave us something to do while we waited. After settling the bill, we went back outside into the misty dusk settling over the town. We walked toward the meeting spot, passing by a museum and some small shops along the road.

Gwyneth stepped out of one of the shops and frowned. "You look familiar. Do I know you from somewhere?" She looked pretty as always, even with the black eye and scratches.

My heart soared at the sight of her. "It's good to see you, Gwyneth."

She grinned. "Good to see you haven't lost your sense of adventure."

"Adventure?" Ambria scoffed. "This is about saving the Overworld, not risking our lives for fun."

"Nice to see you too, Ambria." Gwyneth looked at us appraisingly. "You've all grown since the last time I saw you."

"Did you bring the mini-arch?" I asked, eager to get on with the mission.

She touched the silver chain around her neck. "Of course. Shall we?"

I nodded. "Yes, please."

Moments from now, we'd be right under the noses of our enemies, stealing the very supplies that would help us overthrow them.

CHAPTER 8

Gwyneth led us down a narrow alley. As we walked, a terrible thought occurred to me. *What if she's an infernus? What if this is a trap?*

We stopped at a dead end. Gwyneth pulled the tiny arch from within her shirt and detached it from the chain while I watched from a few feet away, hand on my wand. She closed her eyes and touched the ornament. It spun like a top, rapidly expanding upward and outward until it stood nearly eight feet tall and just as wide at the base of the columns.

"Since you want to use an omniarch, I decided it would be best to portal into an unused waystation so we wouldn't have to worry about arch operators finding us." Gwyneth concentrated on the arch. It hummed slightly. The lights in the nearby shops dimmed and a street light crackled, showering sparks. A gateway split the air within the arch. A dimly lit room appeared on the other side.

"Where is that?" Max asked.

"Thunder Rock." Gwyneth stepped through and held out her hands as if to show everyone it was safe. "Ever since this place was picked clean, nobody bothers coming here anymore."

I went through after her. Almost immediately, my palms tingled and a distant sound hummed in my ears. It took me a moment to realize it came from the massive ley lines running through the ground beneath us. It was as if someone had turned up the volume on the background noise and I was hearing it for the first time. I closed my eyes and aetherated. The itching in my palms grew unbearable so I pushed it all away.

Ambria stepped in front of me. "What's wrong, Conrad?"

I shook my head. "Nothing. This place makes me feel uneasy."

"Me too." She rubbed my arm. "We'll be out of here soon, though."

"Wow, look at this place." Max pointed at the huge black arch veined with white. "I wonder why they call those Alabaster Arches when they're mostly black."

Ambria rolled her eyes. "I'll talk to the committee on arch naming about that, Max."

Rows of smaller arches lay in ruins, as if a tidal wave had swept through and reduced them to rubble. Water dripped and wind howled in the abandoned chamber. I could almost sense the ghosts haunting this ancient place.

Gwyneth closed the portal. The miniature arch fell between the columns of the arch we'd used to enter this place and rolled on the floor.

"That's really neat." Max picked it up and inspected it. "So, this portable arch follows you through the portal?"

"It wouldn't be very useful otherwise," Gwyneth said with a smile. She took it from him and attached it to her necklace. "Underborn believes there are portable omniarches, but he hasn't been able to find one."

"Something like that would be amazing," Ambria said.

Gwyneth nodded. "People would kill for that sort of power." She walked to a niche in the side of the wall where rows of omniarches towered over us. Many were broken and crumbling, the silver rings at their bases slashed with red paint. Gwyneth stopped before one marked green and flourished her hands toward it. "Since you know where you want to go, I'll let you do the honors."

"I'll handle this." Ambria stepped inside the silver ring, knelt, and closed the circuit with a press of her thumb. The air crackled and stray hairs rose ever so slightly from her head as concentrated aether washed past.

My palms tingled and the background hum of magic rose in volume. I opened myself to the magical energy around me. This strange new hypersensitivity opened me up like never before to the fluctuations in the ley lines and the static charge of airborne aether. I wondered if Lulu had done this to me, or if my burned skin just made me extra sensitive to everything.

Eyes narrowed, Ambria stared at the arch. A gateway flickered. The air popped, fizzled, and hummed as the portal seemed to fight its way into existence. Energy cascaded across the arch columns. A boom echoed through the control room and the portal stabilized, revealing rows of shelves on the other side.

The power in the ley lines fluctuated wildly as she struggled to open the portal. When it finally stabilized, the power level held relatively even.

Ambria wiped sweat from her forehead. "Goodness, that was difficult."

"Is something wrong with that arch?" Max regarded the portal dubiously.

"Maybe this arch is slightly damaged." Gwyneth stepped inside the circle and tossed a pebble through the gateway. It landed on the stone floor in the ingredients storeroom on the other side. "Seems to work, though." She put a finger through the gateway and pulled it back. "I think it's safe."

"Then let's get what we came for and go." Ambria dashed through the portal. She gasped, stiffened, and fell to the storeroom floor, flailing violently before going still as death.

85

"Ambria!" I ran for the portal.

Max cried out in horror. "Is she dead?"

I leapt through the portal without thinking, realizing too late that whatever had happened to her might have something to do with the malfunctioning arch. I expected to be struck down as quickly as Ambria, but landed safely by her side. I knelt, rolled her over. "Ambria, are you okay?"

She snorted. Giggled. Her eyes flicked open, brimming with amusement. "I got you."

Gwyneth groaned.

"This is no time for games!" Max balled his fists. "Are you out of your mind?"

I groaned and helped her to her feet. "That was mean."

"You didn't even hesitate, Conrad." Her expression grew serious. "What if the portal killed me? What if there was poisonous gas in this room?"

"I didn't stop to think. I just came." I shrugged. "Next time, I'll throw cold water on you instead."

Ambria squeezed my hand. "Thank you."

"For what?" My forehead pinched. "I didn't do anything."

She cleared her throat and took out a parchment with the list of ingredients on it. "Let's split up and get everything okay?"

Gwyneth took a look at the list. "I'll get the elephant tears and meet you back at the portal."

"I've got the toasted slugs," Max said.

"*Snails!*" Ambria said. "*Toasted snails.* You'd better not get the wrong thing, Max."

He rolled his eyes. "I'll get it right."

"I'll get the acorns and the devil pupfish oil." I looked at the names on nearby shelves. We were in the Rs, which meant I had to run down to the other end of the storehouse.

"That leaves the white avocado to me." Ambria tapped a finger to her chin. "Does that mean it's in the A section or the W?"

"Probably W." Gwyneth jogged down the aisle. "See you in a minute."

Max groaned. "Why didn't Professor Grace put a center aisle in this place? It's stupid to have such long rows without a way to cut through."

"Don't be so lazy, Max," Ambria chided him.

I jogged after Gwyneth since she headed in the same direction. The storeroom was stretched for at least a hundred yards, so it took us a moment to reach the E section where Gwyneth split off from me. I turned right on the next row and jogged past shelves lined with every conceivable potion ingredient that started with the letter D. Burlap sacks, plastic containers, bags, and boxes sat in impeccable order, each one clearly labeled with the contents.

It didn't take me long to find to find small vials of devil pupfish oil tucked in between devil pupfish eyes and devil pupfish urine. I took four of the small vials and stuffed them between folds of cloth in my side satchel, then ran to the end of the aisle so I could go to the A section. I saw Gwyneth jogging back toward the aisle where the open portal waited. Ambria waved at me from the far end as she returned with her ingredients.

I turned left and reached the shelves near the front of the room. I found a large bin full of the acorns and grabbed a handful. Several slipped from my grasp and rolled on the floor. I knelt down and stuffed them in my pouch. If I left them lying around Gideon Grace would know for sure someone broke into his precious ingredients room.

Something clicked behind me. I turned around as the door to the store-room swung inward. Two familiar faces regarded me with wolfish grins.

"Well, if it ain't our little mouse." Talbot bared white teeth.

My heart froze. I backed up a step.

Delilah pulled back the hem of her black duster to reveal a pink wand in its holster. "Don't run, boy. Not unless you want a hole through your leg."

"Don't damage the goods too much, sis." Talbot chuckled. "His daddy won't like that."

"How did you know I was in here?" The corner of the shelf was only inches away. The question was, could I get there before they shot me?

"We got the whole campus warded against portals." Talbot slid back the hem of his duster and put a hand on the hilt of the black wand in its holster. "Ol' Victus wanted to block portals, but we figured, why stop portals when you can catch the people using them?"

"You set off an alarm," Delilah said. "And now you're in our snare."

I'd seen how fast the wandslingers were. Even the short distance I had to travel was too far. I didn't dare reach for my wand, and I didn't have anything on me to get me out. In a matter of minutes, one of my friends might look for me, or shout my name. If I went with the bounty hunters right now, they might not search the warehouse. I didn't want to risk anyone else getting hurt.

On the other hand, I wasn't a novice anymore. Kanaan had taught us a great deal about magitsu and physically conditioned us for emergency situations. I had a chance—a very slim one—but it was better than the alternative.

I put up my hands. "Fine, you caught me."

"Smart boy." Talbot smirked. "Guess your daddy gets you back in one piece after all."

I looked between the bounty hunters and widened my eyes. "Dad, what are you doing here?"

It was the oldest trick in the book. Maybe they thought I was too young and stupid to try something like this, or maybe they were just too cocky to care. Either way, Talbot and Delilah glanced over their shoulders.

I dove for the end of the aisle and slid around it. Then I vaulted to my feet and ran. Ambria stepped out of the row with the portal, a hundred feet away, and put hands on her hips. "What's taking so long, Conrad?"

"Run!" I shouted. "Get through the portal!"

"What?"

A bolt of silver energy exploded against the end of the shelf to my right. Splinters sprayed through the air. "He's got friends, Talbot!" Delilah yelled.

I dove around the shelf for cover as another kinetic bullet thudded into the wood.

"Wandslingers!" Ambria screamed.

"Go without me!" I shouted. "Go now!"

"No!"

"Do it!" I sprang to my feet and raced to the other end of the aisle.

Talbot stood four rows down from me, wand at the ready. Energy flashed. A bin of bird feathers exploded in a cloud. I used the smoke-screen to dash past two more aisles before a silver bolt grazed my shirt-sleeve and forced me back in. I checked the nearest label. *Hypovolemic Herbs.* Ten more rows to go to freedom.

I'll never make it.

A volley of green spheres sang past in the opposite direction. "Son of a bitch!" Talbot said.

"Run, Conrad!" Gwyneth said. "We'll cover you."

"Your boy takes a step toward you and I'll hollow out his chest," Talbot said. "Give him up and the rest of you can go."

"No deal!" Ambria said.

While I appreciated cover fire from my friends, I didn't know how I was supposed to run toward them while they were firing at someone behind me. What if they shot me by accident? I looked up the shelving and had a flashback from the time I'd escaped a secret library patrolled by dogs. These shelves stood nearly twenty feet tall with another twenty feet of clearance to the ceiling. I could probably reach the top, but could I leap the ten-foot gap between the aisles?

Probably not.

I rummaged through the items on the shelf, hoping to find something useful, like a smoke bomb, or a magical shield, but it was like looking for a weapon in a grocery store. Professor Grace had stocked this place with the ingredients to make potions, not ready-to-use magical artifacts.

Think, Conrad, think! Were there ingredients starting with the letter H I could use to make an emergency potion? *Horse tail hair and hemp fibers make magical rope!*

I ran down the aisle, searching the inventory for the ingredients as my friends traded attacks with Talbot up and down the outer aisle. When I stopped to grab the horse hairs I noticed faint grooves in the polished stone near the middle of the aisle. Unlike the other shelves, this one seemed to hover a fraction above the floor. I gave it a gentle push and the shelf slid backward and to the side.

There's a hidden middle aisle! It just had to be opened manually.

A kinetic bullet pinged off the floor. Ambria and the others had held off Talbot, but apparently none of them realized Delilah had flanked me from the other side. I dashed through the opening before she could fire another shot and shoved the middle shelf in the next row. It slid open like the last.

"The mouse found a hole down the middle!" Delilah shouted.

I ran forward, pushed the next middle shelf. Delilah ran down the outer aisle, pacing me, but unable to get off a clean shot before I pushed through into the next row. Unfortunately, each shelf slowed me down a fraction of a second, and she had nothing in her way.

Eight rows. Seven. Six. I was almost halfway home. As I extended my hands to push through the shelf to the fifth, fire seared the back of my calf. I fell forward, slamming into the shelf and shoving it open. Before another magic bullet hit me, I dragged myself into the narrow space between shelves.

"I winged 'im!" Delilah said.

Muddled shouts rose from the direction of my friends, but I couldn't make out what they said.

"There's a middle row!" I shouted above the explosions and pinging kinetic bullets. "Push the shelves!" I peeked around the shelf and saw Delilah stalking down the aisle toward me. Anger heated my chest. I clenched my teeth and gripped my wand. She might be a good shot, but could she penetrate a shield?

I put pressure on my injured leg and bit back a cry of pain. Somehow, I had to shield myself while I ran—limped, rather—to safety. I pushed up to my feet and nearly fainted when I tried to stand on my hurt leg. It felt like something was ripping through my calf muscle from the inside out.

I pulled up the pants leg and saw a clean hole in the outer edge of my calf. Blood trickled down the sides, but the edges looked nearly cauterized. If it had gone clean in and out, why did it feel like something was still in there? Forget running with a shield—I'd have to limp. Another glance showed Delilah only a few yards away.

Hopping on my good leg, I went through the opening. Closing the shelf wouldn't do a thing to stop her and I couldn't shield my back while hopping backward. She'd just shoot my other leg. I fought past the nightmares and formed an image in my head. I flicked the wand through the patterns, weaving them into the shield spell I'd learned from my mother's soul fragment.

Instead of casting it at the tip of my wand, I attached it to the center aisle, virtually invisible except for a slight shimmer. I turned and limped across the aisle to the next shelf. Pushed it open.

"One more step, boy, and I'll put a hole in your ass."

I really wanted to thumb my nose at her, but it was all I could do to keep moving forward. I heard a thump. A fist banging against the shield. A cry of frustration.

"You think you're mighty clever, don't you, boy?" A bolt of white streaked over my head and exploded against the shelves in front of me. The shockwave threw me backward with a painful jolt. "You ain't going nowhere!"

I staggered to my feet. Delilah stepped back a few feet from the shield, aimed her wand and unleashed a fierce volley of explosive charges at it. The shield shimmered and crackled. I hopped frantically toward the next opening and made it through, shoved open the next. *Three more rows!*

But when I pushed against the next shelf, it wouldn't budge. I pushed harder. Suddenly, it rammed into me, knocking me over backward. Fire raced up my injured calf. Max dashed through the opening and grimaced. "No wonder it was stuck!" He grabbed my arm and yanked me up. "Hurry!"

I lurched to my feet and screamed as my weight landed on the wrong leg. Another explosion threw me forward and sent Max staggering backward. "Run!" I shouted.

Max threw my arm over his shoulder and took off through the next opening. Silver energy whizzed past. Ambria appeared from the left, wand arm weaving a shield. Magic bullets pinged off the surface. She and Max dragged me back toward the portal.

"They're escaping!" Delilah shouted.

"I thought you had him!" Talbot yelled back.

I glanced back. Delilah thrust her wand forward. A kinetic bullet the size of a small missile snaked through the middle row, above Ambria's shield, and toward us. If size was any indication, it would blow us to bits. "Run!"

Max and Ambria picked up the pace and tugged me around the corner.

"Keep going, I'm right behind you," Gwyneth shouted.

Max shoved me through the portal. Ambria piled in after me and Max staggered through. The spell rammed into the shelf and obliterated whatever was on it. Ashes and pieces of ingredients rained down. The blast caught Gwyneth as she ran toward us. She flew backward and landed in a lifeless heap.

CHAPTER 9

Gwyneth twitched once and lay still. *She can't be dead.*

"Get her!" I shouted.

Max and Ambria snapped from their dazes and dashed back through the portal. They grabbed Gwyneth by the feet and tugged her like a sack of potatoes across the polished stone floor. I desperately wished to help them, but my calf hurt even worse than before. They dragged Gwyneth through just as another spell smashed into the shelves.

I tried to close the portal, but pain shattered my concentration. Delilah dodged around the corner and aimed her wand. A volley of kinetic bullets streaked our way.

"Off!" Max screamed. The portal closed an instant before the bullets reached it.

I gritted my teeth and rolled onto my knees. Put two fingers to Gwyneth's neck. A strong pulse beat beneath her skin. She took a shuddering breath and opened her eyes. "What happened?"

"Explosion," Ambria said. "It knocked you silly."

"I thought wandslingers just used kinetic bullet spells." Max inspected his singed clothes. "Those were more like magic missiles."

Ambria wiped soot from her cheeks. "They've obviously upgraded."

Gwyneth pushed herself into a sitting position. "Did we get everything?"

Panic gripped my heart. I opened my satchel, grimacing at what I might find inside. Two vials of oil were shattered, but the other two had survived. I sighed with relief. "I got mine."

"Me too," Ambria said.

Max nodded.

Gwyneth removed a vial of elephant tears from her satchel. "Thank god."

"Oh crap." Max grimaced. "I got slugs instead of snails."

"You what?" Ambria's face burned bright red.

Max guffawed and produced a wooden box labeled *Toasted Snails*. "Just kidding."

Ambria shoved him. "I'll turn you into a snail, Maxwell Tiberius!"

I collected the ingredients and stuffed them into my satchel. "We've got another problem."

"What's that?" Max asked.

"Asha and Galfandor don't need to go to the university anymore." I took out my arcphone and hesitated before texting Asha. *Will she be mad that I went?* A part of me didn't care, but another part didn't want her to think I'd gone behind her back. Either way, it didn't matter. Going to campus was far more dangerous than we'd thought.

I tapped out the message. *Do not go to the university. We have everything already.*

My phone rang an instant later.

"Conrad, how did you get the ingredients?" Asha sounded tense.

"An omniarch." I glanced at my injured calf. "We were in and out fast." *At least that isn't a lie.*

"How did you—never mind." Asha said something muffled, probably to Galfandor. "Well, I guess we'll turn around and come back. But you and I need to have a talk."

The tone of her voice rubbed me the wrong way. "Look, you might be my teacher at school, but outside of it, you're my sister. You're not my boss."

"I'm your *older* sister, Conrad."

"I've survived just fine without you and I don't need you and Galfandor acting like we're a bunch of babies." I caught nods of affirmation from Max and Ambria. "If you'd just let us help, we could've saved you a trip."

Asha sighed. "It's just that—" Another sigh. "I like having family, Conrad. I want to keep you safe."

A lump formed in my throat. "I want you to be safe too. Maybe we look like kids to you, but we've been through a lot. Kanaan's given us extensive magitsu training, too."

"You definitely got all the ingredients?" Asha asked.

"Yes." I patted the satchel. "We're about to open a portal back to Stan's. Would you like us to open a portal so you can come back with us?"

"No, Galfandor took us on a small detour to gather some other supplies, so we'll drive back."

"Okay, we'll see you soon?"

"Soon, Conrad." Asha ended the call.

Max rubbed his hands together. "I don't know about you, but I'm anxious to see if Percival can make this potion work."

"He'd better," Ambria said.

I turned to Gwyneth. "I know you don't think Underborn will help us, but can you at least ask him?"

She nodded. "I'll see what I can do."

Max nodded at her necklace. "I don't suppose we could borrow that mini arch of yours?"

"Underborn would be very upset." Gwyneth ran a finger down the chain. "Otherwise, I'd happily let you borrow it."

"He's not a very nice person," Ambria said.

"It's not that he isn't nice," Gwyneth said, "it's that he's self-centered."

"In other words, selfish and mean." Ambria raised an eyebrow in challenge, but Gwyneth didn't pursue an argument.

"Well, thanks for the help." I took Gwyneth's hand. "Are you certain you feel okay?"

"I'm a bit bruised and sore, but it's nothing I haven't been through before." Gwyneth winced as she climbed to her feet. "By the way, Conrad, Liana asks about you all the time."

A heat wave flushed up my neck. Liana was every bit as pretty as her older sister. "Oh, um, I hope she's doing well."

Gwyneth laughed. "You're adorable when you're embarrassed."

"I can't help it," I said. "Fighting my father frightens me, but women can be almost as scary."

"Tell me about it," Max said.

Ambria huffed. "It's time you started acting like men instead of boys."

Max grunted. "I don't know about Conrad, but I want to enjoy being a boy for a while longer."

"Too late," I muttered. "Besides, we might not survive to manhood."

Max's shoulders slumped. "Don't remind me."

Gwyneth hugged me and kissed my cheek. "I'll tell Liana you asked about her." She must have felt my shoulders stiffen, because she giggled. "Don't worry, she doesn't bite."

"I do," Ambria said in a threatening tone.

"Hmm." Gwyneth's gaze wandered to Ambria and back to me. "Sounds like someone already has you in their sights." She knelt and sealed the silver ring around the omniarch, wincing and holding her ribs. "This is going to hurt in the morning." She concentrated on the arch and a gateway opened into an alleyway paved with cobblestones.

"Is that the Grotto?" Max asked.

"Yep." Gwyneth made a thoughtful noise. "The portal opened right away this time. That portal alarm spell at the university must have been the reason it took so long to open there."

I'd noticed the same thing. "Well, maybe we can use that knowledge to our advantage next time."

Max pshawed. "I don't know about you, but I'm not going anywhere near the university without Ivy and Nightliss to back us up."

Ambria smirked. "That's one of the smartest things you've said all day, Max."

Gwyneth waved farewell and stepped through the gateway. It blinked off an instant later. Ambria opened a portal to the field in front of Stan's farmhouse.

Max took a long last look around the arch control room. "Man, I really hate going back to the middle of nowhere again."

"Not for much longer," I said.

Ambria nodded. "Provided Percival comes through."

I prayed he could. *Time to find out.*

I limped through the gateway and into the dark field. The burn in my injured calf had receded to a deep ache, but it still couldn't take much weight. Max and Ambria followed me through and closed the portal behind us. Natalia in leopard form bounded up to us moments later, eyes curious.

"Is it bad that I want to pet her?" Max said.

Natalia bowled him over and stood on his chest.

"I think she'll pet you instead," Ambria said with satisfaction.

Max pushed back to his feet after Natalia let him up. "Geez. Girls are so touchy."

When we went inside, Stan came out of his bedroom already dressed in his pajamas. "Goodness, you're back already?" He looked down at my bloody pants leg. "You've been injured!"

I slumped into a chair and closed my eyes, exhausted and aching all over. "It's not too bad."

"What happened?" Percival said.

I blinked open my eyes. "We've got your ingredients. Can you make the memory potion?"

"What? But I thought Galfandor and Asha went to fetch them." He knelt and pushed up my pants leg to inspect my calf. "You've been shot!"

"Yeah." I suppressed a groan. "Maybe something for the pain?"

"I have just the thing." He darted away.

"No ghost pepper potion!" I shouted.

Max's face paled. "They got you good."

"It's awful!" Ambria gripped my hand and stroked my hair. "Is the pain unbearable?"

I leaned my head against her arm. "I've had worse. Besides, it was worth it."

"How did the bounty hunters find us?" Max asked.

"They told me the entire campus is warded against portals." I leaned down and looked at the hole in my leg. The skin around the edges was puckered and crusted with blood. "That's the reason the portal took so long to open, and when it did, it set off an alarm."

"I didn't realize you could ward against portals," Ambria said. "I thought you had to have portal blocking statues."

"They could've set wards to detect changes in atmosphere," Max said. "When you open a gateway, it's bound to change the air pressure, or something detectable. It's all about hacking a weather spell to suit the purpose."

Ambria tapped her chin. "I suppose you're right. Those bounty hunters are very clever."

Natalia, still in leopard form, sniffed my leg and growled.

"I agree," Ambria said.

"I'm relieved you made it out alive," Stan said. "Did you tell Galfandor and Asha?"

"Yes, I called them," I said. "They're on the way home."

"Good, good." Stan shook his head slowly. "I'll admit, I was worried sick, but here you are, mostly safe and sound."

Percival returned with a green potion that he brushed onto the wound. I winced at the initial sting, but it soon faded to numbness.

He pressed a thumb to the wound. "Feel anything?"

I shook my head.

"Good." Percival applied a thick white gel to the injured flesh on both sides of my leg then wrapped a poultice with cotton. "That should heal up within a few days, but the pain potion will only hold you for a day or so."

I tried to stand, but Percival pushed me back down with a stern glare. "Just because you don't feel pain doesn't mean you should put weight on the injury." He huffed. "Take a breather. I think you've bloody earned it."

"Yes, you should go to bed." Ambria put a hand on my shoulder. "I think we've had enough excitement for one day."

"If Percival had let me up, I planned to limp to bed, not run a marathon." I looked expectantly at the healer.

"In that case, you may go." Percival picked up the satchel of ingredients. "While you slumber peacefully, I'll be hard at work." He frowned and took one of my hands. "Have you been applying the lotion I gave you?"

I nodded. "Yes, why?"

He peered at the skin in the middle of the back of my hand. "It's scarring, and it shouldn't be."

I examined the pale spot of rough skin. "My skin has been peeling. Maybe that's why."

"It's scarring here, too." Ambria rubbed a similar patch on the back of my other hand.

Percival examined my arm, neck, and face—all places I'd been sunburned. "Yes, there's another patch on your throat." He touched the hollow of my neck. "How did this happen?"

I told him about the incident with Lulu.

He huffed. "Sometimes I think you're out to test the limit of my abilities." Percival tapped his chin. "My god, I hope dragon breath doesn't give cancer."

Images of Cora wasting away in a hospital seized in my chest. "Cancer?"

Percival waved a hand. "Probably not. I think the pure aether in her maw probably singed you. Hopefully the scar tissue will recede over time."

I hoped he was right. *Lulu, what did you do to me?* Why had she burned me? Why was I so sensitive to aether now?

Nightliss came downstairs, eyes curious. "What happened?"

Ivy leapt down the stairs behind her and nearly bowled her over. "What's all the excitement about?"

Max's eyes took on a dreamy look. "We sneaked onto the university campus and stole the ingredients for the memory potion! Then the wandslingers found us and nearly murdered us."

Ivy's eyes widened. "Oh, really? Did you blast them to ashes?"

"We're not nearly strong enough to do that." Ambria rolled her eyes. "No, we all ran for our lives, including Max."

"We ran through a hail of magic bullets to rescue Gwyneth," Max grumbled. "I mean, give me some credit."

"Yes, you were very brave, Max." Ambria pushed him toward the stairs. "Perhaps Ivy will reward you with a kiss."

Max's face turned bright red. "What?"

"Oh, a hero's kiss?" Ivy bounded down the stairs and wrapped her arms around Max's neck. "For being a hero, I reward you one big smooch!" With that, she pressed her lips enthusiastically to Max's and held them there until he pulled away gasping for air.

A drunken grin crossed Max's face. He stumbled backward and might have fallen if Ambria hadn't propped him up.

"Did you like it?" Ivy asked.

"I love you," Max said.

Her big blue eyes sparkled. "Aw, that's sweet!"

I looked at Nightliss and found myself hoping she'd give me a hero's kiss too, but considering our age gap, she might consider it inappropriate. The angel did walk over and look with concern at my leg.

"Oh, you're hurt, Conrad." She knelt and touched the skin around the bandage, her cool fingers sending shivers up my leg. Nightliss stood and kissed my forehead. "You are a brave boy. Thank you for helping us."

Boy? I couldn't help but wish that kiss had been on my lips, but I smiled and nodded. "I'd do anything to get your memories back."

Ambria huffed. "Well, I'm going to bed." She stomped upstairs and a door slammed shut.

I instantly felt guilty, and wasn't even sure why.

"She loves you," Nightliss said.

"Friendship love, or love-love?" I asked.

She smiled. "I think you know already."

"Yeah." I sighed. "I do." Part of me felt the same way, but another part felt conflicted. Ambria was my best friend. She was like family to me. Would it change things too much if we liked each other as something more? I wasn't ready to risk our friendship yet.

"Would you like some tea?" Max asked Ivy.

She batted her eyelashes at him. "Like a date?"

He grinned stupidly. "Uh, sure."

I wondered if Ivy would change a great deal when her memories returned. Max's blossoming relationship might be short-lived. It might break his heart, but at least he could have a moment with his crush.

Purah emerged from the kitchen and walked purposefully toward me. She took my arm. "I would speak with you, Conrad."

"Sure." I limped as she guided me toward the kitchen, not from the pain, but to make sure I didn't put too much weight on my injured leg.

Gallifer and Sithain sat at the kitchen table when I came inside, pizza crusts the only evidence of what they'd eaten for supper.

"We heard you returned victorious," Sithain said.

I shrugged. "We survived."

"So modest." Purah pursed her lips. "A mere boy with little power, and yet he throws his spark of life so casually into danger."

I didn't know if she was commending or demeaning me. "I have more power than you right now," I reminded her.

"As you say." Gallifer nodded. "Forgive Purah. She sees mortals as playthings."

"I'm immortal," I lied.

"We know this is untrue," Sithain said. "You are a wizard—a human of limited lifespan."

"We all have limited lifespans," I said. "Seraphim can die just like humans."

"The boy speaks truth," Gallifer said. "He is wise for one so young."

"Not wise, exactly," I said. "I was possessed by a demon that preserved the souls of my dead parents. When the demon was purged, shards of their souls remained behind. Though the shards are now gone, some of their knowledge and memories remained."

"A demon-forged mortal," Purah said. "Remarkable."

I knew this wasn't why they'd brought me in here. "Is there anything else you want to know?"

"Can this Percival truly concoct a cure?" Gallifer asked.

I nodded. "I have faith in Percival."

"That is good." Purah graced me with a smile. "Once we remember our past, we can help you reach Atlantis and beyond."

I returned a confident smile, but my hands trembled with anxiety. The future of Eden rested on Percival and his memory potion. I hoped he could come through.

CHAPTER 10

I spent the next two days relaxing, keeping off my feet as much as possible. Every time I slept, I dreamed of pulsating stars drifting in a void. Each time, they drifted closer to me, threatening to consume me in blue fire. I suspected it was related to the memories of Delectra and the rift guardians—another trauma scarring my soul.

To take my mind off my troubles, I played Granddad Stan in chess nearly half a dozen times, more interested in hearing his stories than playing the game. Percival locked himself in his makeshift lab, coming out only to eat.

Any questions regarding the memory potion were met with short, dismissive responses, or a rolling of the eyes. "This cannot be rushed!" he told me when I caught him getting a bite of supper on the evening of the second day.

Thankfully, his potion and poultice did wonders for my wounded leg. Though it still hurt to put my full weight on it, the puckered flesh evened out, leaving behind only a pale scar. By the morning of the third day, I walked with barely a limp to the breakfast table.

"Where in the world are Asha and Galfandor?" Max said before stuffing a slice of buttered bread in his mouth. "Should we be worried they haven't come back yet?"

"Well, they did say they had a few errands to run." Ambria shrugged. "I'm sure they'll be back soon enough."

"Not like there's much to do here anyway," I added. "I doubt they're in a rush."

Percival stumbled into the kitchen, pale-faced and drooping. He made a shot of espresso with the machine on the counter and tossed it back. Moaning contentedly, he leaned on the counter and stared out the window.

The rest of us shared curious glances, but had learned not to pester him. Percival huffed and turned to face us. "Well, aren't you the least bit curious to know my progress?"

"Of course, but I don't want to get yelled at," Max said.

"Glad you asked." Percival rubbed the dark circles beneath his eyes. "The fusion between the primary potions has completed. Since I don't have my notes, I had to manage the process completely from memory." He raised an eyebrow and pursed his lips.

Sensing this pause indicated he was fishing for a compliment, I said, "That's quite a feat."

Percival nodded knowingly. "Oh, it is. Mind you, it was touch and go for a time, but now, I have this." He produced a tiny vial of electric red fluid from his coat pocket. "A drop of this in each eye will dissolve the memory blocks."

Ambria clapped her hands together and gasped. "Oh, Percival, are you certain?"

He moved his head side-to-side. "Reasonably certain, but I will need a test subject."

Her face fell. "How long will it take to work?"

Percival shrugged. "Minutes, hours—I don't know."

Max dropped his fork and rose from his chair. "I'll get Ivy!"

"We volunteer." Purah stepped around the corner, flanked by Gallifer and Sithain. "Apologies for eavesdropping, but I overhead Percival talking about the potion and was eager to hear of his progress."

"Could the potion harm them?" Ambria asked.

Percival waved away her question. "Absolutely not. I tested it on a rabbit, and the animal is quite unharmed." He regarded Purah and her comrades. "I wouldn't recommend testing all three of you at once, in case there are other side effects."

Ambria looked aghast. "How is a rabbit supposed to compare to a Seraphim?"

"Because it just is!" Percival huffed.

"Very well, I will go first." Purah sat down at the table. "Please administer it to me."

I couldn't help but feel apprehensive at the idea of her regaining her memories and power before the others. Purah obviously looked down on us mere mortals even without her full memory. Once returned to her full strength, how much smaller would we become in her eyes? The only Seraphim I trusted fully was Nightliss.

But what if the potion did have unintended consequences? What if it induced madness or caused harm? In that case, I would much rather it happen to Purah. Her companions shared her knowledge of reaching Atlantis and Seraphina. The best way to handle this was to let Purah take the first dose. If it worked, Nightliss and Ivy would go next.

I needed Purah to be reliant on us until we had absolute assurance that she would show us the way to Seraphina. I blinked and noticed Percival staring at me with a quizzical expression.

"Well, is that okay?" he asked.

"Is what okay?"

"Giving her the first dose." Percival sighed. "Perhaps you need a shot of espresso."

"Yes, yes." I nodded. "It's fine."

"Very well, then. We shall proceed." Percival vanished back into his lab and returned a moment later with an eye dropper. He dipped it into the vial and filled it halfway then dripped a single drop into each of Purah's eyes.

Her irises shimmered with electricity. She gasped, her back arching so hard she nearly tipped over the chair. Gallifer and Sithain gripped her shoulders to keep her in place. Purah's head tilted back and a scream tore from her throat.

Ambria covered her ears. "My god, Percival, you've killed her!"

"Did you put ghost pepper in that thing?" Max shouted above the din.

"Of course not, you little fool!" Percival grimaced and pressed hands over his ears. "I don't know what's wrong!"

Ivy and Nightliss rushed into the kitchen.

"What's wrong?" Ivy said. "Did she eat one of Granddad Stan's spicy sausages?"

Granddad Stan rushed inside the back door. "Good lord, I heard her screams all the way down at the pig barn."

"She tested Percival's potion," Ambria shouted into sudden silence.

Purah went limp and quiet, sagging into the chair.

"You've killed her!" Gallifer exclaimed.

"No, impossible." Percival put two fingers to her neck. "She has a strong pulse, and she's breathing."

Purah's eyes flashed open. Rapid-fire sentences in Cyrinthian shot from her mouth.

Gallifer and Sithain exchanged worried glances.

"Who is King Thussor?" Nightliss said. "What is a bloodstone?"

"I do not know," Gallifer said. "I cannot remember."

"I remember some of these things from long ago," Sithain said. "I do not understand. Is her mind damaged?"

I remembered the strange flashbacks I used to have when still possessed by my parents' soul shards. It seemed as though Purah was experiencing one long flashback. Her abrupt descent into madness suddenly made sense. "She's thousands of years old, and the memory block cut her off from her past," I said. "Everything must be coming back to her in such a rush, her mind can hardly handle it."

Percival snapped his fingers. "Of course. It's like blowing a dam instead of releasing the waters slowly."

"You are the Fallen?" Nightliss's eyes flared. "I remember hearing of you!"

Natalia skidded through the kitchen door, morphing from leopard to naked girl in seconds.

Max's eyes went wide and his mouth hung open. "Clothes?"

"No!" Natalia's eyes widened with fear. "The wandslingers are here, and they've brought a posse!"

Purah's insane babblings filled the stunned silence.

"How in the hell did they find us?" Stan asked.

"Give me that potion." Ivy cracked her knuckles. "Time to blast some baddies."

"No, we've got to get out of here." I jabbed a finger at Purah. "We can't afford for you to end up like her while we're under attack."

"He's right." Percival tucked the vial of remaining potion into his shirt pocket. "It'll only incapacitate you, and we can't afford that while we're under siege."

I ran to the front room and peeked through the curtains. Talbot and Delilah stood in a waist-high field of wheat a hundred yards to the south, flanked by at least half a dozen men and women in dark blue robes. If the sight of the wandslinger bounty hunters wasn't enough to frighten me, another familiar face sent waves of ice-cold terror rippling down my spine.

"Bloody hell, it's Garkin." Max shivered.

Towering above the others, his thick beard laced with gray, Garkin led a group of mages in gray robes. Crimson streaks dripped from the Cyrinthian symbol for strength on each of their foreheads. Only the most devout and powerful of Garkin's mages wore the sign of the blooded. I'd never seen them before, but Kanaan absolutely despised them.

A shimmering portal hung in the air behind the posse, leaving little doubt as to how they'd arrived here. Talbot waved a hand and everyone but Garkin strode toward the house. A scowl on the man's face told me he didn't like Talbot ordering him around. Considering how Garkin had beaten Kanaan in their last encounter, I had little doubt the master of strength could easily handle Talbot and Delilah.

"They must have brought Garkin in case Kanaan was here," I said. "There's no way we can beat Talbot and Delilah without him."

The group halted and one of the blooded waved a wand at the ground. A wall of flame burst from the ground and just as quickly puffed into nothing.

"They're disabling the wards." Stan sucked in a breath through his teeth.

"Do we fight?" Ambria stared with wide eyes through the window. "Or do we run?"

"We should get the car," Max said.

"I knew this day might come." Stan pressed his lips into a thin line. "Everyone get down to the basement." He removed a picture on the wall to reveal a slab of dark wood engraved with symbols. "I'll activate the emergency protocols."

An explosion echoed outside as the mages disabled another set of wards guarding the perimeter.

The symbols glowed as Stan traced each one. The garage door rumbled open and the black Range Rover roared to life and sped away down the road, shadowy figures inside.

"The car!" Max shouted. "Someone took the car!"

Stan chuckled. "Not exactly."

"A decoy?" Ambria said.

"Exactly." Stan motioned toward the stairs. "But we need to go quickly."

Each of the blooded reached into a sack and pulled out a bundle of sticks. They threw them into the air. Wooden limbs unfurled, and stout legs planted themselves on the ground. The sticks formed a ribbed outline that quickly became familiar.

Max gasped. "They're wooden horses."

Garkin and his followers leapt onto the wooden steeds. The golem horses leapt forward, chasing after the car at incredible speed. Within seconds, the strength master closed the gap. He rammed his staff against the backend of the car. A boom echoed and the Range Rover spun out of control, flipping over and skidding on its roof into the ditch.

The golem horse slowed. Garkin slid from its back and held up a fist. His followers halted. Garkin examined the car and shook his head. He tapped a pendant on his robes and spoke, presumably telling the others about the ruse.

"I said go!" Stan shouted. "We have no time!"

That was all it took to get everyone rushing downstairs. Stan traced a symbol on the back wall and it slid aside to reveal a tunnel. Everyone dashed inside. I took a quick headcount. Nightliss and Ivy stood next to Natalia and Ambria, but Purah and her people were nowhere to be seen.

"Wait!" I grabbed Stan's arm before he closed the tunnel. "We're missing four people."

"Where's Percival?" Ambria said.

"Go find him," Stan said. "While you're up there, I need you to grab the high-capacity carpet stored in the closet in his lab. I have regular carpets stashed down here, but it might be better to have one that can carry heavier loads."

"What does it look like?" I asked.

"It's huge, leaning against the closet wall. You can't miss it."

"Yes, sir." I sprinted upstairs and went to Percival's lab. I found him inside lying on the floor. "Percival!" I turned him over. He moaned. Eyelids fluttered open.

"Where is that awful woman?" he groaned.

I patted his shirt pocket. It was empty and I had little doubt where the vial of memory potion had gone. Unfortunately, we had no time to waste. "Percival, do you have any more of the potion?"

He sat up. Groaned and rubbed his head. "Just ingredients."

"Where?"

Percival pointed to a box. "Everything is in there."

I grabbed it and tugged on his arm. "Get up. We haven't got much time." I noticed the closet Stan mentioned hung open. I looked inside, but the flying carpet wasn't there.

The healer staggered to his feet, teeth bared in a grimace. "I just went back to gather my things. The next thing I knew, Gallifer and Sithain demanded I give them the potion."

"Save the story." I grabbed his robe and yanked him after me. "Let's go!"

Percival stumbled after me. Brilliant explosions flashed through the front window as the mages dismantled Stan's wards. Talbot and the others all rode golem horses now, wands drawn, eyes on the house. Garkin and the blooded weren't in sight.

We rejoined the others in the tunnel.

"Where's the carpet?" Stan asked.

Ambria looked with alarm at Percival. "Where are Purah and the others?"

"The carpet is gone," I growled. "So are Purah and the others. They took the potion and ran."

"Ran where?" Max said. "There's nowhere else to go!"

"We don't have time to waste." Stan shooed us down the tunnel. "Go!"

I felt sick to my stomach as we scurried like rats through the narrow tunnel, leaving behind the only people who could help us reach Seraphina. With the memory potion, Purah, Gallifer, and Sithain would regain their memories and leave us behind.

We'll probably never see them again.

I couldn't let that happen. I slowed and stopped. "I'm going back."

"Are you insane?" Percival grabbed my arm. "You can't go back!"

"Why, Conrad?" Ambria stared at me with shock.

"We need Purah and the others. They're the only way to get to Seraphina."

Ivy's forehead wrinkled. "To get my brother?"

I nodded. "If we let them go, we'll never find out how they open a portal to Seraphina."

"Without powers, we can't fight them." Nightliss held onto Ivy's arm. "Conrad, we will find another way to reach Seraphina."

"No, he's right." Ivy shook her arm loose. "I can't blast 'em, but I can still punch them in the throat!"

I threw up my hands like a traffic officer. "No, you can't come with me. Ivy and Nightliss, you have to go with Percival so he can heal you."

"You're not the boss of me." Ivy jutted out her chin. "If you go back, then we all go back."

"Agreed." Ambria mimicked Ivy's rebellious stance. "We all go, or we all stay."

I pressed a palm to my face. "That's not how this works."

"Ooh, I remember my brother doing that a lot," Ivy said.

"Face-palming?" Max chuckled. "I'm surprised Conrad doesn't do it more often."

I paced back and forth. I couldn't risk my friends and the future of our rebellion against my father, but losing Purah and access to Seraphina would be even worse.

"They are the Fallen," Nightliss said. "Purah said it when she babbled. While I do not remember much, I do know the Fallen are ancient Seraphim. Very powerful."

Max groaned. "So once Purah has her memories and powers, it'll be an uphill battle trying to capture her?"

"Even if we find them now, there is no guarantee we can overcome her." Nightliss looked at me with pleading eyes. "Going back is too dangerous."

"I have to agree." Stan patted my back. "Conrad, we have to pick our battles wisely, and this is not one of them."

I stared back down the tunnel, fists clenched in frustration. Nightliss and Stan were right. *We don't have a chance if we go back.* I slumped. "Let's go."

We turned tail and ran, leaving behind the only people who could help us bring Justin Slade back to Eden.

CHAPTER 11

The tunnel ended in a slab of stone. Stan took out his wand and traced an intricate pattern across its surface, leaving behind a slight glow in the rock. The dead-end rumbled aside and light flickered on in the belly of a metal room. The old man rushed over to a tarp and uncovered a pile of flying carpets.

"I hope there are enough for everyone to double up." Stan tossed them one at a time into the air. The carpets unfurled and hovered a foot off the ground. He got on the first one and Natalia hopped on behind. "Would've been nice to have the high-capacity carpet."

I took the last carpet and tossed it in the air. It flopped onto the floor.

"That's not a flying carpet," Stan said. "That's just an old rug I piled the others on top of."

"Get on!" Ivy grabbed me and jerked me onto her carpet before I could protest. "How do we get out of here?"

Ambria reluctantly climbed on behind Max while Nightliss took a seat behind Percival.

Stan flicked his wand and a trap door in the top of the shed slid open to blue skies. "Fly low so they don't see you and follow me."

Something besides Purah's treachery nagged at me, and I finally realized what it was. "Wait. How did the wandslingers find us in the first place?"

Stan shook his head. "I don't know, but we don't have time to figure it out."

"It couldn't have been any of us," Max said. "I don't think even Purah would sell us out."

"I agree," I said. "None of us would willingly lead the bounty hunters here, but what if it was unwilling?"

Ambria grimaced. "Do you think the wandslingers tagged us with a tracker?"

Max face-palmed. "I didn't even think about it."

"But my wards disable trackers," Stan said.

"We portaled into the south field." I rubbed my sore calf. "The wards wouldn't have disabled the tracker until we reached the edge of the field."

"The magic bullet." Percival looked at my dangling leg. "When I healed him, I detected residual active magic. A bullet spell usually dissolves on impact."

Max groaned. "You mean the kinetic bullet carried a tracker spell?"

"It's the only answer." Percival tapped his chin. "The wards must have dissolved the bindings, but the spell hadn't fully faded by the time I inspected the wound. That would definitely explain it."

"So they can't track us anymore?" I asked.

He shook his head. "No, the tracker spell is gone. I'm sure of it."

Stan piloted his carpet closer and scanned me with his wand. "You're clean, Conrad."

I didn't feel clean. I felt awful and dirty. "I led those people to your home, Stan. I've ruined everything."

The old man patted my shoulder. "You're not to blame, son. It could've happened to anyone."

"If they tracked Conrad, why did it take them three days to come for us?" Max said.

"I don't know," Stan said. "I also don't understand why they'd come at us in broad daylight."

"The wards would've warned us even at night," Natalia said. "They probably didn't expect to find a barricaded safe house. They probably thought they'd find us unprotected somewhere."

"True." Stan's lips pressed together. "It's likely the wards dissolved the tracker spell before it gave them a specific location. Probably took them a few days to narrow it down."

"All those wards probably stood out like a beacon to them," Percival said. "Once they found it, they came back with reinforcements."

"I never thought about it that way." Stan shook his head slowly. "The very thing meant to protect us gave us away."

Percival shrugged. "Well, now that we've solved the mystery, perhaps we should flee."

"Yeah, let's go!" Ivy looked up and the carpet jetted toward the hole in the roof. We zipped into open air behind the cover of a small hill. Stan and Natalia appeared a moment later, followed by the others.

"This way." Stan directed his carpet toward a patch of woods.

We kept low and followed him. Off in the distance, sunlight glinted off the roof of a silver pickup truck headed in the direction of the house. It was too far away to make out the occupants, but my stomach twisted when I realized who it might be.

I gripped Ivy's arm. "Is that Galfandor and Asha?"

She narrowed her eyes and peered at the car. "Oh no. It is them!"

I'd completely forgotten about them, and now they were headed straight into a trap. The truck screeched to a stop a few dozen yards from the wrecked Range Rover and made a U-turn on the narrow road. Tires squealed and the engine roared.

Wooden hooves clopped on gravel. The wandslingers, Garkin, and the posse had them in their sights. Despite the head start, the golem horses chewed up the distance between them and their quarry.

"We've got to help." I took out my wand. "Ivy, you steer, and I'll fire."

Ivy clapped her hands together. "Blast 'em good, Conrad!"

"We're right behind you," Ambria called.

Max reached into his side satchel and withdrew small yellow marbles. "Those golem horses are no match for banana peel!"

Ambria groaned. "That's a terrible name for a potion."

"No, it's not." Max changed from a cross-legged position to his knees for better balance. "Just get me in front of them."

"We'll pace you and lay down covering fire," Stan said.

I nodded. "Let's go."

Ivy swooped down toward the road. The posse was too absorbed in the chase to see us coming. All except for Garkin. The magitsu master jumped up in his saddle and balanced on his feet, a thick staff in his hand.

I turned to Max. "Get Garkin first!"

"Got it!" Max gripped two potion balls in his hand and cocked his arm back. "Get me closer."

I fired a storm of kinetic bullets at Garkin, missing by a wide margin since my target was moving so fast. I switched to, *Electro*, a lightning spell I'd programmed into my arcwand. Bolts of electricity rained down in the path of the posse. Garkin snarled and threw up a shield to divert my attacks, giving Ambria a chance to fly over them without return fire.

Max threw two potion balls in front of the galloping horses. A bright yellow slick carpeted the gravel road in seconds, but Talbot, Delilah, and those at the head of the group had time to dodge. Garkin's wooden horse wasn't quick enough. Its hooves lost traction and the golem spun off the road. Garkin vaulted from its back and landed safely on the road, but his magical beast smashed into a barbed wire fence and rolled into a tangle. Several of the blooded went down with their steeds. Wood cracked and splintered, leaving most of them on foot.

"Yes!" Max pumped a fist.

Silver bullets zinged past him as the posse turned its attention to him. Max yelped and toppled backward. A bullet ripped a hole through the carpet and Max fell with a startled shout.

"No, Max!" Ambria reached for his outstretched hand, but missed.

Percival's carpet swooped down. Nightliss reached out and caught Max before he hit the ground. The carpet sagged, losing altitude from the extra weight.

Ivy whooped.

"The carpet can't hold him!" Percival pulled up on the front end of the rug, as if that would do anything to stop their spiraling descent.

Kinetic bullets whizzed past. Ambria cast a shield to deflect them, but it wouldn't hold for long. I fired lightning bolts back at them. Without Garkin to shield them, the battle mages and wandslingers scattered to avoid the attacks.

Asha leaned out from the passenger side of the truck and fired a sizzling orange beam. It struck a mage in the chest. The man cried out and fell from his horse, chest smoking. The golem horse slowed to a stop and stood in place while the rest of the posse skirted around it. Talbot and Delilah unloaded a volley back at Asha. The rear window exploded. Tires popped, and metal pinged.

Delilah flicked her wand in a pattern I recognized from the encounter at the university. She smirked up at Max who still danged from the edge of Percival's carpet. "Dodge this, you little turd!" Glowing white energy wove into a missile the size of her wand and rocketed toward the carpet.

Sizzling red light zapped from Stan's wand, but missed the projectile. I fired, but my shot flew wide and hit the smoke trailing behind it. Ambria flashed beneath Max and spun to a halt. "Drop down!"

Max gulped and let go. One leg slipped off Ambria's carpet, but he grabbed the edges and pulled himself up. Ambria took the carpet into a steep dive. Now freed of the extra weight, Percival's carpet climbed upward. The magic missile veered after him, gathering speed and gaining.

He dodged left and right in a serpentine pattern, outrunning the missile, but unable to get it off his tail. "It's after me!" he cried. "What do I do?"

"Keep running!" Ivy screamed.

Percival aimed for the trees.

The rear tires on the pickup blew. The vehicle skidded off the road and into the ditch.

Talbot laughed. "Got 'em!"

They surrounded the truck and I had no choice but to stop firing for fear I might hit Asha or Galfandor. Ivy pulled back to a safe distance and the others drifted around us, faces tight with anxiety.

"What do we do?" Ambria said.

"We just have to attack them all at once," Ivy said.

"No, we might hit Asha and Galfandor." Stan frowned and looked back down the road. Garkin and his people were nearly half a mile away and walking toward us. "I might have an idea."

One of the mages jumped off his horse and jerked open the passenger door. His jubilant smile faded. "It's empty!"

Talbot chuckled. "I doubt it." He picked up a rock and threw it inside the door.

I couldn't see what happened, but heard a grunt of pain. *They must have camouflaged.*

Orange light blasted the mage nearest the door. He screamed and went down.

Talbot and Delilah aimed their wands at the pickup. "Cease fire and give yourselves up."

Asha emerged first, hands up, and Galfandor struggled out behind her. Blood stained the shoulder of his robes.

Talbot pulled Asha toward him and put his wand to her head. "Well, now. It seems we have something you might want, little Conrad."

My heart palpitated with terror at the thought of losing Asha. *I can't lose my sister!*

Ivy gripped my hand. "Stay calm, Conrad. We'll figure this out."

"What do you want, Talbot?" I shouted in a hoarse voice.

He chuckled. "Why, all of you, of course." He nodded toward me. "Victus is paying well to get his trophies back."

"Are you calling me a trophy?" Ivy shouted. "I'll blast you to cinders when I get my powers back!"

Talbot smirked. "Yeah, well, that ain't gonna happen, princess. Why don't you climb down off that carpet and park your cute little behind on one of these horses?"

Asha bared her teeth. "Don't do it, Conrad! Get out of here before Garkin catches up."

I looked back down the road and saw the bearded man walking stiffly down the road. We had a few minutes to make a decision, but I couldn't imagine leaving Asha in the clutches of these mercenaries.

"Victus wants me more than anyone else," I said. "I'll exchange myself for Galfandor and Asha. Otherwise, we leave and you get nothing."

"These two are worth a pretty penny, but you're right." Talbot glanced sideways at Delilah. "The boy is worth ten times more."

"I'll take that deal," Delilah said. "We can always hunt down the rest of them later."

"True." Talbot nodded and turned back to me. "Just come on down and we'll let your friends go." He flashed his teeth. "Promise."

"No!" Ambria flew her carpet next to mine and grabbed my arm. "I won't let you do it."

"Don't do it!" Asha shouted.

Galfandor struggled uselessly in their grasp. "Fly away, now, Conrad. Don't believe them."

"My word is good," Talbot said in a hurt tone. "I will honor any deal I make."

"How do I know I can trust you?" I said.

"It doesn't matter." Ambria's grip tightened on my arm. "I won't let you go. If you even try, I'll go with you."

"I won't let you go either," Ivy said.

Max nodded. "Me either."

I lowered my voice so it wouldn't carry. "I can't leave Asha and Galfandor."

I heard shouting behind me. "Someone help me!"

I spun and saw Percival flying at top speed from the forest, the magic missile still hot on his tail. Nightliss crouched behind him, eyes wide.

Talbot shook his head and chuckled. "I told you not to fire that damned spell."

"It'll be a hoot when it hits them," Delilah said.

"Yeah, but you'll damage the merchandise." Talbot sighed.

The missile trailed the carpet by maybe ten yards, slowly closing the gap. I thought back to when Delilah fired the missile. It hadn't followed Max when he jumped, which meant it was probably homing in on the carpet and not the people.

"Get me to that carpet," I told Ivy.

"You got it." She leaned forward and our carpet zipped on an intercept course. We pulled even and paced Percival.

I held out a hand to Nightliss. "Trade places with me."

"But the missile—"

"Do it now!" I grabbed her hand and pulled her over, stepping across to the vacated spot.

Percival looked back at me. "What are you doing?"

"Get on behind Nightliss." I nudged him.

"But the carpet can't handle three people."

"It's better than blowing up with this one." I grabbed his sleeve. "Do it."

"Justin, what are you doing?" Ivy said.

My forehead pinched in confusion. "Justin?"

"Oh, I mean—" Ivy shook her head. "I'm sorry, I keep having flashbacks. This feels so familiar."

I grabbed Percival. "Go, now!"

The healer gave me a worried look, then stepped over to the pacing carpet.

Freed of the extra weight, my carpet gained speed, but not enough to outrun the magic missile for long. I veered in a circle and looked down at Talbot. "Hey, you want me? Fine. I'll come to you." I dove straight at them.

The smirks on Talbot's and Delilah's faces turned upside down in a heartbeat.

I raised a fist. "You won't have any of us, you bounty-hunting bastards!"

Talbot held up his wand and opened fire. "You crazy son of a bitch!"

Delilah jerked his arm down. "Don't kill him, you fool! We won't get a bounty!"

I bared my teeth in a grin. Wind whistled past my ears and the ground rushed to claim me. The posse scattered in all directions, the golem horses galloping at breakneck speed away from Talbot and Delilah.

"You'll kill yourself and your friends!" Talbot shouted.

I raised a fist. "Better dead than prisoners!"

Delilah spun her horse and urged it away from Asha and Galfandor. Talbot cast a confused look after her then took off in pursuit, leaving my friends standing next to the truck. I took the carpet lower, aimed it toward the fleeing pair, and rolled off the side. I landed just past the barbed wire fence and at the top of the grassy ditch, rolling down the slope into the tall weeds. I came to a hard stop against the opposite bank.

The breath whooshed from my lungs. I sucked desperately for air. Hands hooked into my armpits and pulled me up to my feet.

"I've got you, Conrad," Asha said.

She pulled me back up the bank toward the fence. An explosion rocked the air as the missile caught up with the carpet. Talbot and the rest of his scattered posse spun back toward us.

Talbot laughed. "You got balls, boy, I'll give you that. But it ain't gonna change the outcome." He spun his golem horse toward us and charged.

We were grounded with nowhere to run.

CHAPTER 12

I finally gulped a full breath of air. "The woods. Go."

Galfandor pushed down on the barbed wire with his hand so we could climb over it. Face white with pain, he lifted his legs over the fence and clamped his hand back over his injured shoulder. We ran for the woods while Stan and the others laid down cover fire from overhead.

The posse fired back, magic bullets rippling through the air, forcing Stan to call for a retreat. The woods were too far away, and even if we reached them, what then? Talbot would just follow us in and track us down. Galfandor staggered and went to his knees. I tried to help him up, but he was too heavy.

"Leave me," he groaned. "Lost too much blood."

"No!" I tugged on him in vain. "Get up and run!"

"I can't, boy." Galfandor wheezed. "Save yourself."

I looked back and saw the golem horses vaulting the fence. Talbot and Delilah grinned with glee, wands leveled toward us while their posse fired volleys into the air to drive away Stan and the others.

A massive beam of white energy, ultraviolet ripples coiling around it, burned a smoking trench in the field between us and Talbot's people. They cried out in surprise, pulling back on the reigns of their wooden horses. Another beam incinerated one of the mages and his golem steed before he could even scream.

A single large carpet drifted over the trees, bearing the Fallen. Purah held up her hand. A ball of white flame danced around it like a miniature sun. "You would do well to leave these people alone, for I shall not allow them harm." Her voice boomed across the field, amplified by magic.

Gallifer wove strands of ultraviolet and white into a great sphere and fired it at the posse. They scattered like smoke in the wind, shouting in fear. The sphere smashed into the ground, leaving behind a crater. I spotted Garkin in the distance, standing still and looking up at the Seraphim. I couldn't see his face, but imagined even he felt fear at this sight.

I felt intense relief. *They didn't abandon us.* And we'd just added immense firepower to our underdog group.

"They came back!" Ivy clapped her hands. "Let's go blast the baddies!"

The high-capacity carpet drifted down to hover a few feet off the ground.

"Thank you." I dropped to the ground next to Galfandor.

Percival jumped off the overburdened carpet with Ivy and Nightliss, casting daggers with his eyes at the Fallen. "You knocked me out and took my potion!"

Sithain ignored him and stepped off the carpet next to the wounded old man. She pressed her hand to his shoulder and closed her eyes. Galfandor gasped. Ice crystals frosted his skin. He cried out and just as suddenly slumped.

"I have mended the wound," Sithain said. "But he must rest."

Percival's eyes went wide. "How did you do that? Can you teach me?"

"Mortals cannot channel," Purah said. "It is beyond you."

Percival glowered. "Well, that's insulting."

"We thought you'd left us," I said. "Why did you steal the potion from Percival?"

"We are not without honor and mercy," Gallifer said. "We used the potion to heal ourselves. Since you saved us from Victus, we have in turn saved you from his minions."

"Consider the debt paid." Sithain got back on her carpet. "We have been away from our realm too long and must return."

"But you promised to help me reach Seraphina." I turned to Purah. "Does your word mean nothing?"

Purah paused for a long moment. "Very well. I promised you, and so it will be. First, we must recover the modified Chalon we use to make portals in Voltis."

"Voltis?" Ambria frowned. "What in the world is that?"

"It is an interdimensional storm that touches all realms—the fringe of the only fragment of the original Earth left after the Sundering." Purah gazed at the fleeing mages racing for a portal in the field to the south of us. "Here in Eden, it is small. In Seraphina it is massive."

I still had no idea what she was talking about. "Once you retrieve your Chalon, you can take us to Seraphina?"

"Yes." She turned her gaze back to me. "We have long traveled the realms, collecting what interests us and living among the denizens to amuse ourselves."

Nightliss held up a hand. "Where is the rest of the potion?"

Gallifer shook his head somberly. "When I took the potion, the memory flood seized me before I could put down the vial. It fell and broke."

"No!" Percival ran a hand down his face. "It'll take me another week to make a new batch."

Nightliss frowned. "Can you heal me and Ivy?"

Purah shook her head. "The memory blocks use demon magic—very difficult to counter without extensive study. The potion works better."

"Just great." Max threw up his hands. "How did Victus even capture you in the first place? I can't imagine he overpowered you."

Purah pursed her lips. "We encountered Victus while searching for ancient artifacts."

Ambria tilted her head. "Like the Relics of Juranthemon?"

Sithain nodded. "The very same. We heard rumor that a collector had gathered a significant number of them. We cannot allow that to happen."

Nightliss raised an eyebrow. "Why?"

Purah answered. "Because if enough pieces of the lost city of Juran-themon are reassembled, they will draw the realms back together. It would be cataclysmic."

Ambria paled. "Didn't Gwyneth mention someone was stealing artifacts of Jura?"

I gave a nod. "I wonder if it's the same person or people."

"Victus was searching for artifacts as well," Purah said. "Somehow—and we do not know how—he rendered us unconscious during our second meeting."

"The next thing I remember is awakening from those coffins," Gallifer said.

I held out my hands. "If you come with us, you can have your revenge on Victus."

"We have no interest in revenge." Purah's voice frosted over. "We are only interested in scattering the relics among the realms and protecting billions of lives."

"I never knew the Fallen were so philanthropic," Nightliss said. "You were banished from Seraphina for crimes I cannot remember."

Purah offered a cold smile. "Do not mistake our desires for philanthropy. Recombining the realms might kill us and it would tilt the balance of power toward the unknown. We simply wish to maintain the status quo."

Ambria huffed. "What if Victus is the one gathering the relics?"

"No." Gallifer shook his head. "Victus was not the collector."

"How do you know?" Ambria shot back.

"We once possessed the Ring of Juranthemon," Sithain said. "It allows the bearer to discern the truth in another's heart, but only if they answer a direct question."

"We asked him if he was the collector," Purah said. "He answered truthfully."

"Does he have the ring now?" I asked.

"No." Gallifer's eyes narrowed. "We left it on Olympus before our second meeting with Victus. It should still be there with our small collection. When we discover artifacts of Jura, we scatter them among the realms that they may never be put back together. There are obscure realms, some without magic, others infested with plagues, that make it nearly impossible for most collectors to reach. Someone powerful is undoing all our hard work."

Max's forehead scrunched. "Wouldn't it be impossible to reassemble the entire city of Juranthemon?"

"The relics come from the focal point of the Sundering," Purah said. "When Saila tried to protect the city from the Apocryphan, the juxtaposition of so much power in one small area split the world into realms. Most of the relics are parts of Saila and anything near her."

"Explains why there's a heart, a hand, and a ring." Asha folded her arms. "How many total pieces are there?"

"The fragments number in the thousands." Gallifer spread his hands. "Most scattered like dust into the realms. But enough pieces of Saila have been discovered over the centuries to pose a threat."

Sithain winced. "Yes, if the statue of Saila is complete, we believe it might be enough to draw the other relics together."

Max's mouth dropped open. "Like an interdimensional magnet?"

"Precisely." Purah shook her head slowly. "Even small combinations of Saila's parts will draw other relics inexorably toward them."

"They will not move on their own, mind you." Gallifer pressed his hands together. "But they will find a way to each other somehow."

"You make it sound like they're alive," Ambria said.

"The magic that destroyed Saila is the very same that gave power to the relics." Purah looked up at the sky. "The pieces wish to reunite." Her gaze snapped back to earth. "But doing so would kill billions of mortals, and destroy life in the many realms."

I frowned. "And this mysterious collector will somehow survive and benefit from that?"

The Seraphim nodded in unison. Purah spoke. "We have evidence the collector works for the Apocryphan who escaped during the war against Daelissa."

"The collector is a long-term threat, but Victus is a much more imme-diate danger to the realms." Ambria put her hands on her hips as if addressing a naughty child. "He sent someone to Seraphina to take it over and he's trying to do the same thing here. We have to stop him, and you could help us do it much faster."

The three Seraphim exchanged glances. Silent communication seemed to pass among them before Purah turned back to us. "We will consider it. For now, we must recover the Chalon we use to make portals through Voltis."

"That's fine." I shrugged. "We'll come with you."

"Very well." Purah clasped her hands together. "Eden aligns with Voltis one month from tomorrow."

"A whole month!" Max scratched his head. "How long does the alignment last?"

"Twenty-four hours," Gallifer replied. "Each alignment is six weeks apart."

My soaring hopes tumbled into freefall. "We can't afford to give Victus another month to do whatever he wants. We need to stop him now."

Purah looked unconcerned. "We will offer you passage to Seraphina, but your feud with Victus is not our concern."

Ivy spun toward Percival. "Make me some potion and I'll help blast Victus. Forget these old fogies."

It seemed my plans were back to square one. Without the Fallen, we had to rely on Ivy and Nightliss. That meant a week of downtime while Percival remade his potion. And what if Ivy and Nightliss didn't want to help after recovering their memories? What if they weren't as powerful as the Fallen? Then we'd have no choice but to wait until the next alignment with Voltis and hope Justin Slade and his army had survived their years of exile.

If they hadn't, then that meant Aerianas ruled Seraphina, and Victus would be unstoppable.

We couldn't afford so many risks. "Please, I'm begging you to help us against Victus." I clasped my hands as if in prayer. "He uses demons to clone people. He's already taken control of the Overworld government. He sent one of his agents to Seraphina to do the same thing there. I know you don't care who rules Eden, but Victus is no ordinary tyrant. If he takes over Seraphina, he'll be unstoppable."

"Take over Seraphina?" Sithain scoffed. "No mortal could succeed where even we failed."

"Agreed." Gallifer shook his head. "We will quash any effort by Victus in our home realm."

"It is your burden to deal with him here," Purah said. "We are not like Daelissa. We do not impose our will on other realms."

My shoulders slumped beneath the crushing weight of stress and worry. For better or worse, we were on our own. I tried not to let it show and asked them the only other question that mattered at the moment. "Where is Voltis in Eden?"

Purah pointed into the distance. "On the tiny island of Kratos in the center of what the mortals call the Bermuda Triangle."

"That's all the way across the Atlantic!" Stan said.

"Indeed." Purah shrugged. "We must make our way back to the Americas to retrieve the Chalon. If you wish to travel with us to Olympus during the next alignment, meet us in Bermuda. She landed her carpet and bent down to pick up a smooth, flat stone. A needle of white energy sizzled from the tip of her finger and carved an address: *Twelve Shore Lane, Tucker Town.*

"Sounds like a weird place for angels to live," Max said.

"It is one of our many abodes," Gallifer said. "This one is most convenient for reaching Voltis."

"Do you have any way we can communicate with you?" I asked.

"We typically use gems," Sithain replied, "but Victus took them."

"Here." Stan put an arcphone in Purah's hand. "Conrad's symbols are already in there. We can use it in case of emergency."

Purah tucked it into a pocket in her jeans. "Very well."

"You know, you could totally redeem yourselves by helping us," Max said. "You don't have to be the Fallen forever. You could be the Risen if you want to."

The corners of Purah's mouth twitched up. "An amusing observation." The large carpet floated up. "We thank you, Granddad Stan, for your hospitality. May our paths cross again."

The Fallen rose and drifted away to the north along the road.

Once again, we were on our own against impossible odds.

CHAPTER 13

"I wonder if the Fallen will take the train," Percival said. "Surely they know better than to be seen on a flying carpet."

"If they've lived among mortals as they said, I'm sure they know how to keep a low profile." Asha sighed. "Speaking of trains, we should probably take one and get as far away from here as possible."

"And take it where?" Max said. "Our only safe house is gone. We don't have anywhere else to go."

"Maybe Gwyneth can help us again," Ambria suggested. "Once we reach a waystation, we can go anywhere."

"First things first." Asha looked down at the slumbering Galfandor. "We need a place to stay the night so Galfandor can recover."

"And I need a place to recreate the memory potion," Percival added.

Max nodded enthusiastically. "Once we get Ivy and Nightliss to full power we won't have to worry about those wandslingers anymore."

I looked around at the group. "Was anyone else injured in the fight?"

Asha inspected black and blue spots on her arms. "Minor scrapes and bruises. Nothing serious."

I noticed a trickle of crusted blood on Ambria's arm. "Hey, what happened?"

"A magic bullet nicked me." She smiled. "It's okay though."

"Are you certain?" I inspected the long welt where it had brushed against her skin. "It looks painful."

Ambria's smile stretched into a grin. "You could kiss it better."

Max groaned. "I think she'll live."

Ambria glared at him. "Maxwell Tiberius, you mind your manners."

He jutted out his chin. "You mind your hormones, Ambria Rax."

Asha burst into laughter.

"Is this flirting?" Ivy cast a confused look around. "I think I tried that once but it didn't work and the boy ran away screaming."

"Yes, dear." Stan patted her arm. "This is flirting."

Asha took a deep breath and quelled her laughter. "Look, we can't afford to just sit here. Those bounty hunters might be watching us from a distance right now. Just because the Fallen scared them off doesn't mean they aren't still tracking us."

"I suggest we head cross-country." I pointed through the woods to the west. "We can use the trees for cover, then head north or south and find a place to settle in for the night. It'll give us time to think and regroup."

Asha nodded. "Let's do that." She motioned to Galfandor. "Someone help me get him on a carpet."

"Percival's carpet blew up," Max said. "How are we supposed to fit everyone on three of them?"

Asha opened a duffel bag she'd recovered from the silver pickup. "I've got an extra."

"We'll have to triple up on two of them," Stan said.

"Lovely." Percival groaned. "Well, let's get going. I have a feeling this will be a long trip."

Galfandor's tall frame took up an entire carpet, so we let his legs dangle over the end while Nightliss piloted. I took my carpet higher with Ivy still on the back and looked where the wandslingers and their posse had retreated. The grassy field in front of the house remained visible from this distance, but I couldn't see if the portal was still there. I hoped Garkin and the bounty hunters had left.

The convoy of carpets was ready to go by the time we returned. Asha, Natalia, and Ambria looked cozy on one carpet, while Max, Percival, and Stan squirmed uncomfortably on their sagging rug.

"This isn't working," Max grumbled. "Can I get on your carpet, Conrad?"

"Behind Ivy?" Ambria smiled innocently. "Do you want to move, or are your hormones talking now, Max?"

"I have potions that can counteract teenage hormones," Percival said. "There are unfortunate side effects, however."

"We don't have time to deal with hormones or uncomfortable carpets," Asha said. "We need to go."

Stan winced. "We'd better keep low to the ground. I don't trust this carpet holding three of us that high off the ground." He took out his wand. "Before we go, I should scan everyone just to make sure none of us were tagged by the bounty hunters."

Asha took out her wand. "I'll help."

It took ten minutes to confirm everyone was clean of tracking spells, but I felt a lot better knowing for sure. It didn't matter how far we ran if Delilah and Talbot knew where we were.

Stan climbed back onboard the carpet behind Percival and Max, his back to Max's so his feet could dangle off the back. "We're good to go."

"Don't have to tell me twice." Percival urged the carpet forward and the rest of us followed.

We threaded between the trees, heading north by northwest toward Florence in the hopes that the big city would grant us some cover from pursuers. Once outside the woods, Percival managed a little extra speed from his carpet, but according to the maps on my arcphone, it would take us hours to reach our destination at this pace.

We kept off the roads and out of sight the best we could, slowing us even further. As the afternoon waned, it became apparent that we'd have to stop in another town for the night. Stan had enough Euros to get us a cabin in a campground in the small town of Monteoliveto. He went into the main office with Max and Percival while the rest of us hid to keep a low profile. Once he secured a key, we sneaked into the small cabin a few at a time.

Three bunk beds lined a wall across from rickety chests of drawers. The bathrooms were in a shared-use facility down the sidewalk from us, and the kitchenette had an empty refrigerator and a microwave. Since we had only the clothes on our backs and no food, we'd have to find a restaurant or a grocer if we wanted to eat.

"It's not ideal, but we can make this work." Stan rolled up each carpet and stored them in the corner of the room. "I'll go to the store for food."

"I'd like to go," Asha said. "Maybe we could make a list of what everyone wants."

"Anything." Max rubbed his tummy. "I could eat a litter of puppies right now."

"Eww, Max!" Ambria slapped his shoulder lightly. "That's awful!"

I helped Nightliss settle Galfandor into a bed. The old man murmured unintelligibly in his sleep, but he hadn't awoken since Sithain healed him four hours ago.

"I would like salad," Nightliss said. "Fruit, too."

"I want a big juicy steak." Ivy rubbed her hands together. "And potatoes."

Stan raised an eyebrow. "Perhaps we could come up with something everyone would like. My funds aren't unlimited."

After a great deal of arguing, we settled on the one food that seemed universal—pizza. Half vegetarian, the other half piled with Iberian ham. Stan left with Ambria, Max, and Asha to get the pizza from the restaurant and pick up other supplies.

"I'm going to scout around," Natalia said after the others left.

"In human or cat form?" I asked.

"Cat."

"People might freak if they see a leopard."

She chuckled. "I've been practicing another form. Let me know what you think." Natalia's forehead furrowed with concentration. Bones and sinews crackled. "Ow! I forgot how much this one hurts."

I winced and Nightliss covered her eyes as the awful transformation continued. Natalia's frame shrunk in up on itself. Black fur sprouted, and her cries of pain turned to yowls. Moments later, an unusually large black housecat looked up at us.

Nightliss's eyes widened. "This seems so familiar."

"In what way?" I asked.

She shook her head. "I cannot place it."

Natalia cocked her head and meowed.

I held up a thumb. "It looks great. You're a little big for a housecat, but not freakishly so." *Although she's close to it.*

She stuck out her tongue and turned in a circle as if to show off her new figure, then stalked toward the door and pawed at it. I opened it for her, and she darted outside. Ivy yelped and jumped off the sidewalk outside. "Wow, that's a big cat!"

"It's Natalia." I moved aside to let her in. "How are the bathrooms?"

"Stinky." Ivy pinched her nose. "Where's Natalia going?"

"To scout around." I dropped into a chair. "Hopefully, we'll get a night of peace."

Ivy's fists clenched. "I'm so mad I can hardly stand it."

"About what?"

Tears sparkled in the corners of her eyes. "I can't remember anything. I don't have any powers, and I felt so helpless when those wandslingers were trying to kill us."

"It's not your fault." I took one of her fists in my hand. Her fingers uncurled and her shoulders slumped.

"I don't like feeling helpless and I don't even know why." She slumped into the chair next to me. "Where is Percival, anyway?"

"He said something about alcohol," Nightliss said. "He seemed distressed about losing the vial of potion Gallifer broke."

"I can't blame him." I blew out a breath. "He worked on that for a long time."

"Well, he needs to get back to it." Ivy quirked her lips. "Maybe we should stay at this campsite until he makes a new batch. I can't take this much longer."

Nightliss sat on a bed across from me and rested her chin in her hands. "I remember bits and pieces of my past. I see flashes. I feel strong emotions." Her green eyes settled on Ivy. "I keep seeing the face of a young man. I think he might be Justin."

"Oh, I wish he was here." Ivy leaned her head on my shoulder. "I wish I could say he always knew what to do, but I can't remember if he did or not."

A contented sigh escaped my lips as I stared at Nightliss's lovely face.

Ivy jerked upright. "Conrad, do you like Nightliss?"

I blinked from my stupor. "I—uh…" My mouth wouldn't work.

Nightliss smiled. "It's okay, Conrad. I like you, but you're a little too young."

I gulped. "I—I understand."

Ivy looked down at her hands. "That's sad."

Nightliss's brow furrowed. "Why?"

"He's brave and strong and nice and you're a super-old woman even if you do look young." Ivy frowned. "It's kind of pervy."

Nightliss tried to speak. "Yes, but—"

"I don't think you want to be pervy, Nightliss." Ivy shrugged. "Besides, I really like Conrad."

Cold sweat broke out on my forehead. "I like you too Ivy, but—"

She shook her head. "I'm not pretty enough, am I?"

"Of course you are." I scrambled for words to make her feel better, but I didn't even know where to start. "Max likes you a lot."

Ivy blinked her big blue eyes. "Really?"

I nodded. "Can't you tell he's infatuated with you?"

She exchanged a confused look with Nightliss. "I guess he's nice and all."

"I think things will change once you have your memories back." I patted the top of her hand. "You're not thinking straight right now."

Nightliss nodded. "Conrad is right. Our personalities might change when we remember everything."

Ivy got up and looked into a mirror. "Max told me I'm supposed to be nineteen or twenty. But look at me. I barely look fifteen because I've been locked away under a preservation spell."

"You look sixteen at least," I said.

"All these years stolen from me right along with my memories." Ivy turned and narrowed her eyes. "No offense, but I want to kill your dad so bad I can taste it."

I offered a sheepish grin. "Be my guest."

Ivy huffed and paced the room. "I can't sit in here. I need to do something." She took my hand. "Let's go on a walk."

I looked over at Nightliss. "Want to come?"

The angel shook her head. "I will watch Galfandor. If he awakens and no one is here, it will confuse him."

"You're right." I got up and looked at my dirty clothes. "Wish I had something to change into."

"We can walk down to the store and get you something." Ivy pulled out a wad of Euros. "Stan gave me some money for clothes."

"That would be great." We stepped outside into the waning sunlight and started walking toward the main road connecting this tiny village to the larger town of San Gimignano just up the road. The others had taken the bus to get groceries, but Ivy insisted we walk instead.

"It just feels good to be on my feet again." Ivy blurred down the road a few yards, spun and came back. "I can't channel a single spell, but at least I have my strength."

I pretended to run in slow motion. "I'm almost as fast."

"You're silly." She punched me lightly in the shoulder. "You could probably run faster with the right spells."

I resumed walking and shrugged. "I hadn't really thought about using spells like that."

"You should. I'll bet it would come in handy." Ivy picked up a rock and tossed it toward the fertile green fields and the rolling hills. The stone buildings of San Gimignano rose on the horizon, seemingly closer than they actually were.

An old pickup truck rattled past in the opposite direction, followed by a tiny red sports car. The screech of tires jerked my attention behind us. The red car skidded to a stop. Talbot sprang from the driver's seat, a malicious grin spreading across his face.

"Well, bless my stars." He tucked the leather duster behind his holster. "Looks like my lucky day."

I didn't even remember drawing my wand. The next thing I knew it was in my hand, firing a storm of electricity at Talbot. His eyes widened with surprise. A hand blurred to his waist and drew his wand. His shield was too late to stop my first attack. Energy crackled and burned a hole in the shoulder of his duster. My other attacks struck his shield, driving cracks into the shimmering surface.

"I'll be a monkey's uncle, boy! You're quick." He shrugged out of his smoking duster and scowled. "That was my favorite coat."

I backed up a step and looked back at Ivy. She wasn't there. "How did you find us?" I wondered if Ivy had run into the bushes to hide.

"Good old-fashioned tracking." He showed his teeth. "You left a trail through those woods a blind monkey could follow. Didn't take much detective work to figure you must be in one of these two towns."

"Where's your sister?"

Talbot stomped on the burnt patch of his coat. "Why don't you throw down your wand and get in my car? Then I'll answer all the questions you want."

I wondered where Ivy had gone. Was she sneaking up behind Talbot, or had she left me behind? Ivy didn't seem like the sort who'd run from a fight, so I imagined she was sneaking up behind Talbot.

"That's not going to happen." I kept my wand at the ready in case I needed to cast a shield or return fire. "I'm more than capable of protecting myself."

"Why don't we make this interesting?" Talbot holstered his wand. "A duel. Me and you, right here."

"Like an old west gunslinger duel?" I backed up a step. "If you kill me, you won't get anything."

"Oh, I won't kill you, boy." Talbot bared his teeth. "I'll just wing you."

"You're really that confident that I won't win?" *Where in the world is Ivy?* I had no intention of risking a wand duel. I might have been quick on the draw when I saw Talbot, but this was a man who lived to fight duels. His hand moved like lightning when he needed to fend off my attacks. I imagined he could beat me in a quick draw, no problem.

"I'll sweeten the pot for you, Conrad." Talbot rested a hand on his holster. "If you win and I survive, Delilah and I will pack our bags and go home. Seeing as how there ain't another bounty hunter worth their salt after you, you'll be home free."

"You'll leave me and all my friends alone?" It actually sounded like a risk worth taking. Maybe I could have the best of both worlds. If I accepted the challenge and lost, Ivy could still save me. If I won, then that would be one less danger to worry about. I holstered my wand. "Challenge accepted."

"That's so cute."

I spun toward the voice behind me, hand reaching for my wand. But a grinning Delilah poked her wand into my chest. I put my hands in the air.

They had me.

CHAPTER 14

I didn't know where Delilah had come from, but I had a terrible feeling about Ivy's disappearance. She wasn't hiding. Delilah must have knocked her out when I had the standoff with Talbot. *He tricked me!*

When Delilah's wand touched my chest, two thoughts echoed in my mind. *They want me alive. If I give up now, I'm done for.*

Delilah was tall, but petite. I had no idea how capable she was physically, but I was about to find out. I dropped into a crouch and swung my leg at hers, just as Kanaan had taught us in our magitsu lessons. She tried to jump, but that only helped me. I swept her legs out from beneath her, and Delilah crashed into the ground.

Using my momentum, I swung around and kicked her wand hand. She shrieked in pain and the wand clattered to the road. With Talbot still at my back, I didn't dare pause to take her wand, or try to knock her out.

"Stop right there, boy!" Talbot shouted.

I spotted a pair of feet poking from behind a bush on the right side of the road and dove for them. I landed next to an unconscious Ivy—at least I hoped she was just knocked out. I couldn't drag her to safety with Talbot and Delilah to worry about, so I took out my wand and fired a jagged bolt of energy at Delilah.

The spell struck her calf and burned through her jeans. She screamed. A breeze blew the odor of burnt flesh into my nostrils. I grabbed Ivy beneath her arms. She was a little shorter than me, but heavier than expected. I dragged her a few feet and gave up on the idea. I couldn't get her upright long enough to get her on my shoulder.

Use a spell, you idiot! I ran through a list in my head, trying to come up with something useful. I flicked my wand through a pattern and pointed it at Ivy. *Levator!* Ivy remained on the ground. Apparently, I'd forgotten how to cast the levitation spell. I tried one last time to pick up Ivy and nearly launched her into the air because she was light as a feather.

I grabbed her hand and yanked her through the air after me. Running and stumbling through the brush, I heard Talbot shouting behind me. I didn't know if he'd stopped to help Delilah, but I wasn't going to stop and find out.

"Huh?" Ivy twisted in my grip. "What's going on?"

I looked back over my shoulder and nearly tripped over a rock. "The wandslingers are after us!"

"Why am I floating?" Ivy gripped my wrist hard enough to make my bones ache.

"Ow, not so tight!"

Her grip loosened, but still held fast. "Why am I flying?"

"Levitation spell," I panted. "Don't worry." I stopped and looked toward the road. It was too far to make San Gimignano, so I doubled back through rows of olive trees toward Monteoliveto. I didn't hear Talbot anymore, but that didn't mean he wasn't right behind us.

Branches crackled. "Ouch!"

I looked back and realized Ivy had floated a little too high. I pulled her down, grabbed her by the waist, and tucked her under an arm.

"This is so weird!" Ivy flailed her feet, but couldn't make them touch the ground.

"Stop wriggling and let me get us out of here." I hid behind a bush and peeked around it while I caught my breath. The thud of hooves and snapping limbs drew my attention to the right.

A golem horse burst through the foliage and raced up a small rise in the middle of the olive grove. I ducked back behind the bush at the fringe of the grove, but not before Talbot's eyes flashed my way. *He saw me.*

The horse thundered straight at us, confirming my fear. I whipped out my wand. Counted to three. Jumped out and fired a blast. Talbot ducked in the saddle, but I wasn't aiming for him. The spell exploded halfway up the front leg of the horse. The wood cracked, splintered, and snapped. Talbot flew headfirst off the horse and crashed through the bushes.

I flicked my wand and engulfed the bushes in flames. Talbot stumbled out, shielding his face with his arms. I fired another spell, but he dove to the side, firing magic bullets. Ivy screamed and went limp. Bubbles of blood sprayed into the air, floating serenely as if there were no gravity.

"Ivy!" Blood seeped from a wound in her abdomen. I pushed her beneath the branches of the bush to keep her from floating away and ran toward Talbot, blasting the tree he hid behind.

Talbot stumbled out. I flicked my wand in a cocking motion and hurled magic bullets at him. One caught him in the shoulder and threw him spinning to the ground. "I'm going to kill you!" I screamed.

A bullet whistled past my ear and thunked into the trunk of an olive tree. I rolled to the side and saw a limping Delilah training her wand on me. *I hate these people!* Rage boiled over. I wove a pattern of destructive spells, layering each one into the other and melded them into the most powerful spell I knew—Fireblade. A beam of brilliant red hissed through the air and sliced the trunk of an olive tree Delilah used for cover. She shrieked and threw up her arms as the small tree toppled onto her, pinning her to the ground.

I slashed viciously at her wrist, but missed and cut her wand off at the base. The spell fizzled and I stumbled, overcome with fatigue. Using Fireblade came at a cost, and I was already tired from running and fighting. More blood bubbles hovered around Ivy. If I didn't staunch the wound soon, she'd bleed out.

Her complexion blanched. For all I knew, she was already dead. I pulled off my shirt and tied it tight around her waist to cover the wound.

"You busted my favorite wand!" Delilah shouted. "I'm gonna tan your hide, boy."

I ignored her shouts and dashed away with Ivy. I burst into the cabin, startling Nightliss. A dazed Galfandor sat on the edge of a bed, blinking blearily and shaking his head.

"Hmm? What's wrong, Conrad?" Galfandor tried to stand, but dropped back onto the bed.

Tears clouded my eyes. "I think Ivy is dying!" I put her on a bed, but she kept floating away.

Nightliss gave me a confused look. "Why is she flying?"

"Levitation spell." I held out my hands helplessly. "I don't know how to get rid of it."

"Basic dispel," Galfandor said. "Unless you used Levator, then you need a strong dispel."

"I'm too tired for a strong dispel!"

He held out his hand. "Might I see your wand?"

I gave it to him. He traced the Levator spell pattern, added a circle, some slashes, and tapped Ivy. The tip of the wand flashed, and Ivy sank into the mattress. Drops of blood still floated in the air.

Nightliss untied my blood-soaked shirt from Ivy's waist and lifted the girl's blouse to reveal a nasty hole pooling with crimson. "She should be healing, but she's not. I don't understand."

"Seraphim have strong healing powers?" Galfandor asked.

"Strong enough to clot the wound by now." Nightliss dabbed the blood with my shirt. "Something is wrong."

Galfandor rubbed his eyes. "Sorry, my mind is still fuzzy." He used my wand to create a suction spell that cleared the blood. Sickly green veins lined the fair flesh beneath. "They laced their magic bullets with a festering spell."

"Can you dispel it?" I asked.

He shook his head. "No, it's already infected the wound. The longer it's in there, the deeper it'll spread."

"We need Percival." I looked out the window, but there was no sign of the others.

I heard scratching on the door and opened it. Natalia in black cat form strode inside and morphed back to human. She stared in horror at Ivy. "What happened?"

"I need you to go get Percival." I gripped her hands, trying to ignore her nudity. "Ivy is hurt badly."

Natalia melted into leopard form and raced through the open door without hesitation. I hoped she didn't cross paths with any noms or she might cause a panic.

"I will go too." Nightliss ran outside.

The seconds ticked past, feeling like hours while Ivy, still unconscious, whimpered. I called Max's arcphone.

"Hey, Conrad, do you want any grapes?" Max asked before I could utter a word.

"Ivy is hurt. Have you seen Percival?"

Max gasped. "What? Hurt how?"

"The wandslingers are here. I escaped, but they shot Ivy." I looked down at her. Galfandor pressed my blood-soaked shirt to the wound and shook his head sadly. "We need Percival!"

"I'll find him." Max hung up.

I stared out the window, minutes passing so slowly but all too fast. I sat back down next to Ivy and stared with horror at my shirt. It was so soaked with blood it probably wasn't helping anymore.

"Can you clear the wound again for me?" I asked Galfandor.

"Why?" He looked at me with gentle concern.

"I have an idea." I grabbed Galfandor's wand off the chest of drawers and handed it to him. "Just keep it clear."

He pursed his lips. Nodded. "Okay, son." Galfandor set my shirt aside and cast the vacuum spell. Blood swirled into a miniature vortex and pooled in the air. I traced my wand, weaving two of the spells used for Fireblade into a less powerful spell. I focused my will and finished the spell. A thin scarlet beam sliced into the infected flesh, cutting and cauterizing. Galfandor's spell drew the cuttings out of the wound as I worked, keeping it clear until I eradicated all the infection.

White bone showed beneath the skin. The magic bullet had apparently been stopped by her hip bone, or it might have spread infection into her organs. Exhausted from the effort, I dropped my wand and slumped backward. The cauterized wound seeped blood but not nearly as much as before.

Galfandor levitated the tainted flesh and blood into my ruined shirt and released the spell. He patted my arm. "That was excellent thinking, Conrad. I don't think I've seen those two spells used in quite that way."

"Destructive spells don't have to kill or maim." I moved to the next bed and lay down. "It's all how you use them."

"Did you learn that on your own?" he said.

I shook my head. "It's something Esma—I mean, Delectra—told me once."

"Purpose is driven by the wielder." Galfandor chuckled. "I remember Esma telling me that once. Had I known she was your mother in disguise, I would have been surprised to hear her say such a thing."

"She wasn't truly evil." I wiped away a tear. "Victus tainted her with demons."

"I believe that now." Galfandor looked at his bloodied hands. "I should wash up. Where is the bathroom?"

I pointed in the general direction. "Down that sidewalk outside. Just don't let anyone see your hands or they'll think you murdered someone."

"Yes, that might prove awkward." He picked up my shirt and tossed it in the plastic-lined rubbish bin. "Unfortunately, cleaning all the blood from the bed and floor is another matter." He gingerly pinched the doorknob between fingers to avoid covering it in blood and went outside.

My eyelids grew heavy, but visions of Ivy jerked me awake. I sat up and looked at her. The wound, nearly the size of a small coin a moment ago, had shrunk a fraction. I hoped that meant her natural healing process was working.

Galfandor stepped back inside and took a chair. "Progress?"

I nodded, managed a smile. "Progress."

Nearly twenty minutes after my call to Max, the others burst through the door, Percival at the lead. Max nearly beat him to Ivy's side, but Percival barred the way with an arm. He knelt next to Ivy, lifted her shirt, and inspected the wound.

"It appears to be healing." Percival frowned and looked over at me. "I thought this was an emergency."

"It was, but quick thinking by Conrad may have saved her life." Galfandor inspected a spot of blood on his long beard. "Unfortunately, the wandslingers have found us again."

"Wait a bloody minute." Percival glared at me. "What did you do?"

"The bullet was infected with a festering spell," Galfandor said. "Conrad cut out the infection before it spread."

"Cut it out?" Percival scratched his head. "Like nom doctors do?"

"So simple, I didn't even think of it." Galfandor shrugged. "Perhaps you should add that to your arsenal of medical wonders."

Ambria sat next to me and shook her head. "Conrad, you're covered in blood."

"I'm out of shirts too," I said. "I don't suppose anyone picked up clothes."

"Max bought nearly a dozen T-shirts," Ambria said. "I'm sure you can borrow one."

Asha sat on the other side of me and took my hand. "My god, what happened?"

Nightliss and Natalia came in behind the others and looked worriedly at Ivy.

"Is—is she okay?" Max pushed his way past Percival and put a hand to Ivy's forehead.

"I think she'll be fine." Percival threw up his hands. "But since the wandslingers somehow found us, I can't make time to concoct the memory potion." He spun to Stan. "Is there anywhere in this accursed country we can go for some peace and quiet?"

Granddad Stan sighed wearily and dropped into a chair. "First we need to know how they found us again."

"Talbot said they tracked our trail through the woods." I burrowed into Max's bag and pulled out a plain white T-shirt.

Ambria watched me slip on the shirt. "What happened exactly?"

"That's what I want to know." Asha grimaced. "We need to lose them."

"Ivy and I were walking to town when a truck and car passed us. Talbot was in the car. Delilah sneaked up behind me." I tried to imagine how she'd gotten behind me. "I guess they must've been watching the road and saw us walking."

"What happened next?" Max asked.

I told them the story.

Stan stroked his chin. "They probably followed our trail through the woods to make sure the Fallen weren't still with us. Since we took the bus to town, they must not have seen us." He made a circle with his finger. "There are hills all around the village, so they could have spotted Ivy and Conrad on the road using one as a vantage point."

Ambria folded her arms. "Sounds like Conrad injured them pretty badly. Maybe they won't mess with us for a while."

"Or they'll just bring in the posse again." Percival mixed a paste together and put it on Ivy's healing wound. "I require a week of uninterrupted work to make the memory potion again. We need to get somewhere safe."

"Doesn't seem like anywhere is safe," Max grumbled. "Maybe we just need to circle the wagons and fight."

Ambria rolled her eyes. "Someone's been watching too many westerns."

"Do you have any better ideas?" Max shot back.

I was so tired I didn't want to think. I also didn't feel safe sleeping when the wandslingers and their posse could show up at any moment. I listened to Ambria and Max argue for a moment, then held up a hand. "We need a car. The carpets are too slow."

"I can get one," Asha said. "There's an SUV parked outside one of the other cabins."

Galfandor raised an eyebrow. "Surely you don't mean to steal it."

Stan tapped his chin. "An SUV won't be big enough for all of us. I noticed a tall white Mercedes vans parked near the vineyards. I don't know if it's a cargo van or filled with equipment."

"I'll go look." Natalia pulled on a blue dress and hurried outside, still barefooted.

Ambria counted on her fingers. "There are ten of us. Maybe we should get two cars."

"It won't take long for the nom police to search for one stolen vehicle, much less two," Stan said.

"I'll charm our stolen vehicle with dissuasion wards." Galfandor twirled his wand. "That should prevent all but the most observant people from looking too closely at the vehicle."

Natalia returned a moment later. "It's a cargo van. Two seats in the front, open space in the back. There are some wooden posts and materials inside, but we could dump them."

Asha tucked her wand into her waistband. "Get ready to move. I'll be back soon."

I touched her arm. "Be careful."

She nodded and left with Natalia.

Weariness wore wrinkles and worry lines into the faces of everyone in the room, even the youngest. Being on the run was already taking a serious toll on us. I just hoped we could find somewhere safe before the wandslingers found us again.

CHAPTER 15

T ires screeched in the parking lot outside.

Galfandor and Stan grabbed Ivy and carried her to the door. Nightliss opened it and the group piled outside. The back door of the van opened and Natalia jumped out, motioning us to hurry. The old men climbed in with Ivy. Ambria and Nightliss got in behind them. Percival ran from the cabin caressing a satchel with all his ingredients inside.

"Hurry up!" Natalia waved him in.

Percival huffed. "I don't know what the big hurry is."

"We saw some people poking around." Natalia's gaze flicked around, her eyes emitting a soft glow. "Might've been nothing, but—"

Magic bullets zinged through the air, leaving silvery ripples. The clomp of wooden hooves on asphalt echoed from the other end of the parking lot.

"It was something!" Max threw his armload of bags in the back of the van and dove in. I shoved Percival inside and climbed in after him.

Natalia slammed the back door shut, turned and shouted. "Go, Asha!"

My sister nailed the accelerator, throwing the human cargo backward.

"So much for warding the van." Galfandor clung to the wheel hump for dear life.

I clawed my way to the front and climbed into the passenger seat. Asha twisted the steering wheel and the van careened around a curve, out onto the main road leading to San Gimignano. A bullet shattered the rear window. I looked back and saw golem horses gallop beneath a street light.

Asha veered hard right and into town. "Which way?"

"I don't know," Stan said. "Just follow the road!"

Asha slowed at a roundabout just enough to keep the van from toppling over and hooked a right on the opposite side. Stone walls rose to either side. We zipped past a street to our left and barreled straight ahead where the road narrowed.

That was when I spotted something in our path. Metal bars blocked our way. "Watch out!"

A wall on the right and a building on the left boxed us in.

"I'm going to ram them!" Asha shouted.

"We can't just run over metal bars!" I summoned all my remaining strength and leaned out the window, weaving Fireblade. Focusing my will, I sheared off one of the bars at the base. My vision wavered, but I fought back fatigue and sliced at the second bar. My body trembled. The spell fizzled out and the rest of my strength left me. I slumped back inside, unable to finish the job.

Asha gripped the steering wheel with white knuckles. "Hold on!"

Iron rang like a bell. The bar snapped and bounced off the front bumper, rolling ahead of us.

"You must have weakened it, Conrad!" Asha steered around the corner.

Galfandor aimed his wand out of the broken rear window and blasted the base of a street lamp. It toppled across the road and came to rest on a brick wall, about chest high to the golem horses. I looked back and saw the posse skidding to a stop. With tall walls on all sides and the street lamp barring the path, they'd have to get off their steeds to go beneath it.

We reached downtown and Asha had to slow for pedestrians crossing the road. She honked the horn and received a flurry of insulting hand gestures in return.

Galfandor flicked his wand at a bus as it passed us. The front tire blew out and the vehicle swerved, blocking the road behind us. "That should hold them for a while."

Granddad Stan cleared his throat. "Asha, perhaps you should slow down so we don't draw too much attention."

"I'm not taking any chances." Asha sped up after we cleared the pedestrians and hurtled around the curve.

A siren wailed and lights flashed from an adjacent road. An instant later a police car appeared behind us.

"So much for not taking chances," Max said.

Galfandor nodded at Max's satchel. "I believe you have something useful in there."

Max's eyes brightened. "Oh, yeah." He took out a yellow potion bomb, blew on it three times and threw it out the back window.

I couldn't see the potion cover the road, but the police car's headlights spun in circles and intersected the trees lining the sidewalk.

"Now will you slow down?" Stan said.

Asha blew out a sigh and let off the accelerator. "Where to?"

I buckled on my seatbelt and fought the fatigue dragging down my limbs so I could pull out my arcphone. I looked at the map and came up with an idea. "Turn here." I pointed right.

Asha followed my instructions. We reached the outskirts of town and circled back the way we'd come, except on a different highway. A gravel road led us between vineyards for several miles until we reached the highway toward Florence.

After fifteen minutes with no signs of pursuit, I allowed myself to relax.

SHINY SCALES *of the purest white coil around a pulsating blue star. A massive earth dragon looks down at me with glowing eyes. The ground trembles and fire rushes through my veins.*

A figure in white robes steps from the star, hand outstretched. "Hurry, boy! Take my hand before—"

"CONRAD, WAKE UP."

My leaden eyelids cracked open to a sad-faced Ivy. I tried to speak, but my mouth felt full of cotton.

"You saved me." She kissed my cheek. "You're my hero, just like my bro."

"I told you to let him sleep!" Ambria sat against the wall of the van across from me, next to a slumbering Max. There was no sign of the others.

My muscles ached and a vice tightened around my temples. I'd used too much magic. Aether poisoning roiled in my guts.

Ivy frowned and looked down. "I'm so sorry I got knocked out, Conrad. I totally failed you. And then I got shot too." Tears brimmed in her eyes. "I'm such a loser!"

I shook my head despite protesting neck muscles. "It's not your fault. They've been a step ahead of us all this time."

"It's not like we were difficult to track." Ambria blew out a breath and glared at Ivy. "Maybe now we'll buy some time."

Percival's face appeared in the broken rear window. "Ah, the boy's awake." He opened the door and rummaged in his satchel. Pulled out a blue pill. "Take this and it should help with the aether poisoning."

I put it in my mouth. It dissolved, leaving behind a slightly sweet taste. "Thanks," I groaned. "Where's everyone else?"

"Making breakfast." Percival produced two glass containers, one with a white substance, the other with dark flakes.

"What is that?" I asked.

"Salt and pepper." He took out a container of red liquid. "And a little bit of hot sauce for the eggs."

Thanks to the medicine, my muscles relaxed and the headache faded. I pushed myself into a sitting position and leaned against the side.

"Is it working?" Ivy stroked my hair.

A pleasant chill worked from my scalp and down my back. "Y-yes. I feel much better."

"Good." Ivy bit her lower lip, blue eyes big and sad. She leaned toward me and pressed her lips to mine. A broad smile lit her face. "You're my hero, Conrad." She scooted out of the back of the van and left.

Ambria stared at me, mouth hanging open. Max, awake now, wore a nearly identical expression on his face.

"She kissed you?" Max's voice squeaked. "But—but..." He blinked rapidly.

"Congratulations," Ambria said in a scathing tone. "You know Max likes her." She got out of the side door and slammed it behind her.

"I'm sorry, Max. I didn't know she was going to do that." I reached over and grabbed his arm. "I promise."

Max shook his head slowly. "I'm not even mad, Conrad. I knew I never had a chance with her, but it was fun to pretend." He swallowed hard. "I wish I could be like you. I wish I could be brave enough to win the heart of a girl like Ivy."

"You are brave, Max." I put my hands on his shoulders. "You've saved me more times than I can list. Ivy would be lucky to have a guy like you."

He managed a smile. "She's lucky to have you." Max shrugged. "You're like my brother, Conrad. I'm happy for you, but"—he pressed a hand to his stomach—"I'm starving. I'm gonna get something to eat." He patted my hand and left.

I sat by myself in the van for a moment, trying to come to grips with what had just happened. *Ivy kissed me.* Ambria had been furious at me, and not because of Max. *She has feelings for me.* Or maybe she was just overprotective, like a sister to a brother. I really wasn't sure what it was, but I didn't want her mad at me. I also knew Max was only pretending to be okay. It had to hurt seeing his heroine kiss me.

I stepped out of the van and into a campground filled with recreational vehicles of all sizes and shapes lined up and down a gravel road. The sun peeked over the treetops of a hill in the distance.

Galfandor chatted with a tall, lanky man at a large RV next door. The man turned sausages on a wide grill. Two little boys played with toy trucks while the mother watched from a lawn chair, a magazine in her hand.

I turned and looked at the van. The window didn't look broken from the outside. The surface wasn't pockmarked with bullet holes. Galfandor had apparently cast an illusion on it.

"Ah, there's the boy." Galfandor motioned me over.

I waved my hand timidly. "Hi."

"A pleasure to finally meet you, Conrad." The man extended a hand and shook mine. I must have looked confused, because he smiled. "I'm Geron, an old friend of Galfandor's."

"You're not noms?" I asked.

He blinked, looked back at the mother and boys. "Those are illusions." He winked. "Just for show."

"Oh." My stomach grumbled at the odor of the sausages. "I hope those aren't illusions."

Geron chuckled. "No, the sausages are real." He plucked one from a plate and gave it to me. "I have a large shower inside the RV if you'd like to clean up." He sighed and looked at the bus-sized vehicle. "Isn't she lovely?"

"Very," Galfandor said. "Thank you for coming to meet us."

"It sounded like an emergency." Geron took in a deep breath and looked out at the view. "You'd never know the world is in crisis from all the happy faces here."

Galfandor stroked his beard. "Have you been in touch with the others?"

"I have." Geron looked at me. "We're gathering everyone. Using the arches is too risky these days, so most resort to nom transportation."

"Like RVs?" I asked.

He chuckled. "This particular RV flies. That's how I arrived so quickly. Unfortunately, Victus probably controls the Overworld Transportation Authority by now." Geron looked up. "Thousands of all-seeing eyes tracking magical flight are up there. If they see me travelling extensively it might raise red flags."

"Does he really control the OTA?" Galfandor sighed. "That seriously limits our transportation options."

"And that's precisely why we need to root Xander Tiberius and his infernus minions from the Overworld by force." Geron returned his gaze to earth. "Our dithering has given him too much time to gain strength."

"I still think stealth is our best option," Galfandor said.

"The time for stealth is over, friend." Geron patted the other man's shoulder. "Even Victus can't stand against us now. If we wait any longer, it will be too late."

Galfandor nodded. "I hope you're right."

"In the meantime, relax and recuperate." He motioned to the lawn chairs. "I've contacted the others to set up a safe house for you in Florence."

Galfandor's brow furrowed. "When does the council plan to take action?"

"Soon." Geron removed the last of the sausages from the grill. "The final preparations are underway. We didn't plan to meet for another week, but now that I've found you, perhaps I should move up the date."

Galfandor frowned. "Why wasn't I informed of another gathering?"

"Because the usual lines of communication might have been compromised." He waved at the RV. "This is why we've started contacting everyone in person."

"Perhaps you're right." Galfandor stared into the distance. "We don't have a choice."

"Are you part of the group that was watching me?" I asked. "Are you the ones who thought I might turn out like my father?"

Geron glanced at Galfandor with a raised eyebrow. "You told the boy?"

"He deserved to know." Galfandor gave him a stony look. "I think he's proven himself."

The other man sighed. "Yes, I believe he has."

Ivy walked from between two campers parked on the row behind us, a delighted smile on her face. "This place is wonderful!" She gripped my hand and pulled me after her. "Have you ever been to a campground?"

"No." I lost my grip on the sausage and it fell in the dirt. My stomach growled mournfully.

"We'll talk later, Conrad." Geron stepped inside the RV with Galfandor, leaving me no choice but to follow Ivy.

She led me down the gravel road, eyes wide with wonder at the families cooking meals on grills, or playing croquet and other lawn games near their RVs. "This place is magical. No worries, just families and love." She stopped, eyes brimming with emotion. "I really miss my family."

I swallowed a lump in my throat. "I miss my mom and Cora."

"Where are they, Conrad?"

"It's kind of a long story, and I'm really hungry."

Ivy giggled. "I'd like to hear about them, but I'll let you eat first." She pulled me toward a large group of people at picnic benches. "Hey, everyone, this is my friend I told you about."

"Hello, Conrad. I'm Linda." A middle-aged woman with a cheery smile pointed to a vacant spot at the bench. "We saved a spot for you two."

"Oh, hi." I put on an uncertain smile. "Thanks." I turned to Ivy and whispered, "Who are these people?"

"Nice ones," Ivy said. "This is why we fight the bad guys, Conrad. It's for good people like them. My brother taught me that just because they're noms doesn't make them any less valuable than anyone else."

"Conrad, good to meet you. I'm Roger." A thick man with an equally thick beard gripped my hand and shook it. "Help yourself to some bacon and pancakes."

I sat down next to him and Ivy slid onto the bench to my right. A young boy and two little girls waved at me. Another older couple introduced themselves. Linda put a paper plate piled with pancakes in front of me.

"You eat as much as you want." She patted Roger's belly. "Roger's had enough."

Roger belted out a laugh. "That's your fault, honey."

My stomach rumbled at the delicious aroma from the pancakes. While Ivy chatted, I stuffed my face.

"Worcester is rather dull, so we enjoy taking our holiday on the mainland," Linda said. "We've come to Italy three times and can't get enough of it."

"Italy is so pretty." Ivy sipped on orange juice and bit into a piece of bacon. "This big breakfast with pancakes and bacon reminds me of someone, but I can't put my finger on it." She sighed and leaned her head on my shoulder. "I have visions of this guy with a cowboy hat. He says weird things like 'Holy farting fairies' a lot."

"Hopefully Percival can get your memories back." My right side felt oddly warm with her touching it. I wasn't sure if I should put my arm on her shoulder or remain still.

Ivy solved the problem by sliding off the bench and stretching. "Let's go on a walk, Conrad." She turned to Linda. "Thanks so much for breakfast. It was wonderful."

"Come by for supper." Roger jabbed a thumb toward a grill shaped like a green egg. "We're smoking a pig."

Ivy's eyes brightened. "Sounds great!" She took my hand and marched down the gravel road.

I tried to keep up, but my exhausted limbs were having none of it. "Could you slow down, please?"

She grimaced. "Oh, sorry. I forgot how tired you are from all the fighting last night." Ivy walked past the end of the road and sat beneath a tree where the hill sloped down into a valley of olive trees.

I sat next to her, my hands folded in my lap. "That was a nice breakfast."

"Yeah, they're nice people." Ivy leaned back against the tree. "Do you think the wandslingers will find us here?"

I groaned. "I hope not."

"I hate them so much." Ivy's hands curled into fists. "I can't wait until I can fight again." She tucked a lock of blond hair behind her ear and sighed, turned her big blue eyes on me. "I feel so helpless. I probably would've died or worse if you hadn't saved me from Delilah."

My mouth went dry and my tongue stopped working, so I just nodded.

"You're a fighter, Conrad." Ivy took my hand. "Those bounty hunters are way older and probably more experienced, but you beat their asses."

I didn't see it quite that way. "I survived."

Ivy laughed. "No, you're a hero." Then Ivy Slade, hero of the Overworld leaned over and kissed me.

CHAPTER 16

A tingle ran down my spine freezing me in place. This kiss was different than the peck on the lips in the van. This one felt real.

Ivy pulled away. "Did I do that right?"

I nodded, unable to speak again.

"I should know all about kissing and boyfriends by now, but I'm just a stupid kid thanks to Victus!" She sagged. "I'm supposed to be almost twenty by now. I mean, technically I am, but he got me when I was four-teen or fifteen." Her forehead pinched. "I can't even remember that for sure!"

"Maybe you know more than you think." I squeezed her hand. "When your memories come back, maybe you'll know as much as an adult."

She kissed me again. "I like you, Conrad."

"I like you too." My hand stroked her cheek. Ivy was so pretty, so soft. Something about her frightened and thrilled me all at the same time.

She pulled me closer and we kissed again. I closed my eyes. Felt her melt against me. Heard her soft sighs. But another face filled the darkness. I jerked back.

Ivy blinked. "Is something wrong?"

I cleared my throat. "I-I'm just tired, I guess."

She put her head against my chest. "I really liked kissing you."

"I liked it too." I got up. "Galfandor wanted to talk to me about something. I'm going to see what it is."

Ivy's eyes narrowed. "Are you okay?"

"Yeah, I'm great." I forced a smile. "I'll see you later, okay?"

Her lips twitched down. "Okay."

I felt bad about leaving her like this. Any sane male would have gladly kissed such a beautiful girl as much as she wanted. I turned and hurried back down the gravel road, hands stuffed in my pockets. I cut between two RVs and over to the road where our stolen van was parked. I was so confused. Ivy was pretty, but I didn't like her like Max did.

Nightliss was achingly beautiful, but far too old. I loved Ambria like a sister, but I'd seen her face when I kissed Ivy. Did I really feel something more?

Romance should be the last thing on my mind right now.

With the wandslingers on our tails, Victus plotting his Overworld domination, and mysterious forces looking to compress the realms back into one, death could come at any moment. If we didn't focus all our efforts on survival and stopping Victus, we'd be too dead for kissing.

Concentrate on what's important.

I looked around at all the happy campers frolicking the late morning sun. Kids played. Adults relaxed and drank. Dogs chased balls and happily returned them to their owners for another toss. I let my worries fade away and just watched. Ivy was right. Moments like this were worth fighting for—worth dying for.

I walked back to the van and saw a lone figure crouched against a tree behind Geron's RV. I knew it was Ambria from her long brown hair and slender figure. Her head leaned on bent knees. She looked so tired and defeated, I want to run over and hug her. But I stopped myself. I'd deal with personal issues later.

Galfandor and Geron sat in the chairs once occupied by the illusionary family members, a half-empty bottle of amber liquid on the table in front of them. I drew up a chair and sat opposite of them.

"I want to know more about this secret order of yours." I was surprised at the steel in my voice, but happy I didn't sound like an impertinent child. "What's it called?"

Galfandor and Geron exchange surprised glances, but Geron nodded. "I suppose you deserve to know after all this time."

"We call ourselves the Night Watch," Galfandor said. "After the way Victus subverted the Arcane Council the first time, we wanted to be ready in case anyone ever tried it again."

"Except Victus did it again." Geron chuckled wryly. "He's a roach. Hard to kill, and can slip through the cracks without you knowing."

"Yes, the infernus are pure genius." Galfandor stroked his beard. "Never would have thought infusing soul fragments with demon flesh could produce replicas of people, but here we are, faced with an Overworld government full of impostors."

"What if I'd turned out like my father?" I asked.

Geron dragged a finger along his throat. "Sorry, lad, but we were ready to nip that in bud."

I tried not to shudder and failed. "It took over two years to decide I wasn't a threat?"

"I proposed changing your status after your first year at the university," Galfandor said.

"The rest of us wouldn't hear of it." Geron offered an apologetic shrug. "Unfortunately, while we were so watchful of you, your resurrected father executed a masterful plan of deceit utilizing Xander Tiberius as his puppet. Now the council is divided among impostors and his willing supporters. The few remaining opponents of Xander are in hiding under our protection."

"How many of you are there?" I asked.

"We have thirty agents in all." Geron poured himself another finger of whiskey. "It may not sound like much, but they're all first-rate Arcanes, well-versed in espionage and covert operations."

"But earlier you said the time for stealth was over." I let that statement linger a moment. "You have no idea how many operatives Victus has working for him. If you come out of the shadows now, you'll be targets."

Geron pursed his lips and looked at Galfandor. "Sounds familiar."

Galfandor raised an eyebrow. "Like I said, going for Xander's jugular is a foolish move without knowing the extent of the corruption. Getting rid of him and his cronies won't accomplish a permanent resolution."

Geron smacked the back of his hand into the other palm. "We know the main players are Xander, Grint, and Quiff. We can easily assassinate them and the infernus on the council before anyone is the wiser. This leaves Victus open and vulnerable."

"It will reveal the Night Watch." Galfandor set down his drink. "Victus will simply use his other operatives to rebuild the council."

"No, he'll come out of hiding and take power himself," Geron said. "And that will leave him wide open for the killing blow."

"You're wrong." My words drew their eyes back to me. "Victus wanted to own the Overworld, so what did he do? He manufactured the Crystoid Incident and tricked the entire Overworld army into going to Seraphina so he could trap them there. As insurance, he sent Aerianas to take over Seraphina with infernus to destroy Justin Slade's army so one day he could rule both Eden and Seraphina." I leaned toward them. "Does that really sound like the sort of man who leaves himself open for the killing blow?"

"Well…" Geron frowned. "Perhaps not."

I pushed on. "Do you really think Victus doesn't have a contingency plan in place if his people are killed?" I didn't give him a chance to respond. "Do you think his people are unprotected? He had Seraphim prisoners. For all we knew, he made demon clones of them and has them in reserve."

"Doubtful." Geron took a sip of whiskey and shook his head. "If he had successfully made clones of Seraphim, he would have already taken power by brute force."

"That's not how he works," I said. "Like you said, the man is a cockroach. He'll infest your walls before he comes out to invade. Even if he doesn't have Seraphim, he's building a monster army in the Dark Forest. How do you propose we beat that?"

"Is he pulling frogres out of the forest to fight?" Geron snorted derisively. "We'd destroy them before they even got close to us."

"But what if that's just the tip of the iceberg?" I hated playing devil's advocate, but I'd lost to Victus too many times to underestimate him. "Victus layers plots within plots."

"Conrad is right," Galfandor said. "Killing Xander and two minor cronies will do nothing to draw out Victus."

"There's another way." I settled back into the chair.

Geron's eyebrows rose. "I'm listening."

"When my father's soul shard was still inside me, I had flashbacks and dreams from his perspective. If I concentrate, I can still bring back memories up until the time the shard left me." My chest tightened at the terrible visions still trapped in my head. "One thing he said more than once is that a baited trap is the best way to reveal your enemies even if it doesn't catch them."

"Traps within traps," Galfandor said.

I nodded. "Xander is an obvious target. He's bait to make Victus's enemies reveal themselves, because you can't kill enemies who are hidden."

"And you know all this from Victus's soul shard?" Geron asked.

I shivered. "I know more than I want to know."

"It's why Conrad is so powerful for someone his age," Galfandor said. "He had the memories of his parents sharing the same headspace with him."

Geron nodded. "And he's the progeny of Ezzek Moore. I've no doubt he'll be as powerful as Delectra someday."

"Even more powerful." Galfandor offered me a faint smile. "Don't let it go to your head, son."

Geron's lips flattened into a line. "What do you suggest we do, young man?"

"I think you should make a go at Xander," I said.

Geron frowned. "But you just said—"

"Yes, I said trying to take out Xander would trigger a response." I let him stew over it for a moment. "Your assassination attempt would bait Victus's response plan."

Geron clapped his hands together. "So we trip Victus's trap to lure his people into a trap of our own."

"It's the only way to outmaneuver him." I shrugged. "The only way to stop Victus is to take out his support structure. Xander and his puppets on the council aren't our primary targets. We need to reveal all the hidden cogs in his machine so we know what we're dealing with."

Galfandor nodded. "The hidden roots of corruption spread deep and wide."

"I'll talk it over with the others," Geron said, "but I think it's a rather sound plan."

"As do I." Galfandor took a sip of his whiskey. "It will not be easy to pull off, but the payoff could be excellent."

"We'll need to leave for Paris in the morning," Geron said. "I'll leave the RV here for your companions to use as a safe house."

I turned to Galfandor. "You're leaving us?"

"I must, Conrad." Galfandor put his glass on the table. "We've called the other members of the Night Watch for a meeting. Naturally, we will also try to convince them to use your plan."

It seemed to me their secret group might be the best chance at holding off Victus until Ivy and Nightliss were back to full strength. "May I go as well?"

The pair looked at each other in silence for a moment. Geron turned back to me and nodded. "Yes, that might actually be a good idea. I think it might raise morale to see the son of the Overlord leading the battle against his own father."

"You're not going to Paris without me." Max folded his arms and glared at me after I told him and the others.

"I'm coming too." Ivy latched onto my arm and kissed my cheek. "I may not have magic, but I can still kick ass."

I shifted uneasily, trying to slip my arm free, but Ivy didn't seem to notice.

Ambria looked down and shook her head slowly. "I won't let you go without me either." Her voice was soft and sad.

"I'm afraid Conrad is the only one allowed to go," Galfandor said. "We cannot simply bring the entire group with us to a secret meeting."

"Why?" Ivy jutted out her chin. "You don't trust us?"

"Either Conrad goes alone with us, or he chooses to remain behind." Galfandor held out his hands helplessly. "That is the way it must be."

All attention shifted toward me. I knew Max and Ambria would want to come, and I wished they could, but Geron and Galfandor had made it clear I had to go alone. I held up my hands. "I wish you all could come, but you can't. This is important, so I'm going alone."

"What if the wandslingers find us while you're gone?" Max said. "What if we have to run again?"

I tapped my arcphone. "Then just call me."

"Percival has the keys to the RV," Geron said. "I also took great pains to ward a three-hundred-yard radius around this area."

Ambria turned her big eyes on me. "Will you come straight back after Paris?"

"Yes." I wanted to reach out and take her hands, let her know I'd be okay, but Ivy held my arm hostage and it would look odd. "I think it's important to meet with the Night Watch. Because a part of Victus lived inside my head for so long, I know him better than anyone."

Max grunted. "You're probably right, but that doesn't mean I have to like it."

"It's not like we can do anything else," Percival said. "I've started preparing the ingredients for the memory potion, but it will take me the better part of the week to finish."

"I think Conrad will be safe." Nightliss took my hand from Ivy and pressed hers over and beneath it. "You are strong and resourceful and a leader."

Her touch made me tingle and gave my heart wings. I shivered and grinned like a fool. "Thank you."

Asha nodded. "You're not a kid anymore, Conrad. I'm proud of you."

"Agreed," Granddad Stan said.

"Sure looks like a kid." Natalia stuck out her tongue at me.

While their compliments filled me with warmth, I just couldn't see what they saw. *I'm just a kid. Victus could kill me in an instant. Those wandslingers nearly killed me.* If not for my mother's intense magical defense classes and Kanaan's magitsu training, I probably would have died already.

Ignoring the conversations around me, I looked at Max and Ambria. If not for them, I would have died two years ago after the late Rufus Cumberbatch captured me and released the demon that bound my soul to those of my parents.

Despite Galfandor's assurances that the Night Watch had decided I was mostly harmless, I still didn't entirely trust them. I had doubts they'd listen to the advice of a teenager or heed my warnings about Victus. As with anything else, I had to plan for the worst-case scenario. The two people I trusted the most were my best friends.

I met Max's eyes and nodded slightly toward the door. Ambria's gaze was harder to capture since she sat down and stared at the floor. Max nudged her. She blinked as if coming out of a dream, looked up at him and nodded.

I stretched and casually walked toward the door while Galfandor spoke with the others. Once outside, I slipped around to the other side of the cargo van. Max and Ambria met me there a moment later.

Max rubbed his hands together. "What is it, Conrad?"

I folded my arms. "I'm not going alone with Geron and Galfandor."

"You mean—"

I nodded. "You two are coming with me."

CHAPTER 17

Ambria perked up. "But how?"

I peered around the van and pointed to Geron's compact SUV. "We're taking that to the train station. From there, we'll take the high-speed rail to Paris."

"Are we supposed to hide in the back?" Max said.

I nodded. "I'll get money from Stan to buy your train tickets."

"Why don't you take Ivy instead of me?" Ambria said. "She's a lot stronger."

I took her hands. "Because you're my best friend and I trust you with my life."

She pulled her hands away. Nodded. "I'll go."

Max frowned at Ambria, but for a change, didn't say anything to start a fight. "I'm with you too."

"Great." I walked toward Geron's SUV. "Let's see where you can hide."

I tested the door handle and it clicked open. The inside was small, but the cargo area behind the back seats offered a little room to hide.

Max opened the back hatch and tried to curl up behind the seats. His longs legs folded until his knees touched his chin. "Both of us will never fit in here." He climbed out and let Ambria try.

She lay in the small depression and bent her knees ever so slightly. With a blanket over her, no one would even know she was there. Ambria sat up. "Will they have suitcases? How far is the drive to the train station?"

"I believe they'll have satchels, and the nearest high-speed rail station is twenty minutes away." I motioned to Max. "Can both of you try to fit?"

He shook his head. "I can't even fit in there by myself. They'll see me right away."

"Maybe you can follow on a flying carpet." I said.

Max looked at me like I was crazy. "With all these noms around? I'd have to walk pretty far away before I could fly, and then I'd have to get off and walk miles before I got to the train station."

I climbed in and curled up, but didn't fit any better than Max. "The back of the seat will hide you. I'll just make sure they don't come back here."

"Bad idea." Max put a hand on my shoulder. "If they find us, they'll send me and Ambria back. Ambria is the only one who can stay hidden. It's better you have her along than no one at all."

Ambria nodded somberly. "He's right, Conrad."

I hated the thought of leaving Max behind, but just having Ambria along to watch my back made me feel immeasurably better. "Fine. Let's make sure we can hide you."

We hunted around for a blanket and put it in the back of the SUV. When Ambria got beneath it, we couldn't even tell she was there. So long as Galfandor and Geron didn't remove the blanket, we might get away with this.

Ambria shoved away the carpet and took a deep breath. "I hope the ride isn't too long, because it's positively stifling under there."

With our plan in place, we walked back toward the RV. Max stopped me. "Have you tried searching your memories again? Maybe you could figure out what Victus's plans are."

With all that had happened, I hadn't given it much thought. "I'll try."

"Maybe use infernus as a keyword," Ambria suggested.

I took a seat in a lawn chair and closed my eyes. *Screams. Blood. Faces of loved ones dying.* I fought past the nightmares to the void. I still heard the screams outside the void, muffled as if underwater.

I focused on infernus and the foundry. Bits and pieces of images flashed past. Zarin carving the demon symbols for the foundry. Someone infusing a soulsphere with aether. Like a television station with bad reception, the visions faded in and out, replaced by burning red symbols. It didn't take me long to decipher the symbols I kept seeing.

I opened my eyes. "Victus must have realized we had a psychic link at some point and warded his mind against intrusion."

Ambria's eyes flared. "Do you think the link was two-way?"

"If it was, we'd probably be dead by now," Max said. "Victus had tons of chances to kill us when he was disguised as Professor Sideon."

"He doesn't want to kill Conrad," Ambria said. "He wants to corrupt him like he did Delectra."

I shuddered. "Let's pray he never has the chance."

THE NEXT MORNING AFTER BREAKFAST, Max distracted Galfandor and Geron while I loaded the SUV with their luggage. Ambria slipped under the blanket and I put the light duffel bags over her. I slid the blanket back from her face.

"If it gets stuffy, just move this corner, okay?"

She offered a wan smile. "I'll do my best not to suffocate."

I chuckled. "Please don't." I leaned over and kissed her forehead. "I need you."

Ambria's eyes grew moist. She flicked the blanket back over her face. "Go away before they get suspicious."

I closed the rear hatch and rubbed my forehead to give Max the all-clear signal. He ended his conversation and walked back into the RV. Geron and Galfandor looked mildly confused at Max's sudden departure but made their way over to the car and climbed in front. I slid into the back.

Galfandor and Geron engaged in small talk during the ride to the train station. When they parked, I hurried out and grabbed the luggage.

"We're running a bit late, but we can make the train if we hurry." Geron slipped the strap to his duffel bag over a shoulder and made long strides toward the terminal. Galfandor lumbered after him, long legs keeping him abreast of the other man. Though I'd gained a few inches over the past year, my legs weren't long enough to match the men's strides, so I jogged behind them, craning my neck to see if Ambria was somewhere behind us.

Geron stopped at an automated ticket machine and used a credit card to purchase our tickets. The departure time was only seven minutes away and we hadn't even reached the terminal yet. The discovery of a cash slot filled me with relief since I'd given Ambria money. *Now if only I knew where she was.* I still didn't see her anywhere behind us.

"Come along." Geron hurried toward an escalator, following signs leading us to platform nine.

I stared out across the crowd as we went up.

Galfandor must have noticed my worried gaze. "Did you forget something Conrad?"

"No." I shifted forward. "Just worried about the others. I hope the wand-slingers don't track them down again."

"I'm sure they'll be safe." Geron patted my back. "Never you worry, Conrad. We have some of the most powerful Arcanes in the Overworld on our side. It won't be long before Victus is no longer a threat."

I certainly hope you're right.

We boarded the train just moments before it left. While the others went to the first-class car, I tarried behind and anxiously watched the platform for Ambria. My heart sank when the doors closed and I still saw no sign of her. The train pulled out of the station and it appeared my brilliant plan to have one of my friends with me had failed.

The top of my hand stung. I looked down and realized I'd scratched the scar tissue until it bled. I'd forgotten to put lotion on it before going to bed, and the skin looked terribly dry. I dug through my pockets and remedied the situation before it got any worse.

Galfandor and Geron had already settled into their seats, the former with a fresh cup of tea, and the latter with a glass of whiskey. I sat down next to the window and stared out at the passing cityscape of Florence.

Galfandor pulled out a newspaper and shook his head. "What a mess these noms make of the world."

"Agreed." Geron had a newspaper of his own. "I still believe a restructuring would do the Overworld and the nom nations a great deal of good."

"A subject we will never agree on." Galfandor unfolded the paper and continued to read the front page. "The noms would never accept imposed rule from the Arcane minority, and there are far too many of them for us to force the issue."

I raised an eyebrow at Geron. "You want to rule the noms?"

"Not rule them, so much as guide them." He shrugged. "The world descends further into barbarism each and every day, and the noms are simply too blinded by partisanship to do what is right."

"That argument sounds just like one Victus used in the past." I suddenly wondered if going to talk to the Night Watch was a terrible mistake. "Is that what your organization is about?"

"No." Galfandor put down the newspaper. "We are committed to protecting free will of the people, be they supernatural or normal. Geron has proposed we intercede at the highest levels of nom government and pull the puppet strings, so to speak. I do not agree with his reasoning, nor do many others."

"Well, don't come crying to me when the seas rise from environmental warming and the lunatics controlling nuclear arsenals drive mankind into extinction." Geron shook his paper and turned to the next page.

"Or perhaps these are natural cycles that govern the rise and fall of nations," Galfandor replied. "Who are we to interfere when we cannot even protect our own government from evil people?"

"I'm going to take a walk." I slid out of the seat and left, heading back toward the car with the cafeteria. Melancholy hung heavy on my heart. I was all alone, on my way to meet with members of a secret organization that seemed to have similar goals to that of my evil father. Perhaps Galfandor was right, and the majority didn't share Geron's views. A dictator was a dictator, no matter the cause.

Lively people and conversation filled the cafeteria. I ordered a tea and sat in one of the tall stools next to the window so I could at least enjoy the view.

"Is this seat taken, sir?"

I set my tea on the table and jumped from my chair. "Ambria, I thought you didn't make it!" I gripped her in a fierce hug. "I was so sad."

She smiled and gave me a quick peck on the cheek before separating herself from me. "I nearly missed it, thanks to those ridiculously diffi-cult cash slots on the kiosks."

"Would you like tea?" I asked.

"Absolutely."

I ordered her one and brought it back to the table. "I can't tell you how much happier I am, knowing you're here."

Her face flushed. "That's what friends are for."

The train ride was not short—nearly ten hours, in fact. I checked in with Galfandor and Geron every so often to make sure they didn't come looking for me, then went to the cafeteria car near the back of the train to sit with Ambria so they didn't accidentally stumble into us.

As we neared the final station, Ambria took out an arcphone Stan had given her. I bumped mine against hers and we shared our locations so we could track each other on the map. That would make it easier for her to follow us at a distance. I still didn't know the security or layout of the meeting site, but hoped I could somehow let her in without arousing suspicion.

I rejoined Galfandor and Geron and we departed a train station near a river my phone identified as the Seine. Geron led the way, crossing the street and entering a small bakery. I expected him to say a secret phrase that admitted us into a back room. Instead, he ordered a croissant and headed back outside.

My stomach grumbled, but I wasn't sure if it was from hunger or anxi-ety. We walked several blocks and took an abrupt turn into an alley.

"Wait a moment." Geron flicked his wand and a small bubble reflected the sidewalk we'd come down.

"Is someone following us?" Galfandor asked.

Geron didn't answer.

My heartbeat sped up. I desperately hoped Ambria wasn't following too close behind. Every second we paused, I grew more nervous. Wiping sweaty palms on my pants I cleared my throat and tried not to sound nervous. "Well, can we continue?"

Geron held up a finger. The bubble blinked green and popped. "Sorry, I thought I saw something earlier. Must have been nothing." He stepped back onto the sidewalk and continued.

After two more blocks, he entered an old hotel. The man behind the desk nodded politely and spoke in French.

"I'm here for the gala conference," Geron said.

The man slid across three key cards. "Rooms four zero seven, seven hundred, and five eighty-one." He slid across a brass skeleton key. "This key will open the third-floor ballroom."

Geron took the keys. "Do you have any neighboring rooms?"

The man shook his head. "I'm sorry, but those are all we have left."

Geron put the brass key in a pocket and handed each of us a keycard. We walked across the lobby to an antiquated cage elevator and slid the door shut. The car creaked and shuddered as it climbed its way up, inspiring little confidence from its occupants.

"I wouldn't be surprised if this lift killed us," Galfandor murmured.

"Riding it is a rather frightening experience." Geron winked at me as if I were the frightened one.

When it reached the fourth floor, Geron handed us the other two keycards and disembarked. "Meet me on the third floor in the morning." He stretched and yawned. "Order meals to your rooms if you wish. I'll cover them."

"Sleep well, friend." Galfandor closed the cage door and turned to me. "Which room do you want?"

I held out a hand. "I'll take seven hundred."

He gave me the keycard and got off on the fifth floor. I continued up to my floor, but instead of getting off, I went back down to the lobby. When the elevator deposited me on the first floor, I went outside and looked around for Ambria. I saw her peeking cautiously around a corner and waved her over.

She peered around suspiciously, then approached. "Is this the place?"

"Yep."

"I'm glad I waited a while when you went into that alley." Ambria scratched her nose. "I thought for sure that was the place, but then you came back out after a few minutes."

"Geron was making sure we weren't being followed." I looked around furtively as if he might be watching. "It's good you stayed put."

Ambria looked through the glass doors. "Are there any guards inside?"

"No." I described the layout. "I have my own room so you can stay in there. I think Galfandor and Geron went straight to bed, so it should be safe."

Ambria nodded. "I thought the meeting was today."

"So did I, but it's in the morning." My stomach grumbled. "Are you hungry?"

"A bit."

"We can order from the room." I took her upstairs. Two queen beds sat against one wall and a red leather couch against another. A rickety old desk hunched in the corner. I ordered food from the front desk. When it arrived, we watched television as we ate, though the language barrier prevented us from understanding much of anything.

Ambria fell asleep in her bed as the television droned on. I turned on my side in my bed and felt comforted, knowing she was here with me.

A young man with a thick white beard and long white hair stands before me. His rugged wool robe rustles as he walks. Bright white fog drifts around us, concealing the surroundings. The man grips my shoulders and speaks, but his words are unintelligible.

I try to pull away, but he's too strong. "What are you saying? I don't understand."

He bares his teeth and speaks with exaggerated movements of his mouth. It takes me a moment to understand what he's saying. "Use more power. Expand your well."

"I already have magic poisoning from overextending myself the last time." Even in my dream I feel weak. "Who are you?"

He gives me a satisfied nod and mouths, "More."

I blinked awake, calm and quiet. *What's happening to me?* I wondered if I still had a link to Victus and if this was one of his tricks, or if it was something else entirely. I couldn't explain it, but this dream felt connected to all the others. *What happens if I use more power to expand my well?* Every Arcane had a well—a psychic reservoir to hold aether for casting spells. By overextending, one could expand the well. In school, the teachers occasionally measured our capacity, but mine hadn't been exceedingly large at my last calibration.

Besides, a well could only expand so much before you reach your limit. I might be the great-grandson of Ezzek Moore, but even he had his limits, no matter what anyone said.

AFTER BREAKFAST in the room the next morning, I got ready to head down to the third floor. "I don't know what to expect," I told Ambria.

"I'll come down in a bit and hide in the hallway." She took out her arcphone and hovered a finger over a red button on the location app she used to track me. "Just hit the panic button and I'll come running." Ambria patted a pouch. "Max gave me his memory fog bombs and some banana peel potions."

I squeezed her hand to calm my nerves. I wondered how many of these people would hate me because of my father. How many still thought I'd follow in his footsteps. "Thank you."

Ambria lifted my hand and kissed the scar tissue. "Everything will be okay."

For some reason, I believed her.

Feeling calmer, I kissed her hand and left. Geron waited on the third floor with Galfandor when I arrived. He nodded. "Good morning. Are you ready?"

I took a deep breath. Nodded. "Yes."

Geron led us to the ballroom. The old key slid into a mortise lock. The door clicked open. We stepped into an empty lobby with a red velvet curtain separating this room from the next. Geron parted the curtain and stepped through. Dozens of people clustered inside. The dull roar of conversation died down as everyone turned to see who'd entered.

Some expressions of delight turned hostile when the gazes shifted from Geron and Galfandor to me, while others regarded me with confusion. I had the distinct feeling my attendance had not been widely advertised.

"I need to use the bathroom," I whispered. "Can I have the key?"

Geron handed it to me. "It looks as though everyone is here. I'll start the meeting now and call Conrad to speak when he returns."

"Yes, I think we should warm up the crowd with discussion first," Galfandor replied. "They don't look terribly receptive right now."

I left them to do their thing and went through the ballroom lobby and out into the hallway.

I looked up and down the hallway and spotted Ambria at the far end. I trotted down to her. "Looks like about thirty people inside. There's a lobby with a curtain just through the door."

"You look pale Conrad." She patted my cheek. "Feeling okay?"

"I was fine until all those strangers looked at me."

Ambria smiled. "You'll do fine. Remember to breathe."

I pressed her hand to my cheek and felt the shakiness subside. "I'm glad you're here."

Her eyelids fluttered. "Me too, Conrad."

I turned and went back down the hall. I hadn't been gone more than ten minutes, but heated discussions rang out on the other side of the curtain.

"You don't know that this boy isn't as bad as his father," someone shouted. "He could be leading us into a trap."

"He's the bloody spawn of evil!" a woman yelled.

"Ridiculous," a calmer voice replied. "The boy is not like his father."

"I'll vouch for the boy," Galfandor said. The shouting faded abruptly.

"I don't trust the boy, but I trust Galfandor," one of the earlier voices said.

"I don't like it, but I'll hear him out," the woman added.

I wasn't sure if that was my cue or not, but I stepped through the curtains and into the ballroom. Chairs circled the middle of the room. Geron and Galfandor sat on the opposite side from me. A few heads swiveled my way. Elbow nudges to neighbors cast more eyes in my direction.

Geron stood and motioned me over. "Come tell them what you told me, Conrad."

I gulped and walked around the circle to the other side where an empty chair waited next to Galfandor. I sat down on my hands so no one would see them shaking.

"I know you have no reason to trust me, but I'd like to see my father brought down as much as anyone else here." I saw a few nods and some encouraging smiles mixed with a nearly equal number of dismissive shakes and glaring frowns. "First, I'll explain how I know what I know." I told them the story of my parents' resurrection and how their soul shards linked their minds to mine. This elicited a number of shocked glances from those who'd glared moments earlier, but I didn't know if it had actually changed their minds about me or convinced them I was tainted. I told them how to best bait Victus into a trap of our own.

"Ridiculous." A man stood. "We're taking advice from a twelve-year-old."

"I'm nearly fifteen, sir." My voice cracked.

"Fifteen. Hmph." He stepped back from his chair. "I've heard enough. Maybe this farce will be over by the time I return from the bathroom."

"Edgar, you've been unreasonable from the moment I first started speaking." Geron stood and spread his hands imploringly. "Why are you so eager to ignore us? Usually, you're among the first to adopt new ideas."

Edgar sputtered. "Because it's Conrad Edison, you fools!" He stormed through the curtains. The door slammed shut a moment later.

"Let me talk to him." The female voice sounded warm and welcoming. "I'm certain I can make him listen to reason."

I glanced around the circle and found a middle-aged woman with short brown hair and a friendly smile.

Geron sighed. "Would you, Melinda?"

"Of course." She left the room.

A portly man stood and spoke in heavily accented English. "I support this idea. We destroy Victus and his cronies, and we do it soon. This time we destroy body. Leave no vessel for evil man."

A burly fellow with a thick mustache stood and smacked a fist into his other palm. "I say we abduct the bloody council and take over the government without all the cloak and dagger."

I recognized a few people from my time at Arcane University, many of whom had spoken out against Xander Tiberius when he ran for Arcanus Primus. Something vibrated in my pocket. It took me a moment to realize it was my arcphone. I took it out and flicked on the screen. Ambria's location on the map blinked red. My heart skipped a beat.

"What's that?" Galfandor asked.

"Max is trying to call," I lied. I got up from my chair, retreated further into the back of the ballroom, and called Ambria.

"Get out of there now, Conrad," Ambria hissed. "There's a traitor!"

CHAPTER 18

T he fear in Ambria's voice froze me to the core. "What's happened?"

"A woman just slit a man's throat in the hallway, and a dozen thugs are waiting outside the ballroom door!"

Mournful howls sent chills down my spine. Huge forms flashed through the curtains on the other side of the room. Claws flashed and cut down the nearest Arcane. Screams. Shouts. Arcanes rose to their feet. Spells flashed and blood splashed. Arcanes fell before the massive werewolves.

"Edison betrayed us!" One of the Arcanes swung his wand toward me. Galfandor punched the man in the face and shoved him away. A mottled lycan sprang on the man's back and bit his head. Blood sprayed.

I focused Fireblade and slashed the head off the lycan. My vision faltered and my knees went weak. I still hadn't recovered from all the magic use in the fight against the wandslingers.

"Try the bloody windows!" Geron shouted above the fray, even as he fired bolts of jagged green light at the lycans.

Galfandor threw a chair against one of the windows. Glass shattered. We ran over and looked out, but it was a three-story fall to concrete.

"We might have to jump," Galfandor said. "Use a levitation spell."

"Well, Geron, it appears your little venture has been nipped in the bud." We turned. Lycans growled before a tight circle of wounded Arcanes. Melinda stood near the door, a smirk on her face. "Did you not think Victus could infiltrate your pathetic little Night Watch?"

"Are you an infernus?" Geron said.

"I am. The real Melinda rots in a mass grave." She put hands on hips. "And now, I rip you stem and root from the ground." Melinda thrust her hand forward.

The lycans pounced. Explosions shook the room and plaster dust rained down as Arcanes responded with shields and spells. Geron put a hand on Galfandor's shoulder. "Get the boy out of here. If we survive this, I'll contact you."

"I won't leave you all behind." Galfandor whirled his wand in a pattern I didn't recognize and unleashed a torrent of silver flames on the lycans. The wolves howled in pain, but Arcanes still died.

I summoned all my willpower, but it refused to coalesce into a spell. Melinda's gloating smirk settled on me. "I will take you alive, child. Your father has plans for you. He—" Her back arched. Blood spewed from her mouth and she went down in a heap. Ambria stood behind her, wand glowing with malevolent energy.

"Why am I not surprised to see her?" Galfandor pulled me along the wall, avoiding the bloodbath in the middle of the room. When we reached the other side, he pushed me toward Ambria. "Go with her, Conrad. I can't leave my companions."

"You can't!" I shouted. "We need you."

"Duty is an oath." Galfandor turned back to the fray and blasted a lycan with a gout of silver flames.

Ambria dragged me out of the room. My legs and arms felt limp as wet noodles.

"We've got to go." She looked up and down the hallway. "I think there are more people on the way."

Shouts emanated from below. We looked over the railing and into the main lobby. I spotted Talbot and Delilah running toward the elevator. The hotel worker lay slumped over the desk, blood pooling around his head.

"Can't go that way." Ambria grabbed my hand and dragged me into the nearest stairwell. Voices echoed and doors slammed shut below us. Ambria grimaced and put a finger to her lips. We tiptoed up the stairs to the next landing and waited.

"Stay here and make sure nobody tries to leave this way." Delilah sounded excited. "Capture the boy if you see him, but don't kill him."

"Affirmative," a male voice responded.

Ambria clenched a fist and shook it. She delicately turned the handle on the door to the fourth floor and eased it open. We slipped through and shut it as quietly as possible. "How did they find you again?"

"Talbot and Delilah didn't." I leaned against a wall. "The Night Watch was infiltrated by an infernus."

"The wandslingers must have portaled here like they did at the house." Ambria reached into her satchel and dug through several pouches inside. She gave me a stick of something green with the texture of cheese. "Eat this. It's for magic poisoning. Percival gave me a supply."

"He knew you were coming with us?" I bit into the stuff hesitantly. It tasted sour, but went down smoothly.

"Yes, I knew we might need more than Max's potion bombs." She smoothed back the hair from my face. "Feeling better?"

I nodded. "I still feel weak, but not as nauseous."

She sighed. "The next question is, where do we go from here?"

I gripped her hands and met her eyes. "Thank you for saving me."

Ambria blinked. Nodded. "You're my best friend, Conrad. I'll always be there for you."

"I'm happy you were here."

"Yes, well, let's save the happiness for once we escape this blasted trap." She tapped a finger on her chin. "The buildings in this area are relatively close together. We could go to the roof and jump to another building."

"I don't think my knees are up to the challenge." The weakness had faded, but I didn't expect to win any marathons.

Ambria dug into her satchel and pulled out two shiny polished stones. "Then it's a good thing I brought these."

"Blink stones?"

"Yes." She handed me one and tightened the straps on her satchel. "You remember how dizzy these things make us. Just be careful not to blink too close to the edge."

"The first blink isn't that bad." Max had used one in rapid succession and promptly thrown up.

"Let's go." Ambria started down the hallway.

"I thought we were going to the roof."

She shook her head. "I have a better idea."

The door to the stairwell opened behind us. We spun. A man in gray robes leveled a wand at us. "Stop right there, Edison, or I'll shoot your little girlfriend."

"I'm not his girlfriend," Ambria growled. She vanished in a puff of shadows. The inside of his skull lit up like a candle. He screamed and fell to the floor, a trail of smoke rising from his right ear.

Ambria stood behind him, a little wobbly on her feet, face white as a ghost. She wiped her wand off on the man's robes. "I'm not little either."

My jaw went slack. "I didn't realize you were so good with the magitsu spells already."

She swallowed hard, as if biting back nausea. "Remember when I couldn't fly a broom well, so I obsessively practiced by myself until I was as good as Max?"

"Yes."

"Well, I did the same after Kanaan's lessons." Ambria looked down at the body and shuddered. "I don't know if I'm sick from the blink, or—" She heaved and threw up on the carpet.

I patted her back. "Magic poisoning?"

Ambria shook her head. "I've killed two people today, Conrad." She wiped her mouth with her sleeve. "I thought the adrenaline would help me not think about it, but I can't." She put a piece of Percival's magic poisoning gunk in her mouth. "I hope this helps with the nausea."

"I know how you feel." I squeezed her hand. "I see death every time I close my eyes."

"I heard a scream," someone shouted from inside the stairwell. "Everyone to the fourth floor."

"No time for weakness." Ambria fused the lock on the stairwell door with a blast from her wand and grabbed my hand. "We've got to be strong."

We jogged down the hall. She stopped near the end and blasted open a door.

The stairwell door exploded into the hallway. Two towering men burst from the stairwell. Each bore the tattoo of a crescent moon on their necks. They morphed into equally huge wolves. Talbot and Delilah

196

dashed through after them, delighted grins on their faces, oblivious to their expired comrade on the floor.

Ambria fired toward the wolves. A fire extinguisher on the wall exploded, driving the beasts sideways.

"Nowhere to go, boy," Talbot called. "Might as well give up peaceably."

Ambria flicked her fingers under her chin like an Italian and shoved me through the door she'd blown open. She destroyed the glass pane in the balcony window and pulled me outside. A chilly breeze pushed the hair from her face. "We have to blink across." She pointed to a balcony twenty feet away on the neighboring building.

I concentrated on the target. The world puffed away like smoke and just as quickly reappeared. My nose pressed against the glass of the French balcony doors. I staggered, dizzy from the blink. Ambria appeared next to me, unsteady on her feet. A flick of her wand and the wood around the door handle splintered.

Howls echoed. The huge wolves leapt the gap.

Ambria shrieked and jerked me inside the doors an instant before the first wolf crashed onto the balcony. The second smashed into the railing and dangled over the side, a single paw clinging to the concrete. Ambria fired a salvo of magic bullets at the paw. Blood sprayed. The claws lost purchase, and the wolf's howls fell away.

The remaining wolf snarled and smashed through the balcony doors. Ambria shoved me behind her and squared off against the huge beast, wand held protectively before her. Her lips peeled back from her teeth. "Come at me, lycan, and I'll burn you to ash."

Saliva dripped from the werewolf's mouth, and his growl deepened until it seemed to vibrate in my guts. But he didn't advance. Ambria backed up a step, pushing me again. I came to my senses and realized she wanted me to keep moving. So I did under the watchful gray eyes of the wolf. I gripped the door handle and opened it.

The wolf sprang, jaws wide. Ambria jumped backed. The beast smashed into an invisible shield so hard the walls shuddered. He staggered to his feet and wobbled, still growling.

Ambria turned and shoved me through the door. "Run!"

We raced down the hallway. The walls shuddered again and the wolf exploded through the plaster. Dust and wooden lathe sprayed across red carpet. Ambria cast another shield spell. The wolf smashed through the wall and went around it. The beast was incredibly fast, but Ambria slowed it with more shields. We reached the elevator alcove. A bell dinged and the doors creaked open. Talbot and Delilah stood inside, wicked grins on their faces.

Ambria yanked my arm and we raced toward a large window at the end of the hallway. Bullets zipped past us. The window ahead shattered.

"Stop or we'll shoot the girl in the back!" Delilah shouted. "I'll kill her dead, boy!"

Ambria flicked her wand and a shield spell blocked the hallway. The wolf smashed into the wall to forge a path around it. Delilah and Talbot followed in its destructive wake.

"Where are we going?" I panted.

"Through the window." Ambria gripped her blink stone. "You need to jump out and blink back across to the other building."

"What's the range on these things again?"

She shook her head. "I don't remember. Just do it!" Still in a dead sprint, Ambria leapt out of the window, screaming like a madwoman. Her body vanished over the side.

I cried out in fear and leapt after her. Time seemed to slow. I looked left and tried to focus on the balcony forty feet away even as my heart seized in terror. Ambria vanished in a puff of shadows and reappeared at the target. I willed myself to the spot by her side.

Darkness. Light.

My feet slapped concrete. Momentum carried me sideways, crashing into Ambria and slamming her into the railing.

She gasped and we went down in a heap. I tried to cast a spell to blast open the door, but nausea twisted my guts. I gripped the door handle. It clicked open. Ambria lay on the balcony, clutching her sides and wheezing. I dragged her inside and closed the door behind us.

French doors on the balcony across from us smashed open. The werewolf morphed into human form and looked at the alley below. Talbot and Delilah stepped onto the ledge Ambria and I had jumped from and looked all around. Ambria's harsh breathing quieted as she finally caught her breath.

She opened her mouth to speak, but I put a finger to my lips and shook my head.

Talbot walked around the corner on the ledge and raised a fist at the wolf on the balcony. "Follow their scent, you damned fool!"

"Their scent is everywhere," the man shouted in a basso voice.

"Because you chased them all over creation." Delilah walked up behind the lycan and smacked him on the back of his shaven head. "Where'd you find these idiots, Talbot?"

"I broke my legs!" a voice shouted from below.

Delilah looked down and spat. "Two grown lycans bested by a little girl. Drag yourself into a corner and heal."

"I'm in agony!" he cried back. "Can't you use a healing spell?"

"Idiots." Delilah fired a magic bullet at the ground. "Ask me again, and I'll heal you permanently."

Despite his size and ferocity, the other lycan looked cowed by the wandslingers even though he probably could have caught them by surprise and torn them to shreds.

I pointed to the bedroom door. Ambria nodded. We slid over the bed to stay out of sight of the balcony doors and crawled behind cover to the exit as the shouting continued. I peered around the base of the bed. The lycan had moved from the balcony, and I didn't see Delilah in view, so I opened the door and we crawled out.

Ambria pulled the door shut. We leaned against the wall, collecting ourselves for a moment. Shouts emanated from the far end of the hallway where the balcony overlooked the atrium.

"I wonder if Galfandor made it." Ambria squeezed my hand. "Do you think he's dead?"

I shook my head. "Should we check?" Sirens wailed in the distance. The police would be here soon and we had to be gone by then.

"Yes. We can't leave here without knowing if he's dead or alive."

I stood and pulled Ambria to her feet. "You were amazing."

A tear pooled in her eye. "Thank you, Conrad."

"I've never seen you so fierce before."

"There was too much to lose." She blinked, and the tear traveled down her cheek. "I knew I couldn't fail."

"The stakes are always impossibly high with Victus." I wanted to lie down and go to sleep.

"So much death." Ambria regarded me solemnly. "I feel as if he's already stolen a part of my soul."

The sirens seemed closer so I grabbed her hand. "Let's check on Galfandor before the police arrive."

We took the stairs to the third floor. Bodies littered the hallway. Blood pooled on the carpet, thick as syrup and dark as death. Fighting the dread feeling frosting my chest, I stepped over body parts and dead wolves to reach the ballroom. Geron lay dead at the far end of the room, his throat torn out. Two burnt lycan bodies lay nearby.

A half-morphed lycan dragged his wolf hind parts with human hands across the shredded carpet, entrails trailing from a huge gash in his belly. I didn't know if he would regenerate or die, but stayed clear of him. We did a quick search of the Arcane bodies, but Galfandor wasn't among them.

Ambria sounded a hopeful note. "He must have escaped."

"I hope so." I edged across the room to a hole blasted through the plaster. I ducked through and into the neighboring ballroom. The door at the far end hung open. I peered through and into a hallway that intersected the main one a dozen feet to the right. A bloody handprint streaked toward an emergency exit to the left.

The sirens sounded much closer now. Ambria jogged down the hallway and opened the door. It led to a dim stairwell we followed down and to a metal door. Ambria pushed against it, but it wouldn't open. I rammed my shoulder against it.

Muffled growls sounded from the other side.

Ambria bared her teeth. "Give it all you've got, Conrad." She counted to three with her fingers and we rammed the door.

A shout of pain answered and the door finally shoved open. The injured lycan lay on the other side, legs twisted at sickening angles. His eyes flashed with recognition. "You little bastards!" Outstretched human hands morphed to claws.

CHAPTER 19

Ambria stomped on the lycan's broken legs. He howled in agony. She rammed her wand in his nose. Magic crackled and the lycan's skull lit for an instant. He fell to the side, smoke rising from nostrils and mouth. Like the others, he wore the tattoo of a crescent moon on his neck.

The wand clattered to the ground. Ambria clenched her stomach and dry-heaved. She staggered back, moaning.

I grabbed her shoulders. "Are you okay?"

Tears streamed from her eyes. She shook her head. "I hate them. I hate what they make me do, Conrad."

My stomach twisted. They'd turned my sweet Ambria into a killer. I picked up her wand and handed it to her. "They backed us into a corner. We did what we had to do."

She nodded. "I know I had no choice, but I hate it."

"There's a difference between you and them." I put a hand on her cheek. "You're a protector. A defender. You shield the ones you care about."

Ambria wiped away tears with the back of her hand. "Killing is awful no matter the reason, Conrad." She managed a wan smile. "But thank you for trying to make me feel better."

I thought about all the lives I'd taken. About what drove me and motivated me to stay alive. I would fight to the death for any of my friends, but...I traced Ambria's cheek with a finger. Tucked her hair behind her ear and looked into her warm hazel eyes. My thumb wandered the curve of lips grown full over the past few years. My Ambria had grown from a ragged little orphan into a fierce woman.

Her eyes held onto mine. A soft gasp rose from her throat.

"I heard him scream." I recognized the voice of the other lycan. "Something happened."

Ambria hissed and yanked me out into the alley. We sprinted to the street and cut around the corner to the left. Police lights flashed on the main road ahead. Ambria turned into an alley on the right. We followed it around a corner and out to the road a distance from the hotel. Curious eyes from passers-by drew my attention to the bloodstains on our torn clothes.

I tugged on Ambria's sleeve to divert her single-minded stride down the sidewalk and pulled her into a clothing shop. The girl who greeted us swept a dismayed look up and down our attire. Though she spoke in French, her disgust broke the language barrier.

"Sorry, English only," I said.

She frowned.

"Pick out something fast," I told Ambria.

I gathered a polo shirt, jeans, and underclothes, and met Ambria at the register. The girl took my Euros without hesitation and didn't seem to care when we changed into our new clothes in the changing rooms. I stuffed our ruined outfits into the bag and we left.

"What now?" Despite her disheveled hair and the bit of soot on her nose, Ambria looked cute in the blue cardigan and dark jeans she'd chosen.

I thought of how soft her cheek felt beneath my fingers. How her lips—

"Conrad?" Ambria snapped her fingers. "Did you hear me?"

I snapped from my thoughts. "Um, yes." I cleared my throat. "We need to make our way back to the train station and rejoin the others."

"Do we have enough money for the train?"

"I believe so." My stomach grumbled. "First, let's get some food."

She managed a smile. "That's a grand idea."

We stopped at a café and ordered by pointing at pictures on the menu. The waitress seemed amused by our attempts to pronounce the French words before answering us in lightly accented English.

Ambria huffed. "It's so frustrating trying to do even the tiniest things when you don't speak the language."

"Is that why you ordered snails?" I asked.

Her eyes widened. "I didn't order snails!"

"I'm sure they'll be delicious."

"Well, maybe I should order snails." She leaned forward. "There's a lot I haven't done. Maybe it's time to live a little."

I snorted. "Instead of surviving a little?"

"Precisely." Ambria leaned a cheek on her hand and stared wistfully through the window. "I'm nearly fifteen and hardly know a thing about the nom world out there. The orphanage didn't teach us much, and Arcane University certainly hasn't filled in the gaps."

The waitress brought us a platter with the escargot I'd ordered, bringing a grimace to Ambria's face. "You really did order it!"

I nodded. "Let's live a little. I'll go first." I picked up a shell and dug into it with a tiny fork. The snail was a small brown lump saturated in butter. I popped it in my mouth, chewed, swallowed. "It's actually quite good."

Ambria wrinkled her nose and uneasily put one in her mouth. Her look of disgust turned to a smile of pleasure. "You're right!" She ate another and another. "They're delicious."

Her enthusiasm lifted my heart. *We should go back to the others immediately.* But I didn't want to. I just wanted to forget the horrors of the day. To forget that we were on the run from bounty hunters and murderers.

For a short time, I did. Ambria and I feasted on wine-soaked hare and enjoyed eclairs for dessert. She looked a little sad when we left. We found the nearest bus stop. I deciphered the map with the help of my arcphone and figured out which route took us to the train station.

Ambria sat on the bench, staring down at the ground. "I don't know how we'll beat Victus now. The entire Night Watch is dead."

I sat next to her and covered her hand with mine. "Don't think about it."

She rested her head on my shoulder. "What else is there to think about? Now we have to stay in hiding until we can go to Seraphina."

I spotted a bus coming toward us and checked the route number. It wasn't the right one for the train station, but on a whim, I took Ambria's hand and pulled her onto the bus with me. She took a seat and stared out of the window, eyes shimmering with sadness. The bus drove across a bridge. Ambria's eyes grew huge when she saw the sight ahead of us.

"It's the Eiffel Tower!" Her gaze filled with wonder. "It's beautiful."

We debarked the bus and joined the throngs of people walking beneath the huge structure. Ambria craned her neck skyward, mouth gaping. "It's so tall!"

I saw a group of tourists milling near stairs and nodded toward them. "Want to climb to the top?"

She nodded eagerly. "Absolutely."

In that moment, her face looked radiant, no longer filled with dejection and sadness. Ambria looked beautiful and my heart grew so full I could hardly speak. Was it happiness? Hope? Whatever it was, it felt so good, I didn't want to let go.

We went up the stairs, animatedly talking about the sights and sounds just like the other tourists. For all intents and purposes, we were no longer wizards on the run from wandslingers, but ordinary noms on an adventure.

Tired and panting, but ecstatic, we reached the second floor at the top of the stairs. From there, we had to take the lift to the top.

"Oh, my." Ambria leaned against the railing and looked down at the lush green mall stretching into the distance where it met a stately old building at the far end. It reminded me a little of Queens Gate.

"It's beautiful."

"It's magical." Ambria hugged my arm and leaned her head on my shoulder. "I'm so glad you brought me here."

As I looked upon her happy, glowing smile, my heart swelled until I thought it might burst. "Breathtaking."

Big brown eyes looked up at me. "Yes, it is."

I shook my head. "No, I mean you."

Ambria blinked. "Conrad—"

I couldn't help myself. I leaned down and kissed her. Ambria wrapped her arms around my neck and pressed her soft lips against mine until we both had to come up for air.

A tear pooled in Ambria's eye, clinging to her lashes and slowly trickling down her cheek. "I thought you and Ivy—"

I shook my head. "I don't think I realized until this moment that there's no one in this world for me except you, Ambria. Ever since our escape from the orphanage, I grew to think of you as family."

"Am I?" she asked in a small voice.

I brushed away her tears. "Yes, and so much more. I just didn't know what I was feeling. It wasn't until Ivy that I realized how she pales in every way compared to you."

"Oh, Conrad." A radiant smile burned beneath more tears. "I've loved you ever since the day you saved me. I never said anything because I didn't want to ruin our friendship." She looked out at the horizon. "You just always seemed too distant, so detached. I didn't know if you felt emotions the same after what your parents did to you."

"Maybe I didn't at first." Tears blurred my vision. "But now I do."

Ambria giggled and kissed me again. "Does this mean I can kiss you whenever I want?"

I chuckled. "As long as we're not fighting bounty hunters or evil wizards."

"You two are so cute!" A woman with an American accent beamed at us. "My god, I wish I could recapture the feeling of that first love." She elbowed a tall skinny man next to her. "Right, George?"

George lowered a camera from his eye and nodded. "Yes, honey."

The woman clasped her hands. "Adorable."

George rolled his eyes and went back to taking pictures of the mall.

Ambria and I giggled and walked around the observation platform hand-in-hand to take in the sights. After a while, we took the elevator back down and toured the mall until our feet ached.

"It's been a wonderful day, Conrad." Ambria leaned against me and sighed. "I suppose we should go back to Italy."

I watched the sun falling lower in the sky and nodded sadly. "I suppose we should."

"Where do you think Galfandor is now?"

I shrugged. "There's no telling, but I'll call Max and let him know everything."

Ambria winced. "We should have done that hours ago."

My finger stroked her cheek. "I think we got a little distracted."

"Shame on us." She kissed my hand and giggled, but her smile slowly faded. "It helped me forget, at least for a little while what we're facing."

"Yes, it did."

Her gaze took in the surroundings. "You know what's amazing?"

"Besides kissing you?" I asked.

Ambria nipped on my finger playfully. "Yes, besides that."

"What?"

"After everything we've seen—Queens Gate, the Grotto, Obsidian Arches, the Glimmer—you'd think a place like Paris wouldn't be that impressive." Ambria shook her head. "But it's every bit as beautiful and amazing, just in a different way."

"It's so wonderfully normal." I shrugged. "I mean, I love magic, but it's nice to take a break, isn't it?"

"Especially with the one you love." Ambria hugged me and leaned her head on my chest. "I love you, Conrad."

My body tingled, and my heart filled with joy. "I love you too, Ambria." I kissed the top of her head. "I love you more than words can say."

I called Max and told him about our adventures, but left out the part about me and Ambria. I wanted to tell him the good news in person.

"What a bleeding disaster!" His horrified face filled my phone screen. "I haven't heard a thing from Galfandor. Are you sure he's okay?"

"I certainly hope so," Ambria said.

I glanced at the time. "We won't be back to Italy until early in the morning. Someone will have to pick us up."

"Just call me and I'll ask Granddad Stan." Max blew out a breath. "My god, I can't believe we're right back to square one. Even with Ivy and Nightliss, I don't know if we can win against Victus."

Ambria's eyebrows rose. "I thought Ivy was the answer to all our problems."

"Well, she's strong, but how are we supposed to fight an enemy when we don't even know who's on our side?" Max ran a hand through his hair. "One traitor just helped wipe out the entire Night Watch. Someone else could stab us in the back at any time."

"We need Kanaan," I said. "I don't know what he's been up to all this time, but I'm going to drag him back."

"Completely agree," Max said. "We need our entire team online if we plan to survive and win."

We said our goodbyes. Once Max's face flicked off, I called Kanaan. The phone rang several times before going to voicemail. "Kanaan, call me back immediately. It's important." I ended the call.

"I'm truly worried about Galfandor," Ambria said. "I put him from my mind all day, and I feel terrible about it."

"Do you think we should return to the hotel and ask around?"

She shook her head. "Too risky. I don't know what to do except go back to the others and hope he contacts us. Maybe he's already on a train to Italy."

"Unfortunately, the nom police are probably all over the scene by now." I wondered how they'd explain the half-morphed lycans in the ballroom.

"Going back also means we might expose ourselves to Talbot and Delilah again. I'm sure they have people watching the area in case we turn up."

"You're right." Ambria deflated a little. "Let's go to the train station."

As we headed back across the mall, I felt a twinge of regret that our brief respite was over. If we survived, I would make it a point to travel to more of these nom tourist traps so we could enjoy what we'd fought for.

Ambria jerked to a halt and pulled on my arm. "Conrad, look."

At first, I didn't know what she pointed at, but then I saw the tall, muscular man standing a distance from us, his nose raised, nostrils flaring. *It's the lycan!*

"He must have followed our scent." Ambria pulled me behind an information booth. "My god, don't those bastards ever give up?"

It suddenly occurred to me that the lycan wasn't even making an effort to conceal himself. Surely he had to know we'd see him standing there, nearly a head taller than anyone around him and a crescent moon tattoo on his neck. I scanned the area and saw the trap already swinging shut. Talbot and Delilah flanked us.

We couldn't go forward, and we couldn't go back.

CHAPTER 20

The crowds around the Eiffel Tower had dwindled, but plenty of noms still wandered the premises. I wondered if the wand-slingers would stay their hands or use magic for all the world to see.

Delilah met my gaze and grinned. She shook her head and patted the wand at her side. *I guess that answers my question.*

I was so sick and tired of dodging these people, but I couldn't confront them in my current state. I spotted police patrolling at the edge of the mall—too far away to hear us if we yelled for help.

"I can't fight all three of them." Ambria clenched my hand. "We have to run."

"Run where?" I saw a couple of openings, but that wouldn't prevent the wandslingers from shooting us.

"We'll angle that way." She nodded her head toward the gap between Delilah and the lycan.

"Hang on." I looked at the police in the distance. "Remember that sound spell you used to make it sound like Max farted?"

Her confused gaze flicked to me. "Shall I frighten everyone with fake farts?"

I shook my head. "This isn't about fighting. It's about getting help." I pointed to the police. "How loud can you make that spell?"

"Ah." Her eyes widened. "I see where you're going with this." She flicked her wand and aimed it diagonally up and toward the police. Explosions thundered. People screamed and scattered.

The lycan and the wandslingers stopped and stared, startled and uncertain. Ambria set off another boom and the police ran toward the sound. Delilah's lip curled into a snarl. She drew her wand and raced toward us. Talbot hesitated then dashed forward. The lycan strode from the other direction, cutting off our retreat.

"Run!" I pushed Ambria toward the police and we sprinted away. Delilah and the lycan angled from opposite sides to cut us off. Talbot, at least, was behind us and would have to catch up.

A magic bullet smashed into a rubbish bin. Ambria cast a shield to protect our right side from Delilah, but the lycan blurred our way in human form, eating up fifty yards in seconds. There was no way we'd outrun him.

The police were still some distance away, rifles drawn and moving cautiously. I hoped we didn't draw fire from them. Delilah fired another salvo. Ambria's shield shimmered and rippled with impacts.

One of the police shouted in French and pointed at Delilah. The wandslinger ignored them and aimed her wand at us. Shots rang out. Bullets smashed into the small trees lining the path. Delilah whipped her wand around and fired a magic missile toward the police. The ethereal projectile left a trail of billowing smoke as it zipped toward them.

The police unleashed a hail of bullets. Delilah screamed. Metal slugs ripped into her chest. Blood sprayed from the back of her head and she dropped like a stone. The lycan broke off pursuit and veered away. The police scattered, but the missile followed a lone target. He dove behind a car, but it did him no good. The missile curved around. He screamed. The explosion rocked the cars parked on the street.

"Delilah!" Talbot screamed his sister's name again. His furious gaze met mine. He roared and charged us. A squad of police in body armor rushed out of cover from behind a building, shouting in French.

Talbot conjured more magic missiles. The police opened fire. Bullets zinged against an invisible shield. The police put up riot shields, but the explosions from the magic missiles flung bodies through the air. The other police charged his position. Talbot wove his wand through the air, hurling magic bullets. "Die, you nom pigs!"

Ambria jerked me to the right. "Run!" We dodged down a street bordering the mall. The police were too busy with Talbot to pay us any mind. People gathered nearby, phones aimed toward the carnage.

One of them stopped us and asked questions in French.

"I don't understand," Ambria said. The man replied in broken English, but Ambria didn't pause and pulled me after her down the street.

We vanished into the crowd and took shelter, this time in an underground metro station. We pushed through the throng, mingling our scent with strangers in the hopes that the lycan wouldn't be able to follow us again.

Ambria pulled me onto the metro and sat down. "Should we take the metro to the train station?"

"Where does this one go?" I consulted the map, but couldn't decipher the tangle of lines. I dropped into the seat next to Ambria and groaned with weariness. "Delilah is dead. I can't believe it."

Ambria bared her teeth. "I hope they kill Talbot too."

I wouldn't shed a tear if they did.

We finally got off the metro in a quaint area somewhere in the southeast part of Paris. Ambria located a hotel and we went inside. The woman behind the counter gave us dubious looks when I asked for a room. She narrowed her eyes and replied in French.

I took out my arcphone. "Phone, can you translate?"

"Yes," it replied.

I repeated my request for a room, and the phone relayed it in French. The woman's eyebrows rose. She replied.

"I need your identification," the phone translated. "You look too young to be wandering around by yourselves."

I shook my head. "I don't have an ID." The phone translated for her.

She frowned and spoke.

"I'm afraid I can't help you then," the arcphone said.

I held up some money. "Please, how much?"

She listened to the translation and shook her head.

Ambria growled. "Forget it, Conrad."

"But—"

"If she won't take our money, then we'll just take a room without asking." Ambria took out one of Max's potion bombs and smiled sweetly at the woman before blowing on it three times and tossing it.

The woman shrieked. Vapors puffed in her face and she went quiet. Ambria pulled me into the lift while the woman was disoriented. We rode up to the second floor and got off.

"Was that a memory fog potion?" I asked.

Ambria giggled. "She won't even remember seeing us."

"You're ruthless, aren't you?"

Her expression sobered. "So is the world, Conrad. Sometimes we have to be ruthless too."

We walked down the hallway. The rooms here used actual keys instead of keycards. Ambria stopped near the end and knocked on the door. No one answered, so she used a spell Granddad Stan had taught us to pick the lock.

I was so tired I took off my shoes and flopped on the bed. Exhaustion claimed me in an instant.

THE MAN in white regards me with satisfaction. He says something. His words sound clearer, but still elude my understanding. Before I can ask him another question, the vision fades to black.

A RAY of sunlight shining through a slit in the curtains woke me up. My head and neck ached and my stomach rumbled. I clicked on the lamp. Ambria wasn't in the room or the bathroom. The clock on my arcphone read seven minutes past noon.

I slept really late. That explained why I felt so ravenous. The latch clicked and Ambria stepped inside clutching bags.

"You're finally awake." She set down a paper bag on the table.

A delicious aroma drew me to it. Croissants with ham and pastries greeted me. I took a huge bite of one and moaned. "You're a life saver."

"Me or the croissants?"

I grinned. "Both."

"I do my best." Ambria dumped clothes from another bag. "I thought we could use another change of attire and fresh underwear."

"Clean underwear sounds heavenly." I stuffed more food in my mouth. Once sated, I sat back and sipped on tea from a paper cup. "I suppose we should head back to the train station."

"I spoke with Max again this morning," Ambria said. "Still no word from Galfandor, but everyone is still safe at the campground."

"That's something at least." I opened the curtains and looked at the quaint, old-world buildings lining the street. "Hopefully that lycan lost our scent. I'd hate to lead Talbot back to our friends—provided he survived."

"Our encounter was all over the news." Ambria removed an éclair from the bag. "Some of the phone videos taken clearly show Talbot using a wand. Unfortunately, he escaped before the police could apprehend him."

I turned on the television and flicked a few channels until I found one of the twenty-four-hour news stations. I set my arcphone to translate again.

Explosions rocked the parked cars where Delilah's missile had hit just after the police killed her. "A weapon similar to the one used by the man was found on the woman's body. Police are still searching for answers in this bizarre incident. Was it terrorism, or something completely different? Twenty-three police lost their lives in the brutal attack."

A frozen image appeared of me and Ambria, our faces tight with terror as we fled from Talbot. "Police are still searching for these children." The camera zoomed in on Ambria's hand. "As you can see, she has a weapon similar to the one held by the man in the background and the deceased woman."

The scene focused on Talbot. Volleys of silver bullets streaked through the air. "Authorities still have no idea how the weapon works. The only bullets recovered from the scene were the ones used by police."

A pair of newscasters appeared on the screen and the image retreated to the upper right of the screen. "Are police really calling those weapons?" the male newscaster asked. "They look like magic wands."

"That's right, Edward," the female replied. "The authorities said the wands are not disguised guns, and they have no idea what fired the rockets." She shook her head. "And yet, we can clearly see those missiles coming from the ends of the wands in the video."

High-definition video of Talbot filled the screen, his lips peeled back in a cry of rage. The playback slowed, showing the magic missiles weaving together from glowing energy at the tip of the wand.

"I know this sounds far-fetched, Ana, but it almost looks like magic."

"People all across the globe are looking for answers, Edward," Ana replied. "Thankfully, we all know there's no such thing as magic."

The video resumed normal speed, but switched back to the newscasters just before the missiles hit the police.

The newscast showed a man in a police uniform standing on a podium. "Our thoughts and prayers are with the twenty-three men and women lost in the attack. I assure the public that we are doing everything possible to discover how and why these attacks took place."

Ambria swallowed a piece of éclair. "This is terrible. If the noms realize magic exists, it might start a war between us and them."

"Why do you think they'll go to war?" I said. "Plenty of noms would love to use magic."

"Perhaps, but just as many will see us as a threat." Ambria switched off the TV. "I hope they convince themselves it was something else."

With my hunger abated, the aches in my neck and head rose to full volume. I lay back down on the bed and groaned. "Do you have any more of Percival's magic poisoning paste?"

Ambria removed some from her satchel and handed it to me. "You're still feeling poorly?"

I put a piece in my mouth and sucked on it. The aches melted away. "I don't feel as bad as yesterday, but I'm still not a hundred percent."

"Is the paste helping?"

"Immensely." I closed my eyes. "Just give me a moment and we can go to the metro."

"Of course." Ambria squeezed my hand and kissed my lips. "There's no rush."

When the pain receded to a dull throb in the background I pushed myself up. Ambria wore a cute red beret and a black-and-white-striped blouse with a red skirt. She twirled. "Do you like it?"

My heart skipped a beat. "You look adorable." I took her hands in mine and pulled her to me. "Beautiful beyond words."

Ambria melted in my arms. "Oh, Conrad. I've wanted to hear you say that for so long." Big brown eyes looked up at me. "I just want to savor every moment just in case—" She shivered.

"In case we die?" I pecked a kiss on her nose. "We'll all die someday, Ambria, but I plan to have plenty of more time with you."

She smiled. "I hope so." Her hand caressed my neck and she pulled me in for a long kiss.

I hope we have more time. But I knew it was unlikely I'd survive the fight with my father. I pushed unpleasant thoughts from my mind and kissed Ambria again. My body tingled and responded in embarrassing ways, so I sighed and released her. "We should go."

Ambria handed me the bag of pastries and a new satchel with my clothes. "Yes, let's."

We boarded the metro and sat across from a man reading a newspaper. Ambria stiffened, eyes wide. "Look."

Our terrified faces filled the picture on the front page. Above it hung a bold headline in French. The question mark at the end likely meant the translation was *Have you seen these people?*

Ambria pulled her beret a bit lower over her forehead and looked down. "I should've gotten you a hat."

A girl staring at a smartphone looked up at us then back down at her screen several times. She discreetly tilted the phone up and I realized she was trying to take a picture. Her phone sparked and a puff of smoke coiled into the air. The girl shrieked and dropped the ruined device.

Ambria tucked her wand back beneath her cardigan, a smug smile on her face. "These noms spend too much time on their phones already."

Unfortunately, I knew the girl was just the beginning of our problems. My arcphone chimed. I looked at the screen and saw a text message. *Louvre. South side. One hour. –Kanaan.*

I checked the contact symbols and confirmed the message was indeed from Kanaan. Relief flooded me. "Look." I showed the message to Ambria.

Her eyes widened. "Oh, thank god, Conrad. We're saved."

I squeezed her hand. "We were already saved thanks to you." I stroked her cheek. "You're quite the badass."

Ambria giggled. "I'd do anything to save you."

A man with a newspaper got up and stalked toward us. He pointed to the picture on the front page and spoke in French.

I shook my head. "I don't speak French."

"You are the people in the picture," the girl with the ruined phone said in a light accent. "I know it is you!"

"Yes!" A teenaged boy said. "I thought the same." Eagerness lit his eyes. "Were those people using magic? Are you wizards?"

"It was magic," the girl said. "I just know it."

"Magic?" Ambria scoffed. "That's ridiculous."

"You are British, no?" the boy said.

The man with the newspaper said something in a loud voice and more people craned their necks our way. The metro slowed to a stop. Several people dashed off the train as if their lives depended on it.

"That's definitely not us in the picture," Ambria said. "We weren't even in Paris yesterday."

A man in police uniform stepped inside. Fingers pointed our way. His eyes narrowed and he said something into a radio.

"This is ridiculous," Ambria said. "We're just tourists."

The boy held up his smartphone, a picture of Ambria zoomed in. The resemblance was undeniable.

"This is getting out of hand," I said as the man with the newspaper started shouting and waving the policeman over.

In a moment, we'd likely be in handcuffs.

CHAPTER 21

Ambria slipped a small sphere into my hand and whispered in my ear. "Get ready to run."

I held up the memory fog bomb.

"What's that?" the boy asked.

The train stopped.

I blew on the potion bomb once, twice, three times.

The doors slid open.

"Go!" Ambria threw her potion bomb toward the policeman and dashed through the open doors.

I ran to the door and tossed the potion bomb to the boy. "Here's the magic you wanted." I jumped onto the platform outside.

Gray smoke filled the car. Waiting passengers shouted and cried out in dismay. People scattered. Ambria and I kept our heads down and ran with the panicked mob. We didn't stop running until we reached street level. We walked several blocks then hailed a taxi. I checked my wallet and realized I barely had enough money for a single train ticket back to Italy.

I hope Kanaan has a way out.

We reached the Louvre fifteen minutes late, thanks to the debacle on the metro and clogged traffic. We walked to the south side of the glass pyramid and pretended to sightsee with the other nom tourists. Thankfully, none of them seemed the least bit curious about us.

Ambria turned in a circle. "I don't see him anywhere."

"I hope he's still here." I sat down on a marble bench and studied the faces in the crowd. Kanaan wasn't among them.

"I am here."

Ambria and I jumped up and found the magitsu master standing behind us. He wore jeans and a black T-shirt. Though his attire blended him in with the noms, it was strange seeing him out of his robes.

"How in the world?" Ambria shook her head. "Never mind. I'm just so happy to see you, I might burst."

"It appears you have made international headlines." Kanaan started walking away from the bench so we followed him across the street and onto a bridge with a spectacular view of the Seine. He stopped in the middle and looked at the water. "We will rejoin the others."

"Do you have a portal somewhere?" I asked.

He shook his head. "Trains must suffice."

"Where have you been all this time?" Ambria asked.

"Watching those associated with Victus. Learning new ways around Queens Gate." Kanaan turned toward her. "It seems the wandslingers have been particularly adept at finding you."

"Lycans and the wandslingers slaughtered everyone in Galfandor's secret organization." Ambria shuddered. "It was awful."

"The Night Watch is no more?" Kanaan's eyebrows rose. "This is troubling."

"I can think of stronger words than that," I said. "They were going to help us fight Victus, but he'd already infiltrated them with an infernus."

Kanaan pursed his lips. "Was Garkin there?"

I shook my head. "Talbot, Delilah, and some lycans."

"Did they bear crescent moon tattoos?"

I thought back to the ink on the back of the dead lycan's neck. "Yes."

"Brothers of the Hidden Moon." Kanaan's lips pressed together. "It appears they have taken a side."

"Who are they?" Ambria asked.

"A cult who believes our moon is but a fragment of the real moon." He turned and leaned on the concrete balustrade. "They believe the hidden moon is in another realm where they will reign supreme." Victus shook his head. "They are lycan supremacists just as Garkin's followers, the blooded, are Arcane supremacists. Though they would usually fight each other, it appears Victus has forged common ground."

"How is it possible to twist hate into a bond?" Images of the carnage twisted my guts. "They're fools."

"Garkin continues to fill his ranks with battle mages," Kanaan said. "Zarin constructs another demon foundry. Creatures of the Dark Forest swell the ranks of the monster army every day." He frowned. "We do not have the numbers for a frontal assault."

"So we have no choice but to wait until we can go to Seraphina?" Ambria threw up her hands. "I don't know how up to date you are on everything, but it'll be weeks before Eden aligns with Voltis and we can even start the hunt for Justin Slade in Seraphina. For all we know, Aerianas already killed him and his army."

"I phoned Max before I met with you." Kanaan stroked his beard. "The

Fallen at least offer us a chance to find more allies. For now, we have few options."

"If Victus gets the foundry back online, he'll clone more important people and infest every supernatural organization until it's impossible to root them all out." I smacked my palm on the railing. "We can't just sit back and wait. Once Ivy and Nightliss come online, we have to attack."

"Attack who, exactly?" Ambria challenged me with raised eyebrows. "Do we know where Victus is? Can we take him out, or should we rush in willy-nilly and fight Garkin and his blooded?"

I turned to Kanaan. "Do you know where Victus is?"

He shook his head. "The facility in Montana is abandoned. I know Zarin works on another foundry because I spied upon the battle mages moving supplies through a portal."

"Where did the portal go?" I asked.

"It was too heavily guarded, even for me." Kanaan folded his arms across his chest. "Garkin and his allies move everywhere with portals, making them difficult to track."

"Portals, hmm?" Ambria tapped a finger on her chin. "Maybe we don't know exactly where they are, but if they're using omniarch portals, that certainly narrows down the possibilities."

"Correct." Kanaan gazed into the distance. "I searched abandoned facilities—the Grand Nexus, Thunder Rock, Three Sisters, El Dorado. I then turned to the public waystations like the Grotto and La Casona. Though many are blocked or guarded, none are actively in use."

"I don't think Garkin would use public waystations to ship battle mages," I said. "That would draw too much attention."

"Precisely." Ambria frowned. "Master Kanaan, are there any abandoned facilities you haven't checked out?"

Kanaan shook his head.

"That leaves two possibilities." Ambria turned to me. "Gwyneth said there are portable omniarches."

"Yes," I said. "But she said Underborn doesn't know of anyone who has one."

"That leaves one other possibility, and it would be the perfect place to set up a secret lair." Ambria arched an eyebrow. "I think they're using the omniarch next to Stoneshire."

Kanaan nodded. "I agree. We should inspect it at once."

Stoneshire, the underground mansion beneath Arcane University, had been built by Justin Slade and the resistance. It was a refuge, a safe place after the mansion aboveground had been destroyed in the battle that claimed the life of Moses.

Max, Ambria, and I lived and trained there for weeks, and at the time it felt more like home than even the house at the corner of Dowling and Bucket. Max had named the underground mansion Stoneshire since it was constructed out of the bedrock of the cavern, and also because he grew tired of calling it the underground mansion all the time. To think that the place we'd once called home might now be the headquarters of pure evil filled me with anger.

"How are we supposed to get there?" I said. "By train?"

He nodded. "Yes. We must travel to London."

Ambria pointed a thumb at herself. "You're taking us with you?" She held up a hand to stop his reply. "Not that I'm complaining, but Galfandor and the others think we're too young."

"Age does not determine ability." Kanaan put a hand on her shoulder in an unusual show of affection. "You have proven yourself a worthy student, Ambria Rax. You are capable."

My jaw dropped open and I felt a tinge of jealousy. "What about me?"

The magitsu master nodded. "You show promise, but you lack focus.

Instead of mastering one talent, you pursue many and excel at none. You also allow troubles of the past to cloud your meditation."

"I'm good with my spells," I protested. "I can still meditate."

"Spells are but one facet of magitsu." Kanaan's hand blurred and something tweaked my ear.

"Ouch." I covered the side of my face with a hand. "What was that for?"

Kanaan's hand flashed again. Ambria twisted and slapped it away before it reached her ear, every bit as quick as she'd been against the battle mage in the hotel hallway.

"You are dead. She is not." Kanaan gave Ambria another small nod. "You have continued to practice."

Ambria beamed and bowed slightly. "Yes, Master Kanaan."

"How much extra practicing have you been doing?" I asked.

"Even before the wandslingers first found us, she found time to train on her own." Kanaan pursed his lips. "In the time left to us, you must achieve greater focus, Conrad."

I looked at Ambria. Instead of jealousy, pride swelled in my chest. "You're glorious, did you know that?"

She giggled. "I suspected it, but I love hearing you say it."

Both of Kanaan's eyebrows rose. "I see you have taken the next step together."

Ambria laced her arm in mine. "If that's your way of saying we're dating, then yes."

The magitsu master's lips quirked into a small smile. "This is good." He took one of my hands and examined the scars. "What happened?"

"Lulu did this to me just before the wandslingers attacked us at the El Dorado waystation." I resisted the urge to scratch the back of my hand. I told him what the dragon said. "Then she opened her mouth and I thought she was going to kill me."

Kanaan pursed his lips and nodded. "This is good."

"Good?" Ambria's forehead pinched. "She said we were on our own and then tried to burn Conrad to a crisp."

"Lulu did this for a reason. If she meant to kill him, he would be dead." Kanaan inspected my palms. "Has anything unusual happened since then?"

I tried not to laugh and failed. "Yes, plenty of horrible and unusual things happened."

Kanaan tapped his temple. "Not without, but within."

"Oh." I shrugged. "Lots of weird dreams, and hypersensitivity to aether. Does that qualify?"

"We must discuss this more, but for now we should go." He turned away and waved us after him. "London awaits."

I THOUGHT Kanaan would ask me more questions on the train ride to London, but he lay down on the bench and went to sleep, so I followed his cue and got much-needed rest.

Kanaan took us to a hotel not far from the hidden entrance leading to Queen's Gate deep below the city. "There are eyes everywhere, so we must disguise ourselves to infiltrate the waystation."

"Galfandor said the wards at the university can detect illusions and even regular disguises," I said.

He nodded. "The perimeter wards do. Once inside, some of the buildings are warded. This is why we will bypass the normal route."

"Hidden tunnels?" I asked.

"No. We will use an omniarch in the waystation." He gazed through the window at the gathering dusk. "Disguises and the morning rush crowds should facilitate entrance. I will procure supplies and meet you here in the morning."

"Where are you staying the night?" Ambria asked.

"Nearby." Kanaan slipped out quick as a ghost before we could ask another question.

I wrapped an arm around Ambria. "Aren't you just the teacher's pet?"

"I have a competitive streak." She pulled me down to sit on the bed. "I called Max on the train. Still no word from Galfandor, and Percival is days away from finishing his memory potion. Otherwise, they seem safe."

"How is Max doing?" I asked.

"Well, he seemed a bit sad he can't join us, but he was also quite happy when I told him that you weren't interested in Ivy."

"Did you tell him about us?"

Ambria shook her head. "You didn't mention it last time, so I assumed you wanted to tell him in person." She laughed. "Not that it'll matter to him."

"He'll probably worry I might team up with you when you two argue."

Her eyebrow quirked. "Will you?"

I shook my head. "You two argue about the dumbest things."

"But I enjoy tormenting him."

I snorted. "Obviously."

"Oh, Kanaan taught me a neat spell you might like." Ambria pulled her wand from the satchel on the floor.

"Yeah? Will it make me the teacher's pet too?"

"Afraid not." She tapped the wand on her head and stepped to the side. A copy of her stepped sideways in the opposite direction. The pair grinned at me.

I brushed a hand at the closest one and found thin air. "That's his illusion spell!"

"I know. Isn't it the best?" She turned and walked to the room door. The illusion walked into the bathroom and vanished. "I know it's not a great demonstration, but the illusion is programmed to take another path once it splits off from you."

"Brilliant!" I took out my arcwand. "Can you send me the code?"

"I already uploaded it." Ambria showed me the shortcut pattern for the spell. "Just do that and tap the wand on yourself."

I stood and tried it out, but nothing happened.

"You have to move." Ambria pushed me back a step. A copy stepped forward out of me. "The illusion will split off and mimic you for a few seconds before taking another path. There's another version that makes you invisible so your illusion is a better decoy, but it requires a lot more power."

"I love it." I headed for the main door and watched my illusion vanish into the bathroom.

Ambria pressed a hand to my chest. "Is the magic sickness gone?"

I conjured a light ball and experimented with a few zaps of electricity without feeling sick. "I think I'm back to a hundred percent."

"You should aetherate as much as you can just to be sure."

I drew in aether. My palms tingled. The pulse of ley lines beat in time with my heart. The faces of the dead swarmed around me until I pushed them back into the void, out of my bubble of meditation.

Usually, it required only a few seconds of steady intake to reach my limit, but this time it took noticeably longer. I felt a distant connection to something else. Something far away, but connected through the network of ley lines. I closed my eyes and tried to touch it. The floor rumbled beneath my feet, nearly shaking me from my concentration.

"Did you feel that?" Ambria asked.

"Probably the subway," I said without opening my eyes. I continued to aetherate until the my well pushed back. Somewhere, just out of reach, I felt a powerful presence. "I'm full." I wished I could push past this wall and discover whatever waited on the other side, but try as I might, I couldn't budge another inch.

Ambria touched my wrist. "Run the calibration spell Ansel gave you."

I recalled the shortcut pattern and activated it, then cast a shield spell and conjured a glowball for measurement. Text glittered in the air. *Cast Efficiency 63%, Aether 823, AP 21.*

Ambria's eyes flared. "That's impossible. Measure again."

I felt like an overinflated balloon, the pressure of aether swelling me to my limit. I ran through the spells again before releasing the pent-up energy. The numbers remained the same.

Ambria blinked several times. "When was the last time you measured yourself?"

"Months ago." I shrugged. "Back before Zarin attacked Ansel."

"What were your stats?"

"Sixty-two percent, somewhere in the five hundreds for aether, and an AP of fourteen."

Ambria blew out a soft breath. "I don't understand." She ran the calibration spell on herself. *Cast Efficiency 81%, Aether 504, AP 13.* "I've only improved a little in the same time."

"It must be from all the times I've overextended myself." I couldn't even count all the magical battles I'd fought. "Fireblade wrecks me."

"Or it runs in the family." Ambria's forehead creased. "You are a Moore, after all. A blood relative of Moses himself."

"I wonder if overextending myself is why I keep having these bizarre dreams, or if it has something to do with aether burn from Lulu." I told her about the man in white and my visions. "Do you think it's connected to the dreams about the stars?"

Ambria tapped her chin. "I think you're having visions, Conrad. Whatever that man is trying to tell you might be important."

"Or he wants me to overextend myself so I'm too tired to fight Victus." A terrible thought gripped my guts. "What if he's one of the bad guys?"

Her eyes narrowed. "Does he seem evil to you?"

I thought back to the dream and couldn't recall feeling anything but fear and curiosity. "No, but that doesn't mean anything."

"Well, there's no harm in improving yourself." She looked at her stats. "My cast efficiency is nearly twenty points higher than yours. If you didn't rely so much on brute strength, you wouldn't overextend yourself as often."

I bowed. "Help me, oh master."

Ambria rolled her eyes. "Precision is key." She frowned. "All the power in the world doesn't mean much if nearly forty-percent of your potential is wasted." Ambria tapped a finger on her chin. "Efficiency is a combination of focus and containment. Let's go somewhere we can practice without destroying the room."

I flashed a grin. "You're going to teach me?"

Ambria smirked. "I'm going to try."

We left the hotel and went a few streets over into Hyde Park. It seemed mostly empty at this hour so we made our way to the Serpentine—a lake in the middle.

Ambria made sure no one was near. "Calibrate again and fire a more powerful spell into the water."

I summoned the statistics spell then cast a shield followed by a gout of fire. My efficiency rose by one point. "Not much better."

"Do it again, but this time, use Fireblade to calibrate."

I repeated it, using all my concentration to cast the destructive spell. Water sizzled and sheets of steam rose where the ruby energy struck the lake. This time, my efficiency jumped to ninety-two percent. I looked at the number with befuddlement. "That doesn't make any sense."

"It makes perfect sense." Ambria watched the drifting clouds of steam. "Delectra's soul shard imprinted that spell so precisely in your mind that your efficiency is nearly perfect."

"That doesn't help my overall efficiency."

"Remember Kanaan's lesson about pinpointing?" Ambria flicked her wand. The tip flashed so brightly it blinded me.

"Ouch." I blinked away the afterimages. "Yes. Something about pushing the spell through a bottleneck."

She frowned. "You obviously weren't listening."

"I could swear that's what he said."

"That was a completely different lesson about throttling the power to a spell so you only stun the target instead of killing them." Ambria sighed. "You get so preoccupied sometimes, Conrad."

"I worry a lot."

"About what?"

"You. Max." Cold fingers gripped my heart. "My dead mother. Victus."

Ambria's lips pressed into a thin line. "We've all seen and done terrible things, Conrad. You've got to forgive yourself for what you've done, and realize that nearly everything else is out of your control."

"I know it's out of my control." My hands tightened into fists. "It doesn't stop it from haunting me."

"How many tragedies have you prevented by worrying about them?"

"Is that a rhetorical question?" I asked.

Ambria gripped my wand hand and pulled it up to eye level. "All that worrying is preventing you from being the best you can be. You're letting Victus cloud your mind. Letting him shut you down without even lifting a wand."

I blinked back a surge of anger. "I can't help it! It makes me sick to my stomach!"

"I know." Ambria's voice turned soothing. "It makes me sick too. But I don't let it interfere." She pressed my hand over her heart. "I overcome the anger, fear, and worry by focusing on the people I love."

It was a lovely sentiment, but I didn't know if I could do it. "I'll try."

"Don't try. Do it." Ambria tapped the end of my wand. "I want you to focus the zap spell so efficiently right here that it pops like mine did." Her eyes bored into mine. "Think about what matters most to you, not about the horrors of the past."

I could almost feel cold, dead fingers clawing at my ankles. "Okay."

Ironically, worry showed in her eyes. "Conrad, we need you. If you use up all your strength with imprecise casting, we'll be on our own. We might die."

CHAPTER 22

The truth was hard to hear, but Ambria was right. I had to improve. If I used up my strength in the first few seconds of a fight, I'd be useless.

Zap was a low-aether cost spell Esma taught us in magical defenses class. Though it wouldn't kill anyone, it delivered quite a shock. For the next hour, I tried to fill my mind with thoughts of those I loved instead of the death and violence I hated.

It only made my focus worse. No matter how much I tried, I couldn't clear my mind of the clutter. Images of the dead, of attacking wand-slingers, and vicious werewolves lingered in my thoughts. Closing my eyes only made the nightmares more vivid.

I'd grown used to pushing aside the ghosts that haunted me. Replacing them with Max, Ambria, and Cora wasn't as simple as I'd hoped. It would take time and practice to completely change the way I'd learned to meditate.

"What's going on up here?" Ambria tapped my forehead. "Even Max's efficiency is higher than yours and he can't stop thinking about food."

I threw down my wand in frustration. "It's not working!" I pinched the bridge of my nose. "How do you do it, Ambria?"

She picked up my wand, but didn't lift her eyes from the ground. "I'm kind of ashamed to admit it."

I lifted her chin. "Tell me. Please."

Her eyes refused to meet mine. "I, um..." Ambria backed up a step. "I think about puppies and kittens playing together and it makes everything else go away."

My mouth fell open. I'd expected something more profound than that. "Puppies and kittens?"

Her eyes finally met mind. "What do you see when you close your eyes, Conrad?"

I tried to put my thoughts into words. "It's just fragments—terrible flashbacks. Blood, death, screams." I winced. "It's always a dull roar in the back of my head."

"Have you tried my method?"

I snorted. "I'm willing to try anything."

"Then do it."

I pictured puppies falling all over each other. Kittens playing with balls of yarn. Then I saw Victus splicing together puppies and kittens. Howls of pain tore through the happy thoughts and jerked me back to reality. I gasped and staggered back.

"Maybe a psychiatrist would be better." Ambria frowned. "How about this? Remember your first lesson with Ansel?"

I shrugged. "Yeah. I made myself sick trying to burn a hole through a diamond fiber chest."

"But it was a trick since diamond fiber is invulnerable to magic."

I nodded. "Well, Ansel seemed impressed that I made a black mark on it."

"I remember." Ambria wiped dirt off the tip of my wand. "You didn't know what you were doing, but you managed to put a mark on what should have been magic immune material."

"True." I wasn't sure where Ambria was headed with this. "But I burned through all my strength and was sick for days."

She smirked. "Well, you did put everything you had into it. You later told me that he asked if you'd used an avatar."

"Yes. But I've tried focusing on my avatars since then and it hasn't worked." My stomach felt a bit queasy just remembering the severe magic sickness I'd suffered after that.

"Ansel never mentioned avatars to me or Max," Ambria said. "In fact, I'd nearly forgotten about that part of your story until now."

I sighed. "Not like it does anything."

"Do you remember exactly what you were thinking?"

"It was over a year ago."

Ambria put a hand on my shoulder. "Think, Conrad."

I closed my eyes, but the darkness filled with horrors—a demon devouring Brickle. Lifeless eyes staring up at me from a mass grave. Lycans tearing Arcanes limb from limb. Victus blowing a hole through Harris Ashmore's chest. I gasped and opened my eyes.

The horror movie of my life, running on a constant loop. "There's too much to forget. So much death."

"I know, Conrad." She kissed my cheek. "It's madness, but we have to push through it." Ambria put a hand on my forehead. "Think back to that day. What went through your mind?"

I gritted my teeth and imagined Ansel's office as I first walked inside.

He'd challenged me to fire off as many spells as I could in quick succession. I'd managed three. He'd told me how the words we used to cast spells had no magic—that it was all from our will and focus. That the strength of a spell came from within us—not the spell itself.

"He said that spells like Ignitus aren't weak, but because we were told they were and believed it, we made them weak."

Ambria nodded. "Yes, I remember you telling me this. What next?"

"He ordered me to burn a hole in the diamond fiber chest. He said if I didn't, he wouldn't teach me."

"How did that make you feel?"

"Angry and desperate." I closed my eyes again and saw myself standing before the chest. "I knew if I didn't pass the test, he wouldn't teach me. I would never defeat my parents." I flashed back to the day Cumberbatch resurrected my parents. Delectra held a cold blade to my throat, a wicked gleam in her eyes as she prepared to end me.

I felt no malice toward my mother. Her innocence had been twisted and corrupted by demonic influence. She had died to save me. Tears burned beneath my closed eyelids. Still caught in the waking nightmare, I turned to face the real enemy—the man who'd bent her soul to his will.

Victus.

My father smirked at me. "Even death cannot stop me, boy. The only limits are the ones we create."

Rage burned through my veins and the tears evaporated. The fears and nightmares haunting me paled in comparison to what would happen if this man took over the world. My hatred burned so bright that I saw only the visage of the man who would be Overlord.

The only limits are the ones we create. Words to live by.

I opened my eyes and cast Zap. The harmless electricity spell crackled like lightning and plowed a furrow into the dirt. Thunder pealed, and the shockwave vibrated me to my core.

"Enough!" Ambria grabbed my wrist to stop another cast. "I think you found your avatar."

My shoulders slumped. "Then my avatar is hate."

Her eyes widened. "What do you mean? Isn't it Cora, or your mother?"

I shook my head. "It's my father."

Ambria's lips peeled back in a grimace. "Well, your efficiency was seventy-nine percent."

I shook my head to clear the angry haze. "That's it?"

"It's above average. Most Arcanes hover around seventy-five percent."

I jammed my wand in its holster. "Doesn't matter. All I need is one spell to finish off the bastard."

"I don't think you found your avatar, Conrad." Ambria hugged my arm. "Anger can help focus, but it's not why you're fighting Victus."

"It's a part of it." I stared at the blackened grass. "If it helps me kill my father, then I'll use it."

Ambria looked up at me with big eyes. "Conrad, are you fighting to destroy the man you hate, or to save the people you love?"

It was a profound question, and to my shame, I couldn't come up with an answer.

She sighed and rubbed my back. "It's okay. Let's go back to the hotel and rest."

THE SCAR TISSUE *on my hands tingle. I scratch and scratch until blood trickles down the sides, but it does nothing to stop the itch. The tingle turns to a burn.*

My flesh bubbles and boils. The scars and blood burn to ash. Blue fire erupts from gaping holes in my palms. I hold out my hands and scream.

I JERKED AWAKE, but not because of the dream. Someone was in our room. I kicked off the covers and sprang to my feet. Ambria shouted and rolled off the side of her bed, wand held at the ready. A man with golden-blond hair stood in the doorway, blue eyes holding us in a friendly stare. He held no weapon, but I didn't let that fool me. Even so, his plaid business suit and bright red bowtie made it difficult to consider him a threat.

"Who are you?" I asked.

"Herbert Jones of the Walla Walla, Washington Vacuum Cleaner Company." He rolled in a suitcase. "Does your house need cleaning?"

"This is a hotel room, not a house." Ambria held her wand at the ready. "Now, identify yourself, or kindly leave."

The man tilted his head slightly. "So, the disguise is convincing?"

"Bloody hell." Ambria lowered her wand. "Is that you, Kanaan?"

"Indeed." He nodded slightly.

"Illusion?" Ambria tentatively touched the suit jacket.

"Contact lenses, dyed hair, and more." He stroked his blond beard and mustache. "No illusion required."

I peered closer at the disguise and recognized Kanaan's eyes despite their new color. "Do we have to dye our hair too?"

"Yes, we will travel as family." Kanaan cleared his throat. "Now, now, children, please go change." His accent sounded convincingly British, a marked departure from his typical concise tone.

Ambria flinched back at the sudden change in voice. "I didn't know you could talk like that."

"I have learned many things over the years, the least of which is magit-su." Kanaan put the suitcase on the bed and opened it to reveal a hideous striped dress and tweed trousers. "Here are your disguises."

Ambria grimaced. "Oh, how awful!"

I took out the trousers and white oxford. "Won't these clothes make us stand out even more?"

"The rush hour crowd in the arch waystation is diverse." Kanaan handed Ambria a plastic bag. "This is the temporary dye for your hair." He gave me one as well. "Simply massage it into your hair, wait fifteen minutes, and rinse."

Ambria sighed. "Wonderful."

Ambria and I went into the bathroom and massaged syrupy liquid into our hair. Fifteen minutes felt like an hour as we waited. I took a quick shower to rinse out the dye and gasped in surprise at my changed appearance. I could have passed for another of Max's brothers with my platinum locks.

Ambria gasped as well when I stepped out into the room. She ran her fingers through my hair. "You don't look half bad, Conrad."

Kanaan pointed to the bathroom. "Go."

Ambria sniffed but did as ordered. I changed into my outfit and stuffed small bits of foam into my mouth to make my cheeks rounder. When I perched round spectacles on my nose and looked in the mirror, I barely recognized myself. "It's amazing how minor alterations change appearance so much."

Kanaan nodded. "The wards will not activate on alterations in hair color since it is so common."

"So we can walk through the wards?" I asked.

"Possibly, but we will avoid them if possible."

The bathroom door creaked open and an angel stepped out. Despite the horrid sailor dress, Ambria looked radiant with fiery red hair cascading around her shoulders. Her hair was straighter and longer than I remembered it, probably because she wore it in a ponytail so often.

"You look beautiful," I murmured.

She giggled. "I sort of like red hair. I might have to get it magically dyed next time."

Kanaan stuffed our meager belongings into the suitcase. "Time to go." With that, he whisked through the door.

We gave each other surprised looks and hurried after him. Kanaan stopped by a shop and bought us biscuits and tea for breakfast, which we gobbled down at his urging. Once done, we walked into the parking deck with the secret entrance to the Queens Gate waystation and took the express levitator down.

My stomach seemed to gain wings as we plummeted deep beneath the city. Ambria's hand gripped mine. "Reminds me of the first time we took this lift," she said.

I chuckled. "Frightened us half to death."

She shivered. "Still does."

The levitator slowed to a stop at the bottom. The doors opened to reveal the huge waystation teeming with people. Cars of every kind filled the parking lot as far as the eye could see. People filed out of a bright yellow double-decker bus and headed toward the massive black arch towering in the middle of the cavern as another bus of similar color pulled in behind it.

"Goodness, I don't think I've ever been here during rush hour." Ambria gazed with wide eyes at the long line leading to the arch. "It must take forever to get your turn."

Kanaan kept walking, gaze surveying everything around us. "No distractions. Watch for suspicious people."

It was hard to see anything except the crowd right in front of our faces, but I tried to be as vigilant as possible. Arch operators in bumble-bee robes—black with yellow stripes—directed travelers into queues separated by destination. A klaxon wailed. A low hum filled the air as the Obsidian Arch powered up. The air between the monstrous columns split open to reveal a similar cavern on the other side. A throng of people from our side hurried through on beasts of burden, in nom cars, or perched on flying carpets or brooms.

Another group entered the portal from the other side and took their camels, elephants, and even ostriches to the large stables just outside the yellow caution circle.

I realized I'd become dangerously distracted and turned my attention back to the crowd around us. Kanaan took us behind the animal stables and into a narrow alley between the wooden structure and a rock wall. He ran his hand along the wall, stopped, and tapped his wand on the spot. A portion of the rock vanished to reveal a metal grill. He tapped a lock on the grill and it clicked open to reveal a long shaft. Kanaan waved us inside then followed and closed the vent behind us. It was just high enough to crouch-walk through the narrow space.

"Is this one of Underborn's secret tunnels?" Ambria asked.

Kanaan put a finger to his lips and led us through the vent until we reached another grill. He eased it open and dropped over the side. Unlike the other vent, this one was several feet off the ground. I swung my legs over the ledge and lowered myself with my arms before dropping to the floor. Ambria followed soon after, landing lightly on her feet. Kanaan flicked his wand and the grill swung shut.

We hugged the wall and followed it to the left. A few dozen yards later, we came to the niche with the omniarches nestled inside.

"What if they're blocking portals?" I whispered.

Kanaan didn't answer. He knelt and closed the circle around an omniarch with a green mark next to it. The hum of the Obsidian Arch and the warning klaxon out in the main cavern grew louder, drowning out the hum of the omniarch. A silver line split the air and flashed open.

"It opened immediately," Ambria whispered. "I don't think the area is warded against portals like the ingredients room."

"It's probably too large a space to detect atmospheric changes," I said.

A gray stone wall stood a few feet away, indistinct from any other of its kind to most people. But I instantly recognized the outside of Stoneshire. Kanaan peered down the central corridor in the control room. A lone arch operator stood nearly a hundred yards distant at the control sphere for the Obsidian Arch, oblivious to our activities.

"The niche should hide the arch unless someone comes back here," Kanaan said. "However, haste is wise."

We followed him through and into the cavern housing Stoneshire. The mansion stretched nearly fifty yards to either side of us. The hum of the Obsidian Arch and the wail of the klaxon emanated from the portal so Kanaan put a muffling spell in front of it to keep the sound from carrying.

The magitsu master hugged the wall and scurried to the left. Ambria and I trailed behind him to the corner. There was no one on the side of the mansion, so we slinked around the corner and toward the front. Gray-robed mages walked in and out of the open front doors as if they owned the place.

My fists clenched. These people desecrated a place I held dear.

A short distance away, a square opening in the wall led to a corridor tall and wide enough to fit two buses side-by-side. Straight across was a gauntlet room used for magic training, to the right, a tunnel led to the Burrows, a maze of ancient tunnels beneath Arcane University. But the crown jewel was down the corridor to the left, a circular room with the omniarch.

Our omniarch.

Or so it had been once. I wished I could burn the poison from these caves with fire.

A group of Garkin's blooded dragged the limp body of a half-naked man through the cavern. Kanaan stiffened, but said nothing. Another cluster of battle mages practiced combat spells in the far corner. Others loitered around the front of Stoneshire, smoking, drinking, and listening to raucous noise that might be music.

The mages were all ages, sizes, and genders. A man with spiked hair spoke to a broad woman with piercings in her nose and cheeks. A group of young people with shaved heads, skin covered in tattoos, strutted toward the mansion while another group of men with long, thick beards sneered at their passing.

I identified the crescent moon tattoo of the lycan supremacist group and the twisted pentagram of the Demonists—a group who willingly gave their bodies up for demonic possession since they despised humanity. I didn't need to know the names of the other groups to know they represented the worst of their kind.

Victus had assembled an army of hate.

They were diverse in belief, but united in cause, even if only barely. Had Victus promised them something, or had he subverted their leaderships with infernus?

This dark army of hundreds was on top of the monsters gathering in the Dark Forest. With Night Watch wiped out and Justin Slade a world away, we had no hope of winning a battle.

CHAPTER 23

K anaan watched for a moment, face grave. Without a word, he turned and led us back to the portal behind the mansion.

"Who was that man the blooded were dragging?" Ambria asked.

"One of my former apprentices." Kanaan's jaw tightened. "He showed promise, but now he is dead. Garkin's thugs hunt those who follow the way of the monkey and the tree."

Ambria bared her teeth. "The man is absolutely evil."

I paced back and forth. "They've got a small army out there. How in the world are we supposed to stand up to that, much less the monsters in the Dark Forest?"

"Maybe we could sabotage the omniarch," Ambria said. "That would slow them down."

"Unwise and pointless." Kanaan looked at the small windows twenty feet up the wall. "Even if we had the power to destroy the arch, they would relocate to another."

"But it would at least delay whatever they're planning." Ambria threw up her hands. "We've got to do something."

As they spoke, my mind wandered to another realization. Massive ley lines ran through this place, a necessity for the power-hungry omniarch and Obsidian Arch in the nearby waystation. Stoneshire was not only perfect for housing Victus's army, but for constructing another foundry.

I held out my hands and tapped into the ley lines, taking advantage of my newfound hypersensitivity. The magical power of the earth hummed in my ears. Aether tickled my scarred hands like electricity. There was so much power here, it sent chills up my spine and raised the hairs on my neck.

Somewhere above us, I felt something else—something familiar and powerful. I reached for it and sensed a presence. *What—who are you?*

Let me show you, came the response.

I whirl my glowing staff and roar a battle cry as I leap over the side of the manor to fight the enemies below. The sky burns crimson, clouds boiling with my rage. I draw upon the primal fount. Pure, sweet, energy courses into my veins. I sweep my staff at the enemy. A meteor smashes into their ranks. Bodies fly. Scores fall like wheat before the scythe. Molten rocks sear flesh. Flying boulders crush bone. The first power flows into me. I focus it into my hands and ram my staff into the ground.

A shockwave drives Daelissa and her army back a hundred feet.

Qualan and Qualas blur toward me. A torrent of Brilliance streams past me and strikes Qualas. She screams in agony and dissolves into ash. I see the Slade boy, still up on the roof of the mansion, drop to a knee after delivering the killing blow. "Fly, you fool!" My words are lost in the roar of battle.

I kill more soldiers. Drive Daelissa and Qualan back. Rain meteors down upon them. The mansion burns. The forest burns. If the Slade boy doesn't escape, the realms will burn. My life buys him precious time.

I am tired. So tired. No man is an army unto himself. I am no exception.

Daelissa and Qualan overpower me. Finally, it is time. At last, I can go home. I look to the skies and shout, "Thesha, I am coming!"

I no longer resist the end. I am ready.

I flinched in pain, jerked back to reality by a slap. Ambria grabs my hands. "Conrad, what are you doing?"

"It's Moses," I said in a shocked voice. "I—I saw his last battle with Daelissa."

"What?" Ambria looked at me like I was crazy. "Why would he see that, Kanaan?"

The magitsu master didn't have an answer. "I do not know." He pointed up. "Moses died almost directly above us."

"I've been to his memorial a dozen times and never felt anything like this." Somehow, I knew it was connected to my strange dreams.

"Perhaps he left you a message," Kanaan said.

"How would he know to leave me a message? I never met him." I tapped back into the ley lines and sensed his presence again. Minute power fluctuations reminded me why I'd tapped into it in the first place. "Hold on." I closed my eyes and diverted attention to the cold fire tickling my palms.

Standing next to the omniarch portal, I heard the distant klaxon of the Obsidian Arch. Felt the power dip in the ley lines as the arch hit full power and opened a portal. The klaxon fell silent and the power level rose once again.

I waited and waited some more. The power level spiked downward so abruptly, the void drew a gasp from me. An instant later, it shot back up. I opened my eyes. "The foundry is here."

Kanaan nodded. "As we suspected."

Ambria's eyes widened. "It is already operational?"

"I don't know." I released my hold on the ley lines and the presence of Moses faded again. That mystery could wait until we figured out what to do next. I slumped against the wall. "Victus is too powerful already. If we don't destroy the new foundry, he'll be unstoppable."

"Impossible," Ambria said. "We need an army."

"Justin Slade might not even be alive." I pounded a fist against my leg. "Even if we wait until the next alignment with Voltis and go to Seraphina, there are no guarantees we'll find what we need."

Kanaan nodded. "Conrad is right. Stopping Victus is paramount."

Ambria put hands on her hips. "How, exactly, do we do that?"

I looked up at the windows. "Cut the head off the snake."

"Assassination would be difficult." Kanaan ran a hand over the stone wall. "But easier than fighting an army."

Ambria's mouth dropped open. "Are you suggesting we break into the mansion, hope we find Victus, and kill him?"

"Well, we're here, aren't we?" I stiffened my back. "If anyone can kill Victus, it's Kanaan." Even as I said it, I knew to my very core that I wanted to be the one who killed my father.

The magitsu master tapped his wand against the stone wall. "I detect no wards protecting this wall." He looked at us. "We already know the layout of Stoneshire. All we require is a disguise."

Ambria held out a lock of her blond hair. "This isn't enough?"

"He means robes," I said.

"Yes, Conrad, I realize that." Ambria gripped my hand. "This is too sudden. We don't even have a plan."

"Yes, but we're here now and we have to try." I waved a hand at the portal. "What if we leave and can't get back to an omniarch?" I pointed at the rocky cavern floor. "Right now, this day, we could put a stake in Victus's heart and end his plans."

Ambria groaned, eyes flicking back and forth from me to Kanaan. "Maybe you're right, but I think rushing in is foolish."

"To leave such an opportunity unexplored would be even more foolish." Kanaan drew his wand. "Hold out your hands." We did as instructed, and he tapped them. "Now the bottoms of your shoes." Kanaan tapped them as well, then did the same for himself. "Go slowly and the spell should hold."

"What spell was that?" Ambria asked.

Kanaan began to climb the wall like a spider, drawing gasps from us.

"Pull up gently when you need to unstick." Kanaan demonstrated by peeling his hand upward off the wall.

"That's a neat trick." Ambria tentatively touched the wall and climbed after him.

I couldn't help but miss Shushiel and wondered how she fared in the Dark Forest. I wondered if she worried about us or if she had problems of her own with the monster army gathering there.

Ambria looked down. "Come on, Conrad."

I reached up and put a hand on the wall. It didn't feel like anything happened, but when I pulled on it, it stuck in place. I jumped and stuck my feet to the wall, then followed Kanaan and Ambria higher and higher. Another time, another place, this might have been fun.

Kanaan reached the first window and tapped on it with his wand. The clear glass dissolved into a shower of glittering sand. He peered inside, flicking his wand this way and that, then climbed through. Ambria and I followed close behind.

We stood inside one of the bedrooms, this one empty except for a lamp standing in the corner. Kanaan tapped our hands and shoes to dispel the spider spell. He eased open the door and looked out into the upstairs hallway then turned to us. "Wait here." The magitsu master flitted into the hallway, quiet as death. He paused briefly to peek into the rooms on either side of the hallway. Three doors down from the grand stairwell, he stopped at a room on the left and motioned us inside.

We crept along the stone floor, careful to keep our shoes from echoing and joined him inside the room. A wooden golem maid dusted the furniture while another made the bed. They paid us no mind as Kanaan opened the wardrobe. Two gray robes hung inside, but they were large as tents.

Kanaan turned to the golem making the bed. "We require fresh robes. Fetch some in our sizes, please."

The golem straightened and paused then turned toward us, the face carved into the wooden head expressionless. After a moment, it walked from the room and closed the door behind it.

"They must have added more servant golems," Ambria said in a hushed voice. "I don't remember seeing these two."

"Judging from the number of empty rooms, I suspect Victus only allows his top people to live here." Kanaan examined the large robes in the closet. "This is Garkin's room."

"Odds are Zarin lives in the mansion too," I said. "I'll bet their army lives in those chambers in the Burrows."

Kanaan nodded. "Agreed."

"If only his top people live here, where is the golem supposed to find extra cloaks?" Ambria said.

I pointed down. "The main laundry is downstairs."

She frowned. "Oh, yeah. I guess they all have to wash their clothes here."

Kanaan went to the window overlooking the front of the estate. "Let us hope Garkin is out for the day."

Ambria shuddered. "I think he's even more dangerous than Victus."

"Dangerous, yes, but more focused in his ambitions." Kanaan turned back to us. "Garkin is strong because Victus is strong. He uses this leverage to root out those he thinks are weak. Without Victus, Garkin would return to his place at the fringes."

"There's more to life than brute magical strength," Ambria said. "Intelligence, for one thing."

"That is of little concern to Garkin." The magitsu master inspected the furniture. He picked up a book on the nightstand and looked at the worn leather cover. The book spine read *The Art of Strength –Moon Zin*.

Ambria stood next to him. "What's that?"

"A treatise on the way of the rock." Kanaan opened the yellowed parchment pages. Worn sheets filled with notes were tucked inside. He read from a page. "Equally important to strength are intelligence and agility. One does not approach a situation with only force as his tool. This is the path of the fool. Intelligence allows one to gain insight into the cause of the situation. Agility allows one to avoid conflict."

"Sounds wise to me," I said.

Kanaan read the sheet of parchment tucked between the pages. "Insight does not matter. Avoidance is weakness. Face the foe. Drive them to their knees. Negotiation is the path of the fool."

I grimaced. "I guess Garkin doesn't agree with the author."

"Moon Zin is one of the original masters. Unfortunately, Garkin follows the teachings of one of Moon's early followers, Yawata." Kanaan closed the book and put it on the table. "Garkin must believe Victus is the way to purge weakness from the Overworld."

Ambria punched a fist into her palm. "So let's purge them first."

The door creaked open. Ambria and I jumped. Kanaan calmly watched the golem burdened with three sets of gray robes enter, and took them from outstretched wooden arms. "Thank you. You may resume your duties."

The golem went back to straightening the sheets while we threw on the robes. Mine were a bit loose, and Ambria's two sizes too large, but they looked close enough to me. Judging from the diversity in age of the battle mages outside, Ambria and I would fit right in, and the disguises Kanaan provided would prevent anyone from realizing our true identities.

"What now?" Ambria asked.

"We scout the rest of the hallway." Kanaan opened the door. "If Victus sleeps here, he might be in his room."

My stomach tightened at the prospect of encountering the man I hated most in this world. "I'm ready."

Ambria squeezed my hand. "You look worried."

"We're in the enemy camp." I tried to smile and failed. "Of course I'm worried."

Kanaan slipped into the hallway and we hurried after. The next few rooms were empty, but the first one on the other side of the grand stairway yielded personal effects. Richly embroidered clothes hung in the wardrobe. A platinum watch encrusted with small diamonds sat on the nightstand.

Kanaan examined the holographic image of a pale, thin woman scowling at us. "Zarin stays here."

"What an awful portrait," Ambria said.

"Aerianas, his sister and lover." Kanaan looked inside the drawers.

Ambria grimaced. "How disgusting!"

"It is the way of Daemos." Kanaan closed the drawers. "Zarin must work night and day to complete the new foundry. With the omniarch nearby, I do not think he would stay otherwise."

"It's literally only a few hundred yards to the omniarch," I said. "Why wouldn't Zarin just portal home?"

"Perhaps he feels more secure here." Kanaan opened the door a crack. Peered into the hallway and stepped out. The other bedrooms held nothing of interest, but the master bedroom at the end of the corridor more than made up for it.

The bed and most of the furniture was gone, replaced by bookshelves and tables. Sheets of parchment clung to the walls, many inscribed with bizarre diagrams or horrendous, inhuman faces. Portraits covered another wall, each face labeled. I went to the nearest one and examined one of a middle-aged woman, her likeness drawn by a skilled hand.

"Eleanor Barnes, cleric for the Ministry of Magical Permits." I looked at the neighboring portrait of an older man. "Jacob Hunt. CEO of International Foods."

"Good heavens." Ambria traced a finger down the drawings. "These must be the people Victus has cloned with infernus."

"Some, but not all." Kanaan pointed to checked boxes beneath several portraits that were left unchecked beneath others. "Our efforts must have halted the conversions."

"This is monstrous." Ambria looked up and down the long span of wall. "There are hundreds of portraits here."

I turned toward the next wall and stumbled over a rolled bundle of leather. At first it looked like the bottom of a fur rug, but the crudely-stitched shapes in the hide sent me shrinking back in horror. The outlines of faces, torsos, arms, and legs twisted my stomach. "What is that awful thing?"

Kanaan untied the leather bindings and kicked it open. The leather unrolled to form a ten-by-ten square. The inside was smooth and pink except for the crimson diagram spanning the center. The pattern made my vision swim, much like the one on the floor of the last foundry.

"Is it a blueprint for the foundry diagram?" Ambria asked.

Kanaan pursed his lips and examined strange symbols on the upper right corner. After a moment, he shook his head. "How is it possible?" Something like surprise flashed in his eyes.

His confusion filled me with dread. "What do you mean?"

Ambria backed away a step. "What is this thing, Kanaan?"

The magitsu master rolled it back up and bound it. "A demon gateway on human leather." He murmured a chant and tapped his wand on the bindings. A soft blue nimbus surrounded the bundle.

"Like a summoning pattern?" I asked.

Kanaan holstered his wands. "The reverse."

Ambria opened her mouth to reply when Victus burst through the door.

CHAPTER 24

Victus was so absorbed in his thoughts, he didn't even glance to the side or he would've instantly seen us. He strode to a table in the middle of the room and dug through a pile of scrolls, his back to us. Kanaan whipped out his wands and stalked across the room, silent as a panther. My hand clenched painfully tight around something. I looked down and saw my own wand in hand.

I'm going to kill him. I'm going to make him pay for what he did to Delectra and Cora!

Before I could move another muscle, Kanaan jammed his wands into Victus's ears. Brilliant blue light lit the inside of my father's skull. A scream died in his throat and he slumped to the floor, eyes bulging grotesquely, smoke rising from his nostrils.

I could hardly believe my eyes. So much destruction. So much death. So much pain. And the man who'd caused it all lay dead just feet away. Why hadn't Kanaan let me kill him? Why wasn't I the one to stand over his corpse?

My wand clattered to the floor. My knees turned to mush. Ambria grabbed my arm to keep me from falling.

"I wanted to kill him." My voice felt rough as gravel. "I wanted him to know I ended his life."

"It doesn't matter, Conrad." Ambria leaned over and picked up my wand, put it in my holster. "He's dead."

"Why did you kill him, Kanaan?" My vision swam. Anger and regret consumed me. "He was mine!"

Kanaan's eyes narrowed. "This is not Victus."

"What?" Ambria staggered back a step, nearly letting me fall.

I sucked in a breath, suddenly aware I'd stopped breathing for the span of several seconds. "It isn't?"

Kanaan turned Victus's head to reveal a small but noticeable mole on the left cheek. He also pointed to the scar over the eye. "Victus does not have a mole, and the scar is an inch too long."

My forehead tightened. "Are you certain?"

Kanaan tore open Victus's oxford to bare his chest. A narrow beam from his wand carved a line down the flesh. Ambria gasped and shuddered. I was still too shocked to react normally and stared in morbid fascination as Kanaan cut open the chest cavity and removed a small glass sphere dripping with blood. He wiped it on a piece of parchment and let it rest in his palm. Gray smoke within hung still around a dimming constellation of aether. The smoke turned black as soot and faded to nothing.

He frowned. "I am sorry, Conrad, but this is an infernus."

White-hot shock seared my nerves. *That bastard is still alive.* I couldn't even fathom why, but the thought gave me relief. *I can still kill him.*

Kanaan seemed to sense my mixed feelings. "Your desire for vengeance overshadows the need to stop your father by any means."

Conflicting emotions held my tongue. I'd admitted my feelings only seconds earlier. As ashamed as I felt to acknowledge them, I nodded. "I want him to know I killed him. I want him to know I did it for Delectra and Cora."

Kanaan raised an eyebrow. "But Cora lives."

I slashed a hand through the air. "She's not the same! After I resurrected her, she barely remembers me. She won't even let me come back into the Glimmer!" My voice grew rougher with every word, my heart heavier. "I want to watch the light drain from that bastard's eyes while I carve out his heart just like he did mine!" Tears blurred my vision, but I didn't care.

"Conrad." Ambria took my hand but I pulled away.

"I want to kill him, Kanaan." I jabbed a thumb to my chest. "You have to let me do it."

"Even at the cost of him escaping or killing you?" Kanaan holstered his wands and watched me. "What if you fail and he lives to destroy even more?"

I knew I was behaving like a child. I couldn't possibly win a fight against Victus, no matter how much I wanted to, but the thought of what he'd taken from me filled me with pure, sweet rage. Electricity stung my palms and traveled up my spine.

I felt that distant flow of pure, sweet energy, just as Moses felt during his final battle.

I hung in a void. A stream of crackling energy hummed just out of reach, azure blue mingling with the purest of white. It stretched endlessly before me. But it remained beyond my fingertips no matter how hard I strained to touch it.

"Oh, my god." Ambria's voice echoed from somewhere outside the void. "What's happening?"

I snapped back into reality.

Scrolls on the table hovered in the air. The heavy oak table rattled as if shaken by an earthquake and leapt off the floor. A deep hum vibrated me to my core.

The tingling sensation vanished. The table thudded down. Parchments, potions, and all manner of objects crashed to the floor.

Kanaan stared at me, his mouth slightly ajar in what could only be described as surprise. Shouts echoed from the hallway outside. Footsteps thudded on distant stairs. Kanaan grabbed the leather bundle off the floor and raced toward a window.

Ambria grabbed my arm and yanked me along, shaking me from my stupor. Kanaan tossed the bundle out of the window then charmed our hands with the climbing spell. Ambria went out first and I followed close behind, breathless with fear.

"Oh no." Ambria hung from the wall by her feet and one hand, the other pointing to our portal. Gray robed individuals rushed from the opposite end of the mansion toward our escape route. Since we were at the far west end of the building, there was no way we'd beat them there. The air shimmered as Kanaan cast a spell to conceal us from the incoming mages. We skittered down the wall like insects and reached the ground well after the horde reached the portal.

"What now?" I asked.

Kanaan traced his wand over the leather bundle. The awful stitches melted away to look like a regular rug which he tucked under an arm. "We blend in and leave through the Burrows."

A group of young mages nearly collided with us at the western corner of the mansion, their group heading toward the back.

"What the bloody hell?" A young man with spiked hair and a gold bone piercing the septum of his nose shoved Kanaan. "Watch where you're going."

Kanaan bowed slightly. "Apologies."

"What's going on back there?" A woman threw back the hood of her robes to reveal a face glittering with dermal implants. "It felt like an earthquake."

"Look, a crack in the foundation!" Another woman put a finger in a long fissure at the base of the house.

"We saw nothing," Kanaan said, and squeezed through the group.

I grabbed Ambria's hand and pulled her behind me. The rest of the punks passed by without incident. We walked slowly, trying to look unconcerned even as dozens of others ran toward the mansion, wands drawn. Every yard seemed to stretch into a dozen. My heart raced with fear that someone would see past our stolen gray robes and discover impostors.

The corridor beyond the mansion cave was nearly empty except for a tight group of mages guarding the entrance to the omniarch room. Several bore the crimson stains of the blooded.

"We cannot get to the omniarch," Kanaan said in a low voice.

Two burly men opened a gap and Garkin himself stalked from the omniarch room, his huge staff striking the ground with every stride. He'd covered nearly half the distance between us before I realized Kanaan was urging us toward the gauntlet room a few feet away. We stepped inside our old training grounds. Burnt and crushed humanoid dummies lay inside dozens of target ranges. The place bore little resemblance to the gauntlets Kanaan used to train us.

A few mages remained, casting destructive spells, cheering when they destroyed a target.

Kanaan stared at the mages. "These people pervert the mystic arts."

Garkin turned into the Stoneshire cavern and we stepped back into the corridor. A scarred face met my gaze. Victus, a red cloak fluttering from his back, emerged from the direction of the Burrows. Zarin, the Daemos, walked at his side, seemingly unconcerned with the loud alarms wailing.

A young mage rushed out of the mansion cave and fell at Victus's feet. "My lord, your infernus was foully murdered."

Victus's eyes flared. "Murdered, how?"

"His skull is a burnt-out husk, and his soul sphere was ripped from his chest."

"And it happened right under your noses?" Victus bared his teeth at the messenger. "Zarin, I'll require another."

"Can it not wait until the daemonculus is complete?" Zarin brushed something off his Victorian-era suit and sighed. "It would considerably decrease the time required."

Victus scowled. "Very well. Construction has been delayed enough already." He grabbed the messenger's hair and jerked back his head. "Where did it happen?"

"Inside the mansion, sir." The man's voice trembled with fear. "The entire cavern shook and brilliant lights flared inside your upstairs study."

"We felt it too." Zarin looked toward the mansion. "Are you certain it wasn't an earthquake?"

"Positive, master." The man paled even more. "There is a portal behind the mansion that leads to the Queens Gate waystation."

"Kanaan," Victus growled. He shoved the messenger's head away and walked toward the mansion. "Search the waystation, the mansion, even the damned Burrows!" Victus shouted. "I want Kanaan's head!"

"Come," Kanaan whispered. "Walk slowly, but deliberately."

We turned left toward the entrance to the Burrows. I couldn't tear my eyes from Victus. Hatred boiled my blood. The evil smirk when he killed Delectra flashed in my mind. I'd given him a scar, but it wasn't enough. I wanted to see him burn. Hear him scream.

"Conrad," Ambria hissed. She gripped my wrist and pulled me after her into the corridor.

"You!"

Ambria froze and turned slowly to face the source of that call—Victus. "Y-yes, master?"

His gloating face filled my vision. The indifference as he watched me with my dying mother. It took everything I had not to draw my wand and silence him forever. If I had been alone, I would have gladly died if it meant I could cut him to pieces in front of his minions.

"Are you searching the Burrows?" Victus continued.

Ambria bowed deeply. "Yes, master."

"Ensure all exits are blocked." He grabbed one of Garkin's blooded mages. "Go with her and make sure she gets it right."

The mage bowed. "As you say, my lord."

Red filled my vision. *This might be my last chance to kill him.* But Ambria would die with me. I looked at her frightened face and the rage cooled. I wouldn't let Victus steal another loved one from this life. I'd finish him on my own.

Victus didn't so much as glance at me a single time during his exchange with Ambria. Apparently, he didn't recognize me with blond hair and fat cheeks. My father turned and led his retinue into the mansion cave.

"Let's go." The blooded mage shoved Ambria toward the western corridor. A gaping hole at the far end led into the Burrows.

Kanaan walked slowly ahead of us by about twenty paces. The mage stalked past Ambria. "Hurry up, you idiots. We need to reach the other end and seal it before the killer escapes." He slapped Kanaan on the back of his head. "You hear me?"

"Yes, sir." Kanaan broke into a jog to keep up.

Ambria and I followed suit. When we stepped into the old dungeons, the blooded led us down a tunnel and into a large room. Rubble lay at the edges and in the center, the beginnings of a complex demon summoning pattern.

The new foundry! Dozens of people with shaved heads toiled at clearing broken rock and sweeping dust. Not one of them looked up at us, or seemed aware we were passing through. Their faces remained blank and expressionless. A man in white robes stabbed the tip of a finger and trailed blood into the grooves of the pattern.

The blooded mage picked up a stone and threw it at a nearby worker. It bounced off his head, leaving a spot of blood. The man didn't even blink. "If we don't catch the assassin, I'll make sure Zarin turns you into one of his drones." The mage sneered. "Got it?"

Drones? What was wrong with those people?

"Yes." Ambria bobbed her head. "We won't fail."

We made our way through the rubble and into a hole broken in the wall. Beyond it lay a series of broken tunnel walls where Victus's people had created a shortcut through the wending Burrows.

"If the killer came through the Burrows, he's got an hour of walking ahead of him." The mage bared his teeth in a grin, made fiercer by his thick beard and bloody streaks on his face. "He won't know about our new secret shortcut."

"Truly genius," Kanaan said. His wands blurred and jammed up the mage's nostrils. Blue fire erupted from the man's ears. Eyes popped from his sockets. A death rattled gurgled in his throat, and a foul odor filled the air.

Ambria shrank back. "My god, I wasn't expecting you to kill him right now!"

"The blooded are an affront to magitsu." Kanaan gripped the corpse under the armpits. "Help me move him."

We hoisted the body and dumped it on a mattress in one of the nearby rooms. Sleeping bags, blankets, and furniture confirmed my suspicions Victus's army used this area as living quarters.

"That'll be a nasty surprise for the occupants." Ambria shuddered.

I walked toward the room with the shortcut. "Victus thinks the assassin is trying to escape."

"Obviously," Ambria said. "What's your point?"

"He wouldn't expect someone to go for the kill now." I pointed behind us. "He didn't even recognize me."

She grabbed my arm. "Don't you dare get yourself killed, Conrad."

"It'd be worth it to stop him." I glanced at Kanaan's impassive face. "We could destroy the start of the new demon pattern right now, too."

He shook his head. "It would take considerable effort without the proper potions, and we do not know how those drones would react."

"Well, with Victus dead, Zarin probably won't complete it."

"There is more at stake here." Kanaan walked past me. "I had not realized it before today."

"Realized what?" I grabbed his robe to stop him from walking. "Look, I can get close enough to kill him. I can end all this in one blow."

"We witnessed the power of Moses back in the mansion." Kanaan folded his arms and faced me. "If you die, that is lost forever."

"The shaking of the house. Everything levitating—" Ambria's eye flared. "That was all Conrad?"

"Yes," Kanaan said.

I tried to remember the details, but the void, the endless energy seemed like a distant dream. "It couldn't have been me. I'm not that powerful."

Kanaan turned toward the room with the shortcut. "Now is not your time to die. We must ensure you reach your potential, for you are more than just Conrad Edison."

"Agreed." Ambria gripped my hand. "You're coming with us, Conrad. I swear if you try to go after Victus, I will tie you up and drag you behind us."

I wanted to argue, but remembering the incident at the mansion filled me with curiosity. "What do you mean I'm more than Conrad Edison?"

"I think that should be obvious." Kanaan ducked through the first broken hole and continued toward the next one. "We will talk more when it is safe."

I resisted the urge to argue and followed him.

We traversed the series of blasted holes and reached the exit to the Burrows within twenty minutes instead of the usual hour or more. Kanaan sealed the exit with a ward and we headed up several flights of stairs and into the university building itself.

Posters of Arcanes battling snarling vampires, lycans, and other supers covered the hallway walls, each one emblazoned with the slogan, *Arcanes First!* A stack of pamphlets sat next to a newspaper stand. I snagged one and stuffed it into my pocket. The newspaper headline also caught my attention: *Vampire Registration Starts Today*. I rolled one up and stuffed it into my back pocket.

Ambria frowned. "What is all this?"

"Propaganda." Kanaan tapped a wand to a poster and the parchment crumbled to dust. "The information war is well underway."

"Where to now?" Ambria said.

"The rear doors." Kanaan pointed in the direction of the gondola that took passengers down the cliff to the waystation. We reached the back entrance and stepped outside. Webbings of energy laced around us and an alarm wailed.

We were snared in a trap.

CHAPTER 25

I gripped my wand. "We tripped a ward."

"I did not think they would trigger on exit." Kanaan slashed a wand at the honeycomb webbing, but it refused to part. He pointed to three joints. "Focus a dispel on these points and cast on my mark."

Ambria flicked her wand through a pattern. "Ready."

I readied the strongest dispel I knew. "Ready."

"Now." Kanaan touched his wand to a joint. Ambria and I tapped our assigned sections. The energy flickered and fluctuated. The honeycomb merged with the one below it, leaving a larger gap in the prison.

"They're the ones who triggered it!" A man in blue security robes led a group of Arcanes down the hallway toward us. "Detain them."

Ambria gripped her wand. "I'm ready to fight."

Kanaan shook his head. "No fighting. More dispelling." He readied his wand. "Once again."

Ambria composed herself and summoned another dispel. We widened the gap, but it still wasn't enough to get through. The security Arcanes closed fast, but the same webbing that held us prisoner, prevented them from reaching us.

"Where's the damned ward master?" the first security Arcane said. "I don't have the dispel token."

"He's coming," another Arcane replied gruffly.

"Again," Kanaan said. "Hurry."

We three hit the joints of the next honeycomb with more dispels. A gap barely large enough to squeeze through formed. Kanaan went first. The hem of his robes touched a glowing line and smoked.

"Stop right there!" The security head fired a wand from his spell, but the honeycomb trap deflected it.

Ambria gasped and gathered her robes so they wouldn't touch the webs. I followed her example and went through. We raced toward one of the gardens as a third guard rushed up behind the others and deactivated the web.

"Where to now?" I said. "There's no way we can reach the gondola."

"We must find brooms and fly across to Science Academy," Kanaan said.

Ambria huffed. "The broom closets are inside the university!"

A large contingent of security Arcanes appeared at the far end of the building near the student keeps and charged our way.

Kanaan sighed. "Then we must fight our way free."

I looked beyond the gardens and the wide field at the tree-covered mountain rising in the center of the Dark Forest. "Maybe we can hide in the forest. If we find Shushiel, she can help us escape."

More security Arcanes emerged from the university building behind us and another group flanked from the west. *We're boxed in.*

"It appears that is our only option." Kanaan sprinted through a garden filled with bushes trimmed into the shapes of unicorns and other magical beasts. The high walls of Colossus Stadium rose several hundred yards to our right, and beyond it, the walls of the Fairy Gardens.

Ambria jogged alongside me. "I don't think the Dark Forest is a good idea. We'll be eaten for sure."

"No choice." I glanced back over my shoulder. Arcanes on flying brooms soared from the turrets of the university and zipped toward us.

Our physical conditioning allowed us to easily outpace the Arcanes on foot, but those on brooms would be upon us within seconds. Spells splashed against the ground behind us, their effects weakened by distance. A pair of flying Arcanes swooped low, blasting destructive spells in front of us.

"Halt!" one shouted. "I'll shoot if you take another—oof!"

A spell from Kanaan knocked the man from his broom. His comrade tried to catch him, but he fell twenty feet and plowed a furrow in the grass. Kanaan flicked his wand toward the shimmering shield holding in the deadly denizens of the Dark Forest and opened a hole. We rushed into the trees and the shadows swallowed us.

Light glowed at the tips of our wands, piercing the gloom so we could see a few feet ahead. Though the underbrush thinned, the canopy overhead only grew thicker. Trees measuring at least twenty feet around at the base towered hundreds of feet into the air. Pulsating clusters of glowing fungus on their trunks offered enough light for us to extinguish our wands.

Ambria shivered and looked around. Chills crawled up my spine. Unseen eyes seemed to watch from all directions. Distant screeches, hoots, and other noises echoed sporadically. The one thing missing from this forest was the constant hum of insect life. What threats waited in these woods if even the insects remained quiet?

Only Kanaan seemed unconcerned, walking down a wide path clear of any underbrush. We covered at least a hundred yards before I broke the silence.

"Where are we going?" I asked in a hushed voice.

Kanaan stopped and held up a hand. He tilted his head as if listening. "We are safe for the moment."

Ambria's eyes flared. "Until something eats us?"

Kanaan looked at me. "I will tell you what I meant now."

My chest tightened. "About why you think I'm more than Conrad Edison?"

"It certainly makes no sense," Ambria said.

"You are a direct descendant of Moses—Ezzek Moore—Jeremiah Conroy." Kanaan took my wrists and examined my scarred hands. "The blood of the first Arcane flows within you."

"Yes, but it also flowed in my mom." I resisted the urge to scratch my wounds.

Kanaan released my hands. "Have you ever heard of the first power?"

The words summoned flashbacks to Victus sending Delectra over the bridge in the rift. "In one of Victus's memories, he thought Delectra could control the rift guardians because she was linked to the first power. Serena thought she was too tainted by demon magic."

Kanaan nodded. "Tell me more of this memory."

I closed my eyes to recall it, and relayed what I remembered without actually reliving it. "Victus wanted the first power for himself, but Serena seemed convinced only Delectra could wield it."

"Very few can even sense the primal fount," Kanaan said. "I believe you have actually touched it."

I remembered the crackling spheres, the infinite beam of energy in the vision at the mansion. "When I had the vision of Moses, he tapped into this incredible energy. I think it was the primal fount."

"I don't understand." Ambria waved a hand to interrupt. "Don't we all draw power from the same source—aether in ley lines and the air?"

"Yes." Kanaan stroked his beard. "The primal forces of the universe are creation, destruction, and equilibrium. The Seraphim call them Murk, Brilliance, and Stasis. The ley lines carry the primal forces, filling the world with aether."

"We studied this in elementary magic," Ambria said. "Arcanes can't isolate the prime forces like Seraphim, nor can we channel. We have to cast using stored aether instead."

"Correct," Kanaan said. "The primal fount is the origin, the first power of the world. It is the wellspring from which all magic flows."

"I thought magic was created in the Gloom by minders," Ambria said.

"That is a source, but not the origin." Kanaan turned his gaze on me. "Moses told Justin Slade how he originally gained his powers. I later read the full account. The earth dragon, Altash, sent Moses deep into a cave to touch a glowing river. I believe the dragon allowed Moses to bind himself to the primal fount."

"Maybe that's why Lulu called to me." I held out the backs of my hands and stared at the scars. "Maybe that's why she burned me with her breath and I started having visions of the bearded man—of Moses."

Kanaan stroked his beard. "Tell me every detail."

There wasn't a lot to tell, but I told him how Moses told me to expand my well and of the twin stars pulsating with magic.

Kanaan stood silently for a moment. "Yes, it makes sense. You are nearly of age so your well is only now able to handle so much pure power. Moses reached out to you from the afterlife so you can claim your birthright."

Could it really be the spirit of Moses? "Is using the fount more powerful than using aether?"

"The fount is pure, its power immeasurable." Kanaan nodded. "It is the source of magic that flows to all the realms."

"This is amazing, Conrad." Ambria took my hand. "You need to do whatever you can to gain this power. Victus won't stand a chance."

"No man is an army unto himself." I gave her a sober look. "That's what Moses thought right before he died."

"Way to ruin the moment." Ambria gave me a small smile. "I suspect you'll need to strain yourself even more so you can expand your well."

Kanaan nodded. "Agreed. Conrad must have the capacity to wield such power. Victus believes he can harness the power through him."

"That's why Victus sent Delectra toward the rift guardians," I said. "He wanted her to gain the power, but she couldn't."

"Why would he send her to get zapped by the guardians?" Ambria grimaced. "It's insane."

"The guardians were created by Moses." Kanaan's gaze seemed to focus inward. "But are they sentient, or merely wards? Would they kill the wielder of the fount or obey him?"

I closed my eyes and recalled the memory, but through Victus's eyes this time. I focused on Serena. The short Arcane was methodical in her study of magic. If anyone could connect the dots, it would be her. As the scene played out in frightening detail, I ignored Delectra's plight so I could focus on the conversation between Victus and Serena.

I cast a shield to push Delectra toward the guardians. Without the demonic influence, she is weak and frightened.

"I'm certain the guardians would recognize Moses or his proxy," Serena said. "They wouldn't attack him, but the taint of demon magic in Delectra might make her vulnerable."

"You speak as if those things are alive." Victus pshawed. *"They are merely wards, conjured from the first power. If they strike Delectra, they will infuse her with their power."*

"Doubtful." Serena hummed tunelessly. *"I would so hate to lose such a valuable asset as Delectra."*

I woke from the memory before they snatched Delectra back from her death. Though I had more information, I still had no answers. "Serena thought the guardians wouldn't attack Moses or his proxy. Victus thought the guardians had to attack Delectra to give her access to the first power. I don't know if either of them were correct."

"Maybe you had the vision of Moses's final battle because of the close proximity of his grave." Ambria shrugged. "Maybe we need to go back there."

"Perhaps," Kanaan said. "Or the rift guardians may be what we seek."

"We're still not terribly far from Moses's grave." Ambria waved a hand to the east. "Can you feel anything now?"

I closed my eyes and reached for aether. Through it, I linked to the ley lines. I sensed a powerful presence, but try as I might, I couldn't touch it. I opened my eyes and shook my head. "It's just out of my reach."

Ambria tapped a finger on her chin. "Lovely. How are we supposed to reach the grave with the entire university on alert for us?"

"They don't know who we are," I said. "They just know some strangers triggered the wards. Maybe we can exit the forest closer to the manor and reach the grave."

"They know we are in disguise." Kanaan held out his wand like a divining rod and let it guide his arm. "I detect arachnids in that direction. Perhaps Shushiel can offer camouflaged escort to the destination."

Ambria seemed to take notice of the shadows again and shivered. "Anything is better than sitting all alone in this awful place."

I took out my arcphone. "Shushiel has a comm pendant. Maybe she can come to us."

Ambria nodded enthusiastically. "I like that idea better than traipsing through the Dark Forest."

I tapped the symbol. "Shushiel?" The range on the pendant was limited, but we were well within range of anyone in Queens Gate. "This is Conrad. Are you there?"

Only the soft hiss of static replied. I tried a few more times before giving up. "She's not answering."

Ambria's eyes filled with worry. "I hope she's okay."

"For now, we follow the wand." Kanaan began walking.

We hiked in the direction indicated by Kanaan's wand, our own wands at the ready in case of attack by lurking monsters. The path turned up a rise toward the mountain in the center of the forest. Even my conditioned legs began to tire from the constant climb.

It seemed like an hour had passed when we finally came upon strands of large webs high in the trees.

"Thank goodness." Ambria stopped and leaned against a tree trunk. "Shall I call out for Shushiel?"

Kanaan shook his head. He flicked his wand and sent a rock sailing up and into a web. A huge eight-legged form skittered out onto the web, a frightening silhouette for any who hadn't met Shushiel.

On the other hand, we hadn't met any of her relatives. "Um, are the other ruby spiders friendly?"

"Unknown." Kanaan watched as the arachnid descended on a strand of silk. "We shall soon see."

Ambria backed up a step, wand at the ready. "I hope they are."

The furry form resolved into shape and color as it grew closer. Even if it had not been a hue of bright blue, I would have known this spider wasn't our friend, Shushiel. Its abdomen was fuller, its legs longer and thicker. The spider's mandibles twitched and a whispery voice drifted from its mouth. "Mages come for more?"

Ambria's eyes tightened. "For more?" She shook her head. "We're friends of Shushiel. Is she here?"

"Friends?" The massive blue spider rotated slightly to face her, its eight eyes blinking calmly.

"Yes." Ambria put a hand to her chest. "We are friends with Shushiel. I didn't realize there were blue ruby spiders."

The spider's eyes blinked several times. "Yes, come." It rotated away from us and trundled forward.

"Oh, thank goodness." Ambria released a sigh of relief. "Let's go."

I'd never met a blue spider, but something about the color nagged at the back of my mind. It seemed as if I'd met one before. *Where have I seen a blue spider before?* I tried to meditate and recall a memory, but kept tripping over my own two feet. Meditating and walking didn't go well together.

A webbed fortress rose in the gloom before us. Dozens of eight-legged forms hung from the trees, shadows against the glow of fungus.

"Is that your home?" Ambria asked.

The spider bobbed once, but its whispery reply was too faint to hear.

The sight of the webbed castle sent a thrill of pride through me. But it wasn't because I felt proud. It was because Victus had felt proud of this place, and the memory lingered somewhere in my subconscious. My steps slowed, mired in dread. I saw the blue spider in Victus's memory. Watched the conversation in my mind's eye.

Victus lays a hand on the spider's bright blue foreleg. "The rubies betrayed me, and for that, they must pay."

The blue spider bobbed. "What would you have of us, master?"

"The cobalts are my chosen. You will be my assassins. Kill the rubies until there are no more."

I snapped from the memory, legs frozen in place.

I grabbed Kanaan and Ambria by their arms and held them back. "These aren't the ruby spiders at all," I hissed. "Victus bred cobalt spiders to kill the ruby spiders after they abandoned him."

Ambria gasped. "You mean—"

Kanaan drew his wand. "This arachnid leads us to our doom."

CHAPTER 26

The spider apparently heard me.

The cobalt leapt and spun around in mid-flight. Dozens of his comrades skittered down the trees all around us. Kanaan set the fallen leaves in front of us on fire and bolted back the way we'd come. We sprinted after him before the cobalts closed off our escape.

Leaves rustled behind. Branches creaked overhead. The spiders darted after us at a terrifying pace, some of them leaping from tree to tree, others pouncing from webs, legs spread open to strike. A susurrus of whispery voices echoed behind us like ghosts.

The only things that kept us ahead was our physical conditioning and the random spells we threw behind us to keep the spiders from closing in.

"They're too fast," Ambria gasped. "There's nowhere to hide!"

A cluster of eight-legged silhouettes dropped from the trees ahead. "And now there is nowhere to run." Kanaan drew his second wand and braced himself for combat.

I resisted the urge to cast Fireblade, for fear I'd exhaust myself too quickly to be of any use. Instead, I readied the strongest shield spells programmed in my arcwand.

Ambria fired a brilliant glowball overhead, lighting the vicinity in a wide radius. The trees behind us literally crawled with brilliant blue monsters. And ahead of us—my heart skipped a beat. The arachnids ahead of us were bright red!

"Rubies!" I shouted.

A familiar shape raced up to us, her eyes blinking in unison. "Conrad, Ambria, Kanaan! I am so happy to see you."

"Shushiel!" I resisted the urge to hug her due to the enormous wave of enemy spiders rushing behind us.

A line of red spiders big as horses trundled past and formed a front line, forelegs raised. Dozens of smaller blue spiders, no larger than Great Danes, formed the opposing spearhead, mandibles twitching furiously as they rushed our giant allies.

A loud hiss from the lead cobalt broke the eerie silence. "The traitors have come from hiding. Now we will end you for the master."

One of the large rubies spoke. "You are our people. Pawns of the evil one. Forsake your alliance with Victus and join us."

"Never," the cobalt replied.

"Never!" The hiss picked up like a rallying cry and spread across the army of cobalts until it sounded like a den of snakes.

Ambria shrank behind Shushiel. "Why didn't you tell us about the cobalt spiders?"

"I did tell you of them before I came here." Her mandibles twitched. "Perhaps I should have gone into detail."

"What now?" I asked. "Do we fight?"

Shushiel swayed back and forth—her way of shaking her head. "No. We do not have enough soldiers. We are a small scouting group tasked with spying on the movements of the enemy army. One of our scouts saw you following the cobalt spider and told us. We came at once."

The line of giant rubies spun around and fired huge webs from their spinnerets, covering the ground and trees between us and the cobalts. The lead cobalt tried to dart across the web, but the silk clung to its legs, binding it in place.

A ruby spider Shushiel's size, but with a black stripe down the middle of its abdomen, struck crystal bangles on its forelegs together three times. Without hesitation, the small force of rubies retreated toward the trees behind us, leaving the frustrated cobalts to circumvent the web traps behind.

Every so often, the giant soldier spiders fired more webs to foil any attempt to follow. A tiny ruby only half the size of Shushiel occasionally stopped to rub its abdomen against a tree.

"What is he or she doing?" Ambria asked.

"Despite our different colors, the cobalts are genetically similar to rubies." Shushiel pointed a foreleg at the blue streaks in the other spider's fur. "Some of us even have bits of blue. Ishlish can mimic cobalt pheromones."

"Putting her scent on the trees." Kanaan raised an eyebrow. "Would this not attract more spiders?"

"Yes. She is leaving a tracking scent used by cobalt scouts and will soon split away from us to lead them in the wrong direction." Shushiel's mandibles twitched with amusement. "Ishlish is very good at her job."

"Thank you, cousin." The tiny spider's whisper was barely audible.

"What about the spider with the black stripe?" Ambria asked.

"Ush is our commander." Shushiel pointed a foreleg to the giant spiders. "Those are our soldiers."

I watched Ishlish steadily angle away from us, rubbing her abdomen on trees as she went. The soldiers stopped spraying the ground with webs and Ush led us up a steep rise. "Shushiel, can any of the others camouflage like you?"

She shook her body. "Few of my kind are capable of perfect camouflage. That is why I was chosen to be a scout."

"Do your people always spy on the cobalts?" I asked.

"Yes. They wish to destroy us, so we can never let our guard down." Shushiel's eyes looked sad. "My people were happy to have me back because this group's last scout was killed by the army."

"The cobalt army?" Ambria asked.

"There is much to discuss." Shushiel pointed up the hill. "I will tell you more when we reach the safety of the outpost. For now, we should be quiet. The cobalts have excellent hearing."

Ambria's eyes flared. "Will we be safe there?" she whispered.

"The enemy has not found us yet." Shushiel crawled over a small boulder as easily as walking on flat ground while we humans had to walk around it.

The hill grew steeper. Leaves and gravel hindered me and Ambria, though Kanaan seemed unperturbed by the terrain. At last we reached the top. It wasn't as high as the mountain in the center of the forest, but it offered a clear line of sight down through the trees in all directions.

At the top of the hill, Ush tapped his bangled forelegs against a rock face. The wall shimmered and vanished to reveal a tunnel.

"Wait, isn't that illusion?" Ambria said. "I didn't think spiders could do magic."

"Galfandor gave us enchanted objects long ago." Shushiel followed the others inside. "This is how we keep our outposts and home web hidden."

Ambria stepped into the wide tunnel after her. "How far away is the home web?"

"On the other side of the mountain, far from our enemies." Shushiel stopped and turned toward us while the other rubies continued on around a bend.

Small glowballs embedded in the stone emitted soft yellowish light. It was the closest thing to sunlight I'd seen since entering the forest and filled me with relief despite the irony of being underground.

Kanaan leaned against the rough-hewn rock. "Explain the situation."

"The monster army grows larger every day." Shushiel's mandibles twitched. "Frogres, viper wolves, giant crows, and more gather to the south."

"It's even bigger than the last time?" I asked.

"Much larger." Shushiel shivered. "Mages placed enchanted totems around the forest to draw out the creatures Victus made. They do not seem to attract drakes, spider bats, or other native beasts."

"What about bistaurs and dragophants?" Kanaan asked.

"Yes, there are some," she replied.

Ambria's breath hitched in her throat. "What about the tragon?"

Shushiel shook her abdomen. "I have not seen him. As one of Victus's first creatures, perhaps he cannot be controlled."

"An army of Overlord minions." I sucked in a breath. "How large is it?"

"Even with all of our eyes, we could not count them." Shushiel sank as if deflating. "Most of the creatures are unintelligent. The cobalt spiders are among the few self-aware species."

Ambria grimaced. "Dare I even ask what a bistaur or a dragophant is?"

"Bistaurs are part human, part bison," Shushiel said. "Dragophants are fire-breathing elephants with reptile scales."

"This is even worse than we thought." I sank to the tunnel floor, completely defeated. "I didn't expect the monster army to be so large. How many monsters did Victus create?"

"Not this many," Kanaan said. "I suspect they have reproduced since their introduction into the wild."

Ambria frowned. "If Victus has such a huge army, why hasn't he taken control of the Overworld yet?"

"Would I use a cannon to kill a fly?" Kanaan didn't wait for an answer. "Victus has overwhelming power to crush his enemies, but he has no need. Subterfuge and the infernus grant him control of the government. And yet, he has an even more insidious way to control public opinion."

Ambria's eyebrows rose. "And that is?"

Kanaan's lips formed a grim line. "Propaganda."

"As in rewriting history to make Justin Slade the bad guy?" Ambria's lips peeled into a scowl. "My god, he's covered every angle."

"Victus uses the poor economy and plight of the average Arcane as the vehicle of hate." Kanaan folded his arms across his chest. "The monster army is most likely a last resort—a looming threat for those who withhold support for the Overlord."

"If we come out against him, he could destroy us in a heartbeat." I stood and paced. "We need our own monster army, and I know just where to find one."

"You want the monsters from the Glimmer, don't you?" Ambria's forehead pinched. "How are we supposed to get there?"

I touched my throat where the anchor stone fragment used to hang on its necklace. "I don't know how, but there must be a way into the Glimmer."

"What makes you think Cora will help us?" Ambria said. "After you resurrected her, she barely remembered you. Then she closed off the

Glimmer to repair all the damage done by Naeve and we haven't heard from her since."

"I don't know, but I have to ask her. I have to try." *Why did you shut me out, Cora?*

"I am sorry, Conrad." Shushiel rubbed a furry foreleg on my shoulder. "Is there no way inside the Glimmer at all?"

"The rift guardians will kill anyone who tries to cross through the crack in the world, and I don't have an anchor stone fragment to sneak through the reflected world." I rubbed my eyes. "There's no other way inside that I know of. And once I get there, what guarantee do I have that Cora will even listen to me?"

"Because she loves you." Ambria gripped my hand. "I hope she still remembers that."

"If the anchor stone hasn't drained her of all emotions." I hoped that wasn't the case.

Shushiel bobbed up and down. "The question remains—how will you get past the rift guardians?"

"Your camouflage won't work, and none of us can cast a shield strong enough to withstand their attacks." Ambria looked at me. "Our only hope is if the first power protects you."

"We have to find out." I turned to Kanaan. "Right?"

"You cannot touch the first power yet." He tapped a finger on my chest. "I do not normally advise this, but you must strain yourself to exhaustion to expand your well and strengthen your psyche to withstand the concentrated power of the primal fount."

Shushiel's eyes blinked. "What is the primal fount?"

Ambria chuckled. "We've got a lot of catching up to do, but I'd rather do it someplace more comfortable."

"Perhaps you should eat and rest." Shushiel motioned us on with a mandible. "You can tell me over dinner."

Ambria walked alongside her. "What do you eat?"

Shushiel blinked. "Mostly spider bat blood."

Ambria grimaced. "Gross. Is that what we have to eat too?"

"Only if you wish to."

Ambria gagged. "Just for the record, I don't wish to at all."

Shushiel's mandibles twitched with amusement. "Come with me." She led us down the tunnel and into a wide cavern. Huge crystals on the ceiling sparkled with the light of glowballs. A blue lake spanned several hundred yards into the distance, its clear waters lit by fungus on the rocky bed. A school of bright green fish leapt over the bowl-shaped edge of the lake and vanished over the side.

"Where did they go?" I asked.

Shushiel took us to the edge of the shore where the cave floor met a dark abyss. A pinpoint of light shone from far below. "They go to the underground," she said. "Another stream feeds back up from below to this lake."

"It's so beautiful!" Ambria splashed a bit of water over the side.

Her smile warmed my heart. I put my hand in the water and was surprised by its temperature. "How is the water so warm?"

"Underground springs," Shushiel said.

Ambria took out her arcphone and took some pictures, using the brilliant flash on the device to peer far down into the chasm. I leaned over the side to see how far down it went, but it was hundreds of meters deep. I cast a glowball spell and sent it hovering over the middle.

"Conrad, you should not do that," Shushiel said. "It is dangerous."

"It's just a glowball." I frowned. "What's dangerous about that?"

The air thrummed. Something huge buzzed up from the chasm, and struck at the glowball. I snuffed it immediately.

Ambria shrieked and rolled backward, dropping her phone in the process. I grabbed her hand and pulled her to her feet as a cricket the size of a horse splashed into the edge of the lake. Giant hind legs rubbed together. The deafening chirp sawed at my eardrums. The next instant, it lunged for us, mandibles flashing.

CHAPTER 27

Ambria dove and rolled to the side, narrowly avoiding the crushing grip of the cricket's mandibles. "It's a giant bug!" She drew her wand and cast a shield to block another attack, but the cricket ignored her and struck at her phone where it lay, casting its bright light upward.

Soldier spiders skittered across the cave floor and lunged at the cricket. The creature thrashed, but webs tangled its legs and it went down. Tiny Ishlish raced up the side of the bug and bit it on the abdomen. Within seconds, its thrashing ceased and the spiders dragged it away.

Shushiel touched Ambria. "Are you okay?"

Ambria put a hand on her chest. "W-what was that thing?"

"A deep dweller." Shushiel pointed a mandible at the phone. "The bright light from the glowball drew this one from the depths." She faced the direction the soldiers took the giant insect. "On the other hand, this will be quite a treat for dinner."

Ambria rubbed goosebumps on her arms. "Are there are more of those things?"

"Oh, yes." Shushiel bobbed up and down. "If you go to the underground, there is a cave so large you cannot see one end from the other. The fungus glows bright as a full moon, and forests and meadows span for miles."

"An underground forest?" I scooped up Ambria's phone and was relieved to find it still intact. "That's unbelievable."

"It is beautiful, but dangerous even for us." Shushiel trembled. "We once thought the underground forest would provide a secret home for us, but the deep dwellers are numerous and deadly. Even the Dark Forest with all its monsters is safer."

"How terrifying!" Ambria took her phone from me and deactivated the flashlight app. "Are there giant roaches, centipedes, and scorpions?"

"Oh yes." Shushiel's mandibles twitched. "They are delicious, but few wander up here."

"Unless drawn like moths to a flame." Kanaan walked over from the lake. "The glowball lured it."

I waved a hand at the glowing fungus. "But there's light everywhere."

"The light from the glowball is far brighter." Kanaan lit the tip of his wand until it shined bright enough to hurt my eyes. "The fungus is not bright enough to attract it."

"It's a good thing only one came," I said.

"Yeah, you don't want a whole fleet of those crickets swarming you." Ambria shivered. "How awful would that be?"

We walked past the lake and into a smaller cave that branched off into chambers. The tunnels seemed to go on forever in all directions. A small group of humans clustered around a fire in the center of this one. I recognized our history professor, Eleanor Beetle right away. She huddled in blankets, face miserable.

Ambria gasped. "Professor Trask?"

An older woman in gray robes stalked toward us, expression stiff. "Conrad Edison and Ambria Rax? What in the world are you doing here?"

"Well, the party keeps growing," a deep voice boomed. Minister of Wildlife, Horace Moon strode over. His thick beard and mustache were gone, but his burly stature gave him away.

"More refugees?" A thin, weasel-faced man came up behind Moon. "I'm surprised children made it this far."

"No ordinary children." Kanaan seemed to melt from the shadows. "Apprentices."

Trask's eyes widened. "Oh, Master Kanaan." She bowed slightly. "An honor to see you."

"Well, that's a bloody pleasant surprise!" Moon boomed a laugh. "We might survive this insurrection after all."

"How could one man make such a difference?" The weasel-faced fellow nodded at Kanaan. "No offense, but even your skills cannot destroy an entire army."

Kanaan raised an eyebrow. "Victus is too well protected to assassinate. His roots of corruption spread far and wide. You are correct. One person is not enough."

Horace threw up his hands. "Wonderful, Gilbert. You've ruined my mood."

"I am, first and foremost, a realist." Gilbert scratched the tip of his long nose. "If even the great Kanaan seeks refuge with us, then the odds are direr than we thought."

"We're not refugees, exactly." I massaged the back of my neck, a bit nervous to talk to professors and ministers as if I was anything more than just a boy. "We're trying to defeat Victus."

Eleanor Beetle finally stirred, giggling like a school girl. "The Overlord was barely defeated the first time, and then we had help from Ivy Slade." She looked me up and down, remaining seated in her chair. "How's a mere boy supposed to defeat Victus?"

Ambria gripped my shoulder. "This *boy* defeated Victus in battle before. He rescued Ivy Slade and Nightliss, the Templar Clarion, from a secret prison. Now we have them on our side."

Trask gasped and flicked her gaze to Kanaan. "Is this true?"

Kanaan nodded. "Even now we seek the help of the Glimmer Queen."

"The what?" Beetle rose from her chair, clutching blankets around her as if they were the only thing preserving her life. "Do you mean the crazed woman who nearly destroyed campus a few years ago?"

"Eleanor, hush." Trask waved away the other woman like a minor annoyance. "Master Kanaan, I would like to hear everything from start to finish." She held up a finger and gave him a stern look. "Leave out nothing." My stomach growled and Trask's expression softened. "Over dinner."

While Shushiel and her spider companions feasted on giant cricket, the humans retreated to yet another chamber furnished with beds, a magic stove, and a food preservation chamber filled with dozens of covered dishes that looked as if they'd been taken straight from the university dining hall.

"I am the director of food services," Gilbert told us as we feasted on steaming roast. "Once a week, a golem delivers a shipment to a ruby spider so we can continue to eat like humans."

"Brilliant," I said between bites. "I was a bit concerned we'd have to eat insects or spider bats."

Trask looked at Kanaan. "Well, let's hear the story."

Ambria's eyes flashed. "How far back, Professor? We discovered the Anchored World our first year in school and saved campus from Naeve, the evil reflection of the real Glimmer Queen. Our second year, we stopped Victus from obtaining powerful relics and brought Conrad's foster mother back to life. Only recently, we destroyed Victus's foundry where he manufactured demon clones of people."

Trask's mouth dropped open slightly. "What nonsense is this?"

Kanaan pursed his lips. "The truth."

The table went silent. Trask and the other adults shared surprised glances.

I swallowed the last of my roast and put down my fork. "I'll start from the beginning—the orphanage."

Trask nodded respectfully. "Yes, Edison. Please do. You'll forgive me for being skeptical, even if Master Kanaan offers his endorsement."

Eleanor Beetle took out a quill and parchment and wrote something at the top of a sheet. "I'm ready."

I gave a brief but thorough account of my life. I started at Little Angel Orphanage and explained how the demon curse that bound my parents' souls to mine killed my foster parents in terrible ways. How Cora, the only foster parent I'd loved like a real mother died of cancer thanks to the curse. Fighting back tears, I led them through the resurrection of my biological parents and onward to my discovery of the shattered world of the Glimmer.

I told them of Cora's evil reflection, Naeve, who ruled the Glimmer after stealing part of Cora's soul. Victus allied with Naeve so he could discover the source of immortality hidden in her realm. We drove out Victus and banished Naeve back to the reflected world.

My recounting of Harris Ashmore's death sent a ripple of gasps through the audience of four.

"But he was prophesied to defeat a great evil!" Horace scowled. "That poor lad."

"If he wasn't the one in Foreseeance Five Thousand, then who is?" Beetle arched an eyebrow and dipped her quill in ink before writing on a new sheet of parchment. "How curious."

"Does it matter?" Ambria said. "It was the most important thing in Harris's life story. It was his destiny." She scowled. "The foreseeance isn't important. What's important is that we bring down Victus no matter what."

"Indeed," Trask said. She looked to me. "Continue, Conrad."

"Yes, professor." So I continued. Recounting everything, digging through all the plots and subplots took longer than I wanted, but it reminded me how much we'd survived despite the long odds. I'd stopped Victus before. Surely, I could do it again. The man was brilliant, but not infallible.

Eleanor Beetle wrote furiously for a moment after I'd finished. "I'd like considerably more detail about the Sundering and these Apocryphan." She stopped writing. "I can't enter this into official record without more fact sources."

"Forget that." Horace Moon swiped the air with a hand. "The boy isn't here to fill the history books with old news. He's here to make history, and we need to help him."

"Make history, or fulfill the foreseeance?" Beetle tapped her quill on the tin of ink. "Or is the prophecy even valid?"

"I think it's preposterous any of you even believe these tall tales." Gilbert sniffed. "This boy and his little friends would have died ten times over if any of it was real."

"Frankly, I don't care if you believe a word of it." Ambria glared at the food director. "But I would like dessert if you have any."

Gilbert narrowed his eyes, but produced a slice of pie and passed it to her.

Trask locked a stern gaze on Kanaan. "Do you really think an alliance with a foreign power is our only chance? This Cora woman might once have been a good person, but it sounds like she forgot everything after her resurrection. What if she decides to ally with Victus or simply takes power as Naeve attempted?"

"Cora shut me out." I tried to hide the pain as I spoke, but my voice still cracked. "Her only concern seems to be the Glimmer. Our only problem will be convincing her to help us."

"Only problem?" Horace chuckled. "I don't know how you plan to reach her in the first place."

"Yes, the rift guardians." Professor Beetle scrawled on her parchment. "Tell me more about them."

The last thing I wanted to do was keep talking. I was tired and my throat hurt. "Maybe later." I put my dishes in a crate with the others and walked out of the room. Though he didn't make a sound, I sensed Kanaan behind me. I turned and faced him. "Are we going to the rift tomorrow?"

He shook his head. "You are not prepared to face the guardians. You must expand your well."

"If I overexert myself again, it'll take days to recover."

"If the guardians kill you, there will be no recovery, and no chance to gain help from Cora."

I tried to counter his argument, but he was right. We didn't have time to wait, but we had no choice. Every day we waited, the monster army grew larger, the foundry neared completion, and Victus's infernus seized more power.

But unless I took the time to prepare for an encounter with the rift guardians, we'd never gain the help of Cora. Somehow, I needed to put the chicken before the egg without killing myself in the process.

Kanaan broke the long silence. "We can try something, but it is dangerous."

I nodded. "I'll do it."

"Do not accept lightly." Kanaan paused as if to let it sink in. "I have seen students attempt this and lose their powers forever."

"Just tell me what it is."

He held up a small vial of purple fluid. "This is the refresher potion I gave you during your early training."

I remembered it. "The stuff you put in our tea for lunch."

"What I gave you was diluted. This is the concentrate. It fortifies the mind. Allows it to go beyond mental limits and up to your physical limit."

I thought back to one of Kanaan's many lessons during our early training. "You told us going to our physical limits could kill us."

He nodded. "It is likely."

My chest tightened. "Why is this better than me simply overextending myself with Fireblade again?" I felt nauseous just thinking about it.

"It is not better. It is faster, but dangerous." Kanaan tucked the potion into his tweed jacket. "Your fingers have grazed the primal fount, but cannot grasp it. Expanding your well once again may allow you to dip your fingers. Twice again, your entire hand. Thrice may be enough to break the surface and allow you to survive the rift guardians."

"That much recovery would normally take a month." I'd thought that one more expansion might be enough, but three more? "Will the potion allow me to do that much overexertion all at once?"

"Perhaps."

"Absolutely not." Ambria stormed out of the shadows. "Conrad, there is no reason to risk your life like that. If it takes a month, then so be it!"

"But we have to get inside the Glimmer now." I balled my fists in frustration. "How are we supposed to do that if I can't get past the guardians?"

Ambria's eyes flared. "The blink stones! I completely forgot I had them."

A ray of hope filled the darkness trying to swallow me. "They're perfect!" I imagined the distance from the halfway point on the rift bridge to the crack on the other side. "It'll take us two blinks to make it through the danger zone."

"And we won't even have to face the guardians." Ambria glared at Kanaan. "Conrad can expand his well safely on his own time."

"I agree. There is no need for Conrad to risk the potion." Kanaan seemed relieved. "You will go and I will study the enemy."

"Ok...good." Ambria seemed surprised by his sudden agreement. "You really think that's the best way?"

"There is no magic bullet for this predicament," Kanaan said. "Our options are limited, and your solution is safer. Had I known about the blink stones earlier, I would have suggested using them."

"Great." A broad grin spread across Ambria's face. "I like coming up with good ideas."

I kissed her cheek. "Great job."

She blushed.

I was exhausted so I told Kanaan goodnight and took Ambria with me to find a place to sleep. Shushiel led us through the human den chamber and deeper into the tunnels where we found small rooms with mattresses and sheets Gilbert's golems had stolen from the university.

"Do not wander too far past this area," Shushiel said. "The tunnels go much further and deeper, and you could easily get lost."

"You could make a spider city down here," Ambria said. "It seems safe."

Shushiel rotated side-to-side. "We desire life aboveground in the trees. There is nothing so beautiful as sunlight reflecting off the webbed city."

"I'd like to see it someday," I told her.

She stroked my arm with a foreleg. "I would love having my friends see my city." Shushiel backed out of the room. "Good night."

"Good night." I flopped down on the bed. Ambria curled up next to me, and her warmth soon put me to sleep.

"CONRAD." The voice is a whisper in the wind.

I open my eyes and see Moses inches from me, his dark eyebrows fierce. "You're almost there."

I jerked upright. Ambria breathed softly next to me. One of the soldier spiders crawled past in the corridor outside, shocking me back to the reality of where I was. I checked the time on my arcphone. It was nearly nine in the morning. *I must have slept like a stone.*

Moses's words echoed in my mind. I did, indeed, feel close to something momentous. I dared to hope that Cora would happily lend her aid and lead a Glimmer army to the university. After a fierce battle, our forces would rout Victus and the Overworld would once again return to normal. Being away from the anchor stone would restore Cora's memories and emotions, and she'd shower me with love as she had so long ago.

What a fairy tale that is.

I might come back empty-handed with little choice but to abandon these plans and hope the Fallen could offer us transport to Seraphina. I tried not to dwell on the stakes too much, or what might happen if we failed.

I called Max and updated him on everything. "How's Percival's potion coming?"

"His first batch spoiled." Max's holographic face grimaced. "I think he got in too big of a hurry to finish it. His next batch should be finished today."

I shook my head. "Even with Ivy and Nightliss back to normal, we don't stand a chance against the monster army and the battle mages."

"True, but if Cora helps, then you'll definitely need us." He quirked his lips. "I'll ask Gwyneth if she can help us reach you. Maybe we can take an omniarch portal to the ruby spider hideout."

"It would be good to have everyone on hand in case Cora does agree." I sent him Gwyneth's symbols along with a picture of the ruby spider cave. "See what you can do."

"Okay." Max's lips pressed together. "Be careful. I know Cora was special to you, but she's been in the Glimmer a while now—long enough to lose her emotions. I hope she's not like Naeve."

"Technically, she is Naeve and was Naeve long before her reflection stole her identity. She was the Glimmer Queen for thousands of years." I managed a wan smile despite the conflicting emotions twisting my insides. "I just have to remind her that she was also once Cora, an extraordinary woman who loved an orphan boy and saved his life."

"That's beautiful, Conrad." Max smiled sadly. "I hope it works."

We said our goodbyes and ended the call.

I went back into the room and nudged Ambria.

She stretched, yawned, and looked up at me. A smile spread across her face. "Goodness, I slept better than I have in ages."

"Me too." The usual nightmares stayed away for some reason, but I wasn't complaining about it. The grinding emotions melted away in the light of her smile. I gladly let them go.

After breakfast, we changed into comfortable clothes for hiking—jeans and T-shirts—but kept the stolen gray robes bundled in our satchels in case we needed disguises. Kanaan wore dark robes that blended with the wooded environment.

Shushiel followed behind us. "I will see you safely to the edge of the forest."

"You're a wonderful friend." Ambria stroked the spider's red fur. "I feel like I'm always being watched by some awful monster when I'm outside."

"You probably are," Shushiel said. "There are many predators who would love to eat you."

Ambria shuddered. "That doesn't make me feel any better."

The tiny spider, Ishlish, perched on Shushiel's back and bobbed up and down. "I will keep you safe." Her voice was a tiny whisper without an amplifying gem.

"Thank you so much." Ambria reached a tentative hand for her.

Ishlish reached out with a foreleg and stroked her skin. "Shushiel has told me much about your grand adventures. I am jealous."

Ambria laughed. "Oh, I wouldn't be jealous about what we've been through."

"You are great heroes." Ishlish looked at me and blinked. "I am happy to be a part of your journey."

Ambria blushed. "Aw, thanks."

I looked away, ashamed. I wasn't anything like Justin Slade or Ivy. If I were a true hero, I would've stopped my father long ago. Instead, I had to rely on everyone else to carry the load. I managed a fake smile and started walking.

It was time to face the rift guardians.

CHAPTER 28

The moment we entered the forest, Ishlish vanished into the trees and Shushiel left us to scout ahead. She appeared every ten minutes or so to tell us the way ahead was clear. We passed the bodies of several dead creatures, mostly viper wolves that Ishlish had killed to protect us.

After two hours of steady hiking, we reached the edge of the forest closest to the Fairy Gardens.

Ishlish dropped from a tree and perched on Shushiel's back. "This was fun. I would like to do it again soon."

"Even if Cora helps us, we'll need all the ruby spiders to fight." I looked imploringly at her and Shushiel. "Please convince your people to help us."

Both spiders bobbed—a strange sight since the smaller one stood on the larger one's back.

"We will send word," Shushiel said. She stroked mine and Ambria's arms. "Take care, my friends."

Ambria hugged her. "You too. Please be careful."

"I like these humans." Ishlish leapt atop Kanaan's head and stroked his hair with her forelegs.

The magitsu master managed to look comical with his new spider hat, despite the stony look on his face.

"Kanaan is not as huggable," Shushiel said, mandibles twitching in amusement.

Ishlish leapt to my head and stroked it. The hairs on the back of my neck rose, whether from pleasure or primal fear, I couldn't say. I managed to smile. "Thank you, Ishlish."

"Of course." She gave Ambria a head hug as well, then leapt to Shushiel's back.

We left our friends and the Dark Forest through a hole Kanaan made in the shield. Across a hundred yards of open field, we reached the cobble-stone path leading to the black iron gate and stone walls guarding the perimeter of the Fairy Gardens.

Kanaan tapped a wand against the lock and the gates swung open. We stepped inside and looked around cautiously. A pond sparkled in the early afternoon sun. Saplings stood tall and bright green in the forest, sprouting straight from stumps. Victus had poisoned the pond and cut down the entire forest, but Evadora had nurtured it back to health again.

Max, Ambria, and I had rescued the Lady of the Pond, Mirjana, and her husband from the poison, and Percival had nursed her back to health. It had been a long time since I'd been back to see her.

"Do you think Mirjana would help us?" I asked.

Kanaan walked toward the forest. "I will ask her after—" He spun and drew wands. A cloud of green smoke puffed and blinded us. Kanaan's voice rose. "Run!"

I took out my wand and tried to cast a wind spell, but the magic slipped from my grasp no matter how hard I tried. Ambria grabbed my arm and jerked me forward. A blade flashed and narrowly missed my ankle. We coughed and stumbled forward, finally free of the smoke.

Kanaan whirled his wands. A breeze lifted the smoke. He threw a packet of sparkling powder into the air, and a hunched form became visible. It had black fur, sharp teeth, and the face and horns of a goat, but its feet and hands were humanlike. One hand clenched a silver blade. Its forked tail twitched back and forth. "I'd heard you were good, mage, but you are even more prepared than I imagined."

"Do you think I have never faced invisible opponents?" Kanaan backed away, wands at the ready. "You are Talin of the Assassin's Guild."

The goat-man's eyes narrowed. "Indeed."

"Victus hired you to kill us?"

"If that were true, you would be dead." He bared pointy teeth. "I am here to watch for intruders."

"I suggest you let us pass," Kanaan said. "I do not desire to kill you."

A foxlike grin spread across Talin's face as his body began to fade from sight. "It is not me you need fear."

The earth trembled beneath my feet. Two monsters burst through the iron gates, ripping them from their hinges. Frog heads perched atop massive muscular bodies. The frogres laid eyes on us and croaked as they lumbered forward, long strides eating up the distance between us. Another four frogres piled through the broken gates after them.

A flock of black birds rose in the distance. Hoots, howls, and roars echoed as the monster army came for us.

Talin's grin widened. "God speed, magitsu master."

Kanaan's wands blurred. A shimmering energy shield slammed into the nearly invisible assassin. He flew a dozen feet and landed in a heap. "I can do little against the frogres. Go to the pond and jump in. We will take refuge with Mirjana."

"No." I jabbed a finger toward the fairy forest. "We might be safe underwater, but we'll be trapped. We can make it through the rift with our blink stones."

Kanaan paused. Nodded. "Very well. I will distract the creatures." He gripped my shoulder. "Good luck, Conrad." With that, he turned toward the monsters and charged. Sparks flew from his wand, blinding the creatures and slowing them.

Ambria and I raced for the sapling forest. A nerve-rattling screech pierced the air. I looked skyward. Crows with ten-foot wing spans dove, wicked talons ready to pierce flesh and bone.

"Illusion spell!" I took out my arcwand and cast the diversion spell. A copy of me sprinted in another direction. I did it again and sent another illusion racing away.

Copies of Ambria ran in all directions. The birds took the bait and dove for the illusions instead of us, even though we continued in the same direction. Crows smashed into trees and each other as they fought for the decoys. The sapling forest provided some cover from the birds. We slowed to catch our breath for the final sprint on the other side.

The path wended through a grassy field. Only a few scattered trees offered cover from here to the charred skeleton of a mansion nearly a hundred yards away. It used to be the estate of the Arcanus Primus, but hadn't been repaired in the decade since Harry Shelton destroyed it. A steep cliff rose behind it—the end of the world as far as Queens Gate was concerned.

I gripped Ambria's hand and released it. "Ready?"

She took a deep breath. "Let's go."

We ran out of the forest, tapping ourselves to leave decoy illusions every few seconds. The giant crows soared overhead in greater numbers, some diving at the same targets only to grasp thin air. There were so many that it didn't take long for some to focus on us instead of the illusions.

Ambria zapped the first crow that came our way with a bolt of electricity. Feathers flew. The bird cawed and veered into a tree. I flashed blinding light at the next crow. It crashed into another bird and the pair tumbled to the ground.

Despite our success against the birds, a group of frogres had broken past Kanaan's distractions, heavy strides thundering. The only upside was that the monsters were too big to fit through the crack in the world.

I fired another flare at a diving crow. It screeched and plowed into the ground right at Ambria's heels. Her foot glanced off the huge beak. With a shriek, Ambria tumbled on the ground. The crow staggered to its feet, snapping its beak in our general direction. I zapped it, frying feathers. It fluttered backward, cawing angrily.

I yanked Ambria upright. Her eyes flared, transfixed on something behind me. "Watch out!"

Before I could react, my feet left the ground. The satchel strap tightened against my throat and armpit. I looked up and saw a crow holding the satchel in its beak.

"Conrad!" Ambria slashed her wand. The strap parted, and I fell five feet to the ground.

"The blink stones are in that satchel!" I struggled to my feet and fired a blast at the crow, even as more of its comrades streaked for us.

The bird squawked and dropped the satchel. I caught it. A stream of fire from Ambria's wand caught another crow in the face.

"Ribbit!" The frogres were nearly upon us. A long pink tongue flashed out and caught a crow, pulling it into the frog mouth like a giant fly.

"Run!" Ambria's shout snapped me from my shock.

We sprinted the final yards to the mansion and went through the skeletal front entrance. Climbed over rubble and dodged around charred furniture. Leapt through a hole in the back wall and entered the grove of trees near the cliff.

An unbroken cliff face waited there. The crack in the world was gone.

"No!" I cried.

"Oh my god, Cora closed the crack!" Ambria ran her hands along the rocky face.

The crows circled overhead. Crashes and thuds resounded as the frogres smashed their way through the burned mansion. Within minutes they'd corner us, crush us, and eat us.

Ambria cast a dispel and another spell to uncover illusions, but the rock revealed no secrets. "It's stone, Conrad. The crack is really sealed."

I had no choice. My wand flicked through the complex patterns, binding multiple spells into one coherent form—Fireblade. Aether tingled through my palms.

Ambria's voice cut through my concentration. "You can't cut down an army of frogres and crows, Conrad!"

"I'm not going to." I aimed my wand at the rock face and unleashed Fire-blade. The orange beam drilled into the rock. Lava trickled from the incision. I traced the beam slowly down the cliff face. Power poured from me and my knees grew weaker by the second. I started another cut just a few feet from the ground, forming a triangle.

My focus wavered and I nearly lost hold of the spell. *Ambria will die if I don't do this.* I clenched my teeth and fought the exhaustion. Aimed my wand at the base of the cuts and finished the triangle. I stopped casting and held the spell ready in case I needed to cut more.

The moment of truth. How thick was the patch? If Cora had sealed the entire crack, we were doomed. "Can you try to break through?"

Ambria fired a concussive shot from her wand. The triangle of stone wobbled and thudded backward. A dark tunnel waited on the other side.

"Thank god." I released the spell and leaned on a tree.

Ambria put a hand to my forehead as if checking my temperature. "Are you okay? You're dripping sweat."

"Yes." I pushed off the tree and stumbled toward the opening. The rock still glowed from heat. "Can you cool it down?"

"Oh, yes." She cast a freezing spell. Moisture turned to frost and dropped on the bottom edge of the cut. The rock hissed as it cooled.

"Ribbit!" A frogre smashed into one of the trees. Its tongue lashed toward us but caught on a branch.

I screamed. Ambria screamed. We dove into the newly opened crack in the world. The bottom lip in the opening had cooled but the triangular slab still burned red hot against my hands and through my jeans. I yelled in excruciating pain. Ambria cried. We scooted across the hot slab, every inch of progress pure agony until we finally reached cool dirt on the other side.

I reached into the satchel with trembling hands and activated a glowball to light the tunnel. Ambria inspected blistered skin on her hands, tears trickling from her eyes. I examined my own and cringed.

"I can hardly hold my wand." Ambria tried to cast one of the anesthesia spells Asha had taught us, but her wand tumbled from trembling fingers.

I gripped my wand feverishly and managed to cast the spell on Ambria's hands. She moaned in relief and numbed my hands with the same spell. I shivered at the respite. Our skin wasn't healed, but the agony was gone.

"Oh, I wish Percival was here right now." Ambria inspected the blisters. "I don't know any good healing spells."

I clenched my hand and wiggled my fingers. The flesh was raw and seeping, but I could still hold my wand. "Maybe Cora can help us."

Ambria pulled up the legs of her jeans to look at her knees, but thanks to the denim, the skin was only pink. She let out a long sigh and leaned back. "I pray she can."

A frogre crashed against the small hole, trying to push its way inside. Though the inside of the tunnel was tall and wide, it couldn't hope to fit through the tiny opening. It croaked and smashed its fists against the stone over and over again. Dust showered down on us. It tried to shove its head through. Its long tongue lashed out, narrowly missing my face. I knew from experience how sticky and strong that tongue was and what would happen if it latched onto me.

Cracks formed in the patch. If it and its comrades kept ramming it, they might actually break through.

It took everything I had to get up. Casting Fireblade for so long had torn through my reserves. I tried to pull Ambria to her feet, but my arms wouldn't cooperate. "Go!"

Ambria ran. I stumbled after her down the tunnel, the croaks fading behind us. Within minutes we reached the cliff at the end of the world. Above, below, and beyond lay the infinity of space. I didn't know what would happen to anyone who fell into that void, and I didn't want to find out. I peered across the wide rift and spotted the crack in the stars that led to the Glimmer. It looked even farther away than last time, but at least it wasn't sealed shut.

Two small stars detached themselves from the tapestry of space and drifted toward the invisible bridge, growing larger with proximity. Energy pulsated across the bluish-white spheres. They looked beautiful and deadly. *Thank god we have blink stones.*

"Can I rest for a moment?" I sat inside the tunnel so my stomach would stop twisting with fear at the sight of the rift.

Ambria sat next to me. "Did you overexert yourself?"

I nodded. "Just give me a minute and then we'll cross."

Thuds echoed down the tunnel as the frogres continued to pound against the patch. They hadn't broken through just yet.

"Of course." Ambria leaned my head in her lap and kissed my forehead.

I tried to sleep, even if only for a moment, but my nerves were tight as drums and the racket of hammering frogre fists only wound the strings tighter. I had no idea how well I could use the blink stones while so exhausted from casting. It looked like I had no choice but to find out.

I pushed up to my feet. "Let's go."

Ambria pulled the stones from my satchel and put one in my hand. "We can do this."

We stepped out into the void. Instead of falling, our feet found the invisible bridge. Max discovered the hard way it was only a few feet wide by nearly falling off the edge during one of our ventures. I kept the crack on the other side centered in my view to keep from getting too close to the edge.

The keening wail of the guardians rose from a background noise to fever pitch as we approached the middle of the bridge. The orbs danced around each other in a figure eight pattern, electricity crackling and arcing between them. Another couple of steps and they'd vaporize us. The first time Evadora brought us here, she'd dodged past the guardians and made it across. If she hadn't been supernaturally fast, they would have easily killed her.

We were nowhere near fast enough to run from them once we made our first blink, especially not with my state of exhaustion. A loud croak cut through the wailing of the guardians. I turned and saw a frogre burst from the tunnel and rush us.

"Go!" Ambria shouted. She vanished in a puff of shadows.

The frogre hurled a stone the size of my head at me. I focused on the spot Ambria appeared and blinked. I stumbled forward and fell to a knee. My head swam and my legs felt like jelly. I looked back and saw Ambria behind me.

The guardians hummed with deadly energy and zipped toward us. It was then I noticed the rock the frogre had thrown sailing far over where I'd been. It crashed onto the bridge and rolled.

"Watch out!"

Ambria spun around and jumped back, but the rock struck her foot and knocked her over. She sprawled on her stomach and the blink stone tumbled from her grasp and fell over the side of the bridge.

CHAPTER 29

Ambria looked at me in horror.

My leaden legs refused to move. Even if I stood up, I'd never reach her in time. I slid my blink stone across the twenty feet dividing us. She grabbed it with outstretched hands. Deadly arcs of destruction struck the bridge beneath the fury of the guardians. Terror choked me and tears stung my eyes.

"Blink, Ambria! Blink!"

Her mouth hung open in horror. "Conrad, no!"

"Do it!" I screamed, the guardians only feet from her.

The wrath of the guardians speared the puff of shadows where Ambria had been an instant ago. I looked behind me and saw her only a few feet from the crack leading to the Glimmer. She was safe.

I held out a hand to her. "I love—" Agony speared through my chest. Intense heat vaporized me in an instant. The world went away.

I stood in darkness. *Am I dead?* My eyes adjusted to the dim light. Stalagmites jutted around me like sharp teeth and stalactites threatened from above. The light in the tight cavern grew brighter gradually, emanating from a tiny puddle in the middle. I pinched myself and felt pain. This wasn't what I'd expected of death.

Perhaps the puddle was a portal leading to the afterlife, or maybe this was a dream, frozen in time at the instant of my death. Oddly, I felt no fear, only curiosity. I walked closer to the puddle and peered into its depths. It sparkled like molten sapphire one moment then became so clear the hole seemed to have no water in it at all.

I got down on my knees and peered into the depths. The light seemed to come from far below, but when I cupped the water in my hands, it glowed with a light of its own.

"Welcome to the fount."

I should have jumped with surprise, but turned, calm and detached to face Moses. His black hair was short, his beard trimmed and neat, and his eyebrows groomed. "Why is your hair different from my dreams?"

He raised an eyebrow. "That's not the first question I expected."

"Yes, it is rather foolish, I suppose."

Moses smiled. "I can fashion my appearance as I wish."

"But you're dead."

He nodded. "My corporeal body is gone. I am in the afterlife."

I pinched myself again. "I'm dead."

Moses held out his hands to indicate our surroundings. "This is not the afterlife. This is what you might call the birthing chamber."

I blinked, confused. "The fount?"

"Yes, the first power, the primal fount." His lips compressed. "Some might even call it the source of life."

My eyes flared. "Is it god?"

Moses shrugged. "If the fount is sentient, it has remained silent on the matter."

I looked down at the puddle. "It's not what I expected."

"Ah, what you see before you is the earthly fount." He stepped beside me, knelt, and took some in a cupped hand. "The fount runs throughout everything, from Eden to the realms, and all the multiverse."

"So, this is just the fount on Earth?"

Moses seemed to flicker, like a ghostly vision, and faded ever so slightly.

"What's happening?" I asked.

"We don't have much time." He motioned me down next to him, so I knelt. "Put your hands in the fount."

I did as instructed and Moses scrubbed the scars on the backs of my hands until blood clouded the water. The water glowed brighter, and the crimson stain vanished. "You're not quite there yet, Conrad, but soon, very soon."

"Soon what?" I said.

"Focus your power here." He slapped my palms. "With these, you don't need a wa—"

Before he could finish, my insides burned in agony and a scream tore from my throat.

"Conrad!" I heard my name screamed over and over again, but it wasn't Moses calling me.

I looked up into the pale fury of the rift guardians. Bolts of energy speared into my palms, bursting from the backs of my hand and riveting me to the bridge. I finally realized I lay on my back where I'd fallen after Ambria blinked away. My veins seemed to run with fire. I screamed and screamed, unable to stop.

The pain vanished and a cry of agony died on my lips. The guardians hung over me, their azure energy calm and subdued. I sat up and saw frogres thudding across the bridge toward me. It took everything I had to push my heavy body upright. My legs dragged, nearly useless. There was no way I'd outrun the frogres.

Ambria blinked to me. She staggered, too dizzy from another blink to stand upright, and grasped my hand. "We'll blink together!"

But it was too late. A tongue lashed out and caught my leg, dragging me backward and Ambria along with me. "Let go!" I said.

"Never! I'll kill the bloody monster if I have to." Ambria drew her wand and fired, but the blasts only enraged the frog monster.

"No!" I shouted. "I won't die to one of my father's monsters!" Yet I was nothing but a fly struggling to escape the spider. There was nothing I could do.

My palms tingled. A jagged blue arc speared from my hand into one of the guardians. It glowed brighter, coming to life and zipped in front of me. I sensed a distant consciousness, as if something awaited my command.

I didn't understand how or why, but the guardian was responding to me. I held up a hand and felt a connection to the second one. A malicious smile split my lips. "Kill these damned frogres."

The guardians hummed like powerful generators. Destructive beams lanced from them, solar flares, spearing through flesh, slicing the tongue of the nearest frogre and sending its smoldering corpse over the side of the bridge. They tore into the next three monsters, reducing them to ashes.

When the final creature was dead, the guardians fell silent once more.

Ambria dragged herself over to me. "W-was that you?"

I nodded. "I don't need Cora. I can destroy Victus's entire army with these things!"

She wiped tears from her eyes. "I thought you died, Conrad! It looked like they vaporized you on the spot."

My forehead pinched. "Wait, what?"

"You were gone for several seconds. The guardians fired these beams into the bridge and then you reappeared." She shuddered. "What happened?"

"I saw Moses, and the primal fount—or at least the fount of Eden." I could hardly believe it had happened, but I told her everything. "Somehow he gave me control of the guardians. I'm going to take them out there and destroy the monster army."

Ambria kissed my cheeks, my lips even as tears dripped from the tip of her nose. "I love you, Conrad. I'm so happy you're not dead."

"Me too, but did you just hear what I said?"

She nodded. "Yes, I'm happy about the guardians, but life would be awful without you."

I sat up and unwrapped the frogre tongue from my jeans. Ambria helped me to my feet and we limped toward the crack leading to Queens Gate. The guardians trailed behind me like dogs on leashes. I felt my mind connect to the sentience inside the miniature stars.

"Go through the tunnel and wait for me on the other side."

Voices whispered at the back of my mind. *We are of the rift. In the rift we remain.*

My chest tightened. *But I need you to fight my enemies.*

We cannot leave the rift, the voices said in unison. *Here we must remain.*

My face must have fallen because Ambria's forehead pinched with concern. "What's wrong?" she asked.

"They can't leave the rift." I wanted to throw up my hands, but was too tired. "They can't fight the monster army."

She offered a tiny smile. "Well, I guess you need Cora after all."

I looked up at the guardians and sighed. "Why can't it ever be easy?"

Ambria chuckled. "I don't suppose we could trick Victus into bringing his army here?"

"I wish." I looked at the long expanse back to the other side and groaned. "I'm so tired, I don't know if I can make it back."

Ambria looked up at the guardians. "Maybe they can carry you."

I connected with them again. *Can you carry me back across?*

Energy laced around my arms and hoisted me into the air. Before I could say a word, the guardians flew across the rift at breakneck speed. I might have screamed if my throat hadn't locked up from fright. They deposited me gently on the other side and hovered nearby.

"Conrad, you left me!" Ambria waved from afar. I sent the guardians to get her. She shrieked when they lassoed her and brought her to me.

"Well, at least we've got this going for us," I said.

Ambria hugged me and sighed with relief. "It's so very strange."

I looked up at the pulsating orbs. *What's out there in the void?*

Other worlds. They spoke in cold, calm unison.

"Are you talking to them?" Ambria asked.

I nodded. "I want to know more about them."

Her eyes widened. "If the Glimmer anchors all the realms together, I wonder if we could reach Seraphina through the rift."

My hopes rose. "That's a wonderful idea." I sent the question to the guardians. *Can I reach Seraphina through the rift?*

You may reach the outer bounds.

You mean like the wall? I walked to the crack in the stars, the tunnel leading into the Glimmer, and patted it with my hand. *Like this?*

Yes.

I asked the next questions out loud so Ambria could hear. "How do I break through the outer bounds?"

We do not know.

"Can you take me to the outer bounds of Seraphina?"

If you know which one it is.

I threw up my hands and relayed the information to Ambria. "I'd have to know which one is Seraphina and figure out a way to break through the wall."

"Perhaps Cora knows how to locate each realm." Ambria pointed her finger straight up and drew a circle as if to draw the anchor stone. "After all, they orbit the anchor stone."

"I wonder if I could reach the realms by flying up to them with a broom." We'd theorized about it before, but had never tested it.

"For now, I suggest we take one thing at a time." Ambria took my hand and locked her eyes on mine. "Let's talk to Cora."

I nodded. "Yes, let's." I stretched my arms and legs. They felt every bit as heavy as they had moments ago. "I'll have to go slow." I looked up at the guardians. "I don't suppose you can heal me or give me more energy, can you?"

We guard.

I waited for more of an explanation, but none was forthcoming. "Okay. Don't let any monsters through here, but if you see Kanaan, he can come."

A vision of the magitsu master flashed into my mind's eye. *This man may pass.*

"Yes." I took Ambria's hand. "Let's go."

We entered the crack. The tunnel beyond was much larger than I remembered it. I ran my hand along the etches and grooves in the tunnel wall. "It looks like something dug at the walls."

"The tunnel on the Eden side looked the same way." Ambria knelt and picked up the tip of a broken claw. The greenish hue gave it away. "A frogre did this."

I found several more broken claws. "More than one." My stomach tightened. "How did frogres get over here?"

"Victus somehow got into the Glimmer during our quest for the Broken Relic." Ambria dropped the claw fragment. "Maybe he still has access."

"I was in the Glimmer only a year ago, and the tunnels didn't look like this." I sniffed the air for telltale signs of frogre stink, but only sensed a musty odor. "You saw what the guardians did to four of those monsters. How could any of them slip past?"

"Victus must have a piece of the anchor stone," Ambria said. "He used it to come through the reflected world and bypassed the guardians."

"But why?" The question might as well have been rhetorical, because I immediately knew the answer. "He planned to invade the Glimmer with his army."

"He'd be a fool to even try." Ambria slowed her steps to keep up with my leaden pace. "Cora controls every living thing in the Glimmer. Even ten thousand of Victus's monsters can't fight that."

We reached the end of the tunnel and stepped into what should have been a forest of crooked trees. Ravaged earth and ash met us. Piles of bones lay in rusting armor. A warhammer nearly the size of my body rested atop the crushed skull of a huge condor skeleton.

Ambria gasped. "This place is a graveyard."

"Victus invaded." I slowly climbed atop a boulder for a better view. The devastation continued for hundreds of yards in all directions. "Maybe this is why Cora blocked me out of the Glimmer. Maybe she didn't want me to see this. Or maybe she wanted to keep Victus out."

"Maybe." Ambria surveyed the damage from my side. "Victus's monsters didn't get very far."

The path we usually followed was gone, replaced by a trail of bones. In the distance, a giant tree bridge rose from the barren land. It arced out across the starry expanse and should have met another tree of the same size leading to the next land fragment. Instead, it ended in splintered wood.

"The bridge is destroyed." I slumped in defeat. "How are we supposed to reach Cora?"

The crooked peak of a mountain rose in the distance and above it hung a giant green moon—the anchor stone. Somehow, we had to reach that mountain.

"We'll find a way, Conrad." Ambria looked around. "Maybe the invaders had flying brooms or carpets. We should look."

I couldn't tear my eyes from the moon. "I hope so."

Sparkling like a crown of jewels, the various realms orbited the anchor stone, held together by its magical gravity. The aura of the moon granted immortality, but it also slowly robbed emotion. Evadora countered the effects of the moon with a bottle of emotions she harvested during her frequent visits to us at the university.

I wondered if she still had it, or if she'd succumbed.

I finally looked back at Ambria. "I don't know why frogres would have flying carpets, but let's look, just to be sure."

We wended our way through the maze of destroyed trees and charred bones, our progress considerably slowed by my exhaustion. I had to stop several times to rest, but Ambria didn't complain once. We found the bodies of mages and even the remains of several flying carpets, but they'd been shredded to ribbons.

We reached the base of the tree bridge, large enough to accommodate several city buses side by side. A small grove of crooked trees and the scaly red snake grass at the bottom of the tree bridge had survived the monster battle

I slumped beneath a tree, exhausted and defeated. "We have to go back to Eden and get a flying carpet."

"How will we get past the monsters waiting on the other side?" Ambria looked around, eyes pinched with worry. "There must be a working carpet here somewhere!"

Bark creaked. Sharp limbs speared the ground around us and in an instant, the crooked trees held us in a prison. Ambria drew her wand, but coils of snake grass gripped her arms and pinned them to her sides. More coils secured my arms against my ribs. Purple vines, their thorns glistening, snaked toward us. I knew from experience they would instantly put us to sleep.

Ambria struggled uselessly. "What's happening?"

I surrendered to the grass, too tired to make a fight of it. "We're Cora's prisoners." I smiled. "Maybe she'll come to us instead."

I felt a prick in my neck and the world faded to black.

CHAPTER 30

Something poked me in the chest. I blinked open heavy eyelids and found a teenaged girl standing over me. Long green hair framed huge amber eyes and silver skin. A gentle breeze brushed back the hair to reveal pointed ears. Her gossamer dress flowed around her like silken clouds.

Evadora looked so much older now. She was every bit as pretty as before, but a flat line replaced the girlish grin and the light in her eyes dimmed to a dull stare. The color of her eyes shaded darker until the irises turned greenish gray. "Conrad."

I swallowed a lump in my throat. Evadora's wild spirit had been tamed by the moon. "How are you, Evadora?"

"Mother told you not to return."

"Because of the battle?" I looked down and was surprised to find my arms and legs were free. Ambria was asleep. A vine thorn pressed against her neck told me it was not by choice. I stood and was surprised to find my legs had regained some strength. Physically, I felt much better than before the grass trapped us.

"Victus invaded." Evadora turned to face the ravaged land. "Many innocents died that day, so Mother decided closing the Glimmer to outsiders was best."

I reached out a tentative hand and touched her arm. Her usual feverishly warm skin was cool to the touch. "Do you still have your bottle?"

"Mother said it was time to forget the ways of the outside and focus on our needs." Evadora looked at my hand without a trace of emotion. "You feel warm. I do miss the warmth of the sun."

"I need to speak with Cora." I took her hand. "Can you take me to her?"

"No." Evadora pointed to a speck against the stars. "Mother comes to you."

I swallowed nervously. "She won't harm us, will she?"

A green eyebrow arched. "Why would she harm you?"

"I mean, she's not like Naeve now, is she?"

"She was Naeve before her reflection took her name." Evadora squeezed my hand ever so slightly. "But she does not go by any name but Mother now."

"Not even Glimmer Queen?" I asked.

"She cannot break the sleep spell Naeve put on the people," Evadora said. "Who is there for her to be queen of?"

I looked back at Ambria. "Can you wake her?"

The purple vine with the thorns withdrew. Ambria's eyes fluttered open. She yawned and flinched when she saw Evadora. "Oh my, Evadora, you've grown!"

Evadora tilted her head curiously. "Have we not all grown?"

"You're beautiful!" Ambria hugged her, but the other girl simply stood there. Ambria backed up a step. "You look so much like Cora."

I looked past the green hair, the silver skin, and the huge eyes and saw some resemblance to her mother. But it wasn't enough to immediately remind me of her.

A condor with the wingspan of a small jet plane appeared from the starry sky and screeched like some prehistoric creature. Its wings flared and it landed gracefully in a clearing free of broken trees and bones.

Cora walked down the bent neck of the condor, her flame orange hair flying in the wind, green eyes reflecting the twilight like those of a cat. She wore a simple white dress that reached to her ankles and barely moved in the wind. My breath hitched in my throat and it took all I had not to throw myself against her in a fierce embrace.

"You have returned, son." Cora took my hands in hers. "I ordered you to stay away, but it is good to see you." Her kind words lacked warmth and emotion. I wondered if she was trying to act as one might expect after the long absence of a loved one.

"Are you truly happy, or are you simply saying it?" I asked, still resisting the urge to hug her.

Cora's face remained impassive. "I am trying to remember how it felt, but even the memories of emotion fade to nothing in this place."

"You should come with me." I pointed in the direction of the crack. "Spend some time in Eden so you can remember."

"I think not." Cora let go of my hands and folded her arms. "Why did you come?"

"Victus is taking over everything in our realm. He's trying to kill me and my friends." I held out my hands imploringly. "Please, Cora, we need your help."

She held out a hand and waved it around the destroyed land. "So this can happen again? So innocent creatures can lose their lives at the whim of a madman?"

"Victus isn't mad." Ambria planted her fists on her hips. "He's building a massive monster army and once he's done with us, he'll come for you again."

"He desires a fragment of the anchor stone," Evadora said. "Immortality."

"Didn't he use an anchor stone fragment to get his army here through the reflected world?" I asked.

She shook her head. "His blond witch found a way to bridge the worlds with a portal." Evadora picked her way through the battlefield and motioned us to follow. She stopped at the edge of a dark pond, now filled with debris, and pointed to the outlines of a pattern burned into the very dirt itself. "We have never seen anything like it."

Ambria gasped, likely because she recognized the pattern just as quickly as I did. "That's the pattern from that sheet of human leather Kanaan took."

I shuddered. "It's a demon portal."

"But how did Victus get here to inscribe the diagram?" Ambria asked.

"He did not." Cora brushed at the pattern with her foot but like a stain, it refused to fade. "It simply appeared."

"That settles it then," I said. "You have to come with me and stop Victus before he invades again."

"I refuse." Cora turned away and looked at the giant moon. "If he sends another army, we will destroy it as before."

"At what cost?" I said. I waved an arm around. "Look at the devastation. You haven't regrown the vegetation and trees because you can't, right? The demon magic spoiled the earth."

Evadora's eyes flared slightly. "You are perceptive."

Cora faced me again, lips tight. "Yes, the demon portal fouled the land. It will be years before it can support life again." She pointed to the tree bridge. "The middle of the bridge was destroyed in the fighting. Even if he returns, he cannot cross to another island."

"If the demon portal operates anything like an omniarch, Victus has to have a clear picture of where he wants to go." I pointed to the fouled pond. "This is where he entered the Glimmer every time he visited. It's the place he visualized the best. That means if he comes back and takes pictures of other places, he could open a portal anywhere and destroy the land there. He doesn't have to cross the tree bridge."

"Then we will strengthen the defenses here," Cora said. "He will go no further."

"Why are you being so stubborn?" Ambria held out her hands as if she choked an invisible person. "Your son needs you, Cora! Eden needs you!"

"You may remain here as long as you wish, but I will not fight your wars." Cora started walking back toward her condor.

"What about you, Evadora?" I gripped her shoulder. "Will you help?"

She hesitated. A spark of emotion flickered in her eyes, but quickly died. "I promised Mother I would not leave her. I cannot break the promise now."

I'd come here knowing Cora might refuse to help, but I hadn't been prepared for the grim reality of it. I walked up behind her and grabbed her wrist.

She stopped and faced me. "Do not make this any more difficult, child."

I could threaten Cora, tell her I'd order the guardians to let Victus's monsters through. I could trick her into following me out into the rift so I could show her my control of the guardians and trap her outside the Glimmer. There were wicked ways I could try to bend her to my will. But if I had to do that, what would be the point of winning? I would only prove that I was as terrible as my father. Victory at any cost was not the answer.

I had one last card to play before I left with a broken heart.

"If you refuse me, you have no more love left in you." I choked back tears. "Your love forged me into the person I am today. You gave me strength when I had none and hope when everything looked hopeless. I loved you so much I journeyed to the ends of your world and recovered a relic to bring you back to life." She tried to speak, but I held up a finger. "I returned a mother to her daughter, and a kingdom to its ruler. Can you not even lift a finger to help me in my time of greatest need?"

A single tear trickled down her ivory cheek. Cora gasped, as if surprised by the tiniest spark of humanity left in her heart.

"Conrad risked everything for you, Mother." Evadora reached into the folds of her gown and produced a glowing bottle of frosted glass. "Can you not risk everything for him?"

"I told you to get rid of that thing," Cora said, voice trembling as she fought for control. "Why do you still have it?"

"To remember." Evadora uncorked it and held it out to Cora. The bottle shaded warm glowing red. "Drink and remember, Mother."

Cora stared at it for so long, I thought she would refuse. But like an alcoholic faced with a free drink, she snatched it and tipped it back. A single drop fell onto her tongue. A tiny smile cracked her hard lips. Her mouth softened, and the smile grew into a grin. Cora threw back her head and laughed until tears flowed down her cheeks. Then she gripped me in a tight embrace and held me until we both cried ourselves dry.

I looked up into the tear-stained eyes of Ambria. It appeared Evadora had taken a dose from her bottle as well because she wiped her wet cheeks.

"I will help you, Conrad." She walked over to the giant condor, removed a pouch hanging around its neck, and fastened the strap around her waist.

"How long will it take you to gather your creatures?" I asked. "We don't have a lot of time."

"I'm afraid getting them here is impossible," Cora said. "It would take me weeks to grow back something as massive as the tree bridge."

"What about mewlies and condors?" Ambria asked.

Cora nodded after a brief pause. "The mewlies, yes. The condors will not fit through the tunnel."

Evadora nodded. "I will come too."

Cora closed her eyes. Piercing shrieks echoed from far away. A black cloud rose on the distant horizon and swarmed our way. A single mewlie landed on Cora's shoulder and rubbed its feline head affectionately against her ear, fluttering its webbed wings for balance.

She opened her eyes. "The mewlies have agreed to help. They will follow us through."

I took Cora's and Evadora's hands. "Then let's go." I led them toward the tunnel.

Evadora ground to a halt. "Don't we need to go to the pond and jump into the reflected world?"

Cora arched her eyebrows. "I took your fragment of the anchor stone, so you couldn't have come that way, Conrad. How did you get here?"

"We went past the guardians." I tugged on their hands. "Come on and I'll show you."

Evadora released my hand and took another drink from her bottle. The frost around her emotions cracked and fell away. Her silver skin flushed pink. She clapped her hands and giggled. "Oh, it's been so long!" She spun in a circle, arms outstretched. "Running past the guardians is so exciting."

Cora's lips flattened. "It is strange seeing so much emotion after all this time."

Evadora held out her bottle. "Want some more?"

Her mother shook her head. "No. There will be time for emotions soon enough." Her hand tightened on mine. "Let's go, Conrad."

We entered the tunnel and walked through it to the cliff at the edge of the rift. The guardians hung a hundred feet away over the bridge.

"They're so close." Evadora's eyes flared. "Oh, this will make it much harder."

"Um, actually—" Ambria didn't have a chance to finish her sentence before Evadora raced for the guardians.

Let us all pass, I told them, just in case my earlier orders hadn't been clear enough.

Evadora blurred beneath them, dodging back and forth. She skidded to a stop and stared up at the unmoving orbs. "What's wrong with them?"

Come to me. I gestured at the guardians and they drifted over to me.

Cora's eyes widened. "What—how?"

I told her what had happened.

"Can they take me out into the rift?" Evadora dropped to her knees, hands clasped. "Please? Oh, please let me ride them into the rift!"

It was a relief to see her back to her unstable emotional self. Only moments ago, I'd feared her spirit lost to the emotion-draining aura of the anchor stone. "Maybe later. Right now, we have to get back into the Dark Forest and meet Kanaan."

"That's a weird name." Evadora skipped by my side. "Is he a monster or a man?"

"A man." Ambria clasped my free hand opposite from Cora. "Shushiel is there too."

"Oh, I love her!" Evadora pranced in circles around us as we crossed the long bridge, heedless of the invisible ledge.

The mewlies fluttered in a morphing cloud behind us, silent as ghosts.

Cora gazed at the charred corpses of the frogres killed by the guardians. "Will the guardians fight with us?"

"They can't leave the rift." I sent mental commands to the guardians to clear the bridge of the dead and they set about dragging the bodies into the void.

I stopped at the entrance to the tunnel leading back to the university. "We were chased in here. I don't know if anything is waiting out there."

Evadora dashed ahead. "I'll find out!"

"No, wait!" But she ignored me and vanished inside.

"Impetuous child." Cora shook her head. "I must admit it is good to see her acting carefree once again."

A question brewed at the back of my mind that worried me. "Cora, have you regained your full powers again?"

"I am not as mighty as I was centuries ago, but I have relearned much that was lost." She released my hand and patted the pouch she'd removed from the condor. "The vegetation in Eden is not nearly fierce enough to fight monsters. I have in here the seeds of everything that grows in the Glimmer."

I hadn't returned with an army, but I'd gained a mother, a sister, and a swarm of flying cats.

I hoped it was enough.

CHAPTER 31

Evadora returned by the time we reached the halfway point in the tunnel to the university. "There were a whole bunch of monsters out there." She giggled. "I ran around the big green ones and they chased me all the way out of the Fairy Gardens and into the big stadium. I lost them in the maze of rocks and came back."

"Did you see any giant birds?" Ambria asked.

Evadora shook her head. "No, but I wish I had. Do they look neat?"

"I wonder if Mirjana would help us fight," Ambria said. "We should go to the pond and ask her."

"She left months ago," Evadora said. "When I came for my last visit, she told me that everything changed for the worst at the university and her time there was at an end."

"I had no idea she left." Ambria sighed. "She wasn't wrong. Everything has changed for the worst."

"I suppose you should tell us everything that has happened," Cora said. "First, let us get into the Dark Forest." She motioned forward and the mewlies streaked ahead toward our goal.

"Agreed." Ambria stepped out of the tunnel and looked up at the cloudy skies. "I'm worried about the crows and that invisible assassin we encountered earlier."

"I'd nearly forgotten about him." The hairs on the back of my neck stiffened as if I were being watched. The nap I'd taken in the Glimmer had been quite restful, but I still wasn't back to a hundred percent. I reached for aether and was greeted by a nausea. It was a terrible time for another recovery phase, but at least I had three strong friends who could protect me.

We made our way through the decrepit mansion and into the fairy forest.

"Oh, they look so much better now." Evadora stopped and whispered to several trees. "You're my favorite. And you're my other favorite. Oh, I'll sing to you very soon!"

It was just like old times.

When we reached the other side, Evadora stopped and narrowed her eyes. "I found the invisible man!" Her eyes followed something. "Don't be sneaky. I see you."

"As do I," Cora said. "You cannot hide from the grass you walk upon, trickster."

Evadora dodged to the left. Flipped backward through the air. She gripped something and a silver blade appeared in her hand. The grass twisted up, grasping invisible limbs. Cora tossed a seed on the ground and a purple vine sprouted, its length covered in thorns. It wrapped around what looked like thin air.

The goat-faced man faded into view, eyes wide with fear. "Who are you?"

Cora showed her teeth in a fierce grin. "I am the Glimmer Queen."

The vine jabbed a thorn into the assassin's neck and he went limp.

"He's just asleep, right?" Ambria asked.

Evadora held the assassin's blade. "I can cut his throat if you like."

Ambria's face blanched. "I've killed in self-defense, but I don't know if I could kill a defenseless man like that."

"There is no need for callous murder," Cora said. "He will remain in a deep slumber until released."

"What if someone cuts the vine?" I asked.

"He will awaken after a time once the thorn is removed from his neck." Cora shrugged. "If he confronts us again, then he will die."

"Agreed," said another voice.

Evadora and Cora gasped and spun at the sound of the new voice.

Kanaan offered them a curt bow. "The way to the Dark Forest is clear."

Evadora's eyes lit with excitement. "How did you sneak up on us?"

"Is it stealth magic?" Cora asked.

"Ancient Chinese secret." Kanaan didn't crack a smile as usual, leaving it a mystery whether this was a joke or truth.

"Conrad spoke of you." Cora looked him up and down. "Thank you for training him and keeping him alive."

"He did well enough on his own," Kanaan replied.

We left the Fairy Gardens through the broken gates. Several times I thought I saw dark wings overhead and braced for an attack by giant crows, but none appeared.

I observed the low-hanging clouds. "It wasn't this cloudy when I left."

Kanaan opened a hole in the shield surrounding the forest. The cloud of mewlies funneled inside and vanished into the trees. "During your absence, I scouted the university and rescued several prisoners.

Professor Grace launched a weather potion into the sky to remove the advantage of a bird's-eye view."

"You rescued Gideon Grace?" Ambria's voice rose in surprise. "I didn't even know he was a prisoner."

"He's always hated me," I said. "I guess that's mostly because he hates my father."

"He fought their propaganda," Kanaan said. "Gideon Grace is rigid in his beliefs, so they locked him and other protestors in the Burrows."

I hadn't even thought about all the other professors that might be held against their will in the school. Without the foundry, Victus couldn't clone anyone else—at least not very easily, so he probably imprisoned anyone he couldn't control.

Ambria frowned. "Hold on a moment. You rescued a group of professors and changed the weather all in just a few hours?"

Evadora giggled. "Hours? You were asleep for two days." She took Ambria's hand and twirled her until the other girl staggered free. "Mother and I talked for a long time about what to do with you."

"Two days?" It seemed like we'd been gone only a few hours. "What else have we missed?"

"I will explain when we reach the caves." Kanaan closed the forest shield when everyone was through. "We must move silently and quickly to avoid detection from the creatures hunting the forest for us."

Shushiel dropped from a tree. "Evadora, it is so good to see you again!"

"My pretty spidey!" Evadora gripped her in a hug. "I haven't seen you in so long."

"Yes, too long." Shushiel rotated toward Kanaan. "Ishlish killed three cobalt assassins not far from here. We must be vigilant."

"Agreed." Kanaan set off at a brisk pace and the rest of us followed.

We passed the corpses of spiders, frogres, and other beasts Ishlish had terminated to clear our path.

Cora stopped to examine a dead frogre. Her lips peeled back in disgust when she touched the slimy green skin. "There is nothing natural about this beast. I had hoped I could exert some control over them, but Victus has thoroughly perverted them."

"What about the trees in this forest?" Ambria asked.

Cora touched the trunk of a massive oak. Like the other trees in the forest, it stood hundreds of feet high—far taller than any of its kind anywhere else. "The trees listen and speak, but they are too large and inflexible to be of use in a fight."

Kanaan put a hand on the trunk. "Can they tell you the locations of enemies?"

Cora's eyes narrowed in concentration. "Only a vague sense. The trees are unhappy with the clouds blocking the sunlight. They pay little attention to the creatures on the ground." She pointed south. "The trees several miles in that direction are uneasy about the large concentration of creatures threatening their roots."

"That's where the army is," Shushiel said.

Kanaan put a finger to his lips. "Something is nearby."

A cobalt spider the size of a dog thudded to the ground a few feet away. Its legs twitched then curled in upon itself. Ishlish dropped down a silken thread a moment later and perched on Kanaan's shoulder. She said something, but I couldn't hear her whispery voice from this distance.

Kanaan nodded. "We need to remain quiet for the rest of the trip."

We continued in silence and reached the ruby spider hideout an hour later. The caves set aside for humans hummed with activity. Gideon Grace's voice echoed down the corridor as he issued orders to the other refugees.

"No one put you in charge, Grace," Horace Moon shouted as we entered the common chamber.

Grace's lips twisted into a scowl when he saw me. "Edison."

I usually avoided confrontations with the man. After all, he was my professor and an adult. But not here. Not now. "I suppose you're going to blame me for my father's actions?"

"You should have been banned from the university the moment we discovered your true identity." He drew his wand. "How do we know you're not in league with your father?"

"The boy is not your enemy." Kanaan stepped into the room and all conversation stopped. "He has brought allies."

In the silence that followed, I realized I was supposed to introduce said allies. "Oh, this is Cora, the Glimmer Queen, and her daughter, Evadora."

Eleanor Beetle gasped. "My goodness. I have so many questions to ask about the Sundering. We absolutely must document everything in case we're all killed in the next few days."

Horace and some of the other professors began speaking among themselves, filling the room with a dull roar.

"Nonsense." Trask's voice cut through the chatter. "Our allies have no time for idle banter, and we have little enough time to plan for war as it is."

Feet pounded down one of the tunnels and Max burst into the room. "Conrad, you're alive!" He buried me in a hug before I could respond. "I thought for sure something awful happened to you."

Ambria huffed. "I suppose you don't care that I survived too?"

He rolled his eyes. "Of course I care." Max hugged her so tightly, her eyes bugged.

Galfandor strode up behind Max. He looked almost ashamed. "Conrad, I am so sorry about Paris."

I held up a hand to stop him. "It wasn't your fault. When did you rejoin the others?"

"I laid low in Paris for several days," Galfandor said. "When I felt certain no one followed me, I took a train back to rejoin the others in Italy."

Max nodded. "Yeah, he got there right when we were getting ready to leave with Gwyneth."

"Is she here?" I asked.

"No." Max spread his fingers and hands apart in a poof gesture. "She got us to the omniarches in Thunder Rock and vanished. I think she was sneaking around behind Underborn's back to help us out."

Another argument broke out among the professors as Gideon Grace tried to bend them to his will. Galfandor huffed and broke up the fight. "People, we must cooperate if we're to survive."

Max watched them for a moment then blew out a sigh and turned back to us. "I thought for sure you guys were dead when they told me you'd been gone two days."

Ambria put her hands on her hips. "Maxwell Tiberius, did you really think Cora would hurt us?"

"I thought the guardians zapped you," Max looked back and forth between me and Ambria. "What happened?"

I hardly knew where to start. "Before we get into that, did Percival finish the potion?"

Max flashed a grin. "Yeah. Percival has it ready but he didn't want to give it to Ivy and Nightliss until we had a place to stay for a while."

My nerves tightened. "Have they taken it?"

"Right after we got here a few hours ago." His grin faded. "Nightliss went into convulsions like Purah. She's asleep now."

I put a hand on his shoulder. "And Ivy?"

Max shrugged. "She just went to sleep. Percival figures since she's so young it won't take her long to recover." His eyes filled with misery. "And she probably won't like me anymore."

Ambria patted his arm. "It's okay, Max. At least you got to be friends with one of your heroes." She smiled. "How many people can say that?"

"I know." He looked down. "I just wish it could be more."

"Speaking of which." I cleared my throat uneasily. "Ambria and I are—"

Max's eyes brightened. "Are you two finally together?"

Ambria's forehead pinched. "How did you know?"

"Duh." Max grinned. "I mean, you share a bond going all the way back to the orphanage. And the way Ambria always looked at Conrad, I just knew it would happen."

Ambria's lips peeled back in horror. "Was it so obvious even you could see it?"

Max snorted. "I'm not that blind, Ambria Rax."

"It's Max!" Evadora skipped over from wherever she'd been, grabbed his hands, and danced in a circle until they were both dizzy.

Max pulled away. "Please, I'm about to fall over!"

Evadora ruffled his platinum locks. "You're so cute, Max." She kissed him on the lips and giggled. "I just want to eat you up."

He cringed backward. "Not literally, I hope."

Evadora burst into laughter. "No, I don't eat humans." She took another drink from her emotions bottle and hummed to herself. "I'm so happy I could just scream!"

Cora stood by impassively watching her daughter dance around the room. "Dangerous times," she said. "But this place fills me with warmth."

Max snorted. "A cave full of giant spiders and refugees?"

"Yes." A tiny smile lit her face. "I remember why I left the Glimmer in the first place, all those years ago. If only I could recall more about my past."

"Do you remember much about us?" I was so frightened of the answer I could hardly ask the question.

"Bits and pieces," Cora said. Her eyes saddened. "What little I remember is very dear to me."

I cleared my throat to get rid of the lump. "Let's go check on Nightliss and Ivy."

"Those names sound familiar," Cora said. "I recall images of a young man and a flying ship for some reason."

"I've seen the very same thing before!" I strained my memory, but couldn't connect the images to anything. "I think the man is Justin Slade. I met him when I was little, but my memory is cloudy thanks to whatever Victus did to me as a child."

Max led us down a tunnel to a room far from the commotion in the main chamber. Percival sat in a leather divan reading a romance novel, tears in his eyes. "Damn you, Jeffrey. Can't you see Melinda loves you?"

I cleared my throat. Percival jerked his gaze up to us. "Just when I finally find time to catch up on my favorite series, you all burst in here like a pack of wild dogs." He groaned and bookmarked his novel. "I see you and Miss Rax returned safely from your journey to the Glimmer."

"Yes." I nodded. "I just wanted to check on your patients."

"You're wasting your time." Percival jabbed a thumb toward a curtained area. "They're asleep back there and I don't think they'll wake until later today or tomorrow. I suppose it doesn't matter to you that good medicine can't be rushed."

"What exactly was wrong with them?" Cora asked.

Percival blinked a few times as if just seeing her for the first time. "And you are?"

Ambria smiled wickedly. "The Glimmer Queen."

Percival paled. "Oh, goodness." He glared at me. "Why didn't you tell me I was in the presence of royalty?" Before I could answer, he bowed to Cora. "Greetings, Your Highness."

Cora frowned uncertainly. "Greetings, healer. What can you tell me?"

Percival straightened. "Well, Your Highness, their memories were blocked by magical manipulation of neurons. It also inhibited them from channeling magic." He picked up a small vial. "This potion repairs the damaged neurons and removes the blocks."

Cora bit her lower lip. "Do you think it could repair memory loss incurred from death and resurrection?"

The healer blinked several times, a blank expression on his face. "I have no idea." He stood and paced for a few moments then faced Cora. "Tell me the exact circumstances."

"I do not remember exactly," Cora said.

I knew the details from Naeve, so I told him. "When Cora first left the Glimmer, she used the reflected world to escape. Her reflection caught her and stole part of her soul. Cora died of cancer in Eden, but since she wore a piece of the anchor stone on a necklace, her soul went to the Soul Tree in the Glimmer."

"Yes, makes perfect sense," Percival said in a tone that indicated it sounded like complete nonsense.

"We captured Naeve and took her to the Soul Tree. I used the Heart of Jura to mend the soul back together within Naeve's body." My voice filled with emotion as I recalled the instant my dear Cora came back to me. "When her soul reunited, it erased Naeve and restored Cora."

"Simple," Percival said. "Our reflections in the reflected world are exact reverse copies of us, but without souls. You brought this woman back into a body that is the mirror image of herself. Her memories are completely out of alignment."

"So her body is backward?" Max asked.

"It's reversed." Percival held up his hands. "In other words, her neurological pathways need minor adjustments so her soul can align with it."

"In other words, your potion won't work," Max said.

"For once, Mr. Tiberius, you are correct." Percival bowed slightly to Cora. "If you would allow me to run some diagnostics, I will see if I can help."

Cora's eyes glistened. "I would be very grateful."

I left her with Percival so I could catch up Kanaan with our latest adventure. I told him about my conversation with Moses and my new relationship with the guardians. I also described the destruction in the Glimmer and the demon portal Victus used to send his troops through.

"This is momentous," Kanaan said in his understated manner. "Once you have recovered, you must overexert yourself again. It is imperative you tap your true potential."

"Is that wise?" Ambria asked. "He needs to conserve his strength in case Victus's monster army finds us."

Kanaan silently stroked his beard for a moment. "In truth, even with Cora and Evadora, Ivy and Nightliss, there is little hope we can defeat his forces."

CHAPTER 32

M y stomach knotted. "We risked our lives to go to the Glimmer for nothing?"

Kanaan shook his head. "I had hoped Cora would bring her own army of creatures to even the odds."

"Hang on a minute," Max said. "Ivy could annihilate all of Victus's monsters."

Ambria rolled her eyes. "Max, you need to take her down off that pedestal and get realistic." She turned to Kanaan. "Can we use that demon portal you stole to our advantage?"

"Out of the question." Kanaan's expression grew grim. "The portal opens a tunnel through Haedaemos. It allows physical beings to travel through the realm of spirits. But without the protection of a powerful demon, any who go through would be at great risk."

"How did Victus use it to reach the Glimmer, then?" I asked.

"I think we know the answer," Ambria replied. "He's a heavy user of demon magic. Surely he has friends in the netherworld."

"A demon lord at the very least," Kanaan said. "Considering the complex design of the last foundry, I suspect a demon overlord."

"Is that the highest rank?" Max asked.

He shook his head. "Baal is the grand overlord of Haedaemos. Few approach him in power." His eyes narrowed. "Even a single overlord might struggle to keep an entire army safe during its passage through Haedaemos. He may have more than one working with him."

"Would Baal have any problems moving an army?" I asked.

Kanaan pursed his lips. "None at all."

"Hold on." Ambria snapped her fingers. "This demon portal can go anywhere in any realm? Could we reach Seraphina through it?"

"As with an omniarch, we would need a clear image of the destination." The magitsu master folded his arms across his chest. "And then we would need to make it through the demon tunnel with our souls intact."

"Have you ever used a demon portal before?" Ambria asked.

Kanaan waved aside the question. "It is not worth the risk."

"Then how are we supposed to win?" I threw out another possibility. "Maybe it's worth the risk to at least try to reach Justin Slade. He's Daemos. Maybe he can negotiate passage through Haedaemos."

"Daemos are not the same as demons," Kanaan said.

Max shuddered. "Yeah, we'd die for sure."

"Then what's the point of all this?" I ran a hand down my face. "If we don't have a chance, then maybe we should just go to Bermuda and wait on Voltis to align with Eden."

"Meanwhile, Victus spawns more monsters, rebuilds the foundry, clones more people, and entrenches himself," Ambria said. "And if we reach Seraphina and find Aerianas in control instead of Justin Slade, our chances of victory will be zero."

Ambria was right. Kanaan was right. Only one other variable remained. "Kanaan, if I'm able to use the first power, will that give us a chance?"

"In truth, I do not know," Kanaan said.

A man screamed. Shouts thundered through the tunnels. We raced toward the source and found several professors standing around the charred remains of a cobalt spider.

"It came from nowhere," Gilbert said.

Horace Moon clenched his wand as if the dead arachnid might awaken at any moment. "There was another one but it got away."

"Which direction?" Kanaan said.

The food director pointed down one of the many tunnels leading out of the chamber. Several of us followed it through a honeycomb of chambers. Most were dead-ends, but some continued on seemingly forever.

Kanaan called a halt after a while. "There is too much to search." He headed back to the main chamber.

I was glad he knew which turns to take because I felt completely lost. "Shushiel told us these tunnels went on for miles."

Cora put a hand on the tunnel wall. "So much dead rock and no place to plant a seed."

"You cannot grow vines here?" Kanaan said. "We may need defenses soon."

"Unless you can crush this stone to dirt, no." Cora brushed off her hands. "Once the roots take hold, they can burrow into the rock. We would have to import dirt from aboveground."

The ruby spiders were on full alert when we returned. Shushiel scurried over to us. "The cobalts must have found another entrance to the network of tunnels. Now that they have found us, it will not take long for more to come."

Any spark of hope I'd had puffed out like a candle in the ocean depths. "Should we evacuate?"

"We have no choice," Shushiel said. "It may already be too late."

"Maybe we could retreat into the underground forest," Ambria said.

My forehead tightened. "The one with the giant insects? That would be suicide."

"No one told me about an underground forest," Max said. "Does it really have giant bugs?"

"Retreating into the Dark Forest would be suicide," Horace said. "At least here we have bottlenecks and wouldn't have to face the entire army."

Kanaan nodded. "A wise observation against a conventional enemy. Victus has an omniarch. If the escaped cobalt can give him an image of the cavern, they can open a portal anywhere."

I turned to Shushiel. "Is that possible?"

"Spiders have eight eyes and excellent memory." She sagged. "The cobalt spider is capable of opening a portal with the omniarch."

"Then we're doomed." Max leaned against the wall. Eaten by giant insects or murdered by giant spiders. What a choice."

"Hold on." I took Cora's hand and led her into the main cavern with the glowing lake and the chasm leading to the underground forest. "Can you sense the bugs down there?"

She narrowed her eyes in concentration. Shook her head. "There is only dead rock between us and the place below. I cannot grow a vine down the side because of the rock."

"There's glowing fungus growing all over this place," I said. "If it found a place to take root, can't a vine?"

"I will try." Cora pursed her lips. "Do you wish me to request help from the insect kingdom?"

"Yes. Can you?"

Cora walked to the lake and put a hand in it. A school of bright green fish swam up and nibbled on her fingers. She laughed. "Oh, you are too kind."

I looked over the side at the pinpoint of glowing water far below. "Maybe you could drop a seed into the lake down there and it'll grow."

"Fungus can cling to bare rock and flourish," Cora said. "A vine needs soil to take root. I cannot tether myself to the forest below without a direct connection." She removed some seeds from her pouch and gave it to a fish. The school darted away and leapt over the side into the chasm. "My new friends promised to drop the seeds where they can grow."

"Can those purple vines grow that long?" I asked.

She smiled. "Oh, this is a special sort of vine."

Kanaan stood at the edge of the lake watching silently. I wondered if his stomach clenched like mine at the thought of Victus's army pouring in here.

"Hey, guys." Max ran over to us, pulling a giggling Evadora after him. "I came up with another idea."

Ambria looked at him expectantly. "Well, spit it out Max!"

"The tragon!"

Evadora jumped up and down, giggling. "I'm going to find the biggest monster of them all!"

"Can you actually talk to that thing?" I said.

"I can try." She twirled around. "Oh, may I, Mother?"

Cora nodded. "Yes, but be—"

Evadora blurred away before she could finish her sentence.

"Careful." Cora sighed. "She was so much easier to handle without emotion."

"Max, are you insane?" Ambria broke into a smile. "Because that idea is crazy good."

"Huh?" Max scratched his head. "Was that a compliment?"

"I just hope Evadora can control it." Ambria turned to me. "Do you have any of Victus's memories of the tragon?"

"Probably. I'll take a look." I closed my eyes and searched for references to the tragon. The memories came in flashes.

Victus discovers the preserved flesh of an earth dragon killed in an ancient war. Using science and magic, he molds it with the DNA of a Tyrannosaurus Rex. He nurses the fetus to life in a birthing chamber. The tiny tragon is born. Pride swells in Victus's chest.

"You are my greatest creation," he says.

The tragon grows exponentially. Despite Victus's best efforts, the creature will not bond to him. It will not obey. When it is barely a month old and six feet tall, the tragon attacks Victus because it is out of food.

"I freed you of instinct and gave you intelligence!" Victus shouts at the caged beast. "Or did I fail even at that?"

The tragon hisses and lunges at him. It strikes against the bars over and over again, almost as if it doesn't understand that it cannot reach its prey. Ego bruised, choking on disappointment, Victus sedates the beast and banishes it to the Dark Forest. Perhaps one day he will try to tame it again.

"I will learn from this mistake and persevere." Victus stares at his marvelous creation for a long time before turning and heading back to the university.

I snapped from the memories. "Victus tried to make it intelligent, but it didn't work. He was never able to control it."

"Let's hope Evadora can woo it to our side," Ambria said.

A distant rumbling shook loose chips of rock from overhead. I grabbed Ambria and pulled her away from the edge of the chasm. "What's happening?"

Kanaan raised an eyebrow. "Interesting."

Unafraid, Cora peered over the lip into the pit. "Ah, my little fishies did their job."

Stalactites broke free from the cave roof and plunged into the lake. Fish scattered and confused cries rose from the people in the cave beyond. Within minutes, a monstrous black stalk sprouted from within the chasm and rammed into the rocky ceiling. Dust and gravel showered down. Smaller vines spread in all directions, roots burrowing into the rock. Stems reached from the trunk, arcing out to bridge it to the cave floor.

I stared in awe at the giant vine. Reached out a finger and touched the smooth bark of one of the stems. "I never saw one of these in the Glimmer."

"Giant beanstalks were a staple crop in the Glimmer at one time." Cora stroked a leafy stem. "I have not grown one in centuries."

Max recovered his wits. "Did you ever give one to a fellow named Jack?"

Cora frowned. "I do not remember."

"Can you sense the bugs now?" I asked.

She pressed a hand to a vine bridge. Her eyes flared. "There are so many, I can hardly discern which is which."

Ambria tapped my shoulder. "I can tell you that frogres will have no problems fighting giant crickets. We need something a bit deadlier."

"I cannot do this from here." Cora walked across a vine bridge to the beanstalk. "I must go below."

I tried to grab her and missed. "But we need something now!"

"I know, son." Cora blew me a kiss, gripped a vine, and leapt over the side. She vanished into the darkness a heartbeat later.

Shushiel rubbed a foreleg on my arm. "Galfandor led the professors to block off the tunnels just beyond their chambers. That should keep out other scouts."

"It won't stop a portal though." I imagined the cobalt spider scurrying through the forest to reach Victus. "How long would it take you to reach the underground mansion if you ran as fast as you could from here?"

"Nearly three hours," she replied. "I could not run the entire way, so it would take longer."

"Victus would have to get his troops to the omniarch in the first place," Ambria said. "I can't imagine him moving that many monsters very quickly."

Kanaan stroked his beard. "Even now, I suspect more cobalt spiders search for other ways in. They will discover tracks leading to the hidden entrance. Victus will march his forces here and break inside. Battle mages will portal within while the frogres attack from without. We will be crushed in between."

Ambria's mouth fell open. "That's horrific."

"The hilltop with the secret entrance is defensible," Kanaan said. "I believe the ruby spiders can defend it while Galfandor and the professors set up wards in here to prevent an internal assault."

"What if Cora fails?" Max said. "What if Evadora doesn't come back with the tragon?"

A flash of blond hair blurred into the cave. Ivy Slade slid to a halt in front of us, a fierce grin on her face. "Look who's back." Sizzling white orbs formed in her hands. "I'm ready to blow up some bad guys."

Max pumped a fist in the air. "Yes!"

Ivy grabbed the front of his shirt and pulled him close for a long kiss.

When she let go, Max staggered on his feet like a drunk. She smirked. "You're my hero, Max."

"M-me?" He rubbed his eyes. "What did I do?"

She nodded and me and Ambria. "All of you are my heroes. Thank you for saving me, and thanks for getting me back to normal."

"It was a team effort," Ambria said. "Kanaan, Percival"—she waved a hand around the room—"all of us had a hand in it."

"How do you feel?" Max asked.

Ivy spread her hands and summoned a miniature sun between her palms. "Amazing."

I backed away from the intense heat washing over me. "Well, that looks amazing."

Ivy dropped her hands and the sphere faded. She looked at me. "I remember fighting your dad and his monsters. I remember seeing his body and thinking it was all over. I started looking for a way to get my brother back from Seraphina, but no one knew how to repair the Grand Nexus." Her shoulders drooped. "A stranger contacted me and told me he had information." Her eyes glowed white. "A man named Cumberbatch."

Max groaned. "Is that how they got you?"

She nodded. "I don't know how he did it, but he knocked me out. The next thing I remember is waking up to you guys."

"Is Nightliss recovered yet?" I asked.

Ivy shook her head. "Percival says it'll take longer for her."

"Well, we need you now," Max said. He caught her up on the events of the past few hours. "We've got to hold off the bad guys until Evadora and Cora get back, hopefully with reinforcements."

Ivy looked with wonder at the huge beanstalk. "Cora grew that thing in just a few minutes?"

"Yep." Max tested one of the vine bridges with a foot. "Seems pretty sturdy."

I turned to talk to Kanaan but he'd vanished. He emerged from a tunnel with Shushiel and the soldier spiders a moment later, and they headed up the corridor to the secret entrance. I walked toward him. "Let's find out where we're needed."

Kanaan saw us approaching and waited for us to reach him. He nodded at Ivy. "I see you are back on your feet."

"And ready to go." Ivy flexed her arm. "Just point me toward the bad guys."

"I believe Galfandor and the professors can defend against portals inside. The rest of you should help the rubies set up a perimeter." Kanaan glanced at me. "Are you rested enough to cast?"

I aetherated and felt only the tiniest twinge of nausea. Two days of uninterrupted sleep had helped "Yes."

"I will join you once I confirm the caverns are secured." Kanaan turned and marched away.

My stomach twisted in knots. We were about to fight a huge battle against impossible odds, unless Cora and Evadora came through fast.

"I can't believe this is happening," Max said. "I've never fought in a war before."

"I've fought in a lot of them," Ivy said. "This one time, Justin and I rode a flying carpet and blew up a goliath. The trick is to blow up their power gems."

"We don't have any decent flying carpets," Max said. "We'll be on foot."

"It's frightening." Ambria shivered. "This will be an onslaught, Conrad. We might die in the first five minutes."

Max groaned. "You're really killing my confidence. We can't go into this thinking we're gonna die. We've got to come up with a way to survive until Cora and Evadora come back."

"I hope they come back soon." I tried to loosen the knots in my chest and stomach, but I was too scared. Fighting Victus one-on-one seemed simple compared to holding off an army of cobalt spiders, frogres and other monsters. Unfortunately, it was something we had to do.

We walked up the tunnel and outside. A ruby soldier dragged the corpse of a cobalt spider down the hill a little way and left it there.

"The cobalts already found the entrance?" I asked.

"I'm afraid so," Shushiel said. "We fought off several of them when we came outside."

The ruby commander, Ush, clacked the bangles on his forelegs and the soldiers scurried down the hill a few hundred feet in all directions and began webbing the trees.

"Can we help?" I asked.

Shushiel twisted side-to-side. "Not right now. We will block off the hilltop and hope it is enough to keep the enemies at bay for a little while. I hope the message I sent to our people reached them."

I climbed up the stony peak above the entrance to the caves for a better view. The forest looked clear for now, but I suspected that would change shortly. Ivy, Max, and Ambria joined me.

A large glowing sphere rose from the trees and arced toward us. It looked like a ball of glass filled with sizzling energy.

"Holy smokes, it's a crucible!" Ivy shouted. "Everyone take cover!"

The crucible crashed onto the hilltop a hundred yards away. Ivy channeled a shield of Murk around us an instant before a blast of wind bent over the treetops and showered the area with rubble and dust.

The battle had begun.

CHAPTER 33

A breeze cleared the dust cloud and revealed a deep crater where the crucible hit.

"It missed us by a mile," Max said.

"No, it didn't." Ambria pointed straight down. "The corridor leading to the caves passes right underneath us." Another crucible arced out over the trees and headed toward the same spot. "They're trying to blow a hole in the top of the cave!"

Ivy maintained a shield and another shockwave washed over it. "They're going to kill everyone inside."

Trask and Beetle staggered out of the cave entrance, coughing violently. More professors rushed outside. Another crucible streaked over the trees and I realized what Victus meant to do—smoke us out of the cave and into the open.

"It hasn't been nearly three hours," I said. "How did they get here so fast?"

Ambria slapped a palm to her forehead. "The cobalt spiders must have communication pendants or something similar."

"Ugh." Max watched the incoming crucible with dread. "That spider probably told them where we were an instant after it escaped."

The crucible slammed into the hilltop. Professors cried out and shielded themselves from heat and dust.

I saw Percival, Galfandor, and most of the others, but two people were missing. "Kanaan and Nightliss aren't here."

"They'll be trapped inside or killed," Max said.

I tapped Ivy's shoulder. "Open the shield."

A narrow opening formed and I slid through it. "Keep them protected."

The shield closed my friends back inside.

"Conrad, where are you going?" Ambria said.

"Stay here. I'm going to help Kanaan." I looked at Ivy. "Don't let her out, okay?"

Ivy looked back and forth between us. "Sure thing, Conrad."

"Let me out of here!" Ambria banged on the shield. "Conrad, get back here right now!"

I ignored her pleas and slid down the rocky slope. Dust filled the tunnel leading inside, so I cast a wind spell ahead of me to clear my vision. I dodged past rubble and over large chunks of ceiling that had fallen. Debris littered the main cavern. It seemed the beanstalk and its network of vines was the only thing holding up the cracked and crumbling cave ceiling. The tunnel leading to the human living quarters was completely blocked off.

I stared at it for a moment. The cave shook with another impact. I scrambled out of the way of falling stones and cast a shield overhead while I wracked my brain for ideas.

"Brute force isn't always the answer." But what was? I couldn't physically move most of the large rocks jamming the tunnel. Cutting through the shattered stone with Fireblade would have no effect. I needed a bull-dozer but couldn't magically conjure one.

Or could I? I wove my wand through several complex patterns and cast the strongest shield spell I knew. But I didn't cast it in front of me. I cast it inside the blockage as a thin wall. Resistance formed in the back of my mind, the physical weight of the rock pressing down on the tiny shield. I focused everything I had on that small presence. In a burst of energy, I willed it to push toward me.

Stone and dust exploded from the tunnel mouth. I shouted in alarm and dodged to the side as my spell worked better than expected. The shield wall scraped the tunnel clean and shot past me before fading away to nothing.

I wiped the sweat from my forehead and headed inside. I cleared another blockage and the next before I found Kanaan with an unconscious Nightliss slung over his shoulder. He raised an eyebrow when he saw me. "How did you get through the cave-ins?"

"I scraped them out with a shield."

Kanaan blinked. "You removed tons of stone with a shield?" He sounded as if he didn't believe me.

"Yes." I cringed as the tunnel shook again. "Can we go now?"

"Of course." The magitsu master strode down the tunnel ahead of me.

Cloudy skies showed through cracks in the ceiling of the main cavern. I wanted to run to the beanstalk and call out for Cora, but it would do me no good.

The impacts had been so evenly spaced, that I found myself bracing for the next hit in advance as we made our way up the rubble-strewn tunnel to the exit. But the next hit didn't come.

"It seems like no matter what plan we make, Victus comes up with something completely different." I used another shield spell to smooth out a pile of rocks ahead of us. "How are we going to beat him?"

Kanaan shook his head. "We can only try our best."

For the first time, Kanaan sounded completely defeated. The only other time he'd sounded anything like this was when he squared off against Garkin and nearly lost. At that moment, I wanted to get my friends and slide down the beanstalk to the underground forest where we'd take our chances against the giant bugs.

I didn't want to give Victus the pleasure of killing us himself.

I took a deep breath and let the moment pass. My hands trembled and my body shook. Oddly, it wasn't fear that gripped me, but rage.

Victus is going to win. He killed my mother and hundreds, maybe thousands of other people. He tricked Justin Slade into exile. *He's evil. He's corruption.* I could not run away from that vile man. Somehow, I had to stop him.

A small aether generator projected a shield outside to protect our meager forces from debris. But no more crucibles came.

"He could kill us all with one well-placed strike," Grace said. "What's he waiting for?"

A silver line sliced the air and spread into an oval portal a few feet away from us. Victus, flanked by Garkin, Zarin, and the wandslinger, Talbot stood on the other side. I recognized the omniarch room near the underground mansion. A shield shimmered in front of them.

An oily smirk spread across Victus's lips. "Hello, son."

I was so angry I could barely speak. "Victus."

"You've had it rough these past few weeks, haven't you?" Victus's eyes flicked to Kanaan and the unconscious Nightliss. "You took things that didn't belong to you."

"People don't belong to you."

Ivy ran toward me, but I held out a hand to stop her before she came into view of the portal. I didn't want Victus to know she was here.

"If one of your friends is trying to sneak up so he can hit me with a spell, I want you to know that I will order another crucible launched, but this one will land right on top of you."

Ivy scowled, but held her ground, outside the range of the portal.

"What do you want?" I asked.

"I'll make it simple, son." Victus pointed at me. "I want you. In return, I'll let your friends live out their natural lives. I know you won't willingly join my side, but I have ways of making you a little more flexible."

"By corrupting me with demon magic." I bared my teeth. "And if I don't, you'll kill us all with a crucible."

"That's one possibility." He shrugged. "I also have an army that could kill everyone except you, and you'd still be mine. So really, you don't have much of a choice either way."

"Don't do it, Conrad." Ambria grabbed my arm. "Please don't go."

"Innocent love. How precious." Victus's smirk returned. "Your little girl-friend can come with you if you'd like."

I was about to reject his offer, but as I looked around at Max, Ambria, and the weary faces, I realized that saying no would sign their death warrants. But could I trust Victus to keep his word?

No.

He would hunt his enemies to the ends of the earth once he had me in his thrall, and he'd probably use me to do it. I only saw one opportunity with his offer, and it wasn't much. *I might be able to buy some time.*

I looked down and slumped my shoulders in defeat. "Can I have an hour to think about it?"

"I'll give you fifteen minutes," Victus said. "Say your goodbyes and kiss your girl, because in fifteen minutes either you leave, or they die."

"Fifteen minutes?" Before I could argue, the portal winked away.

Ambria gripped my arm. "Conrad, I'd rather die than let you go with them."

"Me too," Max said.

Several professors started arguing.

"I want to live." Gilbert's trembling voice rose above the uproar. "Make the boy go to his father."

"If I die, who will record this historic battle?" Beetle said.

Horace Moon growled. "You'd sacrifice a boy for a history book?"

"Quiet!" Gideon Grace's shout silenced the arguments. He glared at me. "Whether the boy goes or stays, we die." He turned the glare on the others. "Do you think for one moment Victus Edison will honor his word? Remember the deeds of the Overlord and be very afraid."

Gilbert gulped. "Oh, god. We're cornered like rats. He'll kill us all."

"We're doomed!" Beetle declared.

Another argument consumed them.

A frustrated shriek cut through the chatter. Ivy Slade conjured a blazing sphere between her hands. "They can try to kill us, but I'll take ten times more down with me."

Down the hill a distance from us the tops of the trees began to sway. Everywhere I looked, a sea of blue spiders leapt from tree to tree. A wall of green tromped on the ground below. A black cloud of giant crows lifted in the distance and flew above the clouds. Guttural shouts rose from the north. Human torsos crudely spliced to buffalo bodies trotted toward the base of the hill. Behind them came elephants with small wings and reptilian scales. Fire blasted from their trunks.

The monster army stopped at the base of the hill as my fifteen minutes ticked down.

Nightliss stirred. "Oh, my head hurts."

"Well, you've woken just at the right time to die," Percival said. He helped Nightliss to her feet. "As you can see, we're doomed."

"What?" Nightliss's eyes seemed to lose focus. "I remember everything. The war. The next war. The crystoid war."

"Welcome to the monster war," Ivy shouted from the crest of the hill. She held out a hand. "You ready to fight again?"

Nightliss stared at her hands as if they belonged to a stranger. An ultra-violet orb flickered into existence. It grew larger until it enveloped her hand all the way to the wrist. She flattened her palm and thrust it outward. The Murk flattened into a wall. She curled her fingers and the shield curved with them.

"I hate to rush you, but we only have eight minutes left until Victus attacks us," Percival said. "Would you like an aspirin?

Nightliss's gaze locked on me. "What has happened, Conrad?"

Her sudden question caught me off guard. "Victus wants me to join him. If I refuse, he'll attack. If I agree, he'll let everyone live."

"Victus is a liar," Ivy said. "He'll kill us no matter what."

"I know. But Cora and Evadora aren't back, and we're almost out of time." I scanned the horizon but saw only enemies. "We can't possibly hold out."

I felt a strange sensation at my back, as if the air pressure changed ever so slightly. Hands gripped me. Ambria screamed and lunged for me. Ivy shouted a warning. The scene warped as if viewed through a bubble and then vanished, replaced by an omniarch in a small room.

I ducked from the grasp of my captor, rolled across the floor and turned. Talbot sneered down the tip of his wand at me. Victus, Garkin, and the others weren't there.

"Damn, that was easy." Talbot chuckled. "Oh, the look on your face, boy."

I stood slowly, easing to the right so the omniarch stood between us. "Where's Victus?"

"Oh, he's just down the tunnel from here," Talbot said. "He thinks you're going to join him so your friends can live, so he went to fetch one of his demon dolls." He shrugged. "After tracking you for so long, I know better. You don't trust your father a bit, and for good reason."

I put up my hands. "Congratulations. You got me." I sensed high concentrations of aether all around me, tickling my hair like static electricity. Talbot had left the circle around the omniarch closed. Unfortunately, if I couldn't reach my wand, all that aether was useless.

The sneer darkened into a scowl. "Damned straight, boy. I don't care about the bounty anymore. You got my sister killed."

"She got herself killed."

He shook his head. "This hunt is over, and I'm gonna make you suffer. Your father can have your bloody corpse when I'm done."

For once, I wished my father was nearby. "Just going to kill me in cold blood? No chance for a fair fight?"

"The time for that is long past." He aimed his wand. "Let's see—should I blow off your kneecaps, or your hands first?"

There was no way I could draw my wand in time. Talbot would kill me and my friends would die.

CHAPTER 34

I had one last chance. The circle around the omniarch was still bound shut. Concentrated aether tickled my senses. Talbot aimed his wand and I reacted with panic. I opened a portal to a place right in front of my eyes just as he fired a magic bullet. From my side of the arch, I saw the destination. From Talbot's side, he saw the same thing—a dark stone wall. It also happened to be the wall right behind him.

His kinetic bullet ricocheted off the wall and struck him in the back. Talbot cried out. I leapt through the portal and stepped out behind him just as he turned to face me. This time I had my wand in my hand.

Talbot sneered. "You bastard." Blood pooled in the shoulder of his robes. His hand moved.

I flicked my wand. A silvery ripple sliced through the air and struck Talbot in the forehead. His eyes rolled up and the wandslinger toppled. I didn't have time to feel anything. A glance down the outside corridor told me I had little time left. Garkin and Victus stood near the entrance to the mansion cavern, engrossed in conversation.

How much time did I have left on his ultimatum? Five minutes? Two?

He'd walk this way any moment. Talbot's trickery had put me in a dangerous place, but it also might have given me an opportunity.

What if I could kill Victus right here and now?

I turned off the portal and reopened it back to the hilltop crest where Ivy had been. Her eyes flashed with surprise. I put a finger to my lips to quiet her, and stepped through.

"Everyone be quiet," I hissed as loudly as I dared.

Mouths gaped at the sight of me. Ambria looked up at me with tear-streaked eyes.

"No time to explain," I said. "I need Ivy and Kanaan. We're going to kill Victus."

Ivy pumped a fist. Kanaan climbed up to us and we went through the portal. I closed it to hide our presence. Footsteps tapped down the hallway. Victus was already on his way back. I didn't dare peek out of the doorway, but assumed Garkin was with him.

Two figures entered the room. One was Garkin. The other wasn't Victus.

Garkin drew his staff just in time to block Kanaan's wand thrust.

"Die, bitch!" Ivy channeled a brilliant beam of power that incinerated the other mage.

Garkin blocked her next burst with a shield, but it buckled beneath her fury and shattered. Kanaan drove him back with a flurry of attacks and took the fight into the hall. Victus glared at us from down the hall.

"How did you get here?" he shouted.

A group of mages rushed around the corner and charged us. Ivy focused her attacks on the newcomers. They shielded themselves but a torrent of Brilliance burned through the first one and blasted a hole in the next mage.

"Victus Edison, you bastard!" Ivy shrieked and attacked the next battle mage. "I'm going to burn you to ash!"

Victus turned tail and ran.

Kanaan and I launched another barrage of attacks at Garkin. With Ivy off his back, he stood his ground, smashing his staff down. The ground rippled beneath us. Kanaan rode the waves. I stumbled and fell. Super-heated stone seared my elbow. I cried out and got to my feet before rolling into another patch.

A battle mage kicked my wand from my hand. I twisted sideways and knocked his feet from beneath him. The man screamed as his face found a patch of burning stone. I leapt on his back and rammed his head against the stone over and over until I panted from the exertion. Blood sizzled as it spread across the floor. I looked for my wand, but it had slid across the corridor to the group of mages battling Ivy.

The magitsu masters squared off again. Kanaan dodged around another shockwave attack and ducked beneath Garkin's defenses. But the master of strength slammed the agility master's wand aside. His fist glowed and glanced off Kanaan's shoulder. Kanaan spun through the air and slid across the floor.

He stood, brushed off his robes and positioned himself for another attack. Already, he wore the same expression he'd had the last time Garkin defeated him. Kanaan didn't believe he could beat Garkin. And he couldn't, so long as he attacked him head-on. But how did you sneak up on a stone?

Kanaan charged. Garkin's eyes narrowed. He slashed his staff through the air and a cascade of aether spread out, revealing an invisible form coming from the side. The illusion of Kanaan shattered, and Garkin met the camouflaged man with a blast of energy.

The agility master flew backward and slammed into the wall. Blood trickled from his nose and a cut on his forehead. He pushed to his feet unsteadily.

I felt completely useless without my wand. I turned over the dead mage. He'd fallen on his wand and snapped it. I took it anyway, but my attempts to focus through it fizzled out.

My palms and the backs of my hands tingled with all the useless aether around me. Without a wand, all I could do was watch. The more I drew in, the more my hands tingled. Blood trickled from the scabs where Moses had scrubbed them.

What had he said before I left him? *Focus your power here. With these you don't need a—a what?*

Kanaan tried to rise, but fell. Blood dripped from multiple wounds. Ivy tried to help him, but more battle mages poured around the corner and it was all she could do to shield herself from their attacks.

"Weak," Garkin growled. "The only way is strength, Kanaan."

Kanaan shook his head, but couldn't even look up as Garkin towered over him. "No one way is perfect, Garkin. You are a blight on magitsu."

Garkin gripped Kanaan's hair and pulled back his head. "Then die a weakling."

"No!" I shouted. Wand or not, I ran at Garkin as his glowing fist swung down on Kanaan's head.

His fist crunched on an invisible shield. Bones splintered and burst through his hand. Kanaan swung lithely up and buried a wand in Garkin's left nostril. The insides of his skull burst into light. His eyes cooked in their sockets. Gray-streaked blood poured from his ears and his teeth shattered in his mouth.

Garkin toppled like a statue, dead as a rock.

Ivy had finished off the other group of battle mages, but sweat poured down her forehead and her chest heaved. She was exhausted.

I grabbed my wand and ran toward the cavern entrance. The area around the mansion was deserted. Victus must have sent the other mages to fight us on the hill. The only way to recall them was through the omniarch and we controlled it—for now.

I darted toward the mansion. The door hung open. I peered inside and a spell sizzled past my head. I ducked and dove inside, rolled left to dodge another attack. Victus stood in the foyer, the grand staircase behind him. His wand crackled with energy.

His lips spread into a wicked grin. "Where are your friends, boy? Did Garkin kill them?"

"Garkin is dead. Your mages are dead." I readied a shield spell. "My friends are coming and you're all out of allies. Give up now."

I saw a blur out of the corner of my eyes. Ducked. Zarin zipped past and tore the wand from my hand. He blurred behind Victus and snapped my wand in half. "I think you're the one who needs to give up."

A roar of pure rage tore from my throat.

Victus smirked, just as he had when he killed Delectra. The tingling in my hands rose to a searing burn. I tried to release the aether, but it kept building and building, pressing against my insides until I couldn't stand it anymore. I tried to stop aetherating, but it was as if a dam had burst. Pure energy flooded me.

My father aimed his wand and unleashed a crackling bolt of energy. I threw up my hands, calling on the shield spell. Light burst from my palms and a shimmering barrier absorbed the blow. Blue fire flared from the scabs on the backs of my hands, sparking like gunpowder. I fought back the pain and deflected another strike from Victus's wand.

"What is this?" Victus roared.

An image of Moses flashed before my eyes and I knew exactly what it was. "It's the first power."

"In a boy?" Victus launched another salvo. I intercepted it with more shields. He fired again and again. It took everything I had to meet his attacks.

My insides burned. Sweat burned my eyes. I wiped it away with a sleeve.

Zarin blurred toward me. I cast another barrier. He slammed into it with a crunch and fell in a heap.

Victus lowered his wand. "Impressive, boy." He bared a smile. "You've proven yourself worthy. Join me. Make me proud."

"You killed my mother. You killed Cora. You've killed too many people, Father." I barely held onto the scalding cauldron of energy in my well. "The only thing I want to make you is dead."

His wand flashed toward me. This time, I didn't try to block his attack. I ran forward and slid beneath a jagged bolt of death. I wove my hand in the pattern Delectra's soul had taught me. Binding together destruction upon destruction. Ruby fire danced in my palm.

I leapt to my feet and cast Fireblade.

Scarlet beams lanced from the ends of my fingers. Victus tried to shield himself at the last minute, but it wasn't enough. I cut through his barriers and slashed off his right arm. Slashed again and his other hand flopped to the floor.

Victus screamed in agony. Fell to the floor writhing.

I abandoned magic. Leapt on his prone form and pummeled him with my fists. Gripped his hair and slammed the back of his head against the floor over and over again. I stopped when I realized he was no longer screaming. No longer struggling.

I held up bloodied hands, shocked at my raw savagery. Victus's eyes gazed blankly up at the ceiling. Crimson pooled beneath his crushed skull.

A terrible thought occurred to me. *What if this is another infernus? What if he's tricked me again?* I couldn't let the questions go unanswered. Macabre as it was, I needed to know. I sliced open his chest with Fireblade. Blood sizzled and poured from the wound. Inside, I found no soulsphere, only organs and flesh.

Horrified at what I'd done, I squirmed backward through his blood and stared at the body.

"Conrad!" Ivy ran up to me and dragged me backward. Blood painted the floor in my wake.

I convulsed. Rolled over and threw up the contents of my stomach. Heaved until only acid dribbled from my mouth.

"Wow, that was savage." Ivy grimaced. "I saw you fight him at the end. You used your hands to cast spells."

I couldn't reply. I was too numb. Too raw. I didn't feel any better with Victus dead. If anything, I felt worse.

"How did you do it?" she asked.

"The first power." Kanaan's voice was rough. He limped in. "There's no time to waste. We must return to the hilltop. Victus's forces may still attack. We can bring everyone here through the omniarch and get them out of harm's way."

Ivy groaned and dragged me to my feet. "I'm so tired."

I wiped the blood on my pants. The thought of Ambria dying to an onslaught of monsters brought me back to my senses and gave me energy. "Let's go." I ran back to the omniarch room, leaving Ivy and Kanaan behind. I opened a portal to the hilltop. Screams and shouts rose from the other side. Explosions rocked the air.

I dashed through. Ambria and Max stood down the crest, fists raised. They weren't screaming in horror. They were cheering.

Scores of massive wasps buzzed overhead, striking down the giant crows. Scorpions the size of cars stung frogres, bistaurs, and drago-phants in the trees below. Towering mantises speared monsters, and twenty-foot-long centipedes coiled around battle mages. Scores of ruby spiders tangled with their mortal enemies, the cobalts.

In the middle of it all, Evadora rode the giant tragon, shrieking with delight as it smashed and burned anything in its way.

Nightliss stood with the small group of professors and my friends. She channeled a translucent shield, blocking the attacks of any creatures who made it past *our* monster army.

The battle was a slaughter and we were on the winning side.

I collapsed, suddenly bone weary, unable to take another step. "They did it," I rasped. "They did it."

Ambria's lovely face filled my view. Tears poured from her eyes. "Conrad, are you okay?"

I nodded. "Victus is dead. You're alive. I'm okay." And then I blacked out.

CHAPTER 35

W e left Victus's dead to rot in the Dark Forest. Cora returned the giant bugs to the underground forest. At the request of the ruby spiders, she brought up a few of the giant crickets for breeding so the rubies could enjoy the delicacies.

Dozens of rubies had died, but hundreds of the cobalts lay dead. With the population of the cobalt spiders decimated in the fighting, the ruby queen sent soldiers to capture the webbed city so they could assimilate the living into their culture instead of killing them.

Shushiel was among those tasked with the effort. Bobbing with happiness, she told us of her new position.

"Do you really think the last of the cobalts will live with their mortal enemies?" Ambria asked.

Shushiel's forelegs rose in the approximation of a shrug. "I don't know, but we have hope. It would be terrible to kill them all."

We hugged her goodbye and watched her and a platoon of ruby soldiers crawl off into the forest.

"Will you just go?" Evadora shoved the great beast, but the tragon thudded after her, whining like a giant dog. She groaned.

"What did you do to him?" Max asked.

Evadora leaned back against a giant tragon leg and sighed. "He was just really happy that I could talk to him. He's a lot more intelligent than Victus thought, but his instinctual drive is so high, he can't always control himself."

"Sounds like a typical man." Ambria nudged me and grinned.

"So, you just asked him to help and he agreed?" Max asked.

"No." The tragon lowered its head and Evadora patted it. He yawned, revealing a maw that could easily swallow an elephant. "Drago chased me around and tried to eat me, so I climbed on his head and started talking to him. It took a while to learn his language, but once I did, he started telling me how sad and lonely he is."

"He's the only one of his kind," Ambria said.

Evadora wiped away a tear. "I know. It's awful."

"I love you, Evie." Ivy clapped her hands together. "You're crazy!"

Evadora grinned. "I think we could be best friends, Ivy."

Max snorted. "You two are the definition of free spirited."

"Does Drago know Victus is dead?" I asked.

Evadora growled and roared in convincing but miniature fashion compared to the giant tragon.

The tragon reared back its head and trumpeted. Fire blasted a hundred feet into the sky. His tiny wings fluttered, and his ridiculous little arms flailed.

"He's pretty happy," Evadora confirmed. "Drago tried to eat Victus once because he was so furious about the size of his arms."

"For real!" Ivy shook her head. "Poor Drago can't even use a spoon."

Max scratched his head. "Why would he ever use a spoon?"

"There are potions for repairing shrunken limbs," I said. "Maybe Percival could make something to grow out Drago's arms."

Evadora's eyes flared. "That would be wonderful!" She relayed the good news to Drago, who nearly burned down a tree in his jubilation.

"So does this mean he's our friend now?" Max asked.

Evadora shook her head. "Oh, no, not at all. He keeps asking to eat you."

Max shrank back. "But I thought he liked us!"

"Yes, he likes you, but only as prey." Evadora giggled. "He's such a brute."

Cora emerged from the entrance to the caves and smiled radiantly at me. "The creatures of the underground forest are back in place." She perched on a rock. "Did you know that there's another underground even below that one?"

"Wow, how deep does it go?" Max said.

"I don't think it's a matter of depth, but a matter of stepping sideways."

Max blinked. "Huh?"

My forehead pinched. "What do you mean?"

Cora waved her arms around at the forest. "Queens Gate is part of Eden, but it is also a part of the Glimmer." She interlocked her fingers. "The two realms overlap where the anchor stone binds them together."

"Just like the Grotto and the other pocket dimensions," Ambria said.

Cora nodded. "What I did not realize is that all the realms seem to overlap here. Just as Queens Gate is underground to Eden, so are the other realms underground to this pocket dimension."

I jumped up and froze when Drago's predatory gaze locked onto me like a cat eyeing a mouse. It took a moment to remember my question. "Does that mean we can reach Seraphina?"

"Yes, and no," Cora said. "The Arcanes of Eden discovered the pocket dimensions and excavated the earth to reach them. I could find no exits from the insect realm, and didn't go down to the next overlap to search for exits. It's possible they exist, but it would require a major expedition to search them."

"That's amazing." Ambria looked toward the cave. "Can you imagine what we might find down that hole?"

"Down the rabbit hole." Kanaan stepped up beside me. "Unfortunately, we cannot rest."

"Yeah, we've got to rescue my big brother." Ivy's lips flattened. "We don't have long before Voltis aligns with Eden, and I don't want to miss it."

"At least the danger to Eden is gone," Ambria said.

"Not true." Kanaan spread his gaze around the group. "I bound Zarin in sleeper cuffs after Conrad's fight with Victus. After the battle, I questioned him. He is also eager to reach Seraphina and find his sister Aerianas, so he answered all my questions."

Dread rose up my throat. "What did he tell you?"

Kanaan folded his arms across his chest. "Victus was in league with a demon overlord. This is how he ferried troops to the Glimmer through a demon portal. Zarin discovered during his construction of the foundry that this overlord is acting on orders from Baal."

"Victus didn't know that?" Max asked.

"Victus cooperated with Baal years ago, but discovered the grand overlord was only doing it to further his own interests." Kanaan let that sink in a moment. "Zarin questioned many demons during his construction of the foundry. He believes Baal may have subverted Victus's plans in Seraphina and that Baal is the one collecting Relics of Jura."

My heart froze to ice. "The most powerful demon of all is trying to reconstruct Jura? He wants to bring all the realms back together?"

Kanaan shook his head. "Unknown. Zarin has agreed to find more information if we go to Seraphina and discover the fate of Aerianas."

Ambria's looked aghast. "Can we trust him even a little bit?"

"Uncertain." Kanaan shook his head again. "This is certain—we must discover the fate of Justin Slade and the realm of Seraphina. We must put a stop to the relic hunter, or worlds will collide and billions will die."

Max groaned. "Just when I thought it was safe to take a nap."

"We have weeks until the alignment with Voltis," Kanaan said. "For now, we rest and prepare."

"What about the rest of Victus's infernus?" I asked. "Who's going to restore the government?"

"Galfandor and the professors have accepted the challenge," Kanaan said. "It is the best we can do for now."

Evadora thrust her hand into the air. "I want to go to Seraphina."

"Yes!" Ivy hugged the silver-skinned girl. "We're going to have the best time ever."

Cora's gaze grew distant. "I was there once, but I cannot remember how or why. Perhaps I should come."

My heart rose. "You would do that?"

She smiled and took my hand. "It would give me a chance to get to know my son all over again."

Tears stung my eyes. "I'd like that."

Kanaan looked at the blackened wounds on the backs of my hands. "We have not had a chance to talk about Victus."

My stomach roiled at the violent images from my fight with my father. I held up my hands and showed the fresh burns on my palms. "Somehow, I cast spells through my hands." I looked at my fingertips, but they were unharmed despite casting Fireblade through them. "Zarin broke my wand so I had no choice."

"Amazing." Nightliss took my right hand and peered at the wound. "I have never heard of an Arcane who could cast without a focus like a wand, a staff, or an arcphone."

"It hurt," I admitted. "I don't think it's good for me."

"Or perhaps it requires more practice." Kanaan pursed his lips. "Nightliss, can you heal his hands?"

"I am not the most skilled Seraphim healer, but I believe I can help." Her hands glowed with ultraviolet light as she pressed them to my left hand. Soothing frost ran into my flesh. I moaned at the sudden release of pain dogging me since the fight. She repeated the same step with my other hand. When she was done, the pain had gone, and the flesh began to scar over on both sides of my hands.

"Thank you," I said.

"It will be unpleasant," Kanaan said, "but we must explore what happened. We must expand your abilities."

"Can't you give poor Conrad some rest?" Ambria said. "He's been through enough as it is."

Kanaan nodded somberly. "He may rest, but I fear there is much more to come."

WE SPENT the next few weeks resting, recuperating, training, and preparing. Ambria and I spent a lot of time together. Ivy and Evadora were inseparable, vanishing for days at a time to go to the Glimmer so Ivy could see it all.

Galfandor and the other professors began the long work of rooting out

Victus's supporters even while they still controlled the government. Xander Tiberius increased security after Victus's death and put out warrants on his political enemies, forcing the movement underground.

We discussed assassinating Xander, Grint, Quiff, and the other Victus lackeys, but they were nearly impossible to reach, surrounded by so many battle mages. If we could return with Justin Slade and an army, we could force the issue.

Percival made a modified version of his memory potion and gave it to Cora. She remembered some things right away, but Percival warned it would take months, perhaps a year, to reconstruct all her reversed neural pathways. I was just ecstatic to know there was a chance to have the old Cora back.

At long last, the time came to meet with the Fallen. I looked up the address on the internet and used the maps app to zoom in for an image so I could use the omniarch to open a portal there.

Kanaan found a picture of a small cove on the beach nearby. "Open the portal there. Less chance of noms seeing it."

The portal winked open to sugar-white sand and sapphire water. Warmth washed over us in the small omniarch room. Ambria went through first, eyes wide with joy. "How beautiful!"

Ivy and Evadora raced through close behind and splashed into the water, heedless of wet clothes. The rest of our expeditionary group, me, Kanaan, Cora, Nightliss, and Max stepped through into the heat.

We wore shorts and atrocious shirts with tropical fruit patterns on them to simulate what noms wore to the beach. Since there was no one in sight on the cove, I didn't know how effective our camouflage was. We still had three days to go before the alignment, but I didn't want to waste any time or risk the Fallen leaving without us.

"Let's go," I shouted to Ivy and Evadora. "You can play in the water after we contact the Fallen."

Dripping but deliriously happy, the pair splashed to shore.

Kanaan inspected the portal. Since it faced the rock and not the water, it wasn't visible unless someone walked around it. "It should be safe to leave open for now, but I will close it before departing to Seraphina."

Ambria hooked her arm in mine. "I'd love a romantic walk on the beach later."

"Me too." It was actually the last thing on my mind. My stomach twisted in knots at the thought of going to another realm. At what we might discover there.

We climbed up a rocky path to the road. This part of the island was meticulously manicured, the houses pristine and huge. I knew from the picture we'd seen in the maps app that the address Purah had given us belonged to a two-story house with a deck overlooking the ocean. White with light blue shutters, it was modest compared to the others along this stretch of road.

A man with a loud machine strapped to his back blew leaves off the road while another man trimmed a hedge at the neighboring house. They paid us no mind as we turned onto the long drive.

But the house wasn't there. All that remained was splintered wood and rubble.

I waved down the man with the blower. He turned it off and gave me a curious look. "Yes?"

"What happened to the house that was here?"

"A freak tornado tore it apart a couple of weeks ago." He looked up the drive at it and shook his head. "The poor people inside were killed."

"Killed?" I tried to wrap my head around it. "Are you certain?"

"I don't think they ever found the bodies, but they were definitely inside." He pointed down the road. "I was working on their lawn when it happened. Most of these houses are just vacation homes for rich people, but I saw two blond women and a man with a head of poofy hair get out of a car and go inside."

"Sounds like them," Max said.

The man continued. "We had clear blue skies for miles. Everything went gray in an instant and a huge tornado dropped straight down on the house." He blew out his lips. "Never seen anything like it."

The door to the neighbor's house opened and a man walked outside. He wore a white linen oxford and matching shorts. His eyes regarded us suspiciously. "Who are you?"

"My name is Conrad. We knew the people who lived in that house."

The man flinched and his irises paled until they looked white. "Please come inside," he said in a stiff voice.

Ambria and I looked at each other then over to Max.

Kanaan followed the man up the driveway without a word. We followed them inside and stood in a wide tile foyer. A tiny dog yipped and ran into the room.

"How cute!" Evadora yipped back and picked up the dog. "Lulu doesn't like the food you feed her."

The man turned stiffly. "This is Purah. I have implanted a message into this man's mind for Conrad. We investigated the relic collector while we waited for the next alignment with Voltis. This drew the attention of the Apocryphan to us and this island. Despite our powers, we are in mortal danger. He is too powerful even for us. We will leave here and find a place to hide until the alignment is upon us."

"Did you fake your deaths?" I asked.

The man ignored the question and continued speaking. "Take the boat, *Angel Wings*, from the boathouse behind this residence. The keys and directions to Voltis are inside. We have also left a Chalon and instructions for opening a portal in case we are unable to meet you there. Go

372

now and do not linger on the island, lest you draw the attention of the Apocryphan to you." The man slumped, as if puppet strings had gone slack and walked over to the divan. He lay down and peacefully went to sleep.

Once again, things were not going to plan.

CHAPTER 36

"I really should leave him a note about Lulu's food," Evadora said. "She absolutely despises it."

"We need to go." Kanaan sounded anxious and that set the rest of us on edge.

"Um, then let's go." Max ran through the house to the back door where a winding sidewalk led to a pier.

The boathouse stood two stories tall and with good reason. *Angel Wings* was a double-decker yacht nearly as large as the house we'd lived in at the corner of Dowling and Bucket in Queens Gate. Long and sleek, it looked like a toy for the super-rich, and the Fallen had left it at their neighbor's dock for us as if it was nothing.

"Whoa, this thing is huge!" Max stepped off the pier and onto the back deck of the boat. The rest of us piled onboard and inside. A staircase took us to the top deck and the bridge. We found the promised directions and instructions in a compartment next to the captain's chair. Beneath them was a cube of clear crystal. In the center was a small black orb etched with lines.

"How curious." Nightliss took the crystal. "There's a Chalon in the center of this gem."

"That's a crystal, not a gem," Max said.

Nightliss turned it over in her hands. "In Seraphina, there are storms so intense, the pressure solidifies the aether into gems."

"Whoa, really?" Max reached out tentatively and touched it. "I didn't even know that was possible."

Nightliss's gaze went distant. "Aether is so abundant on Seraphina, that my home city of Tarissa literally floats on a cloud of magic."

"Ooh, sounds beautiful." Evadora danced in place. "I can't wait to see it."

"Do you know how to use this gem?" I asked.

"As far as I know, the only way to use a Chalon to activate an Alabaster Arch is to sing it into alignment." Nightliss shook her head slowly. "Justin's mother, Alysea, was the only person I know capable of that."

Ambria groaned. "If we have to sing to it, we're doomed."

"I can't sing as good as my mom," Ivy said. "What do the instructions say?"

Kanaan looked at the letter and summarized. "The Fallen call the Chalon gem a volon since it only opens portals through Voltis. A Seraphim must channel through the gem to generate the power for a portal." He handed the instructions to Nightliss and climbed into the captain's chair. "There is plenty of time to read while we travel to Kratos."

He zapped a crystal on the console with his wand and the electronics on the control console came to life. A large touchscreen with a map allowed us to input the destination, and the boat pulled out of the dock of its own accord and started us on the twenty-hour journey.

"Is this boat built with arcnology?" I asked.

Kanaan nodded. "Ironically, it was built by Xander Tiberius's company."

"What?" I couldn't contain my surprise and turned to Max. "Your father owns a ship building company?"

Max looked down. "Arc Corp doesn't just build ships. They make flying carpets, air ships, rocket sticks, and everything in between. His company manufactured hundreds of killer robots for Victus back before he became Overlord."

"You never told us any of this before," Ambria said in an accusing voice. "Why not?"

"Because I hate talking about my family." Max slumped. "Why do you think I never took you to meet them after all this time?"

I patted his back. "I understand Max." I offered him a smile. "Hey, at least the boat is really cool."

Max looked up at me. "Yeah, it is pretty nice."

Ambria sighed. "I understand too, Max. It just seems like a really big thing to not mention."

"It is another reason why removing Xander as Arcanus Primus will be difficult," Kanaan said.

"Maybe we should've taken our monster army to take him down," Max said.

Cora shook her head. "If a foreign power invaded Queens Gate, we would be looked upon as the aggressors, not the saviors. Besides, it takes tremendous effort to control so many creatures who are not of my world. The only reason we had such success is because I literally pointed them at the enemy and unleashed them. If we had other allies fighting beside us, the insects might have attacked them as well."

"Don't worry," Ivy said. "We'll get my big brother and his army and kick Xander's sorry ass when we get back."

"Victus is dead. His army is wiped out." I leaned back into a chair. "Xander can't make things much worse by himself."

"I'd be surprised if he doesn't step down out of fear," Ambria said. "He can't have much support left."

"Xander has always craved power," Kanaan said. "Now that he has it, he will cling to it as tightly as possible."

Max looked down, as if ashamed. "I'm afraid you're right."

By late afternoon the next day, we reached our destination.

The island of Kratos was little more than a hill with a patch of sand and a few palm trees. We anchored offshore and counted down the hours to the alignment. It happened in the early hours of the following morning. A dense fog rose from the water around the island, covering the land, but going no further. Lightning raced up and down the fog, drawing angry hisses when it hit the water.

Kanaan eased the boat up to the edge of the magical storm and put down the anchor again. Nightliss walked to the prow and channeled through the crystal cube. The lines of the Chalon glowed white. Beams of light projected from the other side of the cube and into the fog.

Nightliss focused on an image Purah had left with the instructions. A portal split open. On the other side, a black rock towered above an alien ocean. Beyond it rose an immense gray wall of thunderclouds and lightning. It was Voltis proper, unlike this tiny representation of it here in Eden.

Everyone exchanged frightened looks, but Kanaan steered us through the portal before anyone could voice concern.

Violent waves caught the boat and tossed us toward the huge black rock. Kanaan flicked through an option screen on the control console. *Angel Wings* rose from the water and a shield flickered on to protect us from lashing rain and wind.

Nightliss looked up the endless wall of writhing gray, mouth agape. "Am I supposed to create a portal through that massive storm?"

Kanaan nodded grimly. "Purah's instructions say this boat has handled the journey many times."

"Let's hope she's right," Ambria said.

Kanaan eased *Angel Wings* closer to the towering storm. Despite the gale force winds, sleet, and balls of hail as large as my head, the boat remained unscathed, thanks to the shield. When we were a few yards from the storm wall, Nightliss went to the prow and channeled through the cube again, focusing on the picture of a blue tree in a field of bright yellow grass.

"Where is that?" Max asked.

"We shall soon find out," Nightliss said as the portal flickered open, a portrait of calm in the raging storm.

The ship flew through and landed on a tiny island. But it was no ordinary island. Just like the fragments of land in the Glimmer, this island floated in a sea of clouds, far above the ocean below. Dozens of the floating islands spread into the distance.

Ambria gaped and pointed toward one of the larger chunks of land. Crystal ships of all hues and organic curves hovered in the air around the island. People seemed to be loading the ships. In fact, it almost looked as if everyone on the island was running to the ships.

Far in the distance, black clouds gathered on the horizon. I wondered if it was another storm, or something more ominous.

Nightliss continued to channel into the crystal cube to keep the portal open. "Perhaps we can negotiate with the Mzodi to take us to Pjurna since their ships are much faster than this one. It is likely Justin is with my people." She released the channel and the portal winked away.

Cora gasped. "Mzodi. *Evadora*." She looked at me. "I remember these ships. I used to have one named after my daughter. Perhaps they'll remember me."

"I hope so," Nightliss said. "The Mzodi can be difficult to negotiate with."

"Flying ships, floating islands." Max blew out a breath. "I can't wait to see what else Seraphina has."

Ambria turned to me and graced me with a beautiful smile. "We're actually here in another realm. Can you believe it?"

"Barely," I admitted.

"I can't wait to see my brother," Ivy said. "Oh, I hope he's okay."

"Justin Slade is good at surviving," Kanaan said. "I believe he is."

Cora took my hand. "This brings back so much, Conrad. I remember taking you onto my ship. I remember seeing Justin there."

Ambria leaned her head on my shoulder. "It sounds like we have a lot to discover."

My heart swelled with hope. We had finally reached Seraphina. We'd finished one journey and started another. I pointed to the graceful flying ships in the distance. "Let's go find the heroes of Eden and bring them home."

I HOPE *you enjoyed reading this book. Reviews are very important in helping other readers decide what to read next. Would you please take a few seconds to rate this book?*

WANT MORE? Touch here for more books by John Corwin!

FOR THE LATEST on new releases, free ebooks, and more, join John Corwin's Newsletter at www.johncorwin.net!

ABOUT THE AUTHOR

John Corwin is the bestselling author of the Overworld Chronicles. He enjoys long walks on the beach and is a firm believer in puppies and kittens.

After years of getting into trouble thanks to his overactive imagination, John abandoned his male modeling career to write books.

He resides in Atlanta.

Connect with John Corwin online:
Facebook: http://www.facebook.com/johnhcorwinauthor
Website: http://www.johncorwin.net
Twitter: http://twitter.com/#!/John_Corwin

www.johncorwin.net
john@johncorwin.net

BOOKS BY JOHN CORWIN

THE OVERWORLD CHRONICLES

Sweet Blood of Mine

Dark Light of Mine

Fallen Angel of Mine

Dread Nemesis of Mine

Twisted Sister of Mine

Dearest Mother of Mine

Infernal Father of Mine

Sinister Seraphim of Mine

Wicked War of Mine

Dire Destiny of Ours

Aetherial Annihilation

Baleful Betrayal

Ominous Odyssey

Insidious Insurrection

Assignment Zero (An Elyssa Short Story)

OVERWORLD UNDERGROUND

Possessed By You

Demonicus

OVERWORLD ARCANUM

Conrad Edison and the Living Curse

Conrad Edison and the Anchored World

Conrad Edison and the Broken Relic

Conrad Edison and the Infernal Design

Conrad Edison and the First Power

STAND ALONE NOVELS

Mars Rising

No Darker Fate

The Next Thing I Knew

Outsourced

For the latest on new releases, free ebooks, and more, join John Corwin's Newsletter at www.johncorwin.net!